George Augustus Sala

Under the Sun

Essays mainly written in hot countries

George Augustus Sala

Under the Sun
Essays mainly written in hot countries

ISBN/EAN: 9783337427054

Printed in Europe, USA, Canada, Australia, Japan

Cover: Foto ©Andreas Hilbeck / pixelio.de

More available books at **www.hansebooks.com**

UNDER THE SUN:

Essays mainly Written in Hot Countries.

By GEORGE AUGUSTUS SALA,

AUTHOR OF "PARIS HERSELF AGAIN," "AMERICA REVISITED,"
"DUTCH PICTURES," &c.

A NEW EDITION,

WITH SEVERAL ADDITIONAL ESSAYS.

ILLUSTRATED WITH TWELVE PAGE ENGRAVINGS, AND AN ETCHED
PORTRAIT OF THE AUTHOR.

LONDON:

VIZETELLY & CO., 42, CATHERINE STREET, STRAND.

1887.

TO

LIEUTENANT-COLONEL JAMES E. FORD,

𝕿𝖍𝖎𝖘 𝕭𝖔𝖔𝖐,

IN PLEASANT MEMORY OF DAYS PASSED LONG AGO

UNDER THE SUN,

IS CORDIALLY DEDICATED.

CONTENTS.

—◆❀❀◆—

CONTENTS.

AN ESSAY ON WARM WEATHER.

(PREFIXED TO THE FIRST EDITION OF THIS WORK.)

HAVE the greater need to pen an Essay with such a title as that which appears above, as introductory to UNDER THE SUN, since I sit down to write it on the Twenty-fifth of May—the merry month of May !—with a blazing fire in my study, and the cat dozing on the hearth-rug, instead of enjoying her natural *otium* at this time of the year, in blinking on the coping of the garden wall. The housekeeper has just knocked at the door to say that the coals are nearly "out," and that in view of such "bitter weather," it would be as well to communicate with Messrs. Cockerell without delay. If the men with the sacks do not come, I shall be fain to bite my thumbs to warm them ; and I may well strive to kindle a little mental caloric by writing about Warm Weather, lest—with the thermometer looking at me with the stony stare of a refrigerator—I should forget that there was such a season as Summer at all, or that anything but frost and fog could be felt and seen "Under the Sun."

I have given to this collection of Sketches of Travels and Manners the title they bear, for the reason that the majority of their number have a direct reference to the Hot Climates of the lands in which I have wandered. It may strike the reader (and in a stronger degree the critic) that some of the chapters in this volume are, neither subjectively nor objectively, of a very sunny nature, and have nothing to do with hot countries. I may point in explanation, first, to the reservation "mainly" which appears

on the face of the book; and next, to the facts that I wrote
"Wretchedville" in Rome, and "Stalls" in Spain, under circumstances of an abnormally inflammatory nature. Those essays
were both composed "in a state of siege," and in the midst of
revolutionary crises; and they should properly smell of brimstone
and boiling lava. With regard to the "Hotel Chaos," in which
I have endeavoured to depict the aspect of the city of Metz
during the month of July, 1870, I can scarcely think that even
the severest censor would feel inclined to question that it was hot
enough in Lorraine in the city, and at the time I have mentioned.

So much for my book: but this is not by any means all I
have to say on the subject of Heat. It has long been my ambition
to say something in print on the subject of Warm Weather and
Warm Blood in connection with their influence on the Literary
Style and Character; and I should wish it, in the outset, to be
distinctly understood that I am not addressing myself to the
jelly-fish section of mankind, to whom Weather, torrid or frigid,
is a matter of indifference; nor to those Hyperboreans who revel
physically, in cold; who "tub" in cold water on the First of
January, and even when they are forced to break the ice with a
hammer to reach their bath; who delight in skating, sliding,
snow-balling, sleighing, "curling," and other arctic diversions,
which to me only represent so many varieties of self-inflicted
agony. Those whom I desire to reach should be warm-blooded
animals, swarthy and sanguineous souls, worn black by the Sun's
am'rous pinches. I am not writing for Philosophers of the Glacial
Period, or the shareholders of the Wenham Lake Ice Company,
or the dragmen of the Royal Humane Society.

Many more years ago than I care to name, when I was a
little boy, the house in which I lived used to be thrown into
periodical commotion by sudden and alarming fits of indisposition
with which a near and dear relative of mine used, from time to
time, to be attacked. Such a running up and down stairs as took
place on these occasions is difficult of description. Warm flannels
and hot-water bottles were sent for from the lower regions. There
were no railway rugs—and few railways, indeed, in those days—

but the thickest of shawls and wraps were in request. When the spasmodic sufferings of the invalid in the drawing-room became unusually violent, the doctor would be sent for. I can remember that when the medical practitioner came he was accustomed to smile, and to say that the sufferer would be "all right presently," and that his invariable prescription in alleviation of the symptoms was sherry-and-water hot. And, indeed, when the flannels and bran-bags and water-bottles had been applied; when the patient had had a dozen extra coverings wrapped round her; when she had been laid on the sofa with a pillow under her head; and especially when the fire had been well stirred and the hot sherry-and-water administered—she would rarely fail to fall into a tranquil slumber, and to wake up afterwards quite composed and cheerful, to be, as heretofore, our hope, and comfort, and joy.

I should observe that these visitations always took place in the winter months, and their severity was in a precisely proportionate ratio to the asperity of the weather, and that their most marked symptoms were a deficiency of circulation in the extremities, accompanied by violent shivering. We children, under these terrifying circumstances, used to cower in corners, quaking with appalling misgivings; for we were but five left from thirteen brothers and sisters, and we had very early indeed begun to understand what Death meant. As it happened, my relative survived the severest of her shivering fits (one which took place when I was a very small boy) full five-and-twenty years; and I am glad to conjecture, nay, to believe, now, that ague or palsy had nothing whatever to do with my dear Mother's ailment. She trembled only because it was January, and a hard winter, and she was so very cold. She was a West Indian, and Cold to her was Pain.

I had the fortune, or misfortune, in after years to be sent to a school in which the boys were never beaten—nay, not to the extent of a rapped knuckle or a boxed ear; and to that circumstance, perhaps, may be ascribed the generally imperfect nature of my education, and my inability at this day to master the niceties of Latin prosody. Had I been duly scourged, I might by this

time have become another Codrus, and—in slightly bronchitic
accents—have recited another Theseid. I can nevertheless conscientiously aver, comparing my own experiences with those of
friends educated under the beneficent rule of Doctor Busby,
Professor Thwackum, and Mr. Plagosus Orbilius, M.R.C.P., that
the physical anguish I endured during my school-life was quite as
severe, although not so ignominious, as though I had been beaten
every day into bruises and blains. I was never Warm enough.
From July to September (if the skies were favourable, and there
was nothing the matter with the Gulf Stream) I enjoyed a temporary respite from chilliness. During the remainder of the year
I shivered.

The Getting-up bell (which was rung at half-past five) pealed
on my ear as awfully, in degree, as the dreadful ding-dong of
St. Sepulchre's may peal on the tympanum of the wretch in
Newgate doomed to die : yet, happier he, the knell is audible to
him but once. _I_ heard the Getting-up bell every morning,
clamouring and screeching, "Come out. Come and be cold.
Come and have a blue tip to your nose, and gooseflesh at the ends
of your fingers, and chilblains on all your toes. Come, and
shudder, and clash your teeth together." That was the kind of
invite I heard in the bell. I know that for a length of time I
spent half my pocket-money in bribing a boy, whose seat was
nearer the stove than mine in the class-room, to allow me to
occupy his warm corner, and that I would smuggle additional
clothes into the dormitories, or borrow my schoolfellows' blankets,
to cover myself at night. I know that I have had impositions of
horrible length set me for the offence of going to bed with the
major part of my garments on.

I had a schoolmaster, once, who was a clever and excellent
man, but a little mad, and who had a craze about making boys
"hardy." He was pleased to fix upon me as a "chilly mortal,"
and expressed a determination to "make a man of me." The
process of manufacture demanded that when I was snuggling over
the fire and a book in play-time, I should be driven forth into the
bleak and bitter open "to play." Now I never could play. At

this date, when I am grizzling, I scarcely know a cricket-bat from
a stump, or prisoner's base from rounders. I never could throw
a ball, or catch one, properly ; and in childhood I was utterly
unable even to " tuck in my twopenny " at leap-frog, or to drive
a hoop. So, while a hundred merry lads round me raced and
gambolled, I used to lurk in a corner of the playground and
Shiver.

We had a large bathroom, and (always with the benevolent
idea of " making a man of me ") I was put through a bastard
course of hydropathy. I declare that in the midst of the most
biting winter weather I have undergone the cold douche, the cold-
shower-bath, and the cold sitz ; that I have been packed in wet
sheets ; that I have been made to put a dry pair of socks over a
wet pair, and thus accoutred have been ordered to walk from
Hammersmith to Kew Bridge, before breakfast, in the dark, to
make me "hardy." Unless another boy of the same "hardy"
breed was sent with me to see that I went through my training
properly, I used to perform the journey from Hammersmith to
Kew Bridge by sneaking to the widow Crump's shop at Turnham
Green—she sold fruit, toys, periodicals, and sweetstuff—and sitting
by the fire in her little parlour, drinking warm ginger-beer, and
reading the Lives of the Pirates and Highwaymen.

The puling, sneaking, lily-livered milksop ! I hear the
Hyperboreans cry. I acknowledge the hardest of the impeach-
ments ; and I confess, indeed, that indirectly I defrauded my
parents by my persistent chilliness ; for we had a racquet court,
a quintain, and a gymnastic apparatus at school. We were entitled
to lessons in swimming, fencing, riding, and calisthenics ; and had
I availed myself of all the Olympian facilities at my command, I
might by this time have become a distinguished athlete, well known
in the higher muscular circles in Elis. As it chanced, my good
crazy master did *not* make a man of me. I grew up to be only a
sickly, long-legged, weak-kneed youth, with premature pains in
the bones, which developed in later years into chronic rheumatism
and intermittant neuralgia.

I had some glimpses of Warm Weather when I was a child,

being much abroad, but only in temperate climes. But from the age of thirteen to nearly thirty I lived mainly in London, and you know what Cold Weather, and Warm Weather, in the British metropolis mean. With Creole, Italian, Portuguese, Red Indian blood in my veins (I am afraid that my great grandmother on the maternal side was a squaw, and was tattooed), I was always panting to be Under the Sun—the *real* Sun, not the tepid simulacrum we see in this country—but it seemed as though my wish was never to be gratified. I was always repeating:

> Yet bear me from the harbour's mouth,
>   Wild winds; I seek a warmer sky;
> And I shall see before I die
> The Palms and Temples of the South.

I saw them, and the Sun himself, at last; but I was constrained to seek my goal by a round-about route. The first real, glorious, blazing, sweltering Summer I basked in was in Russia. The cholera was rife in St. Petersburg when I went there. The fashionable season was over, and all the grand folks were out of town. The streets were dusty, the canals were malodorous. What did all these things matter to me? It was Summer, it was Hot. My rheumatism took unto itself wings, and flew away. I could once more feel my blood in its circuits. A long-congealed mind began to thaw, and during that summer in Russia I studied and worked more vigorously than ever I had worked or studied before in my life.

Now and then, among the few favourable things people have been good enough to say about me, I have been complimented on the score of my " industry." Hearing such a compliment, I have chuckled, not bitterly, but with much inward merriment, as knowing myself to be constitutionally one of the most indolent of men. " Ah, monsieur," pleaded the French beggar to the stern economist who reproached him with his vagabondage, "si vous saviez combien je suis paresseux!" If you only *knew* how idle I was; how I have wasted three-fourths of the time at my disposal —after the necessary deductions for sleep, meals, and recreation

had been made—in purposeless "mooning," in hatching vain:
schemes, in covering the margins of books with trivial notes, in
filling commonplace books with useless entries, in making sketches
for pictures I shall never be able to paint ! In the face of a shelf'
full of books, and thousands of newspaper columns I have scrawled,
I know that, so far as Time is concerned, I have wantonly
squandered my substance and wasted my oil. I know, and can
honestly declare, that so strongly is the *far niente* temper ingrained
within me, *that I have never sat down to serious labour without*
reluctance, nor risen from it without exultation. I wonder how
many "prolific writers," "interminable scribblers," "assiduous-
hacks," would make the same confession, were they only candid
enough to do so ?

One cannot, indeed, repudiate one's own handiwork ; and
during a literary course of three-and-twenty years, a man whose
only source of livelihood has been his pen, must needs have:
accumulated a mass of work performed in some manner or
another. The craziest dunce's punishment-tasks will fill many
copybooks. Thus, when I look at the volumes and the news-
paper-files before me, and ask how ever I could have nerved
myself to knead all these stacks of bricks—often with the
scantiest allowance of straw—I remember that I have always
worked better in summer than in winter, and that I have always
worked best Under the Sun, thousands of miles away. The
Summer of 1864 was intensely hot ; yet I managed to do more
work in the United States, in Mexico, and in the West Indies,.
in three months than I had done in all the preceding three
years. I felt my blood in every vein, and it oozed out of my
fingers, and so into my pen's point, into red ink. The glorious
warm weather melted away the mists and fogs by which I had
been surrounded. I had been Hot and Happy. In a kindred
but modified degree I have recognised the same influence of'
Sunshine as encouraging activity in my own individual case—
and what do I know about other people's ?—in Italy, in Spain,.
and in Africa.

I have been at home now, with brief intervals of con--

tinental travelling, for four years, and I have written nothing worth reading. No original book of mine has seen the light for a very long time ; and my publisher had to make my life a torment to me ere he could incite me to collect these papers and correct the proofs. If any persons wish me to be industrious, let them combine in demanding that I should be banished very far beyond the seas, and to the hottest climate procurable. A double purpose would thus be served. Those who disliked me personally would be able to get rid of me ; whereas those who did not hate me might profit by my absence by communing with me from afar off.

GEORGE AUGUSTUS SALA.

BROMPTON, *May*, 1872.

UNDER THE SUN.

I.

UNDER THE GUNS OF THE MORRO.

HERE used some years ago to be a little tobacconist's shop, somewhere between Pall Mall and Duncannon Street, with the sign of the Morro Castle. It was such a little shop, and it smelt so strongly of cedar and of the Indian weed, that itself was not unlike a cigar box. Here I used to think a threepenny cigar about the greatest luxury in which a young man of pleasure could indulge ; but a luxury only to be ventured upon at the occurrence of solemn festivals, and when the treasures of the mines of Potosi, to the extent of a few shillings, lay loose in one's waistcoat-pocket. There *were* threepenny cigars in those days, and they were delicious. I am afraid that the manufacture has ceased, or that the threepennies have lost their flavour, for Ensign and Lieutenant Dickeystrap, of the Guards, declares that you cannot get anything fit to smoke under ninepence, and that a really tolerable " weed " will " stand you in " eighteenpence. Prince Fortunatus, they say, gives half a crown apiece for his Regalias.

The Morro Castle, however, did a very modest, but, I believe, remunerative, business in cigars at from threepence to sixpence each. Well do I remember courtly old Mr. Alcachofado, the proprietor of the Morro—always in the same well-buttoned frock-coat, always with the same tall shiny hat with the broad turned-up brim — always puffing at, apparently, the same stump of a choice Londres. It was well worth while laying out threepence at the Morro Castle ; for, in consideration of that modest investment, you were treated, for at least five minutes, like a peer of the realm. Mr. Alcachofado himself selected your cigar, and, if you approved of it, snipped off the end in a little patent machine, and presented it to you with a grave bow. You proposed to light it ; but this Mr. Alcachofado would by no means permit. He drew a splint from a stack in a japanned stand, kindled it at the gas jet, and with another bow handed it to you. If you wished to fill the heart of Mr. Alcachofado with anguish, and to pass in his eyes for a person of the very worst breeding, you would, when the splint had served your turn, cast it on the floor and trample it under foot. I have seen the proprietor of the Morro glare at people who did this, as though he would have dearly liked to take off his curly-brimmed hat and fling it at their heads. Regular customers knew well the etiquette of the Morro, which was gently to blow out the tiny flame of the splint and place it horizontally on the top of the fasces in the japanned tin box. Then *you* bowed to Mr. Alcachofado, and *he* bowed in return ; and, taking a seat, if you liked, on a huge cigar chest, you proceeded to smoke the calumet of peace.

Did I say that for five minutes you would be treated like a nobleman ? You might softly kick your heels, and meditate on the transitory nature of earthly things, in that snug little shop for nearly half an hour. Threepenny cigars lasted five-and-twenty minutes in those days. Austere personages of aristocratic mien patronised Mr. Alcachofado. They looked like County Members, Masters in Chancery, Charity Commissioners. They looked as though they belonged to clubs. They called the proprietor Alcatchanything, without the Mr. He was gravely courteous to them, but not more so than to humbler patrons. I remember that he always took in the second edition of *The Globe*. I have, in my time, bespoken it, I think, not without fear and trembling, from a baronet. They were affable creatures, those exalted ones, and talked sedate commonplaces about the House, and the crops, and

the revenue, until I used to fancy I had land and beeves and a
stake in the country.

There was only one absolutely haughty customer. He wore a
spencer and gaiters, and sometimes swore. He smoked a costlier
cigar than the ordinary race of puffers ; and one had to rise from
the big cigar chest while Mr. Alcachofado, a shining bunch of keys
in hand, like a discreet sacristan, unlocked this treasure-coffer and
produced Regalias of price. Yet even this haughty man in the
spencer gave me a bow once when I brushed by him in the lobby
of the House, where I had been waiting two hours and a quarter
on a night when Sir Robert Peel was "up," in the vain hope of
getting into the Strangers' Gallery with an Irish member's order.
The haughty man thought he knew me. I felt so proud that I
had my hair cut the very next day, and determined, like Mr.
Pepys, to "go more like myself."

A grave company we were at Mr. Alcachofado's. Now and then
on Opera nights, dandies in evening dress would stroll in to smoke
a cigarette. There was great scandal one evening—it was Grisi's
benefit—when a tall young man, with a white cravat and a tawny
moustache, ordered Mr. Alcachofado to "open him a bottle of
soda, and look sharp." Those were his very words. There was a
commotion among the customers. Soda-water ! Was this a
tobacconist's and fancy stationer's in the Clapham Road ? As well
might you have asked the beadle of St. George's, Hanover Square,
for hot whisky-toddy between psalm and sermon. Mr. Alcachofado, under the circumstances, was calm. He gave the tall young
desperado one look, to wither him, and in slow and measured
accents, not devoid of a touch of sarcasm, replied, " I sell neither
soda-water nor ginger-beer, nor walking-sticks, nor penny valen-
tines, sir." The customers grimly chuckled at this overwhelming
rebuke. There was nothing left for the tall young man but to
withdraw ; but, as I was nearest the door, I am constrained to
state that as he lounged out he remarked that the "old guy,"
meaning Mr. Alcachofado, "seemed doosid crusty."

He is gone, this Grandison of the counter and till—gone, seemingly, with most other professors of the *grande manière*. The

modern tobacconist is loud-voiced and obtrusive ; proposes to send
you home a box of the "Cabaña Kings" of which you have
scarcely tasted one ; and, ere you have been in his shop five
minutes, gives you a tip for the Two Thousand Guineas. This
was not Mr. Alcachofado's way of doing business. By-the-by, why
wasn't he a Señor ?   But he betrayed no symptoms of Iberian extraction ; and when, seeing an engraving of the Morro Castle itself
on one of his cedar boxes, I strove to draw him out, and asked him
if the picture resembled the place itself, he replied, ambiguously,
that he had not visited foreign parts—adding, after a moment's
pause, that he did not approve of their ways. Whence his Spanish
name, then ?   Whence anybody's name ?   I dealt with a greengrocer once who had the self-same appellation as the last prime
minister of Constantine Palæologus. How Mr. Alcachofado had
come to enter the tobacco business—unless he was a retired
custom-house officer—was to me a mystery.   There was a dim
something about him that always led you to fancy that before he
had dealt in cigars he had been in the Church.

The Morro Castle had to me always a fascinating sound. There
were three boys at the school at Turnham Green, where I completed my education—that is to say, where on the last day of my
last "half" I began to discover that I didn't know anything—
three Spanish creole boys, all hailing from Havana. They kept
very close together and aloof from the rest of the school, and
wrapped themselves up in Castilian pride as in cloaks ; indeed, one
of them subsequently admitted to me that, on leaving Cuba, his
papa had given him two special cautions: to beware of the
" Estrangeros," and not to show them—"enseñar"—the Spanish
tongue. We too were rather shy of them at first ; for there was
a received tradition among us that all foreign boys, when moved
to anger, stabbed. Very unjustly we christened the youngest
creole, Dagger ; his little brother, Bodkin ; and the third, who was
a tall lean lad with glittering eyes, Carving-knife. I think a good
deal of nonsense—as could be proved by the police reports and the
Old Bailey sessions papers—has been talked about the "un-
English" nature of the crime of stabbing. It is not the custom to

carry deadly weapons on the person in England, for the reason
that the laws for the protection of life and property are very
stringent, and, in the main, efficiently administered ; *but I never
heard of a drunken savage Englishman, who could get hold of a
knife in a row, who wouldn't use it ;* nor, as regards the softer sex,
are the biting off the nose of an adversary, and the searing of
her face with a red-hot poker, quite "un-English" or un-Irish
practices.

Our schoolmaster, who was an eccentric instructor, half
Pestalozzi and half Philosopher Square, had an idea that all
Spanish children were weaned upon tobacco, and absolutely
permitted these three creole lads to smoke ; on condition, however,
that they should not light up their papelitos until night time,
when the other boys went to bed. How we used to envy them, as,
marching in Indian file to our dormitories, we could see those
favoured young dons unrolling their squares of tissue-paper, pre-
paratory to a descent into the playground and a quiet smoke !
The demoralisation among the juvenile community caused by this
concession to Spanish customs was but slight.   One or two of us
tried surreptitious weeds on half-holiday afternoons ; but the
Widow Jones in Chiswick Lane did not keep quite such choice
brands in stock as did Mr. Alcachofado of the Morro Castle ; and
Nemesis, in the shape of intolerable nausea, very soon overtook us.
It is astounding, at fourteen years of age, how much agony of
heart, brain, and stomach can be got out of one penny Pickwick.
Pestalozzi Square, Ph. Dr., very wisely refrained from excessive
severity on this head. He made it publicly known that a boy
detected in smoking would not necessarily be caned, but that on
three alternate days for a week following the discovery of his
offence he would be supplied at 1 p.m. with a clean tobacco-pipe
and half an ounce of prime shag in lieu of dinner. We had very
few unlicensed smokers after this announcement.

It was my singular good fortune, ere I left the tutelage of the
sage of Turnham Green, to be admitted to the acquaintance, and
almost to the intimacy, of the creoles. I had somewhat of a
Spanish-sounding name and lineage, and they deemed me not

wholly to belong to the "Estrangeros ;" at all events, they talked
to me, "showed" me some Castilian which was subsequently very
useful to me, and told me as much as I hungered and thirsted to
know about the Morro Castle. For, long before I began to deal
with Mr. Alcachofado, I had pondered over a picture of this
fortress, and mused as to what its real aspect might be. So,
softly and gratefully as dried mint falls upon pea-soup, did the
tales of these Spanish boys about the rich strange island of Cuba
fall upon my willing ear. I saw it in its golden prime, all sugar
and spice, and redolent of coffee-berries and the most fragrant of
cigars. I basked in the rich full light of the tropical sun. I
saw the caballero gravely pacing on his Andalusian jennet ; the
lazy negro pausing as he cut the sugar-cane to suck the luscious
tubes ; the señora in her mantilla ; the señorita with her fan. I
revelled in a voluptuous dream of the torrid clime, where you ate
fifteen oranges before breakfast, and a plateful of preserved
cocoa-nut *at* breakfast ; where you never failed to take a siesta
in your hammock during the noontide heats ; where full evening
costume consisted of a suit of white linen, a Panama hat, and a
guitar ; and where, with any little circumspection, you might
win the hundred thousand dollar prize in the lottery.

I longed to go to Havana, or " the Havannah," as it was termed
in our time. Who has not so longed to visit strange countries
when he was young and imaginative, and had no money ?
Byron's words used to drive us crazy to see Sestos, and Abydos,
and Athens. "Anastasius, or the Memoirs of a Greek "—why does
not some one republish that pearl of picaroon romance ?—made us
tremble with eagerness to see the Fanal of Constantinople and the
Bagnio of Smyrna ; and, later in the day, Eothen sent us wild to
catch a gazelle, and bathe in the Dead Sea, and read the *Quarterly
Review* in the Valley of Jehoshaphat. I cannot say the same of
" Gil Blas." Unsurpassed as Le Sage's great work is as a feat of
story-telling, it is to me singularly deficient in local colour. The
Robbers' Cave might be in Italy, or in England in the days of
Robin Hood. The Archbishop of Granada might be resident at
Barchester Towers. I know Doctor Sangrado. He lives in

Bloomsbury. Now "Don Quixote," on the contrary, is odorous of the real Spanish garlic from the first to the last page. But "Don Quixote" is not a boys' book, whatever you may say. It is a book for men.

Well, the great whirling teetotum of life spun round, and one day it fell, spent, athwart a spot on the map marked "United States of America." I packed up my bundle and crossed the Atlantic, but with no more idea of visiting Havana than I have, at this present writing, of going to Afghanistan. I am not ashamed to confess that I had but a very dim notion indeed respecting the topographical relation in which New York stood towards the Island of Cuba. I think there must have been something wrong in the manner they taught boys geography in our time : it was too sectional ; you were made to swallow Mercator's Projection in isolated scraps of puzzles ; and if your eye wandered towards the Gulf of Mexico when it should have been intent on the Bay of Fundy, they boxed your ears. We used to learn all about the West Indies, and Wilberforce, and Clarkson, and Granville Sharpe ; but no stress was laid on the fact that Cuba, and St. Domingo, and St. Thomas were likewise West India Islands ; and they were never mentioned in connection with North America. I think Admiral Christopher Columbus, or the Spanish Concilio de las Indias, must take some of the blame in this matter. What on earth made them call those American, or rather Columbian, islands Indian ones ? I have never surmounted the early perplexity which beset me on the subject, and to this day it is to me incomprehensible why the passage from Halifax to Bermuda should be such a short and easy one ; you ought to go round the Cape, surely, to the Indies.

Round again went the teetotum, and the tip of its tiny staff pointed to the Southern Atlantic. "Havana" was inscribed on the uppermost facet. Again I packed my bundles, and taking passage in a United States mail steamer, sped past Charleston, the which luckless city General Gillmore was then actively engaged in warming with Greek fire, and which Northern preachers were cheerfully and charitably comparing every Sunday

to Sodom and Gomorrah.   On the third day we were close on the
Gulf Stream, and the usual feat of parlour, or rather gangway
magic, was performed by a boatswain's mate, who lowered a
bucket of water over the side and bade us plunge our hands
into it. It was cold as ice. Twenty minutes afterwards he
lowered the bucket again, drew up more water, and bade us dip.
We did, and the water was tepid, almost warm. There was an
increase of thirty degrees in temperature, and we were in that
stream which an irate American politician once threatened to
dam up and divert from the shores of England, thus leaving us
"out in the cold," and freezing perfidious Albion to the glacial
mean of Spitzbergen.

Three times—I do not understand the mysteries of navigation
—we crossed the Gulf Stream. We skirted the coast of Florida
so closely that we could see the pines that made a grim horizon
to that swampy shore—so closely, that you might almost fancy
you could see Secession in arms shaking its fists at the Stars
and Stripes we carried. All this country was, at the time to
which I refer, a land tabooed and accursed in Northern eyes.
It was the coast of a rebellious state.   Below St. Augustine's,
half-way between that and Key West, we saw the coral reefs
and the Everglades. Coral reefs, I may observe, do not make
so pretty a show on the coast of Florida as the material does, in
the form of bracelets and earrings, in Mr. Phillips's windows in
Cockspur Street. In fact, a prudent shipmaster keeps as far
away from the coral reefs as he possibly can.

We should also have sighted Cape Florida Light and Carysfort
Light ; but the Confederates having carefully put the lights out,
to favour blockade running and perplex their enemies as far as
they could, it was rather ticklish navigation after sunset. However, it is but a few days' voyage from New York to Cuba, and
we had a tight ship and great confidence in our captain. Occasionally, when the look-out man signalled a sail, there was a
slight exhibition of nervousness among the passengers.   The
loyal immediately assumed the stranger to be the *Alabama*, and
indulged in dire forebodings that within two hours the steamer's

chronometers would be ticking in the cabin of Captain Raphael Semmes, C.S.A., the ship burnt or bonded, and themselves carried off to some port in the White Sea or the Indian Archipelago, thence to find their way to their destination as best they could. The disloyal, of whom I am afraid we had a considerable proportion among our passengers, generally jumped at the conclusion that the speck on the horizon, momentarily growing larger, was a Yankee gunboat, specially detached from the blockading squadron to overhaul us. What sudden declarations there were of "whole hog" Union sentiments !—what divings into state-rooms, there presumably to make such little matters as revolvers, Confederate commissions, and rebel mail-bags, snug !

The captain was a discreet man, Union to the backbone, but not inveterate against the opposite party. We had one passenger on board who, for all the privacy in which he kept, and the very large cloak in which he wrapped himself, was unmistakably, inside and out, Southern Greyback and "Secesh." To this gentleman in political difficulties I heard our worthy captain remark one morning, "My Christian friend, I'll tell you what it is : as soon as we get inside the Morro I should advise you to clear out of one of the starboard ports, and never stop running till we've got steam up again. The smell of Uncle Sam's mail-bags ain't good for you. It ain't, indeed." The which, I take it, was very sensible and at the same time very kind-hearted counsel.

All this time, while we were eating and drinking, and lounging and smoking, and dawdling over books and newspapers, and card-playing, and listening to the grand pianoforte in the saloon, which was exemplarily punished at least a dozen times a day by Mrs. Colonel Spankie and Miss Alexandra McStinger, lady passengers—and pretending that the time hung heavily on our hands, when, to tell the truth, sluggards as we were, we revelled in our laziness—there was going on all around us, and to a certain extent in our very selves, a curiously phenomenal process called Transformation. You have read poor Hawthorne's delicious book ; you have read "Faust" (with an English "crib") ;

you have seen Lucas Cranach's picture of the Fontaine de
Jouvence in the Berlin gallery ? Well, we and our surroundings had become Transformed.

I had left New York in the middle of January, and in the
rigidest throes of a Northern winter. The snow lay thick in the
streets. They were skating on the lake in the Central Park.
There were midnight sleighing parties on the Bloomingdale
Road. The steamers on the North River had frozen fringes on
the water-lines of their hulls, like the callous raggedness thrown
out from the ends of a fractured bone ; and you could see the
very shapes of the ferry-boats' keels cut out in the quickly part-
ing ice that gathered about the landing-place. I had left Pier
No. Seventy-seven, bottom of I forget which street, swathed in
furs and woollens, and shivering through all my wrappers. I
heaped mountains of extraneous coverlets in my berth that night.
It was not quite so cold next day. On the third it was positively
mild. On the fourth morning, taking my ante-breakfast walk on
deck, I remarked with astonishment that I was clad in a full
suit of the very thinnest nankeen, and that I wore a very broad-
brimmed straw hat. Nankeen, white linen, or thin blue flannel,
was the only wear among my fellow-passengers, and the ladies
had become positive Zephyrs. The smallest children on board
testified very conclusively indeed as to the weather having
become warmer, by removing their apparel altogether, unless
restrained by parents or nurses ; and then I remembered that I
had kicked off all the bed-clothes during the night, and had had
troubled dreams bearing on iced cider-cup. We had all become
Transformed. Where yesterday was a fire-shovel, to-day was a
fan. We looked no more on a gray angry wintry ocean, but on a
summer sea. It seemed ten years ago since there had been any
winter, and yet that was only the day before yesterday.

For four-and-twenty hours did we sigh and swelter and complain of the intolerable heat, and yet think it the most delightful
thing in the world. We dined at four o'clock, as usual ; but the
purser, if he contracted for our meals, must have made rather a
good thing of our repast that day. The first course was scarcely

over before seven-eighths of the diners rushed on deck to see the highlands of Cuba. Yonder, rather blue and indistinct as yet, was the Pan of Matanzas. That day we dined no more ; but, there being a "bar" on deck, forward, with a New England bar-keeper of many virtues and accomplishments in his profession, sundry cheerful spirits adjourned to his little caboose, and, with steadfast and smiling conviviality of countenance, did "liquor up" on Bourbon and old Rye, till the Pan of Matanzas, to which we had come so close that it was clearly visible to the naked eye, must have been to the convivialists more indistinct than ever.

We were yet many miles from Havana ; but by the help of strong opera-glasses and lively conversation and a glorious tropical sunset, they were the shortest miles I ever knew, by land or sea. Coasting along the northern shore of Cuba from Matanzas westward, by high hills and white houses which, without any intervening beach or sand, came right down to the water's edge, like the castle-crowned vine-hills of the Rhine, we sighted, just before sundown, the Morro Castle itself: a great mass of dun-coloured rock, and tower, and battlement, and steep, of which the various parts seem to have grown into one another, like the rocky convent of the Sagrado San Miguel, so that you could scarcely tell which was castle and which crag. From its summit floats the flag of the Most Catholic Queen, blood-red and gold ; and in front, and in the sea, like a tall grenadier on guard, stands the Morro Lighthouse. No Confeds have put *that* out.

We pass between the Morro and a promontory called the Punta, and can see a harbour, forested with masts, and a city all glancing and twinkling with light. We revel in thoughts of landing ; of abandoning our keys to a commissionnaire, and leaving the examination of our luggage until the morrow morning ; of rushing to an hotel ; of bathing and supping and going to the Tacon Theatre, or eating ices at La Dominica, after the band had done playing on the Plaza de Armas. Bless you, we know all about Havana by this time. I seem to have been familiar with the place for years. Did not Dagger and Bodkin and eke Carving-

knife tell me all about it ?   But the Captain of the Port of San
Cristobal de la Habana is a great man—a very great man, under
correction of the Captain-General Dulce be it spoken—and his
laws are stringent.   The sunset gun has been fired ; the last notes
of the warning trumpets have died away from the ramparts.   We
are just permitted to snuggle into the outer harbour ; but there
is no landing for us until six a.m., and under the guns of the
Morro we are bound to remain all night.   A very few years ago
even this privilege would not have been granted us, and we
should have been forced to turn our heads seaward, and anchor
in the roads.

It was tantalising, certainly ; but still it was exceedingly pleasant, and no one felt inclined to grumble.   It was something, at
least, to know that the huge engines were at rest, and that we
should hear their churning and grinding, their panting and
trembling, no more, until, like Poor Jack in Dibdin's song, we
"went to sea again."   So all the call was for coffee and cigars ;
and we idled about the deck and speculated on what might be
going on in the innumerable tenements in which the lights, now
dim, now bright, were shining.   Then out came the moon, like a
great phantom of greenish white, and spread her arms right over
the city of Havana.   We could make out the hoary towers of the
cathedral, and the church where is the tomb of Christopher
Columbus ; we could see the long slanting shadows cast by the
beetling guns of the Morro on the rubbled walls.   Boats came
and went on the glassy waters of the harbour.   There were
lights in the port-holes of the ships too.   What was going on
there, I wonder ?   Skipper drinking cold rum-and-water.   First
officer playing a quiet rubber with the surgeon, the supercargo,
and dummy.   Purser making up his accounts ; foremast men
drinking "Sweethearts and Wives," in the round-house.   Everybody glad that the voyage is over, save perhaps that poor
Northern lady in the captain's state-room, propped up with
pillows, affectionately tended by that little band of Sisters of
Charity who are going to New Orleans, and who is dying of consumption.   Even she, perchance, is grateful that the restless

engines no longer moan and labour, and that to-morrow she may land and die in peace.

As "good nights" and "buenas noches" cross each other in the harbour, you begin to wish you could find a friend to take a second in "All's well." For the waning moon now deserts you, and only the twinkling lights shine out from the black masses of buildings. The lights, too, are growing fewer, and ever since you came into port—which was at about eight o'clock—you have heard from time to time gusts of wild martial music from the shore. These gusts, the captain tells you, are the strains of the military bands playing in the Plaza de Armas. Hark! a most tremendous crash! then what a quaint yet plaintive flow of melody. Is that a Seguidilla, or a Cubana, or one of the hundred variations of the Jota Aragonese? Now comes another crash; the cymbals have it clearly; the bassoons have given out; 'tis the big drum that is making all the running; the cymbals are nowhere; bah, it is a dead-heat, and the *grosse caisse* and the plated dishes come in together. Now the sounds have changed their direction. The soldiers are marching home to their barracks. Now the wild sounds grow fainter; now they die away altogether, and Havana is left to silence and to me.

I walked the deck until long after the ship was wrapped in darkness—all save the illumined binnacles and my fellow deckwalkers' cigar-tips. It was not at all the kind of night for going to bed. It was, the rather, a night on which to stroll and stroll, and indulge in the deleterious habit of smoking, and wonder how many broadsides from the guns of the Morro it would take to blow you out of the water, and try to remember one of the movements of the Jota Aragonese, and at last, softly stealing into the saloon and quite disdaining state-room berth, to fling yourself on a couch and dream till morning of Mr. Alcachofado and the three young creoles of Turnham Green.

II.

The Humours of Havana.

HE morning, you may be sure, did not find me a sluggard on my couch in the saloon. Never rose a lark, or a landscape-painter on his first sketching-tour in Wales, with more alacrity than did I from the steam-packet's scrubby velvet sofa. Early bird as I was, there had been even lighter sleepers ; and the ship, above and below, was full of joyous life. During the few hours of darkness, too, that process of Transformation I lately spoke of had been making rapid progress. I had fallen asleep, it is true, in Spanish waters but in Anglo-Saxon company, but I woke up on board a caravel belonging to the Spanish Armada. The grave, sonorous, and dignified Castilian—noblest and most Romanesque of tongues —resounded on every side ; and although the day wanted several hours of breakfast-time, the blue filmy fumes of the cigaritos were floating about the cabin like aromatic gossamer.

The consumption of chocolate was immense. Only yesterday we had been content with an early morning cup of coffee ; but chocolate is the sole recognised Spanish desayuno, or breakfast; nor, with a glass of cold water and a cigarito afterwards, does it make you so very bilious. Or is it that your liver becomes, on your entrance into these torrid climes, so utterly disorganised that nothing can make you *more* bilious, save the yellow fever which kills you ? "If in doubt, take a drink," says the American proverb. You had better give chocolate the benefit of the doubt, and drink *that;* for although made so thick that a spoon will well-nigh stand upright in the cup, it is a most delicious and refreshing beverage. I noticed, too, that several of

our Transatlantic fellow-passengers, in compliment to the climate
and the Spanish flag, had substituted chocolate for their habitual
"morning glory," or cocktail ; in fact, one gentleman, used to
these latitudes, informed me that he had "swore off" alcohol
altogether, until when returning from New Orleans, whither he
was bound, he should be north of Cape Florida again ; "and
then," he concluded, "I guess I will change my breath, and
nominate my p'ison"—a prudent resolve, and one that Englishmen as well as Americans would do well to imitate in the tropics.
Yellow Jack is a bitter foe, and swamp fever a fearful scourge ;
but I will back Old Rye and brandy-pawnee to sweep off more
Anglo-Saxons in a week than the "vomito" or the fever will do
in a month.

Tables and chairs covered with oranges—come from none could
tell precisely where ; but it seems to rain oranges in Havana—
and the presence of sundry officials in suits of white linen or
faint blue stripe, with huge Panama hats, helped to complete the
idea of Transformation. Are you aware of the beauties of a
Panama hat ? It is of fine straw—straw so fine and so exquisitely
plaited that it appears to be of one united glossy nature. It is
as soft as silk, and as strong as chain-mail, and as elastic as
caoutchouc. If you are caught in a shower of rain, and your
Panama gets wet through, you have only to wring it out as
though it were a towel, and hang it on your walking-stick to dry,
and in a quarter of an hour it will have regained its pristine
shape. The Spaniards declare that a Panama is shot-proof and
an infallible protection against sunstroke ; but of these assertions
I have my doubts. The life of a Panama hat may be measured
by that of a raven. It is supposed never to wear out. At all
events, there is a cunning hatter in New York, who, for ten
dollars, will undertake to return to you, as good as new, a
Panama which is twenty years old, and has been in the wars,
and shipwrecked, and thrown into a lime-kiln, a tan-pit, and a
bucket of tar. This peerless hat is not to be purchased at a mean
price. It is the dearest head-gear manufactured. Red-skinned
maidens have intoned whole cantos of Indian epics while they

plaited and sewed together those minute circles of straw. A
good Panama will stand you in from fifty to seventy-five *pesos
de oro*—from ten to fifteen pounds sterling.

And now, on this first of tropical mornings, did the steamer's
state-rooms give up their semi-dead. Whole families of señoras
and señoritas made their appearance in shiny black and pink
silks, and low mantillas, and pink stockings, and white satin
shoes, and colossal fans, ready for any amount of flirtation,
serenade-hearing, and bull-fight witnessing. Where had those
señoras and señoritas been for the last five days? On their
backs, I trow, in their berths, screeching piteously when the
steamer pitched; moaning dismally when she rolled; imbibing
chlorodyne, cognac, tea, and other nostrums against sea-sickness,
and calling upon many saints. Our Lady de los Remedios
might be the best to invoke under such circumstances, perchance.

There is an immensely stout old lady in violet-coloured satin,
with a back-comb as high as the horn of Queen Philippa in old
illuminations, a burnt-sienna countenance, a cavalry recruit's
moustache, a bright green umbrella, and an oaken casket clasped
with brass under one arm. This is the old lady, I apprehend, to
whom the stewardess used to take in such tremendous rations of
stewed beefsteak, fried bananas, and bottled ale every day at
dinner-time. She suffered awfully. Her cries for "Cerveza
Inglesa" were incessant. She was troubled in her mind one
afternoon when we had a chopping sea on, and sent for one of
the Sisters of Charity; but I am sorry to say that nurse and
patient did not agree, and that the good sister was speedily dismissed with unhandsome epithets. Sister Egyptiaca being of
Irish extraction, fresh from an orphanage in New York—whence
she was going, good little creature, in perfect peace and content-
ment, to risk her life in the fever-haunted wards of a New
Orleans hospital—and speaking nothing but English, and the old
lady only talking Spanish, may have had something to do with
their misunderstanding. However, the old lady is all right now.
She is very voluble; she has given the steward a golden ducat;
and he has kindled a match for her, and she has begun to smoke

a cigarette. It is reported that the oaken casket with the brass clasps is full of diamonds. The stewardess says she always kept it under her pillow during the voyage. She looks a·rich old lady ; comfortably quilted with ounces, moidores, and pieces of eight. I connect her in my mind with a huge sugar estate and teeming gangs of negroes. I would rather be her overseer than her slave, I think.

It is worthy of remark, as another element in the Transformation we have undergone, that our talk is now all of a metallic coinage. Five days ago nobody had anything but greenbacks. The stewards won't look at greenbacks now. Five days ago, the passenger who had hoarded a silver dollar was quite a lion ; he who had an English sovereign hanging to his watch-chain was made much of ; and one thin dry New Englander, who was absolutely the owner of an American gold double eagle—the handsomest coin in the world—kept it in a wash-leather case, like a watch, would only exhibit it on pressing solicitation, and I am led to infer made rather a good thing of it by taking the precious piece forward and allowing the " hands " to smell it at five cents a sniff. But what cared we for paper money now ? Piles of gold suddenly made their appearance. Little bills for stimulants were paid in five-dollar pieces bearing the effigy of Isabel Segunda. For the first time in my life I saw those numismatic parallels to Brobdingnag and Lilliput—to dignity and impudence —the gold dollar, which is about the size of an English silver penny, and the gold doubloon or ounce, which, to the dazed and delighted eye of the possessor, looks as large as one of King Crœsus' chariot wheels, but is in reality about the diameter of a crown-piece and is worth three pounds ten shillings sterling.

They say Havana is the dearest city in the world ; and I cannot help thinking that the costliness of living there is mostly due to the fact of the ounce being held to many intents and purposes the financial unit. It is the creole sovereign. If you stay at a friend's country-house and his body-servant has valeted you, you give the man an ounce ; if you bet on a cock-fight, you bet an ounce ; if a bull-fighter has won your approbation, you send him

C

an ounce ; if the prima donna at the Tacon takes a benefit, you
purchase a stall and pay an ounce—or as many ounces as your
admiration for the prima donna prompts you to disburse. A
whole lottery-ticket—an "entiero," as it is called—costs an ounce.
If you hire a volante and two horses for the day, the driver very
coolly demands an ounce for his fare : in short, I should imagine
that the only wild animal in Cuba must be the Ounce. "I call
that man a gentleman," I once heard a German settler in Havana
remark, "who can afford to lose at 'monté' or 'tressilio,'
every day of his life, four or five ounces." Four or five ounces !
Ingots and goldbeaters' hammers ! to what a Tom Tiddler's
ground had I come !

I went on deck, where everything was noise, bustle, and Transformation, and where they seemed already to be taking in oranges,
bananas, and cocoa-nuts as a return cargo. The skipper only
remained untransformed. He wore the same fluffy white hat,
the same long-skirted bottle-green coat with the same blue-black
velvet collar, and the same shepherd's-plaid trousers in which he
had stood imposingly on the paddle-bridge of his ship, foot of
pier Number Something, New York city, five days since. He
had a heart of oak, this skipper of ours, and I believe was an
excellent seaman and navigator ; but I could never divest myself
of the impression that he had been concerned in dry goods, or
even a wooden nutmeg factory, before he had taken to going
down to the sea in ships. He had made, I daresay, fifty trips to
Cuba, but he couldn't speak Spanish yet. He pressed the doctor
into his service to act as interpreter in a slight dispute with the
health officer. "Ain't posted up in his lingo," he unaffectedly
remarked.

I looked over the side and drank in a spectacle the most
gloriously picturesque I had ever beheld. I have travelled a
good deal ; but there are many spots, even on the map of Europe,
which to me are still *terra incognita*. I have never been to India.
I have never been in Australia. Looking out upon the crowded
port of Havana, I was reminded irresistibly of the market-scene
in "Masaniello"—the Morro Castle doing duty for Vesuvius.

We were close upon a quay swarming with sunburnt varlets in red nightcaps, in striped nightcaps, in broad flapping straw hats, and some with silken kerchiefs of gay colours twisted round their heads. Nearly all wore gaudy sashes round their loins. They were bare-armed and bare-legged ; their shirts were open at the breast ; and if they had jackets, those garments hung loose upon their shoulders, or with the sleeves tied in a knot before them. Dark elf locks, black glittering eyes, earrings, and little dangling crosses round the neck ; baskets of fish and baskets of fruit, crates of crockery, coops of poultry ; cries of gratulation, welcome, derision, defiance, quarrels never ending in blows, general hubbub and confusion ; and over all the hot, hot Sun and the cloudless vault of blue.

But the market-scene in "Masaniello" soon faded away to nothingness. Havana began to assert its own individuality. I saw a town whose houses were painted in all the colours of the rainbow. I saw long lines of gray and crumbling bastions, and curtains and ravelins built in old times by jealous Spanish viceroys, and which I learned, not without pleasure, General Dulce, the then Captain-General, was beginning to demolish, to give the pent-up city of Havana elbow-room. From all these bastions and ravelins the morning drums and trumpets of the garrison were braying and rub-a-dubbing at the most alarming rate. The port seemed as full of shipping as the Pool of London ; and what scant show of blue water there was to spare was packed close as Cowes harbour at a regatta with the shore-boats. Pretty little skiffs they are, with a lateen sail, often decorated with a full-length portrait of San Cristobal, the patron saint of Havana, and with a gaily striped awning aft.

From where we lay was a good twenty minutes' row or sail to the custom-house. Were the Americans to gain possession of Cuba—a consummation which, for many reasons, is most devoutly to be wished, for they would be bound to commence their occupation by the abolition of slavery—they would have twenty piers built in the inner port in less than six months, and the passenger steamers would come quietly up to the pier-foot and discharge

their passengers on the wharves without any boats at all ; but
this is not the Spanish way of doing business. " Mañana," they
would answer, were this necessary reform pressed on their attention. The authorities are of opinion that the harbour boatmen
have a right to live as well as other folks ; so you are not allowed
to proceed from your ship to the shore without the intermediary
of a boatman, to whom you pay a dollar and as much more as
he can argue you out of. He never threatens, never is rude : his
endeavours to obtain an additional four-and-twopence cannot
even be called begging. He puts the case to you as one between
man and man ; he appeals to your sense of justice, your self-
respect, your honour. You are a caballero ; he is a caballero.
This—here he rests on his oars a moment, or objurgates Pepe,
his assistant, who is putting on too much sail—will at once lead
you to accede to his demand. The name of the boat which conveyed me to the shore on this said morning was " La Rectitud."
The boatman was a most unconscionable rogue ; but there was
something in the calm assumption of dignity in the name on the
stern which drew the dollars from us as though we had been two-
years children.

I am reminded that when I use the first person singular I
might with greater propriety use the plural, for in this trip to
Havana I made one in a party of three. I had two genial
travelling companions, both fellow-countrymen, in whose mirthful
fellowship I enjoyed to the full all the humours of Havana, and
with one of whom I was destined to travel to a stranger and more
distant land, of which in process of time I purpose to discourse.
But as these travelling companions happen to be alive and
merry—as they will probably read these papers, and as one in
the Old and the other in the New World are as well known as
Charing Cross—I feel that it would be impertinent to drag them
into a rambling and fantastic narration, full of perverse conceits
and most egregious fancies ; and I hesitate, too, to veil them
under thin pseudonyms or provoking dashes.*

* I may partially lift the veil as regards them now. One of my travelling companions (alas), Don Eustaquio Barron, whom to know was to love,

Let me, then, the old Babbler, be solely responsible for all I put my egotism to ; and as for any other travellers, not my immediate companions, whom I may touch upon, do you set them down as mere brain-worms, abstractions, and creatures of the imagination. Do you know that I was once most savagely handled by the *Affectionate Review* for having made an " unmanly attack " on the character of a lady, in depicting the airiest shadow in the world of a harmless spinster, by name Miss Wapps, with whom, years ago, I journeyed due north as far as Cronstadt ? To please critics of the affectionate school, all travellers should be blind and deaf and dumb, and should write their words in invisible ink and publish them in coal-cellars.

I, then, Babbler, having, after many shouts and with much loss of inward animal moisture, selected a boat from among upwards of fifty applicants, saw my luggage thereinto, and free pratique having been granted by the officer of health, was rowed to shore. I should not have minded that health officer's boat as a conveyance but for the thought that people whose business is mainly with the quarantine and the lazaretto usually carry about with them the seeds of the cholera or the yellow fever, and die thereof. It was a most luxurious shallop, with an awning striped crimson and white, a rich carpet, and cushioned benches. The crimson and gold banner of Spain, with the crown on, floated at the stern ; and under the awning the health officer lolled at his ease, clad in bright nankeen, a red cockade in his Panama, and smoking a very big Puro. My passport, a document with a very big red seal, granted me by Mr. Archibald, her Majesty's Consul at New York, had been left with the purser on board the steamer, and would duly be transferred to the Havana police authorities.

and whose princely hospitality I enjoyed during my stay in Mexico, is dead. Of mingled British and Spanish lineage—he used laughingly to say that he scarcely knew whether it was in English or in Spanish that he thought— his friends declared that he had Two Hearts, and that both were of gold. He was continually travelling about, doing kind and generous and noble things ; and gentle and simple, rich and poor, alike bewailed his untimely death.

The journey to the shore is very picturesque, though somewhat tedious. One man rows; another attends to the sail; both are smoking and occasionally squabble; and you, the passenger, are expected to steer. If you happen to be totally unacquainted with that art and mystery, the possibility of your running foul of other craft in the port is not a very remote one; and sometimes, while the boatmen are quarrelling or singing a little duet about "Juani-i-i-ta, la chi-i-i-quita!" the boat lets you know that she has something to say for herself, by heeling over and capsizing. But I believe no passenger in a shore-boat was ever known to be drowned before he had paid his fare; and if you steer badly, the helmsman in the next boat may be steering worse; and the two negatives make an affirmative, saying "yes" to the question whether you are to get safe to the custom-house. I suppose there are persons who can steer by intuition. I know there are people who can drive mail phaetons, mix salad, and compose charades, without ever having been taught. It is a gift. One is born to it, as to roasting meat and playing the overture to "Semiramide" on the chin.

The custom-house was an apartment as big as a barn—all the rooms in Havana are huge. The floor was intolerably dirty; but the roof was a magnificent open timber one: the timber being in solid beams of delightfully fragrant cedar. So you had the Augean Stables underneath and Solomon's Palace in all its glory above— not an uncommon contrast in Cuba. The custom-house officers gave us very little trouble. I addressed the first gentleman with a cockade I met as "Señor"—I should perhaps have called him "Caballero"—begged a cigar light from him, and slipped a dollar into his hand. He opened one of my trunks, let a little tobacco-smoke into the orifice to fumigate it, and then dismissed me with a very low bow.

Then I was handed to a little grated wicket, where another official—who was smoking so desperately that he sat, as it were, in the midst of a fleecy cloud, like one of Sir James Thornhill's allegories in the Painted Hall at Greenwich—asked me my name and country, and delivered to me a printed license to reside in

Cuba for the space of three calendar months; which was very kind on his part, seeing that I only intended to remain in the island until the West India mail-packet came in from St. Thomas. This license cost a good deal of money—four or five dollars, I think; and I noticed that, when the official had filled up the form, he was a very long time in sanding it from a small pepper-caster, and looked very hard at me. I know from long experience what being intently regarded by an official of the Latin race means, and so "executed" myself without delay. We parted the best of friends, and I was a dollar the poorer.

I was now free to proceed to an hotel; but this was much more easily said than done. In the first place, there were no public conveyances about save the volantes, which are vehicles far too ethereal to carry heavy luggage; in the next, to find any tolerably comfortable hotel in Havana is a labour which, had it been imposed on Hercules, might have caused that strong man to be a little less conceited about his triumph over the Eryman-thian boar and the eleven other difficulties. The wealthy and splendid city of Havana is worse off for hotels than any other in the civilised world. The Antilles, perhaps, cannot be held as belonging entirely to civilisation; but, as the "Queen" of the Antilles, I think Havana might maintain at least one decent inn.

There is an hotel in the Plaza Isabel Segunda, close to the Tacon Theatre, kept by M. Legrand, a Frenchman; but I had heard dismal reports as to its cleanliness, and it was situated, besides, beyond the walls, whereas I wanted to be near the Plaza de Armas and the sea. There is a very excellent boarding-house, clean, comfortable, and well appointed, kept by Mrs. Almé, an American lady; but her accommodation is limited, and her establishment is nearly always as "complete" as a Parisian omni-bus on a wet day. I have been told, also, that there is a slight drawback to the comfort you enjoy at Mrs. Almé's in the fact of the house being the chosen resort of consumptive invalids from the United States, who have fled from the asperity of the northern winter to the warmer sky of Cuba. But they are often in the penultimate stage of the disease when they land; they don't get better ; and it is apt to spoil your dinner—so I was told—when, inquiring for your next neighbour of the day before who talked so charmingly of the last opera and so hopefully of the coming bull-fight, you are informed that he has been dead for some hours, and will be buried this sundown in the Potters' Field.   You grow accustomed to this at last, for it may be said, without exaggeration, life in these regions of "vomito" and fever resembles life on board a man-o'-war in war time.   You are very merry with Jack and Tom overnight ; and on the morrow Jack is "knocked over" and Tom "loses the number of his mess," and you say "Poor Jack !" "Poor Tom !"   Their clothes are sold by auction before the mast, and you forget all about the sad occurrence.

With the exception of Legrand's and Mrs. Almé's, the inns of Havana are all very like what I should imagine the fondas and posadas of Old Spain, away from Madrid, to be.   I had heard such dreadful stories about them, that, blinking the pulmonary drawback, I determined to try Mrs. Almé's.   By this time, with the assistance of several willing and grinning negroes, who danced with delight at the gift of a very small silver coin—I never saw any copper money in Havana—my luggage had been piled on a machine closely resembling one of those miniature drays in England on which a very small barrel of beer is drawn by a very big horse, conducted by a very big man.   The beast of draught was in this case a bullock, with a tremendous yoke, not over his shoulders but right across his forehead.   The poor animal certainly earned his bread by the sweat of his brow ; and to judge from his lean flanks and protruding bones, I should infer that the jerked beef he might furnish, subsequent to his demise, would be dear at threepence a pound.

The conductor, who sat the animal side-saddle fashion, was a wrinkled old negro whose wool had turned white, and whose wicked old head—he was *such* a nasty-looking old man—was surmounted by a ragged straw hat.   He was singing, of course, occasionally varying that recreation by skinning and gobbling the pulp of some oranges, of which he had a pocketful, and on the whole took things very easily. I presume he was a slave. I was bound to walk behind this sable drayman ; for although I might have taken a volante, was it not my duty to follow my luggage ? And but for an uncomfortable fancy that if I stepped on the dray and sat aside my trunk I should look like a traitor being drawn to execution at Tyburn on a sledge, I would have patronised that mode of locomotion.

There was no obtaining admission at Mrs. Almé's. Intending visitors had written for their rooms a month or six weeks in advance ; and the mansion was as full of phthisis as a Ventnor lodging-house. Next I tried the " Fonda de America," a few streets off. There was some room in that hotel, which was under the arcades of a crumpling old portal, not unlike the Covent Garden piazzas, with the aroma of all the Spanish onions, leeks, and shallots of the adjoining market hanging about the staircase :—a despotism of garlic tempered by tobacco-smoke. The landlady was a German—fair, fat, and twenty-five, and was basking in a rocking-chair, enjoying the smoke and the smell of onions with apparently intense gusto. The perfume was almost like Fatherland. She had one huge apartment to let. It was not vacated yet ; but the occupant, a French commercial traveller, who had seemingly just risen, and who was carefully oiling and curling himself before a glass, most courteously permitted me to inspect the room. He was quite affable, indeed, and was good enough to inform me that a packet I saw lying on a side-table contained some of the genuine Amaranthine soap of her Majesty Queen Victoria, patented and gold medalled at the Universal Exhibition of 1855, and that he was just then clearing through the custom-house eighteen cases of Bully's Toilet Vinegar. Ere I quitted his quarters he likewise enounced the opinion that the island of Cuba was *un fichu pays*, and that the landlady of the Fonda de America was a *mégère*.

Heaven bless the Frenchman, wherever in the world's weary journey you find him ! He is always easy, sprightly, confidential, and conversational. Bless him for his grimaces, his airy philosophy, his harmless, naïve vanity. He is, with the exception of the Englishman, the best travelling comrade in the world ; only, for an Englishman to speak to a stranger to whom he has not been introduced, the stranger must be in the cramp-stage of the cholera morbus, or on the point of having his brains blown out by robbers. Then, but then only, the Briton becomes own brother to the man he doesn't know. But the Frenchman waits for no such crisis.

There was room at the "America," but not for all of me. You will bear in mind that I was in triplicate ; and so raw was I then to Hispano-American usages, that I imagined that a traveller with money in his pocket had a right to a bedroom to himself. I had yet to learn that our English word comrade is derived from three Spanish words—" camar a dos," double-bedded lodgings. I took a bath at the "America," for the good of the house and my own (the oftener you bathe before eating, and the more seldom after-wards, in the tropics, the better it will be for you) ; and then the dray and I and the negro, who was a spiteful old man and had lost his temper fearfully by this time, resumed our peregrinations. We tried, I think, at "Los Dos Amigos," "La Reyna de Ingla-terra," "La Corona de España," and other hostelries ; but the answer in all of them was "no room," or "not room enough." I was, for the nonce, El Señor "Ferguson," and not fated to lodge anywhere ; and the negro sitting side-saddle on the bullock began to spit and swear in Spanish like an infuriated old cat.

But to me the time was not all lost. Far from it. I had begun to study the humours of Havana. The time had worn away, it was ten o'clock, and the city had burst into the full blaze of tropical life. The Anglo-Americans rail at Havana because the streets are so narrow and so tortuous ; but ah ! from ten to four p.m. how grateful you are for narrow devious lanes, in lieu of broad staring thoroughfares ! You have the inestimable blessing of Shade. Now and then you must take, perforce, a hot bath and frizzle for a moment in the sunshine as you cross a plaza ; or, turning a corner, the sun, suddenly espying you, cleverly shoots a ray at your head which pierces your brain well-nigh as an arrow would, but you are soon in the shade again.

A STREET IN HAVANA.

Page 42.

The streets of Havana are perhaps as clean as those of most southern European towns. The principal sanitary inspectors are named Garlic and Tobacco-smoke. They are at least determined to keep the other stenches down. The roadway is littered and untidy, but who should complain of litter composed mainly of orange-peel, the rinds of pine-apples, cocoa-nut shells, fragments of melons, and exhausted Indian corn-cobs? I must go to Covent Garden again for a comparison. Don't you know that delightful litter between the grand avenue and the old Hummums —I mean that spot where the orange-boxes are bursting, and the almonds are tumbling out of their sacks, and the Irish market-women sit in the June afternoon shelling peas. The scene is untidy, but grand. I always think of the Garden of Eden run to seed, in consequence of the gardener, Adam, having been turned away for stealing apples.

There is but a ridiculous apology for a foot-pavement in these streets. The average width of the *trottoir* certainly does not exceed twelve inches. It is a kerbstone with nothing to curb. I have fancied this exiguity of path to be a deliberate device on the part of the municipality to keep up the practice of politeness in Havana, for of course, if you meet any one on the *trottoir* proceeding in a contrary direction to your own, you naturally step into the kennel to allow him to pass. You don't give him the wall, you give him the totality of the pavement. This hypothesis, I fear, however, is as fantastical as the one suggested, that the narrowness of the streets in Havana is also due to premeditation, and is designed to allow opposite neighbours to light their cigars from each other's weeds.

Small as is the space between the houses, they preserve, nevertheless, a tolerably perpendicular elevation ; whereas in the town of Algiers, which in the narrowness of its thoroughfares closely resembles Havana, the houses are built on the lean-to principle. Each story seems on the brink of toppling over, and at the roofs opposite houses nearly kiss each other. I have heard that the Moorish architects adopted this style of construction from notions of economy. You see that all but the very narrowest strip of sky *must* be shut out. Why ? The heavens above are for ten hours out of the twenty-four one blazing basin of burnished copper. The Cubans, however, being wealthy, can afford to leave a wider space between their houses ; but while the sun shines they shut him out with vast awnings of parti-coloured stuffs. This aspect of Havana would delight the heart of an Edgington. The populous part of the city is one huge marquee.

Ah, and how shady the shops are ! There are some as dark as the purser's store-room in a cockpit. You enter them, not only to shop, but to bestow yourself in a rocking-chair, to nod, and to take, if you please, forty winks. The shopkeeper never dreams of disturbing you. He puts your nap in the bill ; that is to say, he adds fifty per cent. to the price of the articles you wish to purchase. Of course you beat him down. You bargain for everything in Havana "mayor o menor," wholesale or retail. The apothecary who sells you a blue pill expects an amicable little tussle over the price. What matter ? It fills up the time ; and unless you are concerned in sugar or coffee, you are sure to have plenty of time hanging on your hands. "Are there no beggars at your gate ? are there no poor about your lands ?" the Poet Laureate might indignantly ask. Well, the poor are slaves, and are very fat and shiny and seemingly well cared for (which does not in the least militate against slavery being a stupid, blundering, and accursed anachronism, of which the Spaniards themselves are heartily sick) ; and as for the beggars, I never saw any in Havana ; and had I met one, I should certainly not have presumed to offer him less than a golden dollar.

The tradespeople seldom, if ever, put their names over their shop-fronts. They adopt signs instead—not painted or plastic ones as the Americans and the Germans do, but simply written inscriptions usually implying some ethical allusion. "La Rectitud," our old friend of the boat, is much patronised by the mercers ; but that tradesman in the Calle O'Reilly must have had queer ideas of rectitude when he charged me seventy-five dollars for a dress professedly made of pina or pine-apple fibre, but which subsequently turned out to be a silk grenadine from Lyons, not worth three guineas. Then you have "La Probidad," "La Integridad," "La Buena Fé," "La Consciencia"—all special favourites with the gentlemen of the narrow width and ell wand. Their signs are very pretty, but methinks they do profess too much. Some are simply arrogant, "Todos me elogian"—I am praised by everybody; "Mi fama por el orbe vuela"—my fame is universal: these are over the cigar-shops. The photographer has a flourish about "El Sol de Madrid" and "El Rayo de Luz;" one studio went by the name of "El Relampago"—the flash of lightning; and I never could refrain from laughing at the motto adopted by the proprietor of a shop for the sale of lucifer matches— "La Explosion."

And now, if you please, picture these thread-my-needle thoroughfares, not one of them a third so wide as Hanway Yard, shady to intensity, but yet rich in the tender tints of reflected light, and semitones stealing through the diaphanous awnings overhead, with here and there a burst, a splash, an "explosion," of positive light and colour—where the sun has found a joint in the armour of awning, and made play with his diamond dart; picture these lanes thronged from morning till night with sallow Spanish creoles, in white linen and Panamas, and negroes and negresses gaudy, gaping, and grinning, according to the wont of our African brothers and sisters. Now and then a slouch-hatted, black-cassocked priest, now and then a demure Jesuit father; many soldiers in suits of "seersucker"—a material resembling thin bed-ticking—straw hats, and red cockades; many itinerant vendors of oranges, lemonade, sugar-plums, and cigars; for though every third shop is a tobacconist's, there is a lively trade in cigars done in the streets.

The narrowness of the foot-pavement affects you little. You may walk in the roadway without inconvenience. There is no-thing to run over you save the bullock-drays, whose rate of speed rarely exceeds a mile an hour, and the pack-mules, which are so laden with fresh-cut Indian corn-stalks for fodder that only their noses and the tips of their tails are visible beneath their burdens, and they look like animated hayricks—and the volantes, which are so light and springy that they would scarcely crush the legs of a fly if their wheels passed over him.

I confess that these several and sundry humours of Havana were, when first I viewed them, subordinated to my intense desire to find an inn in which I could take mine ease; and I was on the point of desiring the old negro (who was frantic with rage by this time) to turn his bullock's head to the city gates and journey towards Legrand's, when the odour of a decidedly first-rate cuisine attracted me, and ultimately induced me to put up at a Fonda called "El Globo," in the Calle del Obispo. To tell the truth, I wanted my breakfast desperately.

III.

A Courtyard in Havana.

LEFT my unworthy self and worthier friends and my trunks, so far as I can recollect, just discharged from a bullock-dray at the Fonda called " El Globo," in the Calle del Obispo—let us say Bishopsgate Street—Havana. Something like four months have elapsed since I found that anchorage, and, glad enough to be in any soundings, ordered breakfast. El Globo—not that Cuban inn, but the real rotund habitable globe—has gone round in the maddest of gyrations since I began to talk of the humours of Havana. I have been much tossed about and am brought very low.

It was at Berlin, in a house overlooking the bridge which has the statues of Peace and Plenty, and over against the great gilded dome of that Schloss which the Kings of Prussia find so gloomy that they are afraid to live in it, and have fled to a pleasant modern palace under the Linden—it was there, beneath the darkling shadow of the Prussian Eagle's wings, that I penned the last paragraph of my last paper about the Queen of the Antilles. Then the world began to roll and the teetotum to spin again. Just as I was stepping into a train bound for St. Petersburg, a civil person in uniform put into my hand a telegram containing these simple words, "Please go to Madrid. There is a Revolution in Spain." The next night I was in Cologne; the morning after I was in Paris; at night I supped at Dijon; next morning I breakfasted at Bordeaux, and lunched at Irun; late in the evening a voice cried "Valladolid," and I had some chocolate; and the next day, the fourth, being Sunday, I got to Madrid, and (it being a great saint's day) was just in time to take a ticket in a raffle for

Saint Anthony's pig—"el santo cochinillo," as they call him. I must tell you about that pig some day.

I put it to you, most forbearing of readers, how could I, being for the first time in my life in Old Spain, take up at once the thread of my reminiscences of Spain the New ? Had I striven to do so, the result would have been but a sadly tangled skein. My conscience pricked me sometimes, I admit. Once I had a most dolorous twinge; it was in an old library at Seville, and, turning over a vellum-bound volume—"Marco Polo's Travels," I think—I came upon some marginal notes, written in Latin, and in a bold honest hand. The old canon who was my guide reverently doffed his shovel-hat when the page, full of marginal notes, lay bare. "They are worth ten thousand reals a letter," quoth Don Basilio. "Ten thousand! they are priceless. They are by the Great Admiral."

Yes; these were annotations to Marco Polo by Christopher Columbus. Of the authenticity of the autograph there was no doubt. The old library I speak of belonged to the Admiral's son, a learned, valorous, virtuous man, like his sire, and to the chapter of Seville cathedral he bequeathed all his books. I say my conscience smote me. How had I lingered over the humours of that Havana which Columbus discovered ! There is a picture of the Admiral hung up in the library : a picture painted by a Frenchman, and presented to the chapter by Louis Philippe in exchange for a choice Murillo. Out of the canvas the mild eyes seemed to look on me reproachfully. I fancied the grave, resolute lips moving, and that their speech ran : "What are you doing here? Why don't you go back to Havana?" But it was no fault of mine. I was a teetotum, and to wheel about and turn about was my doom.

Coming out of that strange and fascinating land—the most comfortless and the most charming in the world—I sat down one day in the Frezzaria at Venice and said, "I really must go back to Havana." So taking hold of Old Spain, I cut its throat and tied a Chubb's patent fireproof safe to its neck and a couple of fifty-six pound shot to its legs, and towing the corse out to the

Lido, sank it just under the lee of the Armenian convent of St. Lazaro. It fell with a plash and sank at once. "Back to St. Mark's," I cried to the gondolier; "and lie there, Old Spain," I continued, apostrophising two or three ripples which played above the deed that I had done, as though murder were a thing to laugh at—"lie there; and the fishes may feed on you till I need your bones and dredge you up again." Old bones have their uses. Professor Liebig once stated that all Europe was ransacked to supply England with bones. I have marked the spot where my skeleton lies, full fathom five.

But I could not, somehow, go back to Havana. Cuba was coy. She floated in the air; she danced; she smiled at me, but she would not be embraced. Like unto those strange apparitions which mock the shepherd's sight on the Westmoreland fells, now seeming as the form of one that spurs his steed midway along a hill, desperate—now merging into a gorgeous train of cavaliers with glittering armour and waving standards—and now fading into vaporous nothingness, I could see, remote, intangible, the Phantom of the Antilles; the burnished sun, the coral glowing beneath the dark blue water; the smooth, black sharks waiting about the bathing-places and raging at the walls of planks; the waving palms, the sanguinolent bananas, the orange and pine-apple groves of the rich island. But she would not approach me then. You cannot always make of your mind an indexed ledger which you can open at will, and, under the proper letter, at the proper page, and in the proper column, find the matter you want, set down with clerk-like accuracy, underruled with red, and ticked off with blue ink. There are seasons when you mislay the key of the ledger, or find the leaves blotted, the index blurred, the entries effaced. Sometimes the firm your transactions with which you are desirous of recalling has gone bankrupt, and the accounts are being unravelled by Messrs. Coleman, Turquand, and Young. Cuba, in short, would not come at call, and it was not until I embarked on the Adriatic and went over to Trieste, whence, as you know, there are steamers starting continually for all parts of the world, that I began to feel a little tropical again, and find my Memory.

D

At El Globo they gave us a double-bedded room.   Double-
bedded!   The apartment itself would have afforded ample quarters to five-and-twenty dragoons, horses, forage, and all.   It was
very like a barn, and had an open timber roof, very massive, but
very primitive in its framework.   The beams, it is true, were of
cedar, and smelt deliciously.   I had no means of ascertaining the
peculiar hue of the walls or of the floor, for beyond a narrow
parallelogram of sunshine thrown on the latter when the doors
were open, the apartment was quite dark.   It was one of a series
surrounding the patio, or courtyard ; and the Cuban architects
hold that windows in rooms which do not look upon the street
are mere superfluities.   Their constant care, indeed, is, not to
let the daylight in, but to keep the sun out.   The consequence is,
that a room in a Cuban house is very like a photographic camera
on a large scale.   Magnify by twenty the pretty fresco-painted
little dens which open out of the courtyard in the Pompeian
house at the Crystal Palace, and you will have some idea of our
double-bedded room at El Globo.   By-the-by, you must forget
to sweep it, and you must be rather liberal in your allowance
of fleas.   What matter ?   I daresay there were fleas in the house
of the Tragic Poet, notwithstanding all. the fine frescoes, and
that the Pompeian housemaids were none too tidy.

I was told afterwards that I might consider myself very
lucky not to find in this double-bedded room such additional
trifles as a cow in one corner and a wheeled carriage in another.
Spaniards, old or new, are but faintly averse from making a
sleeping apartment of a stable or a coach-house.   I was slow
to believe this ; and it was only lately, after some wayside experiences in Andalusia, and having shared a room with a pedlar's
donkey, and being awakened in the morning by the hard, dry,
sardonic see-saw of his horrible bray, that I realised to the
fullest extent the strangeness of the bedfellows with which misery
and the teetotum existence make us acquainted.

Of the altitude of the folding-doors leading into this cave
there was no complaint possible.   I came to the conclusion
that El Globo had formerly been a menagerie, and our room

the private apartment of the giraffe, who, it is well known, is a very proud animal, and will never submit to the humiliation of stooping. The tallness of the doors, however, was balanced by the shortness of the beds. My companion was a long way over six feet in height, and the ghost of the celebrated Procrustes might have eyed him as his very long limbs lay on that very short pallet, and longed to reform his tailor's bills by slipping off some superfluous inches of his anatomy. As to *my* bed, it was as the couch of Dryden's Codrus—short, and hard, and miserable : the poet's bed, in fact, and a fit preparation for the flagstone, and the kennel, and the grave.

But the Procrustean eye couldn't have seen that long-limbed captain overhanging the short bed. Why ? Because, when the folding-doors were shut, all, save a bright streak of sun or moonlight at their base, was utter darkness ; and as soon as we kindled our wax-tapers at night the gnats or the moths, the bats or the scorpions, came and flapped the lights out. I don't know how the Cuban belles contrive to get through their toilettes. I think they must hang up screens of shawls in the patios, and come out into the open to beautify themselves. A Cuban bedroom is not a place whither you can retire to read or write letters. You may just stumble into it, feel your way to the bed, and, throwing yourself down, sleep as well as you can for the mosquitos. Besides, the best part of your sleeping is done in Cuba out of your bedroom—in a hammock slung between the posts of a piazza, or on a mattress flung down anywhere in the shade, or in anybody's arm-chair, or in the dark corner of any café, or anywhere else where the sun is not, and you feel drowsy. In Algiers, the top of the house, with a sheet spread between two poles by way of awning, is still the favourite spot for an afternoon nap, as it was in the time of the Hebrew man of old ; but in Havana the house-tops slant and are tiled, and so are left to their legitimate occupants, the cats.

Our folding-doors proved but a feeble barrier against the onslaughts of a horse belonging to the proprietor of El Globo, and

whose proper stabling was in a cool grot with a vaulted roof—
a kind of compromise between an ice-house, a coal-hole, and a
wine-cellar. This noble animal, seemingly under the impression
that he lived at number five—*our* number—made such terrific
play with his hoofs against our portals on the first night of our
stay, that, remonstrating, we were promoted to a room upstairs,
windowless, of course, but the door of which opened on the
covered gallery surrounding the patio. This dwelling, likewise,
had the great advantage of not being plunged in Cimmerian darkness directly the door was closed, for it boasted a kind of hutch,
or Judas-trap, in one of the panels, after the fashion of the
apertures in the doors of police-cells, through which cautious
inspectors periodically peep, to make sure that female disorderlies
have not strangled themselves in their garters. You might look
from this hutch, too, if you chose, and present to the outside
spectator the counterpart of the infuriated old gentleman, presumably of usurious tendencies, in Rembrandt's picture, who
thrusts his head through the casement and grins at and exchanges
savage glances with the young cavalier who has called to mention
that he is unable to take up that little bill.

Never, in the course of my travels, did I light upon such a
droll hotel as El Globo. You paid about thirty shillings a day for
accommodation which would have been dear at half a crown, but
the balance was amply made up to you in fun. I had been living
for months at the Brevoort House in New York, the most
luxurious hotel, perhaps, in the world,* and the change to almost
complete barbarism was as amusing as it was wholesome. Amusing, for long-continued luxury is apt to become a very great bore
—wholesome, because the discomfort of the Cuban hotels forms,
after all, only an intermediate stage between the splendour of the
States and the unmitigated savagery of Mexico and Spain. I was
fated to go farther and fare worse than at El Globo. Our quarters
there were slightly inferior to those to be found for fourpence in a
lodging-house in St. Giles's; but I was destined to make subsequent
acquaintance at Cordova, at Orizaba, at Puebla in America, and

* This was in the year 1864.

in Castile and in Andalusia in Europe, with other pigsties to which that at Havana was palatial.

I am so glad that there was no room at Madame Almé's, and that we did not try Legrand's. I should have missed the sight of that patio at El Globo. It was open to the sky, of course; that is to say, the four white walls were canopied all day long by one patch of vivid ultramarine. A cloud was so rare, that when one came sailing over the expanse of blue a sportsman might have taken it for a bird and risked a shot at it. I used often to think, leaning over the balusters of the gallery, how intolerable that bright blue patch would become at last to a man cooped up between the four white walls of a southern prison; for suffering may be of all degrees, and anguish may wear all aspects. There is a cold hell as well as a hot one. I have seen the horrible coop under the leads of the Doge's palace at Venice, in which Silvio Pellico spent so many weary months. But he, at least, could see the roofs of the houses through his dungeon bars, and hear the gondoliers wrangling and jesting between the pillars, or uttering their weird cries of warning as they turned the corners of the canals. He could hear the splashing of the water as the buckets were let down into the wells in the courtyard by the Giant's Staircase, and sometimes, perhaps, a few of the historical pigeons would come wheeling up from the cornices of the Procuratie Vecchie and look at him in his cell pityingly. But only to gaze on four white burning walls and a great patch of ultramarine, and the chains eating into your limbs all the while! Think of that. How the captive must long for the sky to be overcast or for rain to fall—and it falls but once a year; and what a shriek of joy would come out of him were he to see, high aloft in the ultramarine, a real live balloon! Such burning white walls, such an intolerable patch of intense blue, must a prisoner by name Poerio have seen in Naples in the old Bourbon time.

There was nothing prison-like about our patio, however. It was as full of life as our bedrooms were full of fleas. The oddest courtyard!—the most antique—the most grotesque. I used to liken it to that pound into which Captain Boldwig's keepers

wheeled Mr. Pickwick while he got into that sweet slumber produced by too much milk-punch. It was strewn with all manner of
vegetable and pomicultural refuse, great leaves of plantains, cocoa-
nut shells, decayed pine-apples, exhausted melons, and husks of
Indian corn. Havana is a great place for oysters, and the four
corners of the "pound" were heaped high with votive offerings
of shells.

Nor to the pound was there wanting the traditional donkey.
He would come strolling in three or four times a day, either bearing a pile of Indian corn about the size of an average hay-stack
on his back, or with panniers full of oranges slung on either side of
him. Occasionally a Pepe or a José, or some other criado, would
come to unload him. Oftener he would unload himself, by rolling
over on the ground and tumbling his oranges about in all directions; then a fat negress would emerge from the kitchen and
belabour him about the head with a ladle ; then he would slink
away to the cool grot where the horse lived, to confer with that
animal as to any provender there might be about, and compare
notes with him as to the growing depravity of mankind in general
and Cuban costermongers in particular. By this time his master
would arrive with a sharp stick, or else the big bloodhound that
lived in an empty sugar-cask, and so zealously licked all the plates
and dishes either immediately before or immediately after they
came from the table—I am not certain which—would become
alive to the fact of there being a donkey in the camp, and "run
him out" incontinent.

How they managed to get rid of all those oranges I really do
not know. I had a dozen or so brought me whenever I felt
thirsty, and I daresay the other guests at El Globo were as often
thirsty and as fond of oranges as I ; and there were a good many,
too, cut up in the course of the day for the purpose of making
sangaree and orange-toddy ; but even after these draughts the
residue must have been enormous. You were never charged for
oranges in the bill. They were as plentiful as acorns in a forest,
and you might browse on them at will. In the streets, at every
corner and under every archway, sits a negress who sells oranges,

so they must have some monetary value, however infinitesimal;
but if you bestow on her the smallest coin recognised by the
Cuban currency you may fill your hands, your pockets, and your
hat too, if you choose, with the golden fruit.

When the Cuban goes to the bull-fight he takes with him a
mighty store of oranges tied up in a pocket-handkerchief, just as
we, when boys, used to buy a pound of gingerbread-nuts, more as
a precautionary measure than because we were sweet-toothed, on
entering the confines of Greenwich Fair. Some of these oranges
the amateur of the bull-fight eats ; but the major part he uses as
missiles, and pitches into the ring at a cowardly bull or clumsy
toreadores. There is positively a verb in the Spanish dictionary
signifying to pelt with oranges.

I mentioned the existence of a kitchen just now. It was a hot
and grimy den, not much bigger than the stoke-hole of a locomotive ; and there was a charcoal stove there, I presume ; but the
real culinary business was done in the patio. As to venture forth
during the noonday or afternoon heats is considered next door to
raving madness, and as you necessarily spend much time within
doors, and as you feel too lazy to read, or write, or paint, or sew—
what a blessing sewing-machines must be in Cuba ! before their
introduction most of the needlework was done by coolies—and as
you cannot be always smoking, or dozing, or sipping sangaree, and
as billiards are out of the question, and as gambling—the real
recreation in all tropical climes—is immoral, there are certain
hours in the day when time is apt to hang heavy on your hands,
and you don't know what the deuce to do with yourself. An
infallible pastime to me was to lean over the gallery and watch the
dinner being cooked in the patio. It has been said that a wise
man should never enter his wife's dressing-room, and it has been
likewise remarked that if we entered the kitchen of the Trois
Frères half an hour before dinner, we should see such sickening
sights as would cause us to lose all our appetite for the banquet
served in the *cabinet particulier* upstairs. We must look at
results, says the sage, and not at the means employed to bring
them about.

But these sententious warnings should not apply, I think, to the cooking that is done in a patio—in the open and under the glorious sunshine. There was a rollicking, zingaro-like freedom in thus seeing your meals prepared in broad daylight. Why did they cook in the courtyard ? Because the kitchen itself was too small, or because the gory sun came to the assistance of the charcoal embers and did half the cooking himself. I was told lately, and gravely too, at Seville—though the tale may be very likely one of the nature generally told to travellers—that on the fourteenth day of July in every year there takes place in La Ciudad de las Maravillas an ancient and solemn ceremony in honour of Apollo—a kind of sun-worship, as it were : a culinary person, white-aproned and white-nightcapped, sets up a stall in La Plaza de la Magdalena, and produces a frying-pan, a cruse of oil, and a basket of eggs. Two of the eggs he breaks, sluices their golden yolks with oil, and then, with an invocation to the sun-god, holds the pan towards the meridian blaze. In forty-five seconds the eggs are fried. You must take these eggs, and the story too, with a grain of salt ; but I can only repeat that Seville is a city of wonders—witness the two angelic sisters who, no later than the year 1848, sat on the weathercock of the Giralda, and spinning round and round while Espartero was bombarding the city, warded off the iron storm from the sacred fane.

Now the sun of Andalusia, though a scorcher when considered from a European point of view, is a mere refrigerator when compared with the great fiery furnace set up within the domains of the Southern Cross. I am not prepared to deny that the preparation of some of the stews we had for dinner might have been accelerated by the monstrous kitchen-range overhead ; but I shrink from asserting as a positive fact that the old negress who used to belabour the donkey with a ladle, fried her eggs in the sun. No, I will grant at once that her pots and pans were set upon little braziers full of hot ashes ; but still, without the sun, I don't think her viands would have been cooked to her or our liking. She evidently gloried in the sun, and frizzled in it, bare-headed, while her eggs and sausages frizzled in their own persons.

Not till her work was done would she bind her temples with
the yellow bandanna, or the gorgeous turban of flamingo hue, and,
sitting down in a rocking-chair, fan herself with a dignified air,
as though she were the Queen of Spain and had no legs. The
oscillations of the chair, however, proved the contrary. She had
legs which Mr. Daniel Lambert might have beheld, not unenvious.
Good old black cook! She was like Sterne's foolish fat scullion
dipped in a vat of Brunswick black. She was gross and oily, and
could exhibit a terrible temper, especially towards troublesome
piccaninnies and refractory fowls who showed an ungrateful un-
readiness in being caught and strangled and plucked, and trussed
and broiled, and served hot with mushrooms, all under half an
hour's time; but her little irritation once over, she was—until a
roving donkey called for the ministrations of the ladle—all grins
and chuckles and broad guffaws and humorous sayings. She
would sing a fragment of a song, too, from time to time—a wild
song of Congo sound, and which needed the accompaniment of a
banjo. The refrain had some resemblance to the word ipecacuanha
pronounced very rapidly and with a strong guttural accent, and
yet I daresay it was all about love and the home of her youth
on the burning banks of the Niger.

Where did all those piccaninnies come from? Who owned
them? The landlord of El Globo was a bachelor; the waiters
did not look like married men; and yet, from the youthful brood
strewn about the patio, you might have fancied Brigham Young
to be the proprietor of the place. "Strewn about" is the only
term to use with reference to the piccaninnies. Their age
averaged between twenty and thirty months. Nobody nursed
them; they were too small to stand; and so they sprawled, and
crawled, and wriggled, and lay, and squalled, and kicked, and
basked in the sun like little guinea-pigs. I have seen a piccaninny
in a dish; I have seen a piccaninny in a wooden tray, like a leg
of pork just delivered by the butcher. They were of all colours—
blue-black, brown-black, chocolate, bistre, burnt sienna, raw
sienna, cadmium yellow, and pale creole white.

I am afraid all these piccaninnies, save those of the last-named hue, were Slaves, and the children of Slaves. Not one of the least suggestive—to some it may be one of the most painful—features of bondage is that free white and black slave children grow up together in perfect amity and familiarity, are playmates, and foster-brothers and sisters. The great social gulf which is to yawn between them—so fair and jewelled with flowers on one side, so dark and hideous on the other—is in infancy quite bridged over. The black piccaninnies sprawl about the verandahs and the courtyards, and the thresholds of the rooms of their owners, and the white piccaninnies sprawl in precisely the same manner.

That fat old cook, for instance, made no more distinction between a white and a black urchin than between a black and a white fowl. Before ever she could address herself to the concoction of a dish, two ceremonies were gone through. A piccaninny had to be fed and another piccaninny had to be "spanked." For the purpose of feeding, that invaluable ladle, dipped in a bowl of saffron-coloured porridge, came into play ; the "spanking" was done with her broad black hand. She was quite impartial, and distributed the slaps and the spoonfuls in strict accordance with the maxims of equity. Thus, if a piccaninny yelped, it was fed ; but if it yelped *after* it was fed, it was spanked. And subsequent to both spooning and spanking, the fat old cook would catch the child up in her arms and sing to it a snatch of the famous song that ended with ipecacuanha.

So have I seen many dinners cooked. So I have seen my made-dish running about the patio with flapping wings and dismal "grooping" noise, to be at last caught and sacrificed to the culinary deities, and to appear at the evening meal, grilled, with rich brown sauce. And so at last the drama of the day would be played out ; as on going home late, and leaning once more over the rails of the gallery, I would gaze then on the patio all flooded in moonlight of emerald green : pots and pans and plates and crates and baskets and braziers and vegetable rubbish, all glinting and glancing as though some fairy "property-man" had tipped their edges with the green foil-paper of the playhouse.

IV.

The Volante.

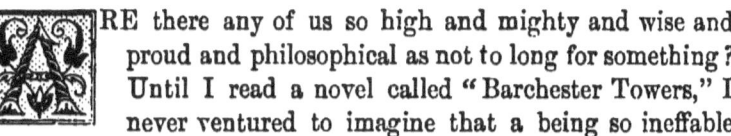RE there any of us so high and mighty and wise and proud and philosophical as not to long for something? Until I read a novel called "Barchester Towers," I never ventured to imagine that a being so ineffable as an English bishop could long for anything. Under the shovel-hat and silken apron, I thought, must dwell supreme indifference to the toys and gewgaws for which a grosser laity struggle and intrigue. Yet, what a delicate touch of the lancet between the under muscles of the human mind is that with which Mr. Trollope shows us poor little henpecked Dr. Proudie, in his grand palace at Barchester, longing, not for the see of Canterbury, not to be a second Wolsey or a new Ximenes, but merely to be able to write his sermons and sip his negus in a warm cosy large room above-stairs, from which he has been banished by his imperious bishopess.

Yes ; a bishop may long. A bishop! Who shall say that his Holiness the Pope has not coveted, within these latter years, the lot of one of his own flunkeys? It was in the disguise of a pos-tillion that the poor old gentleman fled out of Rome in 1849. Quite feasible is it to surmise that his memory has oft reverted to the day when he cracked his whip and rose up and down in his saddle, mechanical, on the dusty road to Gaeta, and that, looking wearily on all his tiaras, and copes, and stoles, and peacocks' feathers, he has sighed and thought that happiness might be found in an obscure post, good wages, a jacket with sugar-loaf buttons, and tight buckskin small-clothes.

We generally long for the thing which we are least likely ever to possess. The ugly woman longs for beauty. The drunkard, in his waking moments, longs for the firm tread, clear eye, and assured speech of the temperate; and I have often conjectured that thieves are beset at times with a dreadful longing to become honest men. I was born to go afoot. When Fate condemned me to the footpath, she also presented me with a pair of bad legs; for Fate seldom does things by halves. The consequence is that I have always been longing to ride in a carriage of my own. Of my own, mind. Let that you have be yours and nobody else's. I have longed for my own carriage this many a year, and have gazed so enviously intent on some of my acquaintance riding high horses or careering along in the chariots of the proud, that my toes have been menaced by their chargers' hoofs, and my last carriage has promised to be a stretcher to convey me to the hospital after being run over.

My longings vehiculary have been catholic, and perhaps a little capricious. In childhood I longed for the lord mayor's coach, so grand, so golden, so roomy. What happiness was his who, with a fur porringer on his head and a sword held bâton-wise, looked from that coach-window like Punch from a glorified show! There was a story related to my detriment during nonage, that I once expressed a longing for a mourning coach. I will own that the cumbrous sable wagon, so repulsive to most persons, exercises over me to this day a strange fascination, and that I have some difficulty in refraining from stealing down the stable-yards of funeral postmasters and peeping into the stuffy cloth caverns, and seeking for strange sights in the shining black panels, as the superstitious seek for apparitions in the drop of ink of the Egyptian magician, and wondering at the uncouth leather springs and braces, and watching the harnessing of the long-tailed round-barrelled Flemish steeds, with their obsolete surcingles and chestbands. The which leads me, with a blush, to admit that there may be some truth in the report that in youth "my sister Emmeline and I"—her name was *not* Emmeline—were in the habit of performing funerals in the nursery, and playing at Mr. Shillibeer.

But these, and the glorious mail-coach, with the four thorough-breds, and a guard and coachman in blazing scarlet and gold, and the brand-new harness and reins, which used to burst on our sight on the evening of the king's birthday long bygone—these were but childish longings, airy desires akin to that which children show for the Royal Arms on a shop-front, or the moon in a pail of water. Not until manhood did I feel that full fierce longing, the longing which is mingled with discontent, and is own brother to envy, malice, and all uncharitableness. I have given the Drive in Hyde Park a wide berth, and have gone out of my way to avoid Long Acre. The sight of other people's carriages made me sick. I never owned so much as a one-horse chaise. I have not even a perambulator.

My longing has varied with the countries in which it has been my lot to long. I have longed for a droschky with a bearded Istvostchik in a braided caftan and a long-maned alezan from the Ukraine in the shafts. There is a droschky, I think, among the specimens of wheeled carriages in the Crystal Palace, but I never longed for an Istvostchik at Sydenham. I coveted the Russian vehicle only while I was on Russian soil. When I went away, I began to long for something else. Nor, I fear, shall I ever possess a droschky of even the humblest kind, which is nothing but a cloth-covered saddle, on which you sit astride, with splash-boards to protect you from the wheels; for in the latest edition of "Murray" I learn that droschkies are going out of fashion, and that the Petersburg railway stations are now beset by omnibuses and hack cabs.

I never longed for an Irish outside car, although I have seen some pretty private ones; and crinoline may be displayed in its widest sense and to its greatest advantage on a "kyar," say between two and five in the afternoon, in Grafton Street, Dublin. My soul has often thirsted for a private hansom. What luxury in the knowledge that those high wheels, that stiff and shiny apron, all belong to you! I think I would have a looking-glass in the splash-board, and I am sure I should be always pushing open that trap in the roof and bidding the man drive faster. And I have

longed for a mail phaeton—not so much for the sake of the two
proud steppers and the trim lamps with their silvered reflectors,
as for the sake of the two grooms who, in black tunics, cockaded
hats, white neckcloths, and pickle-jar boots, sit in the dickey with
their arms folded, like statues of Discipline and Obedience.

I knew a gentleman in the city of Mexico, and he owned such
a mail phaeton with two such statuesque grooms as I have described. Little did he reck, good hospitable man, that the guest
he was wont to drive out in the Paseo de la Vega envied him,
with a green and spotted jealousy, his mail phaeton and his trim
grooms. He had encountered the most appalling difficulties
before he could find two human beings who, even after long
drilling and for liberal wages, could be induced to sit in the
dickey—or is it the rumble ?—and fold their arms without
moving. The Mexicans are a very lazy people; but neither the
Spaniards, nor the half-castes, nor the Indians understand sitting
behind a horse. They prefer sitting across him. My friend sent
to the United States for grooms. They returned him word that
there were no grooms in the Union who would fold their arms. A
lawsuit took him to New York, and he had another mail phaeton
built for the Central Park; but the grooms were still lacking.
He tried Irishmen and he tried negroes. Tempted by abundant
dollars, they would consent to wear the cockaded hats and the
pickle-jar boots, but they could not be brought to fold their
arms. 'To attempt to subject a native American citizen to this
indignity was, of course, out of the question. When I remark that
I have seen a citizen clad in a red shirt and a white hat driving
a hearse at a public funeral, you will recognise the impossibility
of any statuesque arrangements in connection with mail phaetons
in the States.

For any native Yankee carriage I never longed. I held the
Noah's-ark cars on the street railways in horror, and considered
the Broadway stages as abominations. As for a trotting "wagon"
—by which is meant a hard shelf on an iron framework between
two immense wheels, to which a railway locomotive at high
pressure, but disguised as a horse, has been harnessed—I never

could appreciate the pleasure of being whirled along at the rate of about eighteen miles an hour, with the gravel thrown up by the wheels flying about you, now bombarding your eyes, and now peppering your cheeks. Thoroughly do I agree with the general criticism passed on trotting wagons by an old steamboat captain who had endured for a couple of hours the agony of the iron shelf. " The darned thing," he remarked, " has got no bulwarks."

There is rather a pretty American carriage called a Rockaway —not from any peculiar oscillatory motion it possesses, but from a watering-place hight Rockaway, where it was first brought into use. The Rockaway is in appearance something between the French *panier à salade*, in which the *garçons de bureau* of the Bank of France speed on their bill-collecting missions, and the spring cart of a fashionable London baker. Add to this a grinning negro coachman, with a very large silver or black-velvet band to a very tall hat, and the turn-out, you may imagine, is spruce and sparkling. But I never longed for a Rockaway. The American carriage - horses are the prettiest creatures imaginable out of a circus, and are as prettily harnessed. They are almost covered in summer with a gracefully fantastic netting, which keeps the flies from them.

Much less have I yearned for one of the Hungarian equipages, about which such a fuss is made in the Prater at Vienna. An open double or triple bodied rattle-trap, generally of a gaudy yellow, with two or four ragged, spiteful, profligate-looking little ponies, and the driver in a hybrid hussar costume—a feather in his cap, sky-blue tunic and pantaloons, much braiding, and Hessian boots with long tassels. This is the crack Hungarian equipage, the Magyar name of which I do not know, nor knowing could pronounce. The Viennese hold this turn-out to be, in the language of the mews, very " down the road ; " but it fails to excite my longing. Hungarian ponies look wild and picturesque enough in Mr. Zeitter's pictures ; but a gipsy's cart without the tilt is not precisely the thing for Hyde Park ; and the " proud Hungarian " on the box-seat reminds me too forcibly of the " Everythingarian," who in cosmopolitan saw-dust continues the traditions of equitation handed down by the late Andrew Ducrow.

When, in the days of Donna Isabella, I was looking from a balcony overhanging the Puerta del Sol in Madrid, and used to hear, at about three in the afternoon, the clangour of trumpets from the guard-house, at the Casa de la Gobernacion opposite, as the carriages of the royal family, with their glittering escort, drove by to the Prado or the Retiro, I would question myself as to whether I felt any longing for the absolute possession of one of those stately equipages. I don't think I did. They were too showy and garish for my humble ambition. If a slight feeling of longing came over me, it was for the coach which conveyed the junior branches of the royal family. Imagine, if you please, a spacious conveyance all ablaze with heraldic achievements, and crammed to the roof with little infantes and infantas ; Mr. Bumble on the coach-box ; and the beadles of St. Clement's Danes, the ward of Portsoken, and the Fishmongers' Company, hung on behind, abreast—for long laced coats and huge laced cocked-hats are the only wear of flunkeydom in Spain. Harnessed to this astounding caravan were six very sleek, very fat, and very supercilious-looking mules. To the beadles before and the beadles behind must be added the beadle of the Burlington Arcade, on the off-leader, as postillion. Yea, more. The beadle of the Royal Exchange trotted on an Andalusian barb as outrider. A squadron of lancers followed, to take care that the infantes and infantas were not naughty, or that the naughtier Progresistas didn't run away with them.

On the whole, I don't think I longed much for this sumptuous equipage. There is another coach, in the royal stables at Madrid, much more in my line—a queer, cumbrous, gloomy litter, with a boot as big as a midshipman's chest. It is a very old coach—the oldest, perhaps, extant, and nearly the first coach ever built, being the one in which Crazy Jane, Queen of Castile and Aragon, used to carry about the coffined body of her husband, Charles of Anjou.

There is yet another coach in my line—the Shillibeer line, I mean—which may be hired for a franc an hour at a certain city

on the Adriatic Sea, opposite Trieste. There are about four
thousand of those coaches in the city—a very peculiar city, for
the sea is in its broad and its narrow streets, and the seaweed
clings to the door-steps of its palaces. How I have longed to
have one of those coaches for my own private riding ; say in the
Surrey Canal or on the Serpentine ! The Americans have got one
on the lake in their Central Park ; but the toy once placed there
has been forgotten, and it is dropping to pieces. It is the only
coach of which use is practicable in Venice. It is black and
shiny and hearse-like, and its roof bristles with funeral tufts, and
the carving about its doors and panels is strictly of the undertaker's order of decoration. It is called a gondola.

But where would be the use of a gondola in London ? The
Surrey Canal is not in a fashionable district, and the Serpentine
has no outlet. The chief purpose of your own carriage, I
presume, is to drive about to the residences of your friends
and acquaintances, and strike despair into their souls by flashing your liveries and appointments in their eyes. You could
scarcely put your gondoliers into buckskins and pickle-jar
boots, although, upon my word, I remarked once, at Venice,
that the Count of Chambord, otherwise the Duke of Bordeaux,
otherwise Henry the Fifth, King of France and Navarre—
who lived, when he was not at Frohsdorf, at one of the most
beautiful palaces on the Grand Canal, and kept half a dozen
gondolas for his private recreation—had been absurd enough
to dress up his boatmen in tail coats, gold-laced hats, plush
breeches, and gaiters. Truly, the Bourbons have learnt nothing
and forgotten nothing. Incongruity of incongruities ! Imagine
Jeames de la Pluche on the Grand Canal.

As one could not drive down to Ascot in a gondola, or take
it to the Crystal Palace on a half-crown day, or keep it waiting
for an hour and a half at the door of a Pall Mall club—and
as the linkman at the Royal Italian Opera would be slightly
astonished at having to proclaim that Mr. Anonymous's gondola
stopped the way, I must abandon all hopes of possessing a
marine Shillibeer until I can afford to take a palace at Venice.

E

But if my longings are not to be satisfied in Europe, there
is in the Spanish West Indies a carriage to be longed for :
ay, and the longing may be gratified at a very moderate expen-
diture.   In the city of Havana, and in Havana alone, is to
be found this turn-out.   It is but a "one-hoss shay;" but
it is a chaise fit for princes and potentates to ride in.   It is
the queerest trap into which mortal ever mounted.   It is
unique and all but inimitable.   Those who have visited Cuba
will understand that I allude to the famous conveyance called
the Volante.

The rooms looking on the street in Havana are necessarily
provided with windows, but these casements are garnished
with heavy ranges of iron bars, behind which you sit and
smoke, or eat, or drink, or yawn, or flirt your fan, or transfix
the male passers-by with dreamy yet deadly glances, precisely
as your habits, or your sex, or the time of the day may prompt
you.   Skinny hands are often thrust between these bars ; and
voices cry to you in creole Spanish to bestow alms for the sake
of the Virgin and the Saints.   Sometimes rude boys make
faces at you through the gratings, or rattle a bamboo cane in
discordant gamut over the bars, till you grow irritable, and
begin to fancy that Havana is a zoological garden, in which
the insiders and outsiders have changed places ; that you have
been shut up in the monkey-house ; and that the baboons are
grimacing at you from the open.

I was sitting at the grated window of El Globo's restaurant
after breakfast, dallying with some preserved cocoa-nut—a most
succulent "goody," and which is not unlike one of the spun-
glass wigs they used to exhibit at the Soho Bazaar dipped in
glutinous syrup—when, across the field of vision bounded by the
window-pane, there passed a negro, mounted on horseback.
The animal was caparisoned in blinkers, and a collar, and many
straps and bands, thickly bedight with silver ornaments : which
I thought odd in the clothing of a saddle-horse.   But it might
be "un costumbre del païs," I reflected ; just such another
custom as that of plaiting up the horse's tail very tightly,

adorning it with ribbons, and tying the end to the saddle-bow. An absurd custom and a cruel custom ; for in the tropics the horse's tail was obviously given him for the purpose of whisking away the flies, which sorely torment him.

The black man bestriding this tail-tied horse grinned at me as he rode by, touched his hat, and made a gesture as though of inquiry. That, also, I conjectured to be a Cuban custom. Those big placable unreasoning babies called negroes are always grinning and bowing, and endeavouring to conciliate the white man, whom they respect and fear, and love too, after a fashion. This was a stately black man—a fellow of many inches, muscular, black as jet, and shiny. He wore a straw hat with a bright ribbon, a jacket of many colours, a scarlet vest, white breeches, very high jack-boots—so at least they seemed to me—with long silver spurs, and large gold rings in his ears. He carried a short stocked whip, with a very long lash of many knots, and he rode in a high demi-peaked saddle, with Moorish stirrups, profusely decorated, like the harness, with silver. I could not quite make him out. The Postillion of Longjumeau, a picador from the bull-ring, Gambia in "the Slave" on horseback, struggled for mastery in his guise. He moved slowly across the window, and I saw him no more.

I forgot all about this splendid spectre on horseback, and returned to my dalliance with the preserved cocoa-nut. Time passed. It might have been an hour, it might have been a minute, it might have been a couple of seconds—for the march of time is only appreciable in degree, and is dependent on circumstances—when, looking up from the cocoa-nut, I saw the plane of vision again darkened. Slowly, like the stag in a shooting-gallery, there came bobbing along a very small gig body, hung on very large C-springs, and surmounted by an enormous hood. Stretched between the apron and the top of this hood, at an angle of forty-five degrees, was a kind of awning or tent of some sable material. Glancing between the hood and the awning, I saw a double pair of white-trousered

legs, while at a considerable altitude above, two spirals of
smoke were projected into the air. "Surely," I exclaimed,
"they can never be so cruel as to make their negro slaves
draw carriages." I rose from the table, and standing close
to the bars, gained a view of the street pavement. But no
toil-worn negro was visible, and, stranger to relate, no horse,
only the gig body and a pair of wheels big enough to turn
a paper mill, and a pair of long timber shafts, and a great
gulf between. Mystery! Was it an automaton, or Hancock's
steam-coach come to life again? Had my field of view been
less confined, I might have discovered that there was, indeed,
a horse between the shafts, but that he was a very long way
off. He was the identical horse, in fact, ridden by the black
postillion who had grinned at me. I had seen a Volante.

I became intimately acquainted with the volante ere I left
Havana, and I learned to long for it. I have yet faint hopes of
acclimatising it in Hyde Park. Some slight difficulty may be
experienced in climbing into it, for the C-springs are hung very
high, and are apt to wag about somewhat wildly when the weight
of one or two human bodies is pressed upon them. I would recom-
mend a few weeks' practice in climbing into a hammock ere the
volante is attempted; but the ascent is, after all, much more
facile than that to the knife-board of a London omnibus. Once
in the curricle you are at your ease, and happy. You are rocked
as in a cradle, and may slumber as peacefully as a baby; or, if you
choose to keep awake, you may catch glimpses, between the canopy
of the hood which screens the nape of your neck and the crown of
your head, and the black linen awning which shelters your face
and eyes from the blinding rays of the sun, of strips of life and
movement—foot-passengers, or riders in other volantes. To keep
a gig was declared on a certain well-known occasion to be an
undeniable proof of respectability. But to ride in a gig drawn
by a horse with a plaited tail and silver harness, and conducted by
a postillion in a many-coloured jerkin and jack-boots, I consider
to be the pinnacle of glory.

It behoves me to offer two brief explanations with regard to the black postillion's attire. When you come narrowly to inspect him, you discover that he is not entirely a man of truth. There is a spice of imposture about him. Those breeches and those boots are not wholly genuine. The first, you discover, are mere linen drawers, instead of leathers ; indeed, to wear buckskins in the tropics would be a torture, the hint of whose possibility would have filled the hearts of the managing directors of the late Spanish Inquisition (unlimited) with gratitude. I could readily forgive the negro for his trifling fraud as regards the leathers, the exigencies of climate covering a multitude of sins ; but what shall we say of a postillion who pretends to wear jack-boots which turn out to be nothing but stiff leather gaiters or spatterdashes ? These hypocritical boots are truncated close to the ankle, even as was that boot converted by Corporal Trim into a mortar for the siege of Dendermond. At the ankle these boots do not even diverge into decent bluchers or homely shoes. The bare feet of the black man are visible ; and on his bare heels and insteps are strapped the silver spurs with their monstrous rowels. Now jack-boot, I take it, is not a thing to be trifled with. It is either a boot or no boot. This volante appendage is a hybrid, and consequently abominable.

The black postillion may urge, it is true, several pleas in abatement. First, nature has provided him with feet quite as black, as shiny, and as tough as the extremities of any jack-boots that could be turned out by Mr. Hoby, Mr. Runciman, or any other purveyor to her Majesty's Household Cavalry brigade. Next, the Moorish stirrups into which he thrusts his feet are not mere open arches of steel, but capacious foot-cases—overshoes hung by straps to the saddle. Finally, negroes are said to suffer more than white people from the insidious attacks of a very noxious insect common in Havana—a vile little wretch who marries early, and digs a hole in the ball of your toe, in which he and his wife reside. Mrs. Insect lays I know not how many thousand eggs in the hole under your skin, and inflammation, ulceration, and all the other ations— even sometimes to mortification, the last "ation" of all—ensue. Pending the advent of a nice fleshy great toe in which they can construct a habitation, the young couple dwell, after the manner of the little foxes, in any holes and corners that offer ; and the toe of a jack-boot would present a very comfortable lodging until they moved.   So the negro postillion sensibly cuts off the foot of his boot, and his enemy cannot lie perdu, awaiting him in a leathern cavern.

For this queer vehicle, the volante, I conceived a violent longing ; and one of these days I mean to have a specimen curricle neatly packed in haybands and brought to Southampton per West India mail steamer.   A black postillion I might obtain through the friendly offices of the Freedman's Aid Society; and for money you can have silver-adorned harness made to any pattern in Long Acre.   I am not quite certain whether the metropolitan police would thoroughly appreciate the inordinate length of the volante shafts, although in the case of a block in Cheapside the space intervening between the horse and the gig body would give impatient foot-passengers an opportunity to duck under and cross the street comfortably ; and I don't know whether I should get into trouble with the Society for the Prevention of Cruelty to Animals if I plaited my horse's tail up tight, and tied it to the saddle-bow, when summer heats were rife and flies were plentiful.

The volante ! It is such a pretty name too ; and, Shakespeare's doubt notwithstanding, there is much in a name.   Southey and Coleridge and Wordsworth were bent on establishing their Pantisocracy on the banks of the Susquehanna—not because they knew anything of the locality, but because Susquehanna was such a pretty name.   It is a very ugly river, and, curiously enough, it is the home of a bird possessing at once the most delicious flavour and the most grotesque name imaginable—the canvas-back duck.

The Cubans have a genuine passion for the volante.   Volantes are the common hack cabs of Havana ; but then the horse is often but a sorry jade, and the negro postillion a ragged profligate " cuss," the state of whose apparel would have shocked Miss Tabitha Bramble, had she travelled so far as the Antilles.   But the private volantes as far exceed the public ones in number as they do in splendour.   Everybody who can afford it keeps a volante, and many who cannot afford it keep a volante. It is the one luxury, the one expense, which, next to a cigar and a bull-fight, is dearest to the Spanish creole heart, and which, by fair means or foul, must be procured.

I believe that the middle-class Cubans would sooner live on beans and cold water, dress in rags, and lie on straw like Margery Daw, than go without a volante. Fortunately, Providence has been very good to them. Their beautiful island runs over with fertility. All the world are eager to buy what they have to sell, and what almost exclusively they produce—sugar and tobacco. So they make huge piles of dollars and gold ounces, and are enabled not only to keep volantes in profusion, but to give capital dinners and treat strangers with a generous hospitality very rarely shown in starched and stuck-up Europe.

We have all heard of the fondness which the Bedouin Arabs show for their horses. We know that the Prophet Mahomet has written whole chapters of the Koran on the breeding and rearing of colts. We know that the young Arab foal is brought up in the tent with the little girls and boys, and that when he grows up to be a horse he is petted and caressed. The children hang about his neck and call him endearing names; the Arab mother strokes his nose and pats his cheek, fetches him sweet herbs, makes his bed, feeds him with bread and dates, and strips of meat cured in the sun. Well, the affection which the Arabs manifest for their horses the Cubans manifest for their volantes. They can scarcely endure that the beloved object should be out of their sight. Make an evening call—all fashionable calls in Cuba are made in the evening—and in a dim corner of the reception-parlour you will probably see a great pyramid covered up with brown holland. It is not a harp, it is not a grand pianoforte; it is a volante. I must hint that Cuban reception rooms are immensely large and lofty, and are always on the ground floor; otherwise I might be supposed to be availing myself too extensively of the traveller's privilege, in relating that the drawing-room of a Cuban lady is not unfrequently a coach-house as well.

V.

HAVANA CIGARITOS.

HEREABOUTS, I wonder, did those wonderful literary gentlemen of the seventeenth and eighteenth centuries, who were in the habit of writing epic poems, and more amazing still, who persuaded people into reading them, keep the Muse whom they so frequently invoked ? Did she stand at livery with Pegasus, and the bird of Jove, and Juno's peacocks, and Phœbus's fiery steeds, and other curiosities of natural history, always ready to be trotted out when it occurred to the literary gentlemen that a Somethingiad in Twelve Cantos would be precisely the kind of thing to take the town, make the fortune of Mr. Osborn or Mr. Tonson, or extract a score of gold pieces from the Peer of the Realm and Patron of the Muses to whom the Somethingiad was to be dedicated ?

I want to know what that Muse did when she wasn't under process of invocation. It is my opinion that she was a lazy Muse ; for we frequently find the literary gentlemen bidding her, with some sharpness, Arise, or Awake, or Tell, or Say something which, according to their divination, she had to communicate. She seems also to have been a Muse who had something to give, and was worth flattering, since the literary gentlemen often addressed her by such endearing epithets as Gentle, Heavenly, Benign, and Discreet. But they never told anybody where the Muse lived, or how she was to be "got at." I fear she was to be heard of most frequently in the neighbourhood of Grub Street, at the sign of the Satchel, where the Greek translators lay three in a bed, and the gentleman who did Pindaric odes could only go out on Sundays through terror of the bailiffs, and the watchful landlady kept the ladder of the cockloft occupied by the Scholar and Divine who did High Church polemics for Mr. Lintot for half a crown a sheet.

We have been told a vast deal within these latter days about the Curiosities, the Pursuits, the Amenities, the Miseries, of Literature; but the polite world has yet much to learn concerning that Muse. Was her inspiration to be had for the paying for, and did she give credit? By-the-by, she was sometimes called Coy, and I have heard her designated as Intrepid; but that was in a birthday ode about the battle of Dettingen. Her personal history, manners, and customs are, however, shrouded in mystery. The sum of what the literary gentlemen have told us in her regard is this: that she played upon a Lyre and resided on a Mount.

It is a very painful and humiliating thing to be fain to confess that, on the threshold of an article which will not contain one line of poetry, but will be of the very plainest prose on the very plainest of subjects, I would give my ears to find a Muse who, for a reasonable consideration, would permit me to invoke her, and would Inspire my Lay and enable me to get to the end of it without committing five hundred blunders. Is there a Muse of Memory? I am afraid there is not: but it is a Muse of that kind I wish to apostrophise. And if I addressed her as Snuffy, or as Smoky, or even as Cloudy, I should be deemed either stupid or irreverent. Still I desire no less than a Muse who is given to taking tobacco, a Muse who smokes a pipe, a Muse who can twist a cigarito; but chiefly a Muse who will make me remember things. It is my ardent wish to return once more to the Island of Cuba, and to relate as much as I can call to mind about the famous cigars of Havana. I mentioned recently that I was a teetotum. I have spun round most violently since I last took that liberty. Dear me! where *is* Havana and all my lore about cigars? My note-book is at the bottom of the Lake of Garda; and I know that I began an article on cigars one morning at Trieste, wrote the next paragraph at Milan, and cancelled both, as too digressional, at Samaden, in the canton of the Grisons.

Just now, as I sit down despondingly and wish I had attended

the lectures of the professor who discourses on memory at the
Royal Polytechnic Institution, the bells of Santa Maria della
Salute at Venice strike twelve at midnight, and my Muse, hitherto
coy to churlishness, appears and grants me all I wish.   She is a
nut-brown Muse—nay, darker than the nut : as dark as chocolate.
She is round, and smooth, and graceful, and is deliciously
fragrant. I take her up very tenderly between my finger and
thumb, and pressing her to my lips, bite off her nose. Then do I
apply the flame of a waxen taper to her feet, and I begin to
smoke my Muse. Straightway, in the spiral whirls of blue
incense curling from my last cigar, the inspiration which I needed
glides softly down upon me. Cuba comes back. The ghosts of
a hundred memories start up and drum cheerfully on the lids of
rose-coloured coffins. Wars and rumours of wars, camps, cities,
seas, storms, and sick-beds, all fade away, and here I am in the
Calle del Teniente Rey at Havana, bargaining with a volanté-
driver to take me and a companion to the great tobacco-factory
of La Honradez.

I remember it all. I went over the establishment, say only
yesterday. First, we found out a dark counting-house in a
darker street down town—both made artificially sombre by screens
and curtains, for the sun was salamandering about with his usual
ferocity outside—and sought Don Domingo. Most courteous of
clerks in a Cuban banking-house was he. A tawny man with a
close-cropped head of silver-gray, like an over-ripe orange slightly
mildewed at top, his thews and sinews all dried in the sun like
South American dried beef, but given, like that under the action
of warm water, to become quite soft and tender when you were
admitted to his intimacy. Don Domingo was intimately acquainted with the proprietors of La Honradez. To judge from
the very high-dried odour which continually hung about him, he
must have spent at La Honradez, himself, a handsome annual
income in snuff and cigars. He gave us a Regalia apiece, to keep
us in good spirits until we reached the factory, and then we
picked our way through a maze of packing-cases and strong
boxes, and reaching La Calle del Teniente Rey, bargained, as I

have said, with a volante-driver, and were soon set down before the portal of which we were in quest.

I think the place had been, prior to the suppression of the monastic orders, a convent. It was large enough to have been that, or a barrack, or a penitentiary. The walls were amazingly thick; but the windows, few as they were in number, were neither so rare nor so thickly grated but that the odour of fresh-chopped tobacco came gushing through them, like telegraphic messages from the State of Virginia and the Vuelta de Abajo. Have you ever driven along the Paris Boulevards at very early morning? Have you ever noticed the fragrance issuing from the cafés on your line of route—the smell of the coffee roasting and grinding for the day's consumption? The garçons bring their mills on to the pavement, and from six to seven a.m. the Boulevards smell like Mincing Lane. Substitute tobacco for coffee, and you have the street savour of La Honradez.

Penetrating into the great courtyard, the aroma became perhaps a trifle too forcible. It was as that, say, of the most delicate devil's dust thrown up by the sweetest shoddy mills. It was as though you were off some guano islands, the haunt only of birds of paradise. It is nevertheless certain that the air was laden with impalpable powder; that a sirocco of small-cut speedily filled your mouth, ears, and nostrils, and the pores of your skin; and that your first salutation to La Honradez was a violent fit of sneezing. The courtyard was full of broken boxes and the banana-leaf or maize-straw wrappers of tobacco bales— tobacco long since minced, and twisted, and smoked. There was an immense deal of litter and rubbish about; for, it must be owned, tidiness is not a thing you must expect to find in the tropics.

There were also a number of the Sable Sons of Toil, and the Hapless Children of Bondage, lying about in attitudes suggestive to the artistic student of every conceivable variety of foreshortening. They were asleep, and dreaming, probably, of pumpkin. Slavery I hold to be the dreariest and most detestable of treadmills; but in Cuba the thralls doomed to the degrading discipline of the "stepper" seem to be oftener off than on the wheel, and either exercise or the want of it has a tendency towards making them comfortably fat. As a rule, if at broad noonday you see a negro awake, he is Free. If asleep, he is a Slave.

At La Honradez only cigarettes, cigaritos, papelitos, or whatever else you choose to call the little rolls of tissue-paper containing finely chopped smoking tobacco, are made. The process is very simple; and we took the place only as a whet or relish before the more serious tobacco banquet which we were subsequently to enjoy at the great cigar manufactory of Cabaña.

We passed through numbers of barn-like rooms, vast and dim, where, squatting on the floor in groups, negro men, women, and children were sorting the tobacco, stripping the leaves from the stalks, and arranging them in baskets for the chopping-mills. There exists a notion that any kind of tobacco is good enough to make cigaritos with, and that, on the principle said to be adopted in some sausage-making establishments, anything that comes near enough to the machine, be it beef, or pork, or a dog, or a cat, or a man, is forthwith sucked into the vortex and converted into polonies or saveloys. This notion, so far as it regards cigaritos, is, I am happy to believe, groundless.

Very great care seemed to be taken in the assortment of the leaves and the selection of the prime parts; and I was assured that the paper cigars of La Honradez were made from the choicest Havana tobacco obtainable. They are certainly very delicious to smoke. La Honradez is itself modestly conscious of its own merits, and on the little chromo-lithographed wrappers which surround each bundle of twenty-five cigaritos you read this motto: "Mis hechos me justificaran"—"My works shall justify me." Other factories are more self-laudatory and less modest. "Todos me elogian"—"All praise me," says one, on its wrappers. This may be true, only the establishment ought not to say so. "Mi fama por el orbe vuela"—"My fame is world-wide," exclaims a third. This again is a little too self-asserting; for I would bet a reasonable number of gold ounces that my present respected reader never heard of that particular establishment for making cigaritos.

The paper cigars of Havana are not perfect cylinders, closed at one end with a dexterous twist, and provided at the other with a mouthpiece of twisted cardboard and a morsel of cotton-wool to absorb the essential oil. Those are the famous Russian cigarettes, made at St. Petersburg or Moscow, of Turkish, Syrian, and Bessarabian tobacco. The Havana cigaritos consist mostly of so much finely-chopped tobacco placed in the middle of a little square of very thin paper, neatly rolled up into bâtons about an inch and a half long and an eighth of an inch thick, and closed at each end. The art of making them lies in there being just enough loose paper at the ends, but no more, to make the required twist, and in there being a perfectly homogeneous consistency of tobacco throughout the entire length. If the roll be too tight, or if, on the other hand, the tobacco be not evenly distributed, and it bulges in one part and is loose in another, the cigarito is useless. Indeed it must be made with almost perfect nicety to satisfy consumers : for almost every Spaniard has in his own fingers an innate gift for twisting and rolling his own cigaritos.

We have grown quite familiar, owing to the French "sans nom" paper which for a season or two obtained immense vogue in Paris, with the tiny blank books from which leaves of tissue-paper could be torn to serve as envelopes for the tobacco. Neither the French nor the Germans, however, ever attained great proficiency in this most difficult and delicate art. The Italians abominate cigaritos, preferring to smoke the more abominable cigars of native manufacture ; and I think that the majority of Englishmen could more easily learn to curl hair or play on the mandolin—two arts in which they are never very likely to excel—than to roll cigarettes. To the Spaniard the trick comes naturally. He would roll up a papelito and twist it faultlessly, in a third-class carriage in the middle of the Box Tunnel. The old Spaniards however, it must be owned, are the best hands, or rather the best digits, at papelito making. The tropics "take it out" of a man, and the creole Cuban is fain to allow his slaves to manufacture his cigars for him. Moreover, in Cuba, cigarettes are but a pastime. His real repast is in the Puros, or Havanas of the weed itself ;

whereas in Old Spain, genuine Havanas are, through the idiotic
financial policy of the government, so difficult to obtain, and
cigars of native manufacture are so execrable, that the Castilians
smoke cigaritos in self-defence.

Picking, sorting, and chopping tobacco, and packing it up in
the little squares of tissue-paper, constitute only one section of the
art cultivated at La Honradez. Some hundreds of young women
and children, blacks, mulattoes, and quadroons, are employed
in cutting and folding the paper and in packing the cigarettes
into bundles and gumming the wrappers. These wrappers
themselves necessitate the maintenance of a very large chromo-
lithographic establishment ; and in an airy studio—the sun's rays,
however, tempered by screens of white gauze—we found a number
of creole Spaniards at work, busily designing on stone the fantastic
devices and pretty little vignettes, enveloped in which the far-
famed cigaritos of La Honradez go forth to the world.

The workmen who print these designs in colours, and manage a
very elaborate steam lithographic press (made, as I deciphered
from a cast-iron inscription, at Pittsburg, Pennsylvania, United
States), are a very odd kind of people indeed. They are not
negroes, they are not mulattoes, they are not quadroons, still less
are they Criollos or creole Cubans, or Peninsulares, that is to say,
European Spaniards. They are not precisely slaves ; yet they cannot exactly be termed free. There is one of these odd workmen
perched on a high stool by the side of the machine, and intent on
adjusting the pins to the due and proper register of one of the
coloured wrappers. He is a limber-limbed young fellow, very
thin, with very long, slender fingers, the which, with patient
deftness, he knows well how to use. His complexion is of uniform
pale saffron, of the texture of parchment, and he is perfectly
beardless. He has very long, lustrous black hair falling over his
shoulders. In the centre of his countenance, which in its yellow
smoothness does not ill resemble a boiled batter-pudding, show,
like currants in the said pudding, a pair of little sharp black eyes.
His forehead is very low, his cheek-bones are very high, and
about his lips there lingers continually a scarcely definable yet

ineffable simper of complacent beatitude, due perhaps to an inward consciousness of merit, or to opium, or to sheer innate imbecility.

Where have you seen that parchment face, those eyes, that upturned calmly conceited smirk before ? On a tea-tray ? On a tea-chest ? On a fan ? On a rice-paper view of the Porcelain Pagoda at Nankin ? To whom, in fine, should those features and that complexion belong, but to a brother of the Sun and Moon, a native of the Flowery Land, a native of the Celestial empire ? They appertain, indeed, here to a Chinese coolie. Where, you may ask, are his shaven poll and his pigtail ? That question is easily answered. The coolies in Havana let their hair grow, and are soon persuaded to discard their umbrella hats, nankeen knickerbockers, and bamboo shoes for the ordinary white linen habiliments of the West Indies. More than this, and strange enough to say, they do frequently submit to be baptised, to change their Celestial designations for names taken from the Christian hagiology, and so become, to all outward appearance, very decent Roman Catholics.

Among Protestants, in California and Australia, the Chinaman clings most tenaciously to his native idolatry and his native customs, which are very nasty. He sticks to his pigtail, he sets up his joss-house, he burns perfumed paper to " the gods of genteel morals," he eats with chopsticks, and even imports dried ducks and other culinary offal from Canton or Chusan, to feed upon. But in Cuba, no sooner does he submit his queue to the barber's shear, and allow the priest to change his name from Kwang-Low-Fung to José Maria, than he becomes at least as good a Christian as the negro : which is not saying much. To the end of the chapter, however, he remains essentially an odd fish.

He is a capital workman, patient, cheerful, cunning, and industrious enough when he chooses ; but he does not always choose, and is subject to capricious intervals of monkey-like laziness and of a disposition to mutiny; always in a restless, spiteful, monkey-like manner. It is quite useless to reason with him, for he has his own notions of logic and his own code of ethics. By

the law he cannot be flogged ; but his masters sometimes take the
law into their own hands. If he be thrashed, he goes out and
commits suicide. He whose forefathers may have been over-
civilised some thousands of years ago, and the negro, who seems
never to have been civilised at all since the world began, are
about the most hopelessly impracticable beings ever created to be
the curse and despair of philanthropists and missionaries. The
more honour, perhaps, to the courage and devotion of the missionaries and philanthropists who persist in trying to reclaim the
irreclaimable, and to wash the blackamoor white, and to take
away the spots from the leopard. Brave hearts ! May they go
on trying, and never say die !

There are two hundred thousand of these coolies, it is said, in
Cuba. The vast majority of them are " up the country," in the
tobacco and sugar plantations. They are the substitute for
slavery, as electroware is the substitute for silver. They are as
difficult to keep in good order and as generally unsatisfactory as
substitutes for anything are generally found on trial to be. In
the towns they are employed to a considerable extent as mechanics
and as cooks ; in more than one private house I have found
Chinese footmen and body-servants. They are said to be not
unlike cats in their characters : necessary, harmless—till they are
crossed—sharp, quiet, noiseless, contemplative, and very deceitful.

There is a kind of jail or market for coolies at a place called
El Corro, near Havana, and there they are sold—I mean, there
" contracts " can be made with their " trustees " for their labour
for a stated term. At El Corro you may see them in their native
dress and with their crowns shaven, all but a tuft on the top—
the stumps of their departed tails. A coolie may be purchased
or " contracted " for, at a price varying between three and four
hundred dollars. You are bound to pay the Chinaman you have
bought four dollars per month, and to give him his victuals and
two suits of clothes per year. For this he is bound to you for
eight years. The contract is put in writing before a "juez de paz,"
and two copies are made, one in Chinese and the other in Spanish,
to be kept respectively by the seller and the sold. The strongest

CHINESE COOLIES IN CUBA.

Page 80

guarantee for the Chinaman receiving decent treatment at the hands of his master is the almost certainty of the former's committing suicide if he be beaten. Why the Celestial, who in his own country has been weaned on a course of bamboo, and has " eaten stick," as the Arabs say, every day of his life, should so bitterly resent corporal punishment at the hands of the stranger, I am unable to explain. This, however, is the fact.

For my part, I thought the Chinaman had done very well to change his name from Kwang-Lew-Fung to José Maria, and let his·hair grow, and sit on a high stool printing coloured labels. Chromo-lithography is one of the prettiest pursuits imaginable ; and surely it was better to follow it here in peace, and with something like a hire for one's labour, than to be fishing for ducks from a barge on the Canton river, or painting miniatures on the coffin of your grandmother, against that respected person's decease, or addressing hieroglyphic compliments in Indian ink to " the gods of genteel morals." After all, the alcalde is preferable to the local mandarin, with his incessant bamboo.

We went to see the place where the coolie workmen of the Honradez were lodged. The dormitories were, for Cuba, wonderfully clean and airy ; and under proper discipline, I was told, the Chinaman could be made to observe extraordinary neatness and propriety. The beds, or bunks, were in tiers one above the other, as in a passenger steamer, but were much more spacious. Every coolie had his locker for his clothes, and a shelf for his platter, pannikin, and drinking-mug. Above every bunk was printed the name of its occupant. I read a most orthodox catalogue of José Marias, Andres, Augustins, Basilios, Benitos, Beltrans, Cristobals, Manuels, Eustaquios, Gils, Enriques, Jacobos, Pepes, Jaymes, Juans, Domingos, Lazaros, Mauricios, Pablos, Filipes, Rafaels, Estebans, Tadeos, Tomases, Vicentes, and Guillermos. There was one Eusquilo, or Æschylus, and one Napoleone, who—the last—was described as the biggest rascal in the whole gang : the which reminded me that names very seldom suit their possessors, and that the only man I ever knew who had been christened Virgil was a most egregious donkey.

F

We were not allowed to leave La Honradez without an "obsequio" or complimentary offering, and, according to the etiquette of
Spanish politeness, this backshish was administered in the most
delicate and artful manner. We were asked to sign our names
and addresses in the visitors' book, and then, on some pretext or
another, we were taken to a remote apartment. Just as we were
quitting the establishment, and were thanking the superintendent
for the great kindness and courtesy he had shown us, a coolie
stepped forward, and, with a low bow and an inimitable simper,
presented each of our party with a packet of cigaritos, on whose
labels, flourishing in chromo-lithography, were our Christian and
surnames, printed at full length. The operation had been effected
in about six minutes. It is certain that they have a very nice
way of doing things in Havana.

VI.

Havana Cigars.

HE wakes. She is all alive. I have got my Muse fast at Florian's, on St. Mark's Place, Venice, and on a sumptuous summer night. The great full moon hangs over our heads, imminent, like the sign of the World Turned Upside Down. I have regaled my Muse with iced coffee and macaroons. She has even partaken of a "bicchierino" of maraschino. A bicchierino—isn't it a dainty name for a dram ? Then, rubbing my hands in uncharitable glee, to think that yonder white-jerkined Tedesco officers have nothing choicer to smoke than three-halfpenny "Virginias"—the actual Virginia of their birth being probably the Terra di Lavoro, or the Island of Sardinia—I produce from that private case, which has hitherto eluded the lynx eyes of the German Zollverein, the Spanish Duana, and the Italian Dogana, a real cigar—a Regalia Britannica, "Flor fina, Maduro : Havana, 1864." My Muse lights up at once, and pours forth memory in clouds.

You need not be in the least shocked at the idea of this young lady from Parnassus, otherwise a most decorous person, graduate of the Hyde Park College, and who has been nursery-governess in a nobleman's family, indulging in a cigar as big as a BB pencil, at ten o'clock at night, in front of a public coffee-house. Between ourselves be it mentioned, there are many ladies in Venice who are to the full as inveterate smokers as the ladies of Seville. My Muse, perhaps, is the only high-born dame who puffs in the open Piazza ; but then she is invisible to the vulgar, and an Immortal. You shall scarcely, however, take an evening airing in your gondola without observing numerous fair and graceful forms at their open windows, or in their balconies, enjoying, not the pretty puerility of the papelito, but the downright and athletic exercitation of the full-grown cigar.

About sundown, on most evenings, our gondoliers row us from the Ponte de' Fuseri to the Giardini Pubblici. We strike the Grand Canal a little below the garden of the Palazzo Reale. At the left-hand corner of the canal from which we emerge there is a pretty little mansion, Venetian Gothic in style, and, for Venice, in excellent repair. It is precisely the little mansion which, if its bodily eradication, shipment to Liverpool, and removal to London, on the American system of rollers, was judged impossible, I should like to cause Mr. Barry, R.A., to build for me in Curzon Street, Mayfair; and then, with the title-deeds of the freehold in my strong-box, and the bins of my bijou house well ballasted with curious hocks and peculiar clarets, I would lead a chirping life, entertaining my friends, drinking even mine enemy's health, and wishing him better luck the next time he went out stabbing. At a charming oriel window of this tiny palazzetto there is sure to be, about this sunset hour, a plump, jovial-looking little lady—very like the portraits of the Countess Guiccioli—and who is pulling at a cigar at least half an inch longer and stouter than my Regalia Britannica. I think the plump little lady smokes Ambasciadores —a kind of cigar which you hesitate about consuming habitually unless your income exceeds fifteen thousand a year.

In about an hour after sunset we glide back from the Giardini towards the Rialto, and there, at the same oriel window, we are sure to find the same plump little lady pulling away as vigorously as ever at her weed. It is not, I am afraid, the same cigar. Even in an Ambasciador there are not more than forty-five minutes' steady and continuous smoking. It has grown dark by this time, and through the open casement I can see a delicious little salon with a frescoed ceiling, containing that "copiosa quantità d' amoretti" which Cardinal Maurice, of Savoy, was so anxious that Albano, the painter, should supply him with. I see a chandelier, glittering with crystal pendants and wax-lights—the good old candles of *yellow* wax, not the meagre, bleached, half-

hearted gentilities the chandlers sell us too often nowadays. I
see walls with silken draperies, and choice pictures, and rare
Venice mirrors, with frames like a whole horticultural show carved
in gold. The furniture of the salon is of precisely the pattern I
should wish Messrs. Jackson and Graham to send me into Curzon
Street :—sparing no expense, and asking no questions about
settlement.

I hope that the eyes which have thus dived into the penetralia
of a Venetian dwelling-house are not impertinent. Where is the
use of having pretty things if you don't allow the world outside
to admire them? and are not all the really nice people who
possess pretty things always ready to exhibit their treasures?
Finally, at the window of this enchanting chamber, amidst flowers
in boxes and flowers in vases, and with a sprightly little Maltese
dog snoozing in her sleeve, is the prettiest picture of all—the
plump little lady, blowing her placid cloud :

> " Se non son più Sovrana,
> Son sempre Veneziana,"

she seems to be warbling between her whiffs, in that endearing
dialect of the Adriatic which is as soft as *crème à la vanille*, and a
great deal healthier.

I salute you, noble lady of Venice ! Did I dare to launch into
familiarity—did I presume to indulge in slang, I might say what
I think—that you are a " brick." In any case, I prefer you to
Medora in her bower, to Mariana in the South, and to the Lady
of Shalott. I would bow to you, Lady mine, were not bowing
under the coved roof of a gondola almost as difficult a feat as
bowing in bed. More than once the little lady has waved a
smoke-spiral amicably towards me. There is a certain freemasonry
among smokers. I am thinking that to-morrow evening I shall
wave my handkerchief to her, when I am violently pulled back on
to the cushions of the gondola, and the boatmen are instructed in
a passionate feminine voice to row faster homewards. There is no
harm, surely, in wishing to wave one's handkerchief to such a
remarkably plump and jovial-looking little lady.

Yes, red-sashed boatman, even with my ears boxed, take me

home ; and then, when I have filled my inkhorn and nibbed my pen, take me, if you please, back to Havana. Never mind the heat. We shall be hotter before we are through this day's work. Never mind the dust. The sea-breeze will blow some time after gun-fire, and if you can exist unsmothered until then, you will be refreshed. Let us hail the first volante, whose dark and merry-faced postillion invites us to enter, and drive to the cigar manufactory, world famous and unequalled in the world, perhaps, of "La Hija de Cabaña y Carvajal." For shortness it is called "Cabaña's."

There is no longer a palpable Cabaña in the flesh. Firms remain, but partners pass away. Is there a Child ? Is there a Fortnum, or haply a Mason ? Is there a Chevet, or a Widow Clicquot ? Did you ever see Swan and Edgar walking together ? There has not been a Cramer for twenty years ; and what contemporary man ever knew Boodle ? The actual representative of the great Cuban house of Cabaña is the Señor Anselmo del Valle. I had had the advantage of a special introduction to this gentleman at his retail establishment ere I visited his factory. The monarch of Nicotine sat enthroned among odoriferous cedar boxes and cigars yet more fragrant, serene and sweet-smelling, like an old Turk merchant in the Bezesteen among his shawls, and chibouks, and spices, and rose-attar. A lissom, dusky, oily-looking man, if I remember aright, with a lustrous, bush-like moustache, and who, reclining in a low chair, and in a full suit of white linen, was gently perspiring. The chief monarch of the great mosque of Araby the blest, this Señor Anselmo del Valle. What a halcyon existence ! A mattress of lotus-hair—a continuous and diaphanous drapery of grateful incense hanging round. Nothing to do all day long save to loll in a rocking-chair, and take gold ounces in exchange for boxes of superfine Cabañas. For the cigar business is essentially a ready-money one. So many cigars as you make you can sell ; and so many cigars as you sell do you get paid for, in Havana, on the nail.

I have often thought that to be a brewer of pale ale at Burton-on-Trent must be the acme of human felicity. You have only to

go on brewing barrels of beer, and an ever-thirsty public will go
on buying and paying. Dr. Johnson had an inkling of this
when, taking stock, as executor under Thrale's will, of the great
brewhouse which was afterwards to become Barclay and Perkins's,
he told Topham Beauclerk that he had at last discovered the
"source of boundless prosperity and inexhaustible riches." When
I went to Havana, however, I was fain to place the vat in the
second rank. The superlative degree I reserve for the cigar trade.
"Boundless prosperity and inexhaustible riches" are, in the case
of a Cabaña or an Anselmo del Valle, associated with something
even more productive of happiness. The cigar merchant can pass
at least eighteen hours out of the twenty-four in the delicious
occupation of smoking his own cigars. Now the Burton brewer,
however fond he may be of the famous decoction of hops, malt,
and the water of the Mendip Hills, fermented on the placid banks
of Trent, can scarcely go on drinking his own pale ale all day
long. Nature wouldn't stand it. The brain and stomach would
alike revolt from this perpetual state of beer.

As a rule, traders are averse from consuming their own wares.
Some, sagacity warns off; others, satiety sickens. Your provincial innkeeper does not share with a very good grace, and
with a chance guest, the bottle of red ink, logwood, and spirits of
turpentine which he sells as claret, and charges ten-and-sixpence
for. The grocer's apprentice soon grows tired of filching figs and
munching raisins—ah! how nice they were when, as children, we
were allowed to stone the plums for the Christmas pudding, and
stole more than we stoned!—on the sly. The pastrycook's girl
runs to the counter, indulges in a revel of patties and jam tarts;
but in a fortnight she becomes palled, and a wilderness of sweets
rarely invites her to browse.

It is different with the merchant who sells good cigars. He
knows when he is well off, and makes the most of his opportunity. "Carpe diem" is his motto, as it was that of the Regent
Orleans. Heart-complaint, paralysis, liver-complaint, dyspepsia,
cerebral disease in its thousand-and-one forms, may menace those
who smoke too much; but the merchant knows when he has a

good article on hand, and continues to smoke the choicest weeds
in his stock. A cigar merchant who did not smoke seems to me
quite as much of a monster as that French bibliomaniac of the
eighteenth century, whom La Bruyère knew, who had a library
of eighty thousand volumes, splendidly bound, and who confessed
that he never read a book. "I think," says La Bruyère, in his
mention of this person, "that he only amassed volumes because
he liked the smell of new leather. But why, then, didn't he turn
tanner instead of bookworm ?"

I have a distinct impression that after Señor Anselmo del
Valle had squeezed my hand—he squeezed everybody's hand—on
my being presented to him, he left in my palm a Cabaña Regalia.
They give away cigars in Cuba as they give away pinches of snuff
elsewhere. I went into the back warehouse to choose a case of
Prensados for ordinary smoking, and the warehouseman gave me a
handful just to try what their flavour might be like. These are
among the "obsequios." When I got home to mine inn that
evening, I found even a more splendid *obsequio* from the Cabaña
factory, in the shape of a beautiful crystal casket framed in gilt
bronze, inscribed with my name—"Caballero Ingles" being
added as a dignity—and containing one hundred of the superlative cigars known as Excepcionales. These are said to be worth
in England half a crown apiece, and are, indeed, only manufactured in order to be dispensed to crowned heads or presented
as *obsequios* to tourists.

I am ashamed to say that—sentiments of gratitude apart—
I would grudge sixpence for the best Excepcionale that ever
was made. Their mere fabrication is beyond compare. They
are perfect convoluted cylinders of tobacco-leaf mathematically
symmetrical, showing not a join, a vein, or a pimple—with the
broad end as round and smooth as that of a Cumberland pencil ;
with the narrow end as sharply blunt—a paradox, but a truth,
for all that—as the agate burnisher used for embossing diapers in
illumination. I think that were you to throw an Excepcionale
into the midst of Westminster Hall, it would not break, nor lie,
but the rather rebound, elastic, and come back to you at last,

intact, but bent, boomerang fashion. Its defect is that it is a world too light—that is to say, too mild in flavour—and that like all mild cigars, it is hot in the mouth. To the thorough smoker there is no more feverish tobacco than the lightest Latakia, and no cooler than the strongest Cavendish. Mild-tobacco smoking leads to drinking : witness the Turk, with his continually replenished coffee-cup, and the German, who washes down the chopped-up hay-stacks which he crams into his pipkin of a pipe with innumerable mugs of beer.

From the hospitable retail establishment of the señor to his factory, or rather that of the Hija de Cabaña y Carvajal, is a drive of about twenty minutes. The Fabrica is a grandiose building of white stone, and of the architectural style which may be described as West Indian Doric : that is to say, with plenty of porticos and columns and vestibules, erected much more for the purpose of producing coolness than pictorial effect. There are at least a thousand operatives employed here ; but the mere number of hands is no test of the importance of a cigar manufactory. At the huge Reale Fabrica de Tabacos, in Seville, over four thousand men and women, nearly half of them gipsies, find employment. The Régie at Algiers gives daily work to over fifteen hundred hands. The cigar factories of Bordeaux, Barcelona, Anceno, and Venice are on a corresponding scale of magnitude ; but please to bear in mind that the staple of the things made in the usines I have named is mere muck, rubbish, refuse ; whereas the Hija de Cabaña y Carvajal turns out only choice and fragrant rolls of superfine tobacco.

If anything could improve on the dreamy balminess which falls on the contemplative mind in these vast halls, all devoted to the treatment and preparation of tobacco, it would be the fact that the ceiling of every room is of cedar. 'Tis in the groves of Mount Lebanon, or if you choose to be more prosaic, in an atmosphere of lead-pencils, that your weeds are made. I confess that ere I had been half an hour in the Cabaña factory I became immersed in a kind of happy fog or state of coma, such as ordinarily incited Messrs. Coleridge and De Quincey—in the good

old days when it was thought no harm to crack a decanter full of
laudanum before dinner—to literary composition. This must
serve as my excuse for the very vague manner in which I am
enabled to describe the process of making cigars.

I know that I saw great bales and bundles of tobacco, just
brought in from the plantations, being weighed in one long hall
by negro women. The stuff was piled into monstrous scales, like
those used in their dealings with the Indians who had furs to
sell by the crafty traders in old Manhattan—who laid down the
axiom that a Dutchman's foot weighed ten pounds, and popped
their foot into the scale accordingly. I know that I subsequently
saw tobacco in all stages of being cleaned and picked and
sorted, the finer leaves being reserved for the coverings or sheaths
of the cigars, the less choice being used to form what magazine
editors call "padding," and the Cubans themselves, when speaking of cigars, "las tripas"—a term not quite translatable to
genteel ears, but which I may render in a guarded manner as
"insides."

If you offer a Spaniard a cigar—not with a view that he
should smoke, but that he should criticise it—he will, after
expressing the preliminary wish that you may live a thousand
years, produce a sharp penknife and slice the weed through
diagonally. Then with a strong magnifying-glass he will
scrutinise "las tripas," and tell you as confidently as any London
or Linnæus could, the precise order of vegetation to which the
cigar belongs—whether it is of the superfine "vuelta de abajo,"
the Clos Vougeot of Nicotia, or of some inferior growth, either
from the Island of Cuba itself, or from Hayti, or Porto Rico, or
Virginia, or Maryland, or the Carolinas, or haply from the
south and east of Europe ; for vast quantities of Hungarian,
Austrian, Sardinian, and Bessarabian tobacco do find their way
to Cuba, and come back to us in the guise of prime Havanas
—that is certain. A minute investigation of "las tripas" may
also lead to the painful disclosure that the cigar is not composed
of tobacco at all. The periodical reports of her Majesty's
Commissioners of Inland Revenue point out, pretty plainly,

what vile stuff is sometimes foisted on the public as genuine tobacco.

You run no risk, of course, of having a sophisticated cigar from the factory of the Hija de Cabaña y Carvajal. Their wares are of different qualities—just as claret is, and the quality perhaps takes as wide a range as Bordeaux takes between ordinary Medoc and Château Lafitte. But a Cabaña cigar—bought at Cabaña's, *bien entendu*, or at any reputable dealer's in London (no foreign cigar merchant I ever met with could be trusted even so far as I could see him)—is sure to be made of genuine tobacco. You are quite safe, also, with a cigar from the Partagas factory—and there are many amateurs who prefer Partagas to Cabañas ; you are equally safe with an Alvarez ; with a Cavargas ; with a López ; with a Cealdos (of the Guipuzcoana manufactory), and especially with a Figaro. Some persons imagine the name of " Figaro " to be that of a brand or form of cigar, such as a " Henry Clay " or a " Londres ;" but it is really that of a factory. I may mention our " Lion " and " Romford " breweries by way of analogy. I need not say that there are scores more respectable traders in Havana who make good and unadulterated cigars ; but the names I have set down are those best known and most popular with smokers.

On the broadest principle of classification, the cigars which are really brought from the Island of Cuba to Europe may be divided into three great groups. First, genuine Havanas, of various degrees of fineness, but, from stem to stern, sheath and "tripas," made of tobacco grown, cured, and rolled in the Island of Cuba. Second, cigars composed inside of United States or of European tobacco, imported into the island, but with an outside wrapper of Havana leaf. Third and last, cigars brought ready made into Havana from Europe—mostly from Bremen and Switzerland— passed through some export house unfair enough to be an accomplice in such dealings, and re-exported to Europe. You rarely meet with these doubly sham cigars in England ; but they form the staple of the article retailed at extravagant prices to travellers at continental hotels. They smoke so abominably that the con-

sumer usually jumps at the conclusion that they are simply
" duffers," with forged brands and labels on the boxes ; but if he
imparts this assumption to the waiter, that functionary may in his
turn often assume an air of injured innocence and virtuous indignation. He can tell the complainant the name of the wholesale
dealer from whom he has purchased the cigars ; nay, he is often
enabled to point out on the box the actual government stamp, and
the amount of duty paid on the contents as foreign cigars. I
have gone down with a waiter to a custom-house and seen him
clear from the ship and pay duty upon the cigars he has sold me,
and yet have found them afterwards to be the merest rubbish. It
is unjust to make Cuba responsible for the prevalence of such
trash. The rubbishing cigars have been to Havana, but were not
made there. What is it the Bulbul in the Persian poem remarks
relative to the rose ? I think he observes that he is not that
flower, but that he has lived near her. So Bremen, which has
paid a flying visit to Havana, may be regarded as a kind of
rascally Bulbul.

This species of fraud is too clumsy and too slow for the great
English people. We, who are so very hard on the Americans for
their " smartness," habitually resort in trade to perhaps the most
ingenious swindles, the most impudent deceptions, and the
meanest and most detestable "dodges" of any nation in the world.
We adulterate everything. We forge everything. We would
adulterate the mother earth which is thrown on our coffins when
we are buried, if *that* fraud would pay. There is not a petty
tobacconist's shop in a London back street without a stock of
cigar boxes, whose brands, whose printed labels—down to the
bluntness of the Spanish type and the poverty of the Spanish
wood-engravings—are cool and literal forgeries of the Spanish
originals. These brands and labels are forged quite as neatly as
bank-notes are forged ; but this is a " trick of trade " which has
not yet become felony. I have seen with my own eyes, in a great
English town, and in a cigar factory employing three hundred
men, the brands ready for heating and stamping—a kind of
chamber of horrors—where there were no less than ninety different

trade-marks purporting to be those of leading houses in Havana, and all of which were false.

The excuse of the people who resort to these wretched artifices is, that they vend the wares thus spuriously branded and labelled as "British," and not as "foreign" cigars. What's in a name? they ask; and so they call a cabbage a Cabaña, just for the fun of the thing. But would it be fair, I may ask, to stamp the little figure of the "perro," or dog, which is the trade-mark of the real Toledo blade, on the haft of a carving-knife made at Liége, or to brand "Moët et Chandon" on the cork of a bottle of cider? There are, doubtless, numbers of highly trustworthy cigar manufacturers in England who make their cigars of the very best foreign tobacco that can be imported; but I must refer again to the reports of the Commissioners of Inland Revenue for some very ugly revelations made from time to time as to fines inflicted on manufacturers who adulterate their tobacco; and in any case the practice of marking the boxes which contain home-made cigars, even if they be of good tobacco, with the names and brands of celebrated Havana houses, is unfair, untradesmanlike, and immoral. I daresay, however, that I am but fighting with wild beasts at Ephesus in alluding to such matters, and that I shall get but scratches for my pains. Only, to unwary people who happen to be young and wealthy I will say *this*: whenever you have anything to do with cigars, or with sherry, or with pictures, or with horses, look out. Some advisers would include women and diamonds in their caveat; but I halt at horses. They may have a flaw in them, but a woman is a woman and a diamond a diamond, and you can tell paste at once.

A visit to Cabaña's manufactory, although it failed in enabling me to describe with terseness combined with accuracy the process of cigar-making, had at least one beneficial result in disabusing my mind of a variety of absurd stories which I, and I daresay a good many of those who read this paper, had heard regarding the process as pursued in the Island of Cuba. To believe these legends, cigar-making is one of the nastiest, nay, the most revolting of handicrafts, and the manner in which the tobacco is rolled and shaped by imperfectly clad young ladies of the African race and in a state of servitude is, to say the least, shocking. There may be small manufacturers at Havana who own but two or three slaves, or employ but two or three workwomen, and they may do their work in a brutish and uncleanly manner ; but so far as my own experience at the Hija de Cabaña y Carvajal's renders me a trustworthy witness, I may vouch for the scrupulous cleanliness and delicacy with which every single stage in the process of cigar-making is conducted. I have seen barley-sugar made and I have seen bread made, and I certainly consider the manufacture of cigars to be a nicer transaction than either bread or sweetstuff making.

Nothing can be more orderly, more symmetrical, than the appearance of the cutting and shaping room. The operators sit to their work and make the cigars with their fingers, but do *not* roll them into shape by attrition on their sartorial muscles, as is popularly supposed. Every operator has his counter or desk, his sharp cutting tools and his pot of gum for fastening the tips, with his stock of assorted tobacco-leaf in baskets by his side. It is a competitive vocation. The best workmen are best off. Payment is by results. Many of the hands employed are negro slaves, or were so when I was in Havana ; but the finer cigars, the prime Cabañas, the Napoleones, the Excepcionales and Regalias, are made exclusively by white creole Spaniards, who are paid according to the number they can turn out a day, and many of whom realise very handsome wages.

Good cigars are very dear in Havana. You may get a weed for a penny or three-halfpence ; or sometimes, by industriously rooting among the small manufacturers, you may pick up cigars very cheap indeed, which if you throw them into a drawer and allow them to season for six months, may turn out to be tolerable ; but an approved and warranted cigar from a first-rate house will always fetch its price, and our heavy import duties notwithstanding, is not much. cheaper in Havana than it is in England. I may add that it is generally understood in the cigar trade that the very finest and choicest qualities of Havana cigars go to

England simply because the largest prices can be commanded there; yet I believe I am rather under than above the mark in stating that there are not thirty cigar dealers in London from whom fine and choice Havanas can be procured. It has been computed—although I have no official authority for the statement—that of the cigars manufactured by the Hija de Cabaña y Carvajal at least forty per cent. go to England, thirty per cent. to the United States—California taking the largest quantity— ten per cent. to Brazil, five to Russia, five to France, five to Spain, two to Germany, two to Australia, leaving one per cent. for Italy and other fractional consumers of real cigars; and yet the Italians are the most inveterate smokers in Europe. They prefer, however, their own home-made Cavours, which are a halfpenny apiece and slowly poisonous, to the more wholesome but more expensive Cabaña.

I forgot to state that, before I left the Cabaña premises, I smoked and enjoyed very much a full-flavoured Regalia, for whose structure I had myself selected the leaves, and which I saw rolled, shaped, gummed, and pointed, with my own eyes. It was like being at Joe's in Finch Lane.

VII.

A HARD ROAD TO TRAVEL.

T was part of the ineffable system of sweetness and light known as the wisdom of our ancestors, to whip all the children on the morning of Innocents' Day, "in order that the memorial of Herod's murder might stick the closer." The wisdom of our contemporaries, while it has discarded the brutal practice of annually reacting the Massacre of the Innocents on a secondary scale, still retains a trace of the disagreeable mediæval custom, in respect of the strict connection maintained in many households between Biblical study and afflictive punishment, and the intimate alliance between chapters from Jeremiah to be gotten by heart, and bread and water and dark cupboards. Who the philanthropic discoverer of child torture as a prelude to a church festival may have been, is uncertain; perhaps he was a near relative of the bright spirit who hit on the ingenious devices—to which the puddling of iron and the glazing of pottery are but trifling puerilities—of confining black beetles in walnut shells and binding them over the eyes of infants; or of that ardent lover of his species—connected with the educational profession—whose researches into the phenomena of physical pain led him to the inestimable discovery that by boring a hole or any number of holes in a piece of wood with which a child's hand is struck, a corresponding number of blisters may be raised on the smitten palm.

Our good ancestors—can we ever be sufficiently grateful for the rack, or for the whirligig chair framed by medical wisdom for the treatment of acute mania!—blended the Innocents' Day custom with many of the observances of social life. If they were wicked, these ancestors of ours, they were at least waggish in their wickedness. If the boundaries of a parish or the limits of an estate needed accurate record, they laid down a boy on the ascertained frontiers, and flogged him so soundly that he never forgot where the parish of St. Verges ended or where that of St. Brooms began. Fifty years afterwards, if he were summoned as a witness at Nisi Prius, he would relate, quickened by the memory of his stripes, every topographical condition of the limits under discussion. The phantom of this sportive mode of combining cruelty with land-surveying yet survives in the annual outings of charity children to "beat the bounds." Formerly the charity boys and not the bounds were beaten ; but now even the long willow wands with which bricks and mortar are castigated are falling into desuetude, and although the ceremony is still kept up in some parishes—the rector in his black gown and a chimney-pot hat, and bearing a large nosegay in his hand, being a sight to see—it is feared that beating the bounds will, in a few years, be wholly abolished, owing to the gradual but sure extinction of Beadles, as a race.

Another vestige of what may be called Innocenticism lingered until recently in certain pleasant municipal excursions termed "swan hoppings," when some corpulent gentlemen, with a considerable quantity of lobster salad and champagne beneath their waistcoats, were sportively seized upon by the watermen of the Lord Mayor's barge, and "bumped" on posts or rounded blocks of stone. The solemn usage had some reference, it is to be presumed, to the liberties of the City, as guaranteed by the charter given by William the king to William the bishop, and Godfrey the portreeve. Or it might obscurely have related to the Conservancy of the Thames. Substantially it meant half a crown to the Lord Mayor's watermen.

In the south of France there may be found growing, all the year round, as fine a crop of ignorance and fanaticism as the sturdiest Conservative might wish to look upon. The populace of Toulouse would hang the whole Calas family again to-morrow if they had a chance. The present writer was all but stoned once

G

at Toulon for not going down on his knees in the street in honour of the passage of an absurd little joss, preceded by a brass band, a drum-major, a battalion of the line, and a whole legion of priests.   The country people still thrash their children mercilessly whenever a gang of convicts go by on their way to the *bagne*, and especially on the morning of the execution of a criminal.   And it is a consolation to arrive at the conclusion, from patent and visible facts, that wherever wisdom in its Ancestral form triumphantly flourishes, there dirt, sloth, ignorance, superstition, fever, pestilence, and recurring famines do most strongly flourish too.

It may seem strange to the reader that, after venturing upon these uncomplimentary comments on our forefathers' sagacity, the writer should candidly proceed to own his belief that the human memory *may* be materially strengthened as to facts and dates by the impressions of bodily anguish suffered concurrently with a particular day or a particular event.   Such, however, is the fact, although of course it cannot be accepted as a plea in extenuation of the most barbarous cruelty.   For example, if the next time a tramp sought hospitality at the Guildford union the guardians forthwith seized upon such tramp and caused him to be branded with a hot iron from head to foot, and in Roman capitals, with the words, "The guardians of the Guildford union refuse to relieve the Casual Poor," the stigmatised vagrant would, to the day of his death, remember that Guildford union workhouse was not a place whereat bed and breakfast should be asked for.

Still there is no combating the fact that the remembrances of agony are lasting.   I have a very indistinct recollection of things which took place twenty or even ten years ago ; and I often ask myself with amazement whether it is possible that I could ever have written such and such a letter or known such a man or woman.   Yet with microscopic minuteness I can recall a yellow hackney-coach—the driver had a carbuncle on the left side of his nose—which, once upon a time, conveyed my nurse and myself to the residence of a fashionable dentist in Old Cavendish Street, London.   I can remember the black footman who opened the door, and the fiendish manner in which he grinned, as though to show that *his* molars needed no dentistry. I can remember the dog's-eared copy of the "Belle-Assemblée" on the waiting-room table; the widow lady with her face tied up, moaning by the window; the choleric old gentleman in nankeen trousers who swore terrifically because he was kept waiting; the frayed and threadbare edges of the green baize door leading to the dentist's torture chamber; the strong smell of cloves and spirits of wine and warm wax about; the dentist himself—his white neckcloth and shining bald head; his horrible apparatus; his more horrible morocco-covered chair; the drip, drip of water at the washstand; the sympathising looks of my nurse; the deadly dew of terror that started from my pores as the monster seized me; and finally, that one appalling circular wrench, as though some huge bear with red-hot jaws—he has favoured us all in dreams—were biting my head off, and found my cervical vertebræ troublesome: all these come back to me palpably. Yet I had that tooth out eight-and-thirty years ago.

A hard road to travel! I should have forgotten all about *that* road by this time but for the intolerable pain I endured when I was travelling upon it. I have crossed Mont Cenis a dozen times, yet I should be puzzled to point out the principal portions of the landscape to a stranger. I could not repeat without book the names of the Rhine castles between Cologne and Mayence. I am sure I don't know how many stations there are between London and Brighton. And I am not by any means "letter" or "figure perfect" in the multiplication-table, although the road up to nine times eight was in my time about as hard travelling as could be gone through by a boy with a skin not quite so thick as that of a rhinoceros. But every inch of the hard road I happened to travel in the spring of 1864—a road which stretches for some three hundred miles from the city of Vera Cruz to the city of Mexico—is indelibly impressed on my memory.

Since then I have journeyed many thousands of miles over roads of more or less duresse; and in the Tyrol, in Venetia, in Spain, in Algeria, I have often tested by sudden inward query the tenacity

remaining in the reminiscence of that road in Mexico. You turn
to the right from the great quay of Vera Cruz, passing the castle
of San Juan de Ulloa. You drive to a wretched railway station
and take the train (I am speaking of 1864) to a place called La
Soledad, some five-and-twenty miles inland. There you sleep.
Next morning at daybreak you start in a carriage along the great
Spanish highway, and by nightfall make Cordova. At four on
the following morning you drive to Orizaba—you are taking
things quietly, mind, in consequence of the road—and pass the
day there. Again on the morrow you start at four a.m. from
Cordova for Sant' Augustin del Palmar, where you dine and
sleep. The next day's journey brings you by sunset to Puebla.
The next day you make Rio Frio, in time for breakfast, and at
about five in the afternoon you pass the Garita, or customs-
barrier, and are in the city of Montezuma, the capital of Mexico.
That is the road. I spent, going up, six days on the journey; but
I was an inmate of a private carriage. I came down again in a
public diligence in three days; but for reasons I shall explain
afterwards, the agony of the private travelling carriage far
surpassed that of the stage-coach.

Ostensibly I had no reason for grumbling. I was the guest of
a kind friend whose carriage had been built in New York with a
special view to Mexican highways, and who, being a great friend
and patron of the contractor for the Imperial diligences—Mexico
was an empire in '64—was certain of relays of mules all the way
from the sea-coast to the capital. We had a good store of wine
with us, and plenty of Havana cigars; and in the way of edibles,
the commissariat of Mexico is as abundant as that of Old Spain is
meagre.* The route was singularly clear from highway robbers at

* It is curious that in countries where wine is plentiful there should be
nothing procurable to eat, and that in non-wine-growing, but beer or cider-
producing countries the traveller should always be sure of a good dinner.
Out of the beaten track in Italy, a tourist runs the risk of being half
starved. In Spain, he *is* starved habitually and altogether; but he is sure
of victuals in England, in America, and in Russia. Even in the East,
fowls, eggs, kids, and rice are generally obtainable in the most out-of-the-
way places; but many a time have I been dismissed hungry from a village

that time ; the French being in force at Cordova, Orizaba, and
Puebla, and patrolling every league of the way, not only with
their own dragoons, but with local levies known as contra-
guerrilleros. Finally, we had taken the precaution of leaving
behind us in safe care at Vera Cruz, our watches, gold *onzas*, and
other valuables, keeping only a few loose dollars for the expenses
of the journey. I even left my clothes and servant on the coast,
and during the six weeks I remained in Mexico city was not only
boarded and lodged, but washed and clothed by my generous host :
even to the articles of purple and fine linen, lapis-lazuli wrist-
buttons, a Mexican hat as broad as a brougham wheel, and a pair
of spurs with rowels as big as cheese-plates. So, if we had been
robbed on the way, the guerillas would have found very little of
which to plunder us.

    The pain, the misery, the wretchedness I endured, almost
without intermission for six days—at night you generally dreamed
of your bumps, and suffered all your distresses over again—were
entirely due to the abominable road upon which we entered, for
our sins, at La Soledad, and which we did not leave until we came
to the very custom-house barrier of Mexico. Ten years * have
passed since I travelled on the Czar's highway and found it bad.
I have waded through the Virginian mud since then ; have made
acquaintance with muleback on the banks of the Guadalquivir ;
have tried a camel (for a very short time) at Oran. But I can
conscientiously declare that I never found so hard a road to travel
as that road between Vera Cruz and Mexico, and I am confident
that, were I to live to sixty years of age (the Mexican railway by
that time being completed and paying fifteen per cent. on its
stock, and a beautifully Macadamised carriage road running beside
it for three hundred miles), and I were questioned as to what the
Mexican highway was like in 1864, I should, on the "beating
the bounds" principle, preserve as lively a remembrance of its

hostelry in France with the cutting remark: "Monsieur, nous n'avons plus
rien." There is an exception to the rule in Germany—I except Prussia—
which bounteous land runs over with wine, beer, beef, veal, black and white
bread, potatoes, salad, and sauerkraut.

* This was written in 1866.

horrors as I preserve of it now, a peaceable and contented daily traveller on the Queen's highway and the Metropolitan railway.

Had I not been somewhat obtuse, I might have noticed on board the steamer which brought us from Havana that my friend was nervous, even to uneasiness, as to the form my earliest impressions of Mexican travelling might assume. I must expect to "rough it" a little, he remarked. I answered that I had tried an American ambulance wagon and a M'Clellan saddle, and that I could not imagine anything rougher than those aids to locomotion. "Our roads are not quite up to the mark of Piccadilly," he would hint sometimes. "You see, since the French came to attack Juarez everything has been knocked into a cocked-hat." However, he always wound up his warnings by declaring that we shouldn't find a single robber on the road, and that we should go up to Mexico "like a fiddle." If the state in which I eventually reached Mexico bore any resemblance to the musical instrument in question, it must have been akin to that of the fiddle of the proprietor of the bear in "Hudibras," warped and untuned, with my bow broken, a fracture in my stomach, another in my back, and my strings flying all abroad.

I sincerely hope that I shall never see Vera Cruz again :—the ill-omened, sweltering, sandy, black, turkey-buzzard-haunted home of yellow fever! I shall not forget, however, that I was hospitably entertained there, and especially I shall never lose consciousness of a long telescope in the saloon overlooking the roadstead, to which I am indebted for one of the drollest scenes I ever saw in my life. There were three or four French men-of-war stationed at Vera Cruz at the time, but they could not lie in the harbour, which is not by any means landlocked, and has but an insufficient breakwater in the castle of San Juan de Ulloa. The Spithead of Vera Cruz is off Sacrificios, a place which owes its name to the horrible human sacrifices perpetrated there up to the time of Cortes' invasion. Sunday being the Frenchman's day of joyous recreation all over the world, leave had been granted, with some liberality, to the crews of the war-ships in port; and from our window we had seen, during the morning and afternoon,

THE CITY OF VERA CRUZ, FROM THE ROAD TO ORIZABA.

Page 102.

numerous parties of gallant French Jack-tars—they are so picturesquely dandified in appearance that they more closely resemble patent blacking than common tar—swaggering along the strand, peeping under the mantillas of the women, kissing their hands to tawny old Indian dames smoking their papelitos in shadowy doorways, and occasionally singing and skipping, through mere joyousness of heart and exuberance of spirits.

Many of the men-o'-war's men were negroes from the Mauritius, and it was very pleasant to remark that their colour did not in the least interfere with their being hail-fellow-well-met with the white seamen. But you would very rarely see an American and a black foremast-man arm-in-arm. These fine fellows of the Imperial French navy had, I hope, attended service at the cathedral in the morning ; but as day wore on, they had certainly patronised the "aguardiente" shops with great assiduity ; and spirituous intoxication, following perhaps on a surfeit of melons, shaddocks, and pineapples in a tropical climate, is not very good for the health. Touching at St. Thomas's once, I said inquiringly to the captain of the mail steamer, " And this is the white man's grave, is it ? " " No," he answered, " *that* is ;" and he pointed to a brandy-bottle on the cabin-table.

I don't think I ever saw so many tipsy tars as I did that Sunday at Vera Cruz. Portsmouth, with a squadron just in from a long cruise, was a temperance hotel compared with this tropical town. It is difficult to repress a smile when one is told that Frenchmen never get tipsy. All that I have seen of French soldiers and sailors on active service leads me to the persuasion that they will drink as much as they can get ; and in their cups they are inexpressibly mischievous, and not unfrequently very savage. Yet although rowdy, insolent, and quarrelsome, they rarely fall to fisticuffs, as our men do.* On this particular Sunday

* You will find in Algeria, at the military penitentiaries, "disciplinary battalions," formed almost entirely of incorrigible drunkards. The excesses committed by the French in Mexico, and which were generally induced by libations of aguardiente or commissariat brandy, were atrocious ; in fact, they bore out the reputation given them by the Duke of Wellington in his evidence before the Royal Commission on Military Punishments. Five out

they so frightened Vera Cruz from its propriety—the inhabitants being mainly an abstemious race, suffering from chronic lowness of spirits in consequence of civil war and the yellow fever—that pickets of infantry were sent out from the main guard to pick, up inebriated mariners and pack them off on board ship again. The French are very quick at adapting themselves to the usages of the country they visit, and short as was the time they had been in Mexico, they had learnt the use of that wonderfully serviceable instrument, the lasso. The pickets, wearing only their side-arms, went about lassoing tipsy sailors right and left, most scientifically; and after they had caught their men in running nooses, they " coralled them "—that is to say, they would encircle a whole group of nautical bacchanalians with a thin cord, which being tightened, the whole body of revellers would be drawn close together. Then the pickets would, with mild applications of their sheathed bayonets astern, run the captives down to the waterside and tumble them into the boats which were to convey them on board their respective ships.

This afternoon's entertainment had continued for some time, and the last boat-load of topers having been dispatched, Vera Cruz was once more left to the blazing sunshine and to the black scavenger buzzards. My hosts were all in their hammocks (slung in the corridor) enjoying their siesta. I could not sleep, and bethought me of the long brass telescope on a tripod in the balcony. I got the lens adjusted to my sight at last, and made out the castle of San Juan ; the tricoloured flag idly drooping from the staff on the tower ; the shining black muzzles of the cannon looking out of the embrasures of the bastions, like savage yet sleepy mastiffs blinking from their kennels ; the sentinel, with a white turban round his shako, pacing up and down ; the bright bayonet on his rifle throwing off sparkling rays.

of ten soldiers who massacred the citizens of Paris on the boulevards in the December of 1851 were drunk.—(P.S.) I wrote these remarks in 1866. Since then we have seen the war of 1870 and the insurrection of 1871, and a great deal more of what the "temperate" French can do in the way of tippling.

But beyond the castle, some two miles distant, there was nothing to see. Sacrificios and the squadron were "round the corner," so to speak, and out of my field of view. The native craft were all moored in-shore ; and Vera Cruz is not a place where you go out pleasure-boating. There was nothing visible beyond the arid, dusty foreshore, but the excruciatingly bright blue sky and the intolerably bright blue sea : Jove raining down one canopy of molten gold over the whole, as though he thought that Danaë was bathing somewhere in those waters. I fell a musing over poor Alexander Smith's

> " All dark and barren as a rainy sea."

The barrenness here was as intense ; but it was from brightness. You looked upon a liquid desert of Sahara.

Ah ! what is that ? A dark speck midway between the shore and the horizon. The tiniest imaginable speck. I shift the telescope, try again, and again focus my speck. It grows, it intensifies, it is—with figures large as life, so it seems, finished with Dutch minuteness, full of colour, light and shade, and animation—a picture that gross Jan Steen, that Hogarth, that Callot, might have painted. A boat crammed full of tipsy sailors. There is one man who feels very unwell, and who, grasping his ribs with either hand, grimaces over the gunwale in a most pitiable manner. Another is argumentatively drunk, and is holding forth to a staid quartermaster, who is steering. Another is harmoniously intoxicated. Then there is a man who is in a lachrymose state of liquor, and is probably bewailing La Belle France and his mother. Suddenly a negro, who is mad drunk, tries to jump overboard. Such a bustle, such a commotion ! They get the obstreperous black man down and lay him in the sheets, and he too begins to sing. It is as though you were a deaf man *looking* at the "propos des buveurs," in Rabelais. And in the midst of all this the boat with its stolid sober rowers goes pitching and bounding about the field of the telescope, sometimes swerving quite out of it and leaving but a blank brightness, then coming into full focus again, in all its wondrous detail of reality.

After a night not entirely unembittered by the society of mosquitoes, we rose ; took the conventional cup of chocolate, crust of dry bread, and glass of cold water ; and bidding farewell to our entertainers, drove to the railway terminus. I didn't expect much from a railway point of view, and consequently was not disappointed. We have all heard of things being rough and ready. There was plenty of roughness here, without the readiness. It was nearly noon, and the industrial staff of the station, represented by two Indians in striped blankets (serving them for coat, vest, and pantaloons) and monstrous straw hats, were sleeping in two handbarrows. The station-master, a creole Spaniard, had slung his grass hammock in a shady nook behind the pay-place, and was sleeping the sleep of the just. There was a telegraph office, recently established by the French ; and the operator, with his face resting on his arms, and those limbs resting on the brand-new mahogany instrument from Paris, snored peacefully.

It was the most primitive station imaginable. There was one passenger waiting for the train, a half-caste Mexican "greaser," fast asleep at full length on the floor, and with his face prone to it. He had a bag of Indian corn with him, on which, for safety, he lay ; and he had brought a great demi-pique saddle too, which rested on his body, the stirrup leathers knotted together over the pummel, and which looked like a bridge over the river Lethe. Where was his horse ? I wondered. Did he own one, or had his gallant steed been shot under him in battle, and was he on his way to steal another ? Altogether, this rickety ruinous railway station, with the cacti growing close to the platform, and with creepers twining about every post and rafter, and bits of brick, and stray scaffold-poles, and fragments of matting, and useless potsherds, and coils of grass rope littered about in the noontide glare, reminded me with equal force of an Aztec building speculation overtaken by bankruptcy, and of a tropical farmyard in which all the live stock had died of yellow fever.

The time for the train to start had long expired ; but there was no hurry ; so my travelling companion lay down with his head on the half-caste's saddle and took a little nap. I wandered on to the platform, and there, to my pleasurable surprise, found one man who was awake. Who but a French gendarme ? One of a picked detachment of that admirable force sent out to Mexico to keep both invaders and invaded in order—combed, brushed, polished, waxed, pomatumed, booted, spurred, sabred, belted, cocked-hatted, gauntleted, medalled—a complete and perfect gendarme. He was affable, sententious, and dogmatic. " Mexico," he observed, " was a country without hope." I have since inclined to the belief that the gendarme did not dogmatise quite unreasonably on this particular head. He further remarked that discipline must be maintained, and that in view of that necessity he usually administered *une fameuse volée* in the shape of blows with the flat of his sword to the station-master.

· He accepted a cigar, to be reserved for the time of his relief from duty ; and not to be behindhand in politeness, he favoured me with a pinch of snuff from a box bearing on the lid the enamelled representation of a young lady, in her shirt-sleeves and a pair of black-velvet trousers, dancing a jig of a carnaval-esque kind. " I adore the theatre," said the gendarme. " Monsieur has, no doubt, seen ' La Belle Hélène ' in Paris ? " I replied that I had witnessed the performance of that famous extravaganza. " Ah ! " continued the gendarme, with something like a sigh. " They essayed it at Mauritius ; but it obtained only a success of esteem. Monsieur may figure to himself the effect of a Belle Hélène who was a mulatto. As for Agamem-non, he did not advance at all. *J'aurais bien flanqué trois jours de salle de police à ce gredin-là !* I intend, Monsieur," he concluded, " to visit the Bouffes, and to assist at a repre-sentation of the work of M. Jacques Offenbach, when I reim-patriate myself and enter the civil." Honest gendarme ! I hope the " vomito " spared him, and that he has reimpatriated himself by this time, and seen not only " La Belle Hélène," but " Orphée aux Enfers " and " La Grande Duchesse de Gérolstein."

The station-master woke up about one o'clock, and it appeared that he had sent a messenger down into the town to ask my friend at what time he would like to have the train ready. There was no other passenger save the half-caste, who would very cheerfully have waited until the day after next, or the week after next, or the Greek Kalends. My friend said he thought we might as well start at once ; so half a dozen Indians were summoned from outhouses where they had been dozing, and we proceeded to a shed and picked out the most comfortable carriage in the rolling stock, which was but limited. We found a "car" at last, of the American pattern, open at either end, but with cane-bottomed instead of stuffed seats, and Venetian blinds to the windows. The engine also presently came up puffing and sweating to remind us of a fact which had, at least, slipped my memory—that we were living in the nineteenth and not in the ninth century ;—a locomotive of the approved American model ; blunderbuss funnel ; "cow-catcher" in front ; pent-house in rear for the driver ; warning bell over the boiler, and "Asa Hodge and Co., Pittsburg, Pa.," embossed on a plate on the "bogey" frame. Everything in this country which in mechanical appliances can remind you of civilisation, comes from the United States. New York is to Mexico as Paris is to Madrid.

The machine had an Indian stoker, and uncommonly like a gnome, or a kobold, or some other variety of the demon kind did that Indian look, with his coppery skin powdered black with charcoal dust, and his grimy blanket girt around him with a fragment of grass-rope. But the engine-driver was a genuine Yankee—in a striped jacket and a well-worn black satin vest—a self-contained man, gaunt, spare, mahogany-visaged, calm, collected, and expectoratory, with that wonderful roving down-east eye, which always seems to be looking out for something to patent and make two hundred and fifty thousand dollars by. But for the Mexican sombrero which he had donned, and the revolver which he wore conspicuously in his belt, you might have taken him for a law-abiding manufacturer of patent clothes-wringers or mowing-machines from Hartford or Salem. He "passed the time of day" to us very civilly, and confirmed the good news that there were no guerrilleros on the road. "The French have fixed up a whole crowd of 'em about Puebla," he said, "and they don't care about being hung up by the score, like hams round a stove-pipe. I ain't been shot at for a month, and I've loaned my Sharp's rifle to a man that's gone gunning down to the Cameroons."

The long car we had selected was attached to the locomotive, and a luggage van coupled to that, in which a fatigue party of French soldiers who had just marched into the station placed a quantity of commissariat stores for the detachment on duty at La Soledad. We got under way, but, the line being single, were temporarily shunted on to a siding : the telegraph having announced the coming in of a train from the interior.

A few minutes afterwards there rumbled into the station a long string of cars, which disgorging their contents, the platform became thronged with, at least, five hundred men ; stranger arrivals by an excursion train I never saw. The strangers were mostly tall athletic fellows, clean limbed, and with torsos like to that of the Farnese Hercules. Noble specimens of humanity ; and every man of them as black as the ace of spades. They were, in slave-dealers' parlance—now happily a dead language—"full-grown buck-niggers." They were uniformly clad, in loose jerkins, vests, and knickerbockers of spotless white linen; and their ebony heads—many of them very noble and commanding in expression, straight noses and well-chiselled lips being far from uncommon—were bound with snowy muslin turbans.

These five hundred men, shod with sandals of untanned hide, armed with musket and bayonet, and the short heavy Roman "tuck" or stabbing sword, and carrying their cartouch-boxes in front of them, formed a battalion of that noted Nubian contingent, of whom there were three regiments altogether, hired from the Viceroy of Egypt by the French government for service in Mexico. They had come down from La Soledad to reinforce the wasting garrison of Vera Cruz, of which the European portion were dying of " vomito " like sheep of the rot. The sergeants and corporals were black ; but the commissioned officers were Egyptian Arabs, sallow, weazened, undersized creatures in braided surtouts of blue camlet and red fez caps.   They compared very disadvantageously with the athletic and symmetrically-built negroes.

These Nubians, my friend the gendarme told me, were good soldiers, so far as fighting went, but irreclaimable scoundrels. They were horribly savage, and jabbered some corrupted dialect with Arabic for its base, but Mumbo-Jumbo for its branches, and which their own officers could scarcely understand.   The system by which discipline was preserved among them had been beautifully simplified.   If a Nubian soldier didn't do what he was told, his officer, for the first offence, fell to kicking him violently.   If he persisted in his disobedience, the officer drew his sabre and cut him down.

Think of a Mahometan Khedive letting out his two thousand Pagan negroes to a Roman Catholic emperor, in order that he might coerce the Spanish and Red Indian population of an American republic into recognising the supremacy of an Austrian archduke ! As the Enemy of Mankind is said to have remarked on a memorable occasion, "It's a queer lot, and the cards want sorting."

VIII.

THE DIVERSIONS OF LA SOLEDAD.

HE Imperial Mexican Railway, in the year 1864, was in its infancy. The entire line of route had been carefully surveyed and beautifully mapped out ; all engineering difficulties had been disposed of, on paper, and vast numbers of labourers were employed on cuttings and embankments ; but nine-tenths of the line yet remained to be made. A considerable impetus had been given to all kinds of industry in the normally distracted country just then. The unfortunate Maximilian had accepted the crown from the commission of Mexican "notables" who waited on him at Miramar ; and General Almonte had been appointed president of a Council of Regency until "El Principe," as the emperor elect was called, should arrive. As for Don Benito Juarez, he was nobody, and, in sporting parlance, might be said to be "nowhere." He was supposed to be hiding his diminished head in the neighbourhood of Brownsville, on the frontier of Texas, and I have heard him spoken of innumerable times by Mexican politicians (who are, I daresay, very ardent Juarists by this time) in the most contemptuous terms. The mildest epithet with which he was qualified was "El Indio," the Indian ; President Juarez having scarcely any European blood in his veins. More frequently he was called "the bandit," or the "banished despot."

So everything looked very bright and hopeful in Mexico ; a strong French force occupying the country ; and the railway (which was already open for traffic as far as La Soledad) was being pushed forward towards Paso del Macho. We jogged along

pretty steadily in our omnibus car ; but, until we reached a place
called Manga de Clavo, I thought that Mexico must be the
counterpart of the Egyptian desert. For miles the line was
skirted by sandhills. There were more sandhills in the middle
distance, and the extreme horizon was bounded by sandhills ; the
whole of which, illumined by a persistently ferocious sunshine,
offered the reverse of an encouraging prospect. Luckily there
was no sirocco, or the sand would have invaded the carriage and
choked us.

But with magical rapidity the scene changed, and the desert
bloomed into fruitfulness amazing. The train plunged into a
densely wooded country. We saw thick clumps of trees spangled
with blossoms or bending under the load of bright-hued tropical
fruits ; the foreground was literally one parterre of variegated
flowers, and the " cow-catcher " of the engine scattered roses as
we marched. I began to warm into enthusiasm. We hurried
by palm trees, cocoa-nut trees, lemon and orange groves, and
forests of the banana. That tree with its broad blood-stained
leaves, and its body reft and bent by the last hurricane and
the last rainstorm, swaying and bulging, but abating not one
jot of its ruby ruddiness, should furnish a potent liquor ; but
the fruit of the banana is in reality very mild and suave
conveying to the mind, in its dulcet mawkishness, the idea of
sweet shaving paste. It is most tolerable when fried, and served
as a savoury dish.

And here I may remark that the majority of tropical fruits are
productive of most grievous disappointment when eaten. From
the shaddock downward, I don't think I met any which caused
me to think disparagingly of the central avenue at Covent Garden
in London, or of the Marché St. Honoré in Paris. Abnormal
size is the principal characteristic of tropical fruits. They are
intensely sweet ; but the saccharine matter has an ugly propensity
to turn acid on the stomach and kill you. The flavour is generally
flaccid and insipid. From this general censure must be always
excepted the *sweet* lemon—not the lime—a most exquisitely tooth-
some fruit.

Ever and anon, in the density of this new and delicious landscape, there would occur an opening revealing a little valley vividly green, studded with flowers, and perchance with a few scattered wigwams built of palm branches and thatched with palm leaves. The Indian women in their simple costume—almost invariably consisting of two articles, a chemise of coarse white cotton cloth called "manta" and a narrow petticoat-skirt of red and black, or black and yellow striped stuff—looked, at a distance, picturesque enough. Round about all the palm-branch wigwams there were seen to be sprawling groups of Indian papooses or babies of the precise hue of roast fowls well done. Their costume was even more simple than that of their mammas. Mexican scenery, save where the massive mountain passes intervene, is one continuous alternation. Now comes a belt so many miles broad of wonderful fertility. Indian corn—the stalks as tall as beadles' staves, the cobs as large as cricket bats—oranges, lemons, bananas, sugar, coffee, cotton, rice, cinnamon, nutmegs, and all manner of spices. Then, for many more miles, you have a belt of absolute barrenness, a mere sandy desert. What I saw of Mexico reminded me of a tiger's skin—dull yellow desert barred with rich dark brown stripes of fertility. The land is like a Sahara diversified by slices from the valley of Kashmir.

The sun was throwing very long blue shadows indeed from the objects which skirted our track, when we brought up at the straggling structure of deal boards, palm branches, and galvanised tinned iron, or zinc sheds, which did duty as the railway terminus of La Soledad. We found a number of very hospitable gentlemen waiting to receive us ; the sleepy telegraphic operator at Vera Cruz having apparently made himself sufficiently wide awake to notify our coming. He had done us good service. A cordial welcome and a good dinner awaited us. Our hosts were the engineers and surveyors engaged on the works of the railway ; and the engineer is always well off for commissariat supplies. He is the only foreigner, the only invader, on whom the rudest and most superstitious races look without disfavour ; for from the lord of the neighbouring manor to the parish priest—nay, to the meanest day labourer—everybody has a dim impression that the bridge, or the aqueduct, or the railway will do the country good, and that every inhabitant of the district will, sooner or later, "get something out of it."

Our friends of La Soledad were accomplished gentlemen, full of traditions of Great George Street, Westminster; pioneers from the Far West; rough Lancashire gangers and hard-handed Cornishmen. They were banded together by the responsibilities of a common undertaking and by the consciousness of a common danger; for until within the last few weeks every man had worked with his life in his hand. The station of La Soledad had been attacked by banditti over and over again; and it had been a common practice with the guerrilleros to lie in wait in the jungle and "pot" the passengers in passing trains. Even now the little group were lamenting the loss of their managing engineer, who had been shot while riding along an unfinished portion of the line. "The colonel lasted six days after they'd hit him," an American overseer of workmen told me; "and it was a desperate cruel thing, seeing that he left a wife and three small children; but he'd had a good time, I guess, the colonel had. 'Brown,' he ses, turning to me, and clasping my hand as he lay on the mattress in that hut over yonder, 'they've done for me at last; but I reckon I've shot eight of 'em since last fall.' And so he had."

There were two other points in which our railway friends were cheerfully unanimous. They all concurred in despising the Mexicans and disliking the French. "As for the half-castes and Spaniards," the American overseer remarked, "they're right down scallywaggs. Hanging's too good for 'em; and the only thing that makes me bear the French is, that when they catch a Mexican guerrillero they cowhide him first and shoot him afterwards, and hang him up as a climax. As for the Injuns, they're poor weak-kneed creatures; but there's no harm in 'em. About a hundred will do the work of ten stout Irishmen. I used to try licking of 'em at first to make 'em spry; but, bless you! they don't mind licking. They just lie down on the turf like mules.

Well, I recollected how the mayoral of a diligencia makes his team to go when they're stubborn ; he just gets down and walks behind, and he fills his pocket with sharp little stones, and every now and then he shies a stone which hits a mule behind the ear,· and he cries ' Ha-i-a-youp !' and the mule he shakes his head and gallops along full split. When I see my Indian peons shirk-ing their work I just sit on a stone about fifty yards off, and every minute or so I let one of 'em have a pebble under-neath the left ear. The crittur wriggles like an eel in a pump-log, and falls a working as though he was going to build Babel· before sundown."

Why the French should have been so intensely disliked I could not rightly determine. That the Mexicans should have hated them was feasible enough ; but I rarely found an Englishman or a German in Mexico who would give the army of occupation a good word. I have frequently expressed my opinion that a Frenchman in a black coat, in light pantaloons, in straw-coloured kid gloves, in a blouse and sabots, even, is a most agreeable, friendly, light-hearted creature ; but make his acquaintance when he is on active service, in a képi and scarlet pantaloons, and I fear you will find that a more arrogant and more rapacious swash-buckler does not exist. That is the character, at least, which the French warrior has gotten in Mexico, in Algeria, in Germany, in Italy—his transient spell of popularity in '59 excepted—and in Spain.

I remember that the ragged assemblage of maize, and palm-straw, and mud-and-wattle huts, which forms the town of La Soledad, lay in the midst of a broad valley, the sides shelving to a rocky base, through which ran a shallow river. I came to this place on the last day of February. There had been heavy rains a few days previously, and there was some water, but not much, in the bed of the river. In the summer the rivers of Mexico are as dry as the Paglione at Nice ; and the bridges seem as useless as spurs to the military gentleman in garrison at Venice. There was a detachment of French infantry at La Soledad, whose cheerful bugles were summoning the wearers of about two hundred pairs of red trousers to the evening repast, of which ratatouille, a kind of gipsy stew, forms the staple ingredient.

This evening meal is called the "ordinaire," and is made up of the leavings of the day's rations, and of such odds and ends of victual as the soldiers have managed to purchase or forage. There is no such evening entertainment in the British army. Our men eat their clumsily cooked rations in a hurry, and often pass long hours of hunger between their ill-arranged meals. The bugle-calls of the French brought from the shingly shores of the river numbers of moustached warriors who had been washing their shirts and gaiters—socks were not worn by the army of occupation—in the stream. It was very pretty to watch the red-legged figures winding along the paths running upward through the valley, with boards laden with white linen on their heads. There was a grand background to the picture in a mountain range, rising tier above tier : not in blue delicate peaks and crags, as in the Alps, but in solid, sullen, dun-coloured masses. I can recall one now, with ribbed flanks and a great shelving head, that looked like an old brown lion couchant.

The railway gentlemen resided at a little cantonment of timber and corrugated zinc huts, the last of which, although weather-tight and agreeably repellent of various insects (which swarm in wooden structures), were, when the sun shone, intolerably hot. As the sun so shone habitually, without mercy, from eight in the morning until six in the evening, the corrugated zinc huts became by sunset so many compact ovens, suited either to baking, broiling, or stewing the inmates. However, life in Mexico amounts, in the long run, only to a highly varied choice of evils ; and devouring insects being somewhat more aggravating than a warm room, the engineers had chosen that evil which they deemed the lesser. I suffered so terribly, however, during my sojourn in this highly rarified country from determination of blood to the head, that I entreated my hosts to be allowed to sleep under a palm thatch in lieu of corrugated zinc. My wish was acceded to—to my partial destruction.

We dined sumptuously on hot stews, made much hotter with chiles and peperos, the effect of which last condiment on the palate I can only compare to that of a small shrapnel shell going off in your mouth. We had plenty of sound claret, and, if I remember right, a flask or so of that white-seal champagne which at Trans-atlantic tables is considered preferable to Veuve Clicquot. A bottle of "Sunnyside" Madeira, warranted from a Charleston "garret," was also produced. We were too recently from Havana to be unprovided with Señor Anselmo del Valle's fragrant mer-chandise ; and let me whisper to the wanderer, that he who spares no efforts to be provided with good cigars in his baggage will be at least enabled to make some slight return for the hos-pitality he will receive. For in these far-distant cantonments the stock of cigars is liable to run out, and can with difficulty be renewed.

After dinner we talked Mexican politics—a conversation which generally resolved itself into three conclusions. First, that when things come to the worst they may mend. Second, that things had come to the worst in Mexico. Third, that Maximilian and his empire might last as long as the French occu-pation continued, and as long as his own stock of gold ounces and hard dollars held out. I can aver that on this last head I never heard any more sanguine opinion expressed dur-ing the whole time I was in Mexico. Then we played a hand at poker, and tried a rubber at whist, then songs were sung, and then we went out for a walk.

The French tattoo had sounded, and most of the moustached warriors had retired to their huts ; but there were strong pickets patrolling the streets, and double guards posted at every gate. When I speak of the "gates" of this place, I allude simply to certain booms or logs of timber placed athwart blocks of stone at intervals, and by the side of each of which was a French guard hut. When I allude to La Soledad's "streets," I mean simply that the palm-branch and mud-and-wattle huts of the Indian and half-caste population had been erected in two parallel lines, with a few alleys of smaller hovels, with succursals of dunghills branching

from them.   Once upon a time, I believe La Soledad had possessed
a plaza, several stone houses, and two churches ; but all that
kind of thing had been, to use the invariable American locution
when speaking of the ravages of civil war, " knocked into a cocked-
hat " by contending partisans.

In La Soledad we lived in an easy fashion.   We dined without
any table-cloth, and with a great many more knives than forks.
We occasionally carved a fowl with a bowie-knife.   Our claret had
been drawn direct from the wood into calabashes of potters' ware,
kneaded and fired on the spot, and the white-seal champagne had
been opened by the simple process of knocking the neck off the
bottles.   It was very unconventional when we sallied forth on a
stroll to see the mats which served as doors to the Indian huts all
drawn on one side, and the inmates making their simple preparations for retiring for the night, such preparations consisting
chiefly in everybody taking off what little he had on, and curling
himself up in a ball on the straw-littered ground.   The family
mule was tethered to a post outside, and the background was filled
up by the family pigs and poultry.   It was the county of
Tipperary with a dash of Bedouin douar, and a poetic tinge of the
days of the Shepherd Kings of Palestine.

Everybody had, however, not gone to bed.   There was life at
La Soledad ; life half of a devotional, half of a dissolute kind.
The stone churches, as I have said, had been " knocked into a
cocked-hat," but Ave Maria was sounding on a little cracked bell
suspended between three scaffold poles, and a dusky congregation
—all Indians—were kneeling on the threshold of a wigwam
somewhat larger but fully as rudely fashioned as its neighbours,
where an Indian priest was singing vespers.   There could not
have been a more unconventional church.   The poor celebrant
was desperately ragged and dirty, and his vestments were stuck
over with little spangles and tarnished scraps of foil paper ; but
he had a full, sonorous voice, which seemed to thrill his hearers
strangely.   Two great twisted torches of yellow wax were placed
on the altar, which looked like a huge sea-chest.   Another torch,
of some resinous wood, flamed at the entrance of the hut, and

threw the kneeling worshippers into Rembrandt-like masses of light and shade. On the altar were the usual paltry little dolls— not much paltrier than you may see in the most superb fanes in Italy or Spain—but there was one singularly unconventional ornament. The poor cura of the church, I was told, had waited on the railway officials and begged for something to adorn his fabric withal: something "European," the honest man wanted. They had given him a few dollars and a couple of those enormous coloured lamps which at night are fixed in front of locomotives. One of these, a red one, another a green one, he had fixed on either side of his altar ; and there they were, glaring out of the wigwam like two unearthly eyes.

Close to the church was a public gaming-house, to justify Defoe's

> "Wherever God erects a house of prayer,
> The Devil always builds a chapel there."

It was contemptuously tolerated by the French, on condition that no soldier of their nation should be suffered to play in it, and that if any knives were used on the disputed question of a turn-up card, the proprietor should be liable to be hanged. But the Mexicans are admirable gamesters, and very rarely stab over their play. They prefer lying in wait for you in the dark, and admonishing you by a puncture under the fifth rib, or a ball in the occiput, that you had best not be so lucky at cards next time. The gambling-house had nothing of the conventional Frascati or German Kursaal aspect about it. It was just a long wigwam, open in front, and with some rough planks on tressels running along its whole length. It reminded me of a hastily improvised refreshment booth at a cricket match. There was no "*tapis vert*," unless the sward on which the tressels rested could pass muster as a "green carpet."

There were no pure Indians present. Gambling, cheating, and robbing are the business of the Spanish half-castes. These exemplary gentry lined the long table, erect, statuesque in their striped blankets and great coach-wheel hats, motionless save when they extended their long skinny hands to plant their stakes or to grasp their winnings.   With the exception of an occasional hoarse cry of " Tecoloti "—referring to a chance in the game—" Gaño todo," " I win all," or " Pierde el Soto," " The knave loses," there was silence.   The game was monté, of which it is sufficient to say that it bears a vague affinity to lansquenct and to blind-hookey, and is about one hundred times more speculatively ruinous than vingt-un or unlimited loo.   At La Soledad the stakes were dollars, halves, and quarters, and even copper coins.   I saw one man win about five pounds on a turn-up.   He lost all and more within the next five minutes, and stalked away apparently unconcerned : whether to bed or to hang himself or to wait for a friend and murder him, I had no means of ascertaining.

Not many days afterwards I had the honour of being present at several entertainments, of which monté was the object, in the city of Mexico.   There we were quite conventional.   We gathered in full evening dress.   We had wax lights, powdered footmen, and cool beverages handed round on silver salvers.   In lieu of the poor little silver and copper stakes of La Soledad, the piles of gold ounces and half doubloons rose to a monumental height ; but there was no difference in the good breeding of the players. The blanketed rapscallions of La Soledad were just as phlegmatic over their monté as the wealthiest dons in Mexico.

We watched this small inferno for some time ; and I was much amused to observe that one of the most sedulous of the punters was a gaunt half-caste boy who, in a ragged shirt and raggeder drawers, had waited on us at dinner.   The young reprobate must have risked a year's wages on every turn-up, but his employers did not seem to think tthat there was anything objectionable in his having adjourned from the dining-room to the gambling-table.

About ten o'clock the establishment was closed in a very sum-mary manner by a French patrol, who marched along the length of the booth, sweeping out the noble sportsmen before them as though with a broom that had a bayonet in it.   And life at La Soledad being terminated we went to bed.   For my part I sincerely wish I had walked about all night, or had laid down in front of the great fire by the French guard-house. I must needs sleep in a wooden hut with a palm thatch, and I was very nearly bitten to death. There were mosquitoes, there were fleas, there were cockroaches—unless they were scorpions—and finally, O unutterable horror! there were *black ants*. I sometimes fancy that a few of those abominable little insects are burrowing beneath my skin to this day.

IX.

THE CITY OF THE ANGELS.

"THEY call it," quoth the Canonigo, "Puebla de los
Angelos; but for my part," he continued confidently, "I don't think it would do this City of
the Angels much harm if the verdugo were to
come hither and hang every man, woman, and child at Puebla
to a gallows forty feet high. Hombre!" went on the Canonigo,
"I think Puebla would be all the better for it; for, look you,"
and here he sank his voice to a whisper, "everything that walks
on two legs in this city and who is not a guerrillero—a brigand—
is either a gambler or a receiver of stolen goods."

These were hard words indeed to hear from a patriotic
Mexican gentleman, and a dignified ecclesiastic to boot, concerning a city so ancient and illustrious as Puebla. But the
Canonigo knew what he was about. It was at the little village
of Amosoque, a few miles from our destination, that our clerical
friend uttered the strictures recorded above on the character of
the Pueblanas. Now I knew nothing as yet of Puebla; but I
should have been quite prepared to agree with anybody who had
told me that a little hanging—with perhaps a trifle of drawing
and quartering—would have done a world of good to the people
who congregated round our carriage window of Amosoque.

"Mala gente! mala gente!" murmured the Canonigo, looking at the Amosoquians who trooped up to the coach window, and
stared in at us with sad fierce eyes mutely eloquent with *this* kind
of discourse: "I should like a wheel; I a horse; I that stout
man's coat; I his hat; I his dollars; and I his blood." "Mala
gente!" cried the Canonigo, drawing his head in somewhat

abruptly as an Amosoquian of very hungry aspect uttered the
word " Caridad ! " in a tone which far more resembled a curse
than a request. " Por Dios, amigo," quoth the Canonigo, " I
have nothing for you. Mala gente ! " he concluded, sinking
back on the cushions and taking a very vigorous puff at his
cigar, " Mala gente"—which being translated, may be accepted as
signifying " blackguards all : a bad lot."

Whenever you halt in a town or village of Old Spain your
equipage will be surely surrounded by silent, moody men, wrapped
in striped blankets or tattered cloaks, and with shabby hats
slouched over their brows, who will regard you with glances that
are sad, but not fierce. But faded as is their aspect, they have
a quiet and resigned mien, not wholly destitute of dignity.
Yonder tatterdemalion of the Castiles seems to say : " I am destitute ; but still I am a Don. Poverty is not a crime. I involve
myself in my virtue, and have puffed prosperity away. I am
bankrupt, but it was through being security for a friend. I
am Don Dogberry, and have had losses. I held shares in
the Filibuster's Company (limited). The company is being
wound up, and another call on the contributories will be made
the day after to-morrow. If you like to give me half a peseta
you can."

But New Spain ! But Amosoque ! That small, wiry, leathery,
sooty-looking fellow is a half-caste. Watch him scowling at you
in his striped serape—further south called a poncho—his huge
coach-wheel hat like a cardinal's whitewashed, and minus the
tassels ; his loose linen drawers bulging through the slashes in his
leathern overalls. Salvator might have painted him, but Salvator
should have made some preliminary sketches in a Seven Dials
slum and a Bowery whisky cellar to get his hand in. The man
of Amosoque utters nothing articulate save an occasional grunt of
" Caridad ! " but his eyes are full of speech. They say, " Your
throat is precisely the kind of throat I should like to cut. I have
cut many throats in my time. I am a bankrupt, but a fraudulent
one. My father suffered the punishment of the 'garotte vil ;'
and my brother-in-law is a garotter in Orizaba. Give me a dollar,

or by all the saints in Puebla, I and Juan, and Pepe and Fernan here will follow the coach and rob it."

Amosoque is a great mart for spurs. The "Espuelas de Amosoque" are renowned throughout Mexico, and the spur makers, I conjecture, allow the beggars to take the goods "on sale or return." They thrust them in, four or five pairs in each hand, arranged starwise, at the windows, reminding you, in their startling spikiness, of the hundred-bladed penknives with which the Jew boys used to make such terrific lunges at the omnibus passengers in the old days at the White Horse Cellar. These spurs of Amosoque are remarkable for nothing but their length and breadth—the rowels are not much smaller than cheese plates ; but you can no more get clear of the place without purchasing a pair of espuelas than you can leave Montélimar in Provence without buying a packet of *nougat*. I have forgotten the name of that village in Old Spain where fifty women always fly at you and force you to buy embroidered garters. A similar assault, though a silent one, is made on you at Amosoque.

But our mules are buckled to again, and the mayoral has filled his jacket pocket with a fresh supply of pebbles to fling at their ears if they are lazy. Bump, bump, thud, thud, up the middle and down again. We are again travelling on the hard road. This kind of thing has been going on for many days ; and this kind of village we have halted at over and over again. Ojo de Agua was very like Nopaluca ; Nopaluca was very like Acagete ; and all these were very like Amosoque. We are out of the dark defiles of the Cumbres—horrifying mountain passes, gray, jagged, arid, cataractless ; no "tierra caliente" has greeted our eyesight since we left Orizaba. The open has been mainly desert, intolerable dust and caked baked clod producing nothing but the nopal and the maguey, the prickly pear and the cactus. The former is picturesque enough, and besides it yields the juice, which fermented, the Indians and half-castes call "pulque," and on which they get swinishly intoxicated. An adult maguey is very stately to look upon, but goodness keep all nervous ladies, and people given to dreaming dreams, and young children from the sight of the Mexican prickly pear. The plant assumes the most hideously grotesque forms. It is twisted and bent and gnarled like metal scroll work which some mad giant has crumpled up in his fingers in a rage. It is a tangle of knotty zigzags interspersed with the prickly fruit, which can be compared to nothing but the flattened faces of so many demon dwarfs, green with bile and thickly sown with bristles. The prickly pear to me is bogey.*

Let me see ; where was it, between Orizaba and this evil place of Amozoque, bristling with spurs and scoundrels, that we picked up the Canonigo ? Ah ! I remember, it was at Sant' Augustin del Palmar. We reached Sant' Augustin at about two o'clock in the afternoon, just as the diligencia from Mexico had drawn up at the door of the principal fonda, and precisely in time for the diligence dinner. Now I would have you to understand that the chief dish at the coach dinner in all regions Iberian, both on the hither and thither side of the Atlantic, and even beyond the Isthmus and under the southern cross, is the PUCHERO†—print it in capitals, for it is a grand dish—and that the puchero is the only thing in Old or New Spain concerning which tolerable punctuality is observed.

You have heard no doubt of the olla-podrida as the "national" dish of Spain, but so far as my experience goes it is a culinary preparation which, like the rich uncle in the comedy, is more talked about than seen. While I was in Mexico city my eye lighted one day on a placard in the window of a *bodegon* or eating-house in the Calle del Espiritu Santo, setting forth that on the ensuing Thursday at noon " una arrogante olla " would be ready for the consumption of cavaliers. I saw this announcement on Monday morning, and for three days I remained on tenter-hooks

* It may be mentioned that the heraldic cognisance of the Mexican nation bears intimate reference to the prickly pear. The legend runs that Cortes the Conquistador, during his march to Mexico, descried an eagle perched upon a nopal ; and when the country achieved her independence four centuries afterwards "the bird and bush" became the "Mexican arms."

† The names of both the national dishes of Spain are derived from the utensils in which they are served. A puchero is a pipkin, and an olla an earthenware pot. Podrida means simply "rotten"—observe the singular corruption of sense in the French "pot pourri," a vase full of dried roses and fragrant spices.

expecting to partake of this arrogant olla-podrida. I concealed
my intention from my hospitable host. I was determined to do
something independent. I had travelled long in search of beef;
there might be, in the arrogant olla, a bovine element; and the
efforts of long years might be crowned at last with success. I went
on Thursday, but the vinegar of disappointment came to dash my
oil. "Hoy, no," said the keeper of the bodegon, "mañana se
abra." There was to be no arrogant olla that day; there would
be the next. Mañana means to-morrow; and to-morrow to a
Spaniard means the Millennium. I have never tasted an olla,
arrogant or submissive.

But of the puchero I preserve the pleasantest remembrances.
There is beef in it—boiled beef—the French bouilli, in fact.
There is bacon. There are garbanzos (bróad beans) and charming little black puddings, and cabbage, and delicate morsels of
fried banana. It is very wholesome and very filling; and there is
no use in your complaining that an odour of garlic pervades it,
because the room and the table-cloth and your next neighbour
are all equally redolent of the omnipresent ajo. The puchero
(poured from its pipkin) is in a very big platter; and what you
have to do is to watch carefully for the dish as it is passed from
hand to hand; to take care that it is not diverted from you by a
dexterous flank movement of a cunning caballero manœuvring
behind your back, or by the savage cavalry charge of the German
bagman opposite. Seize the dish when you can, and hold on to
it like grim Death with one hand till you have filled your plate.
Never mind if the lady next you looks pleadingly, piteously, upon
you. She is the weaker vessel. Let her wait. Fill yourself with
puchero; for you will get nothing else in the way of refreshment,
save chocolate and cigars, for the next twelve hours. There is a
proverb which justifies the most brutal selfishness in this regard,
and which I may translate thus :   .

> "He who lets puchero pass
> Is either in love, or asleep, or an Ass."

Clutch it then, for when it has once glided away you will never
see it again.

For a wonder the puchero at the diligence dinner at Sant' Augustin del Palmar was not punctual. We had had soup ; we had had frijoles (black beans fried in oil), we had had a seethed kid ; but no puchero made its appearance. The traveller next to me, a stout black-whiskered man, in a full suit of black velveteen, enormous gold rings in his ears, and with a parti-coloured silk sash round his waist, grew impatient.

"Caballeros," he cried, after another five minutes' delay, " I am a plain man. I am a Catalan. Juan Estrellada is well known in Barcelona. But human patience has its limits. I propose that if the puchero is not at once brought in that we rob this house and throw the landlord out of window." The proposal was a startling one ; but the Catalan looked as if he meant it, and I was much moved to remark that a murmur, seemingly not of disapprobation, ran round the table. A gentleman in a cloak two guests off, remarked gutturally, " Es preciso," which may be taken as equivalent to " Ditto to Mr. Burke," and to an opinion that robbing the establishment was the right kind of thing to do. You are so continually falling among thieves in Mexico that your moral sense of honesty grows blunted ; and you feel inclined, when people come to you for wool, to send them away shorn. Fortunately for the landlord, the majority of the guests were philosophers, and had betaken themselves to smoking ; and for-tunately for ourselves, just as the Catalan seemed to be preparing to put his resolution to the vote, two gingerbread-skinned Indian boys came staggering in with the charger of puchero between them, and we fought for the meal like so many wolves, and I didn't come off the worst, I can assure you.

It was when I had secured, with great internal joy and content-ment, the last remaining black pudding in the dish, that I noticed that my right-hand neighbour—the Catalan was on the left—had suffered the puchero to pass. He told me that he ate but once a day, that he preferred to dine at six or seven, and that this was a fast day, too, and that he must keep his ayuno. I had noticed him, when we alighted, clad in a black cassock and a tremendous " shovel "—which brought the Barber of Seville and Basilio to my

mind at once—trotting up and down, saying his breviary, and
puffing at a very big cigar. This was our Canonigo. The good
old man ! I can see his happy beaming face now, his smile calm
as a mountain pool environed by tall cliffs, his clear, bright, trust-
ing eyes. I can hear his frank, simple discourse ; not very
erudite, certainly, often revealing a curious inexperience of the
world and its ways, but infinitely full of candour, and modesty,
and charity. He held a prebendal stall in the cathedral of San
Luis Potosi, to which he was now returning, viâ Puebla and
Mexico city, having journeyed down to Jalapa to see a brother in
high military command, who lay sick in that unwholesome city.

I call him "our" Canonigo, for my friend and travelling
companion, who had been separated from me by stress of company
at the inn dinner-table, rejoining me when we went into the
colonnade to smoke, recognised the prebendary of San Luis Potosi
as an old friend, and embraced him affectionately. The old
gentleman was travelling in a rusty old berline of his own, but
gave heartrending accounts of the hardships of the road he had
endured since he left Jalapa. The post-houses were indeed very
short of mules to begin with ; some thousands of those useful
animals having been impressed by the French commissariat and
transport corps. We had been tolerably successful in the way of
mules, simply because my friend, among his other attributes, was
an army contractor, and had most of the post-masters under his
thumb ; but the poor Canonigo had been frequently left for hours,
destitute of cattle, at some wayside venta. It is not at all
pleasant, I assure you, so to cool your heels and your coach wheels,
while the Indian hostess sits on the ground tearing her long
black hair, and wringing her sinewy brown hands, and crying out
that the "mala gente"—the brigands—are in the neighbourhood,
and will be down in half an hour to smite everybody hip
and thigh.

Nothing would suit my host but that the Canonigo should take
a seat in our carriage and be of our party up to Mexico. The
good priest was nothing loth, for he owned that he was dreadfully
frightened of the brigands, who had been committing frightful

atrocities lately on the Jalapa road. I might have mentioned to
you ere this that we had brought with us from La Soledad a
sufficiently imposing escort, in the shape of an entire company
of French infantry, who journeyed with us on the "ride and tie"
principle : half of them crowded inside and outside a kind of
omnibus we had picked up in the post-office at Orizaba, and half
of them hanging on to the wheels—the omnibus often required
pushing up hill or dragging out of a rut—or riding on the mules,
or trudging through the sand or over the pebbles with their
shakoes on the points of their bayonets, and their blue cotton
handkerchiefs tied under their chins, with perhaps a damp
plantain leaf superadded. These were the merriest set of fellows
I ever met with ; and they laughed and smoked and sang songs
and capered all the way up to Mexico. They never asked us for
drink-money, and were uniformly respectful, polite, and cheerful.
They had a little boy-soldier with them—an *enfant de troupe* in
training to be a drummer—who was their pet and plaything and
darling, and for whom, when he was tired of riding in or outside
the omnibus, they would rig a kind of litter, made of knapsacks
and ammunition blankets laid on crossed muskets, and with a
canopy above of pocket-handkerchiefs tied together and held up
by twigs. And they would carry the little man along, the
soldiers singing and he joining in, with a "Tra, la, la! Tra,
la, la !" and the rest of the company beating their hands in
applause from the top of the 'bus.

There were but two officers with the company—the captain,
who rode with us, and a sub-lieutenant, who preferred occupying
the box seat of the longer vehicle. The captain was a pudgy
little man, who, his stoutness notwithstanding, wore stays. He
had been in Algeria, and, according to his showing, whenever
he and Abd-el-Kader met, there had been weeping in the Smala
and wailing in the Douar. He had been through the Crimean
campaign, and, not very obscurely, insinuated that he, and not
Marshal Pélissier, should, if the right man had got his deserts,
have been made Duke of Malakoff. In fact, the fat little captain
would have bragged Major Longbow's head off. He overflowed

I

with good-humour, however, and had a capital baritone voice.
The sub, on the other hand, was a moody, gaunt man, whose
solitary epaulette seemed to have made him at once low-spirited
and lopsided. It was as well, perhaps, that he did not form one
of our party; for he evidently hated his captain with great
fervour, and when they met off duty, there was generally a
squabble. "I know my duty, but I also know my rights," the
sub used to mutter, looking fixed bayonets at his superior officer.
He was scrupulously attentive to his duties, however, and never
missed saluting his pudgy chief. I think the captain would have
been infinitely rejoiced had the omnibus toppled over one of the
yawning precipices in the Cumbrera, and had the dismal chasm
comfortably engulfed that cantankerous sub-lieutenant.

But the Canonigo had a berline. Well, that was very soon
got rid of. The post-master, who was also landlord of the fonda
where we dined—I remember that he expressed a hyperbolical
wish to kiss my hands and feet at departing, and that he obliged
us with two bad five-franc pieces in change for the napoleon we
tendered him—would have none of the canonical equipage.
"Vale nada," it is worth nothing, he said, contemptuously. He
hoped that the Canonigo would leave it "until called for,"
and that he would never call for it. But he was not destined to
profit by the relinquishment of the vehicle. At first I suggested
that it should be devoted to the use of the cantankerous sub-
lieutenant, and that fatigue parties of light infantry should be
harnessed to the pole, and drag it; but this proposal did not
meet with much favour—especially among the light infantry—
and the sub himself vehemently protested against making his
entrance into Mexico, " before his chiefs," in a carriage which he
declared to be fit only for a quack doctor. "There may be
some," he remarked, with a sardonic glance at the baritone
captain, "who would like to play Dulcamara, or imitate Mangin
in a Roman helmet, selling pencils in the Place de la Concorde;
for my part, I know my duties and I know my rights."

In this dilemma Pedro Hilo was sent for. Pedro, a rather
handsome half-caste, was the administrador or steward to the

lordly proprietor of a " hacienda"—a maguey plantation in the neighbourhood. He was accustomed to buy everything, even, as my friend hinted, to the portmanteaus, wearing apparel, and other spoils of travellers who had been waited upon in the stage-coach by a select body of the "mala gente." Pedro came, saw, and purchased. He was a man of few words. "Twenty dollars" —"pesos fuertes"—he said, and he drew a gold ounce from his sash and spun it into the air. "Arriba !" cried Pedro Hilo, "Heads." Heads it was, and the administrador stuck to his text of twenty dollars. A doubloon—scarcely four pounds—is not much for a berline, albeit the thing was woefully the worse for wear ; but what was to be done with it ? The bargain was concluded, and the Canonigo pocketed the gold ounce.

As we were leaving Sant' Augustin del Palmar, our omnibus escort making a brilliant show with their scarlet pantaloons and bright guns and bayonets, we passed the determined Catalan, who was girding himself up to ascend the roof of the downward-bound diligence. " I wish we had a few soldiers with us," he remarked, as he took in another reef of his parti-coloured sash. "A prod from a bayonet now and then might remind the postillion that it is his duty to drive his mules, and not to go to sleep under his monstrous millstone of a hat. Who ever saw such a sombrero save on a picador in the bull-ring ? In Barce-lona such hats would be put down by the police. I have paid for my place in the interior," he continued, " but the malpractices of the postillion and the mayoral—who, I am assured, is in league with all the gangs of brigands between here and Cordova—can no longer be tolerated. I intend to mount the roof ; and the first time that pig-headed driver goes to sleep again, I propose to myself to blow out his brains." So he went away, significantly slapping a pouch of untanned leather at his hip, and which I surmised contained his Colt's revolver. A determined fellow, this Juan Estrellada from Catalonia, and the very man to be useful in a street pronunciamiento. I fancy that he was some-what nettled that no practical upshot should have followed his proposal to rob the fonda and throw the landlord out of window, and that he was anxious, before he reached Vera Cruz, to do something the memory of which posterity would not willingly let die.

The Canonigo was excellent company, but his excessive temperance somewhat alarmed me. His "desayuno"—literally breakfast —would be taken at about four o'clock in the morning ; for we always recommenced our journey at daybreak. Then he would take a cup of chocolate—a brown aromatic gruel mixed thick and slab—with one tiny loaf of Indian corn bread. And nor bite nor sup would he take again till sunset. The worst of it was that we were not always sure of finding supper when we reached the town or village where we had elected to stay the night. The Canonigo, however, seemed totally indifferent to our lighting upon an Egypt without any corn in it. His supper was always ready, and it seemed to serve him in lieu of dinner, and lunch, and all besides. He produced his grass-woven cigar-case and began to smoke. Not papelitos, mind. Everybody in Mexico—man, woman, or child, Spaniard, half-caste, or Indian—inhales the fumes of tobacco wrapped in paper, all day long. But the Canonigo was a smoker of "Puros," the biggest of Cabañas. They didn't make him sallow, they didn't make him nervous ; and he never complained of headache—at least through smoking.

On one occasion the worthy gentleman made the confession, "Tengo mala cabeza"—"My head is bad." It was on the night before we arrived at Amosoque. We chanced to put up at a venta kept by a Frenchman, whose wife was a capital cook, and whose cellar was, moreover, stocked with capital wine. He gave us an excellent supper, and we subsequently "cracked"—I believe that is the correctly convivial expression—sundry bottles of that very sound Burgundy wine called Moulin-à-vent. Well, we were four to drink it, and the temperate Canon could scarcely count as one. He had a thimbleful, however—two thimblefuls, perhaps—nay, a bumper and a half—and the cockles of his good old heart were warmed. In his merriment he sang a wonderful song, setting forth how a donkey, wandering in a field, once fell upon a flute in which a shepherd had "left" a tune. The donkey tootled, and the tune "came out;" whereupon—"Aha!" brays the conceited animal, "who shall say that donkeys cannot play the flute?"

Then the Canonigo, merging into another mood, like Alexander at his feast, began to tell us about the saints—of the wonders worked by St. Lampsacus and St. Hyacinth, St. Petronilla and St. Jago of Compostella. And then he fell asleep, and I can't help thinking that he woke up the next morning slightly flustered about the "cabeza," and that the Moulin-à-vent might have had something to do with the severity with which he spoke about the inhabitants of the City of the Angels. "However," I said, as we drove into Puebla, "we shall see—we shall see."

We duly entered La Ciudad de los Angelos; but the Teetotum Laws forbid that I should proceed to tell you what we saw there. The fingers of Fate gave another twist to the Roulette-wheel of life. Round whirled the ball; round spun the teetotum, and down it came at last, with Africa uppermost.

X.

Moorish Houses at Algiers.

". . . . Nec ab Icosio taciti recedamus; Hercule enim illæ transeunte,
viginti qui a comitatu ejus dixiverant, locum deligunt, faciunt mœnia, ac
ne quis imposito a se nomine privatim gloriaretur, de condentium numero
urbi nomen datum. Porro urbs Icosium sic vocata fuit a viginti Herculis
comitibus qui illam condiderunt, nam εἴκοσι, græce, latini viginti significat."
(C. IVLII SOLINI, &c. BASILEÆ, 1538, in-4.)

> "Old Hercules (the Libyan),
> They say (or any other man),
> While marching up the Afric coast
> Was clean deserted by his host—
> That is to say, by twenty villians
> Who thought they'd like to turn civilians.
> They chose a site, and built a city,
> Which is the subject of my ditty;
> But lest one of their scurvy band
> Should give *his* name to all the land
> (And claimants to it there were plenty),
> They called the city Number Twenty,
> Thus snubbing individual pride,
> While one and all were glorified.
> You'll find the Latin if you'll seek for 't,
> *Viginti;* εἴκοσι's the Greek for 't,
> From which Icosium we indite
> The modern Algiers:—Am I right?"

Hudibrastic translation of Solin,
by a gentleman's butler.

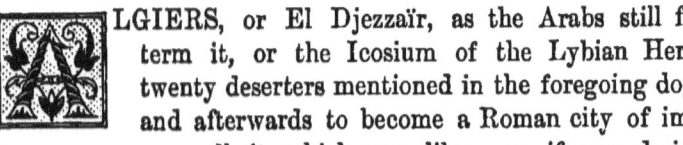

LGIERS, or El Djezzaïr, as the Arabs still fondly
term it, or the Icosium of the Lybian Hercules'
twenty deserters mentioned in the foregoing doggrel,
and afterwards to become a Roman city of importance—you may call it which you like; or if you desire an
additional qualification, the Signor Torquato Tasso will help

you to one. "Algieri, infame nido di Corsari, nutrice di leoni e d' elefanti "—" Algiers, infamous nest of pirates, nursing mother of lions and elephants." The Signor T. T. is ungallant, but he wrote in the sixteenth century, which must be his excuse.

There is a Yankee locution descriptive of a process which implies ruthless and wholesale demolition and devastation, known as "knocking things into a cocked-hat." The Goths and the Vandals and the Anythingarians, the Moors, the Arabs, and the Turks did, during many succeeding ages, knock Icosium into a cocked-hat. Then it retained stability for some centuries as the Mahometan city of El Djezzaïr. Then the French seized it, and from an architectural point of view they too have knocked it into a cocked-hat as battered and shapeless as that of a parish beadle who has been maltreated by a mob of mutinous paupers. But the French have made some amends. Although they have demolished the most romantic portion of Algiers, they have built it up again in the approved Paris boulevard fashion. For the ancient Moresco turban Louis Philippe substituted the *képi* of a chasseur d'Afrique ; and to this Napoleon III. superadded the *petit chapeau* of Imperialism.

Its partial devastation, and more deplorable restoration, notwithstanding, Algiers is yet delightful. Enthusiasts declare it to be adorable. It has been likened to a stately pyramid of white marble, of which the base is flanked by venerable, dusky hills, like old brown lions couchant. Another critic has discovered that it resembles a huge Pentelican quarry scooped out of the bosom of a mountain. The resources of comparison have indeed been well-nigh exhausted in the search for similes to describe El Djezzaïr as it appears from the sea. To one—a mathematical tourist this—it is as a quadrant sharply cut out of plaster of Paris. Another genius of a nautical turn likens it to the mainsail of some huge argosy, or "tall ammiral" stretched on the beach. To a gentleman whose mind was more prosaic, but still akin to his immediate predecessor, it occurred that the thickly-piled and snowy-hued buildings of Algiers looked

like nothing so much as a fortnight's washing laid out on the
shore to dry, with heavy stones at the corners to keep the sheets
and table-cloths from "flopping."

The city is in truth from a distance of most sepulchral
whiteness—whiter than Genoa, whiter than Naples, whiter even
than Stamboul from the Golden Horn. And thus a bard in
"milky white numbers" sings:

> ". . . . Un soir
> La blanche Alger dormait comme un grand encensoir
> D'argent qui fume encore après le saint office."

The idea is certainly pretty, "the scented smoke curling from
a silver censer when mass is over." Only it is nullified by the
fact that no vapour curls from the silver censer of El Djezzaïr.
The Algerines smoke incessantly, but their houses never, save
when they catch fire and are burnt down. The enfumed poet
was obliged to explain, indeed, in a foot-note that the smoke he
meant came from the adjacent lime-kilns of Bab-al-Oued. I
know *their* stench to be awful; and they are suggestive of
anything but silver censers.

The houses of El Djezzaïr are as white as brand-new dice,
and the little peepholes of windows in them stand for the pips.
I question if there ever lived such a nation of inveterate whitewashers as the modern Moors, who have been incited perhaps
to profusion in the use of the double-tie brush by their French
masters. Inside as well as outside the Moorish dwellings are
thickly covered with glaring white distemper paint. At least six
times a year every wall and every ceiling are whitewashed: to
the horror and despair, one would think, of the fleas. There may
at the same time be fleas that like walking upon walls and others
that prefer to roost in warm garments. The Moors whitewash
their inner courts and living rooms persistently, often to the
concealment beneath heavy layers of body colour of the most
exquisitely beautiful sculpture and tracery, the work of less
enlightened but non-whitewashing ages. I wonder how many
acres of fresco and encaustic painting on the walls of old English
churches lie equally perdu, daubed over by the Protestant

brush ? Surely there must be "un infierno blanco," a Tophet
kept alway at a white heat, for those horrible Ostrogoths and
Visigoths, the whitewashing churchwardens of the last century,
and "lubber fiends" to restore and beautify them with white
lead boiling hot.

I have often fancied that when a Moorish lady has nothing
to do—she never has much, still smoking, eating lollipops,
making coffee and love, and twanging the mandolin, do take
up a reasonable part of her time—she calls in the whitewashers
"pour passer le temps." You shall hardly toil up one of the
steep lanes of the Moorish quarter without seeing the white-
washer swinging high in air, as one who gathers samphire, sitting
on a little bit of wood, pendant by ropes from the wall—a human
hanging bookshelf. You shall hardly stand a moment to gaze
sorrowfully on some delicate morsel of stone undercutting he is
filling up with chalky pigment without being bespattered by the
droppings of his brush ; and then a mysterious door opens and
there issues forth, not an Arab cavalier or Moorish damsel
dreamily veiled, but a big negro, brush in hand, his teeth
gleaming as snowily as the whitewash in the bucket he carries.
All this interminable whitewashing is avowedly for the purpose
of keeping the houses sweet and clean, and keeping off at once
the fleas and the cholera morbus.

Let us slowly ascend those precipitous flights of steps bordered
by whitewashed houses, gaunt, silent, and suggestive, which in
the upper town, or old Moorish quarter, are called "streets." Do
you know La Rue des Mâchicoulis at Boulogne ? Put the
bare-legged fishergirls into trousers and haiks, and the fishermen
into burnouses, and the Mâchicoulis would very much resemble
a street in the Moorish quarter of Algiers. In the technics
of the building trade, when the superstructure of a wall leans
away from you, it is said to be "on the batter." The storeys
of these Moorish houses lean, on the contrary, towards you.
They are irreclaimably top-heavy, forming a kind of serrated
vault over you. There is no need to shore them up as we do
tottering fabrics in the old streets out of Cheapside. The

opposite sides are so near touching each other, that little danger
would accrue from their tumbling further forward. You would
only lose that narrow ribbon of bright blue over head, placed
there as you think to let you know that there is such a thing
as a heaven above this " città senza sole," just as in the most
intricate of the back alleys behind the Merceria at Venice you
will always find a thread of white marble meandering along the
centre of the pavement, and which, if you follow it sedulously,
will lead you to St. Mark's Place.

Many of these streets—ladder-lanes rather—are not more than
six feet in breadth. They would, were they on a level surface,
be as fever-haunted as the abominable wynds and closes in the
Canongate at Edinburgh and the Trongate of Glasgow ; but
being built on the steepest of inclines, they are compulsorily
drained. For the rest, the sanitary precautions insisted upon by
the French authorities are excellent. The police would have few
scruples in walking into a Moorish house, were it reported to
be in a filthy state, only they *can't* force the male population to
wear clean burnouses, or to undress when they sleep. The Moors
certainly do their best to keep their houses free from Giaour
intrusion. With very great difficulty they have been brought
even to submit their " état civil," or births, deaths, and marriages,
to registration at the Mairie. Before 1830 there was simply
a Beït-et-Mal, or "chamber of goods," which took cognizance,
with a view to the administration of property, of the deaths of
the population. If you ask an elderly Moor when he was born,
or married, or when his first child was born, he will answer,
either that Allah knows, not he, or that these events took place
about 'the time of such and such an earthquake, or invasion
of grasshoppers, or when this dey came into power, or that pasha
was strangled.

Narrow, and dark, and steep, and tortuous as are the streets
in the Jewish quarter, the houses are in their way—in the
artistic way—gems. In the eyes of Gallic authority they are
simply so many abominations, which need to be swept away to
make room for the *alignement*. The French would pull down

the Alhambra or the Taj-Mehal. It is well that the Russians burnt Moscow about the ears of their invaders. Otherwise, and had Napoleon kept his footing there, composite columns and allegories of victory would soon have replaced the Byzantine cupolas of the Kremlin.

The Moors, in the opinion of non-French critics, have always excelled in architecture; yet, curious to say, the "maallum," or professional architect, is regarded in Arab society less as the professor of a liberal art than as a mechanic. My masonic brethren will remember that the master mason who built the Second Temple was its designer as well; but he was no magnifico; only a working man. Many of the principal edifices in old Algiers were built under the direction of Christian slaves, who, "pour encourager les autres," were occasionally bastinadoed or strangled if the edifices were not finished in time, or if the outlay exceeded their estimates, or if his Highness the Pasha-Dey did not like the house when it was finished. There is one legend of an Italian architect—the constructor, indeed, of the Great Mosque —who was impudent enough to cross its threshold after it had been consecrated to the Mahometan worship! He was dipped into a vat of boiling oil, and then hung up—to dry, I presume.

The Moorish house—the dwelling house—as it is still to be seen in what remains of old Algiers, and to a greater extent in Oran and Constantinople, is simply the house common to Old and New Spain—ay, and to the old East, and oldest Scripture perchance. There is the "patio," or open courtyard, the arched corridor around it, the arched galleries above, and the "azotea," or flat roof. You see in the Moorish house a pretty close illustration of the divergence between Oriental civilisation and ours. For a Moor, his house can scarcely be too shabby and melancholy-ooking without, or too splendid or luxurious within. The house is, in short, a symbol of Mussulman life, with its dreamy and impenetrable mysteries.

The front door looks like the most rearward of back doors; it is like the stage door to a shut-up theatre, or the portal to a gambling-house in the day time; half the paint scraped or kicked off, splashed with mud or whitewash, which it is nobody's business to clean off; bolted, barred, chained, and, it would seem, nailed up. In one panel, head high, is a little Judas trap, with an iron grating before it. There is never a bell; and when there is a knocker, it is usually bolted down to the woodwork. If you wish to make your presence known to those within, you must thunder at the door with a cudgel, or bang at it with your foot. After some ten minutes of this exercitation, the trap may be slowly opened, and the great grinning face of a negress appear at the aperture. In some Moorish houses, in addition to the Judas trap in the doors, there are spy-holes in the wall—sometimes, and designedly, of considerable size—and you may become aware of a moon-face with kohl-stained eyelids, surrounded by tresses interwoven with coins, and crowned by a dainty "chachia," or skull-cap, beaming down upon you. It is only a "Rikat." It is but Jezebel, with her painted face.

In the old days, when to be a Jew in Algiers was to be a despised and persecuted wretch, the Moorish ladies used occasionally to vary the monotony of their existence by having a little bit of fun with an Israelite—after this wise. There were then, as now, numbers of Jew pedlars—vendors of jewellery, gold lace, cosmetics, and other feminine fal-lals—wandering up and down the precipitous thoroughfares of El Djezzaïr. Then the cruel law decreed that no Jew, on pain of forfeiture and the bastinado, was to be suffered to enter the house of a True Believer. But as the Jews sold precisely the commodities most dearly desiderated by the She-believers, they were fain to come to their front doors, and, holding them ajar, transact their business there. The little bit of fun consisted in getting possession of the Jew's merchandise, promising to pay him for it, then slamming the door in his face, and, sliding open the Judas trap, laugh at the poor pedlar's beard, tell him that he was a son of Sheytan, and bid him go to Eblis. This was very funny, was it not? The unhappy Sheeny, thus "left out in the cold," was powerless to regain possession of his property; for another cruel law forbade him to knock at a Mussulman's door. All he could do was to stand in the street, whimper, yell, stamp, dance, tear his hair and beard, and invoke Moses and the prophets.

If it were evening, the watch, perhaps, would come round. Then probably the Jew would be beaten for making a noise; but he was in luck's way indeed if the commandant of the patrol took it into his head to do him justice, by thundering at the True Believer's door, forcing the dishonest inmates to disgorge their booty, and returning it to the pedlar with a deduction of seventy-five per cent. for costs and trouble taken. The good old times of El Djezzaïr. They remind me of an exordium to an article I once read in a Review. "It was formerly the wholesome custom in England, at the seasons of Christmas and Easter, to stone and beat the Jews." And there are a good many people, I daresay, who unfeignedly regret the abrogation of that and many other equally wholesome customs.

The traveller Shaw was of opinion that the houses of Palestine, in scriptural times, were precisely similar to those in the modern Algiers. It is indeed startling to find in a Moorish house the vestibule or "gate" in which Mordecai sat; the "housetop" on which the apostle dreamed his dream, and the "third loft" from which Eutychus fell. But to discuss these matters is not my province. I leave them to the Palestine Exploration Society.

All Moorish houses are built on the same model. The wealthiest make no pretence of exterior façades or porticoes. Everybody—the richest and the poorest—lives in a cube of stone or plastered brick; the only difference between the dwellings of a sheikh and a cobbler is that of size. Here and there a little wooden balcony, not unlike a chicken coop, may project from a window; but, as a rule, the surface of the walls is entirely flat. The door I spoke of just now is a most massive construction, and garnished with huge convex-headed nails. Here and there the panels may contain some carving in an antique geometrical design, and over the lintel a full-blown rose is sometimes cut in marble.

One curious ornament you are sure to find, either painted or carved, in the neighbourhood of the front door. That is the

representation of a human hand, cut off short at the wrist. I was
told that this manual symbol was always affixed by the masons or
painters to a Moorish house, at the moment of its completion,
to preserve its inmates thenceforth and evermore from the
influence of the evil eye :—the " gettatura " of the Neapolitans.
The prows of the pirate ships which used to sally forth from
Algiers were, in a like intent, decorated with the representation
of a human eye.

It is desirable to correct the mistake into which some tourists
have fallen respecting the rude representations, in gold and silver
gilt, of human arms, legs, hands, ears, eyes, and noses which are
exposed for sale in the shops of Algiers. These effigies, reminding
the Englishman of Miss Kilmansegge and her precious leg, have
nothing to do with the superstition of the evil eye. They are
votive offerings, to be purchased by people who have been cured
of hurts or affections of the members to which they have reference,
and to be hung up in the Catholic churches. There are numbers
of Maltese and Spaniards and Southern Frenchmen in Algiers, all
as superstitious as pagans ; and these simple-minded fools—for is
not superstition one of the principal features of simplicity of
mind ?—are the great offerers of offerings at the shrine of Notre
Dame d'Afrique and other popular idols.

I remember a droll story related, on this head, by worthy
M. Douz, the jeweller of the Rue Soggémah. The captain of an
Italian brigantine, whose leg had been broken by his falling into
the hold, determined, so soon as he was well enough to get about
on crutches, to offer up a silver leg as large as life at the shrine
of his favourite saint. He called on M. Douz and ordered the leg
to be made. It was to cost a thousand francs. In a week afterwards he called again. Was the leg finished ? he asked. No ; the
model in wax was only just completed. Well, he had changed
his mind, and he felt a great deal better, and he thought a leg
half the size of life would do. In another week he was again at
Douz, much better, and with a mind again changed. Suppose
M. Douz made him a foot ? After all, it was only the ankle-
joint which had been fractured. Whereat M. Douz grew wroth,

and told him that as in another week he would probably be able to walk without crutches, and would then further diminish his order, he had better let him make him a silver toenail, and be off the leg bargain. In this compromise the captain of the brigantine joyfully acquiesced ; but he must have got very well indeed afterwards, for he never came to the Rue Soggémah again, and the saint who ought to have had a whole leg did not get so much as a toenail.

XI.

COCKPIT ROYAL.

"IX days of the week they do nothing, and on Sunday they go to the bull-fight." Such is the awful charge I have heard brought against the inhabitants of Madrid. But something after all may be urged in favour of a bull-fight. It is a national, a royal amusement. Ferdinand the Seventh established a school of Tauromachia at Seville. Bull-baiting, too, is one of the oldest of English sports. Something approaching it used to take place in the streets of London every Monday morning within very recent times, and until, indeed, the cattle market was removed from Smithfield to Islington, nay, even since the aforesaid removal, I have occasionally seen much sport got out of a lively young bullock between Farringdon-Street and the Old Bailey, to the imminent peril of Mr. Benson's shop windows. Perhaps there may be also a trifle to be said in favour of the bull-ring. You will not hear it said by *me*, for I have gone through my course of tauromachia, and hold a corrida de toros to be the most brutal, cruel, and demoralising spectacle to be seen on this lower earth, after the King of Dahomey's " great custom." Still there are people who like it.

So much for Bos ; but who dares to defend cock-fighting ? No one, I should hope. It is undeniably cruel, and as undeniably demoralising ; since it leads, in England at least, to gambling and to the undue consumption of alcoholic liquors. Again, a cock-fight not unfrequently ends in a man-fight. That the heinous turpitude of the thing is deeply impressed on the English mind is obvious from the proverbial expression employed to denote anything unusually and superlatively profligate and audacious—that

" it beats cock-fighting." Very properly, this barbarous sport has been put under the special ban of the English law. It is reached by the provisions of the Act for the Prevention of Cruelty to Animals, commonly known as " Dick Martin's." Lawyers, cunning of fence, have sometimes striven to show in appeal cases that the cock is not a domestic animal ; but the judges all ranged in Westminster Hall—a terrible show—have decided that chanticleer is as much an animal as a donkey; and more than one amateur of the cockpit royal has expiated his fondness for the gallinaceous tournament in county jail.

There was that poor young marquis, for instance, who indulged in the luxury of a private cock-fight in his own grounds on a Sunday morning. Soon did Nemesis, in the shape of a Society's constable, overtake that sporting peer. There was a terrible scandal. It is true that the marquis was not sent to the treadmill ; but the case against him was proved, and his lordship, if I remember aright, was fined. That, at least, was something. I dwell the more particularly on this case, as, the moment I found cock-fighting and Sunday morning associated in the phrase I had penned, my ears began to tingle and my cheek to blush with remorseful shame. Ah ! I should be the last wretch in the world to moralise on the wickedness of cock-fighting, for, not many years since, I deliberately attended a cock-fight. It was on a Sunday morning, too. I may as well make a clean breast of it, and allow the whole sad truth to be known. I was born to be a " frightful example" to the more virtuously disposed of my species; and I have little doubt that all the misfortunes I have since undergone, or which I may be doomed to undergo, spring directly from, or will spring from, that cock-fight. The only thing I can plead in extenuation is, that the combat I attended did not take place within the London bills of mortality, or within the sound of English church bells. The deed was done on the shores of the Mediterranean Sea, and on the coast of Africa.

It was at Algiers. I had just been reading in the English papers how a whole bevy of noblemen and gentlemen, disguised under the most plebeian aliases, had been arrested at a sporting

K

public-house—Jemmy Somebody's—in London, and marched
ignominiously through the public street to the police-court, where
they were each fined five pounds : all for cock-fighting. The
case against them was clear. The plumed bipeds, the metal spurs,
the weights and scales, the pit itself, had all been found, and duly
produced in court by inexorable inspectors. It was shown that a
great deal of money had been laid on the combat. " Serve them
right," quoth a stern gentleman, to whom I read the report of the
case. " I'd have sent every man Jack of them to prison for six
months, with hard labour." This downright opinion was necessarily provocative of argument. Another gentleman present, a
mild and genial person, remarked that he really did not see much
harm in cock-fighting. The birds, he added, evidently liked
fighting ; and so long as the natural spurs only were used—— But
the stern gentleman wouldn't hear anything in palliation of that
which he termed an abominable and degrading exhibition of
cruelty and ruffianism.

It had now grown to be about twelve at noon ; and it so fell
out that Abdallah, the guide attached to the hotel, sent to ask,
with his duty, what amusement the gentlemen would like to have
provided for them that present Sunday : adding that a capital
cock-fight was to come off at two o'clock precisely at the Café de
l'Ancienne Kiosque, on the road to Moustafa Supérieur. We had
been arguing so long on the pros and cons of cock-fighting without arriving at any satisfactory conclusion, that Abdallah's pro-
position came upon us like the refreshing spray from a hydropult
on a dusty day. The Gordian knot was severed. The stern
gentleman and the mild gentleman, and your humble servant,
were unanimous that the best thing to be done was to proceed to
the scene of action and compare notes on what we saw. So we
hired a carriage and went off to the Café de l'Ancienne Kiosque.
I beg to repeat that all this took place in Africa. In England we
should not have dreamed of doing such a thing ; nor, dreaming,
should we have dared.

But it *was* Sunday. Long years have passed since, in pages
precursors to those in which I now write, I was permitted to

discourse on the aspect of Sunday in London, and on the different Sabbaths which men in their pride, or their strict conscientious-ness, or their sheer indifference, had made to themselves. I have spent five hundred Sundays in twenty different lands since I first took pen in hand and told how I had heard "Sunday bands" playing in the Parks ; how I had heard English mechanics enjoy-ing their "Sunday out" in suburban tea-gardens. And am I, or are you, or is our patron Society any nearer now the solution of the vexed question of how Sunday should best be spent, and which of our human Sabbaths is most acceptable to the Divine Ordainer of all things ? That the seventh day, or the first day—for we are scarcely agreed as to whether it is properly number one or number seven—should not be spent in cock-fighting seems clear enough ; but remember, again, that what I am telling of took place in Africa, in a country governed by a Roman Catholic power, numbering among its subjects Turks, Jews, heretics, fire-worship-pers, and pagan negroes.

Man was made for the Sabbath, they tell you, grimly scowling, north of the Tweed. The Sabbath was made for man, they hold in latitudinarian France, and even in Lutheran Germany. But how is a government to impose a Sabbath upon so many races of men, and of so many ways of thinking ? Religious politics run as high in Algeria as elsewhere. The Mahometan Arabs call the Christians, dogs. The orthodox Turks are continually expressing a desire to defile the graves of the fathers and mothers of the heterodox Moors, and both concur in hating the schismatical Kabyles. The negroes are mere idolaters and Obeahmen. Turks, Moors, and negroes concur in loathing and despising the Jews. The Gallicans in Algiers hint that the Catholicism of the Spaniards who colonise Oran is tinged with strange heresies and excessive mariolatry ; and the Maltese sailors resolutely refuse to pray to the saints in the French calendar. The resident British community import tracts ; try a little proselytism without any apparent results ; squabble among themselves, and make no secret of their convictions that their neighbours are going to Jehanum. As for the Jews, they look upon Moslem and Nazarene alike, with the feelings harboured from time immemorial, but harboured in an occult manner. And yet, amidst this confusion of mosques, cathedrals, chapels, synagogues, and Mumbo-Jumbo houses, Trappist convents, and marabout koubbas, nobody in Algiers, extraordinary to relate, thinks of quarrelling or fighting about Sunday. Everybody enjoys his Sabbath as seemeth him best.

To what causes must the absence of dispute as to the observance of the Algerine Sabbath be ascribed? To the warmth of the climate? To the indolence or placability of the people? To the tolerance of the clergy? Scarcely, I conjecture. Hot as is the climate and lazy the people, there are enough activity and energy about to make Sunday the noisiest day in the week. The clergy are just as intolerant as the authorities permit them to be; and the priests of one sect, not being allowed to burn or plunder those of another, console themselves by preaching against and cursing their neighbours. The real reason is that a casting vote in all matters, secular or ecclesiastical, is given by the dominant power—by the eminently tolerant, unprejudiced, and unbelieving French government. I hope I am not libelling that government by hinting that, theologically, it is a little more than sceptical. Sunday is a day when everybody is allowed, and indeed expected, to make merry; and the Gaul being at bottom a light-hearted and mercurial soul, he sees nothing very wrong in the social organisation of a colony in which there are three Sabbaths instead of one.

I will not say that I pursued precisely this train of thought as the carriage bore us along the very dusty road leading to the Café de l'Ancienne Kiosque, and ultimately to Moustaïa Supérieur; but the roadside was fertile in materials on which future reflections might be founded. It was Sunday out on the most extensive scale, and with the oddest combination of Oriental and European characteristics. Group after group of French soldiers, military coveys of red-legged partridges, were scattered along the broad highway; and in the keen zest in which they were evidently enjoying their Sunday, offered a very marked contrast to the English warriors whom you meet listlessly wandering about the streets of provincial towns, and whose mental condition never seems to me to extend beyond these stages: first, that of despair at not having money enough to get drunk; second, that of having it, and being drunk; third, that of having got sober, and wanting to get drunk again. The third stage is analogous to, but not identical with, the first. The British private, who has tasted the sweets of the beer-shop, is in a position more fully to appreciate the poetical reminder that the sorrow's crown of sorrow is in the remembrance of happiness.

Ah! if under some blessed fiscal dispensation the English soldier could only be supplied with cigars three for a penny! He would still visit the canteen, I suppose; but I would lay any odds that he would not get tipsy half so often; that he would not be half so brutal, so stupid, or so disorderly; and that he would not find time hang with such awful ponderosity on his hands. Cigars three a penny! My panacea is a cheap one. I have but one addition to suggest: a theatre for twopence, in lieu of the filthy public-house and the blackguard music-hall. With cheap cigars and cheap theatrical amusements you would soon find a sensible diminution in your number of courts-martial, in the inmates of your barrack cells and the number of your punishment drills, your extra guards, your stoppages, and your bloody stripes laid on the backs of poor brave fellows who get into trouble because they do not know what to do with themselves.* Cigars three a penny, I say, and "Box and Cox" for twopence, in preference to the "Memoirs of ⦿tenant Melchisedec Bethel," that sainted subaltern of foot, ⦿he "Beatified Baggage-wagon Woman," price thirteen ⦿gs per thousand for distribution.

⦿gars three a penny were very common in the mouths of the French warriors on the road to Moustafa Supérieur. Scarcely a private but had his cheap roll of tobacco; nor did his officers seem to be too proud to smoke cigars at the same price. Tobacconists in Algiers will sell you so-called Londres

---

* Flogging, thanks to Mr. Otway, exists no longer in our army.

and Regalias at as high a price as you are foolishly willing
to give; but the prices are essentially "fancy" ones, and the
cigars themselves but the sweepings of the French Régie.

Given a fine Sunday afternoon, and several hundreds of
military men swaggering or strolling along in the direction of
a café where a cock-fight is about to take place, the odds in
England, I opine, would be laid on all those military men
being intent on witnessing the cock-fight in question. Did
your betting lay that way in Algeria, however, you would
lose. Every nationality here has its special and exclusive Sunday amusement; but cock-fighting is not one to which the
French are addicted. "*Comment!*" they would cry. "Spend
two hours in seeing two miserable birds peck one another
to pieces: *mais c'est une horreur!*" The Frenchman's Sunday
means a long day of dawdling, of staring at shows and sights,
of ogling pretty girls, of sipping moderate and thin potations,
and of winding up at billiards or the play. The French officers
have an occasional bout at partridge-shooting or pig-sticking,
and, at outlying stations, can cultivate perilous laurels, if they
choose, in hunting the lion; but ideas of "Le Sport," as it is
understood in France, have not yet penetrated to Cæsarean
Mauritania. Horse-racing languishes. Many of the Mahometan
gentlemen have magnificent studs of thoroughbreds, but they
decline to enter their full-blooded Arabs for plates unless the
French owners of racehorses can exhibit a faultless pedigree
with each of the horses they enter. And a racer must have
a very long lineage to match with one in the stud-book of
Arab sheikh. The native gentry, too, are great falconer
the French scarcely know a hawk from a hernshaw, and
regard a falcon as a kind of semi-fabulous bird, not oft
out of heraldic scutcheons, and which ladies used to w
their wrists like bracelets some time in the dark ages.

The Arabs understand cock-fighting, and among themselves
can enjoy it keenly; but, on the whole, they prefer the contests
of quails, and even of pheasants—which are here "game" to
the backbone, and desperately pugnacious—to those of cocks.

Moreover, they never bet; and to Europeans a cock-fight without money won and lost is as insipid as card-playing for "love." The real amateurs, "aficionados," as they call themselves, of cock-fighting are the Spaniards, of whom there are some thousands domiciled in Algiers, either as agriculturists, as mechanics, or as shopkeepers. They wear their national costume; speak very little French; scowl at the Arabs as though they were the self-same Moriscoes whom they were wont to persecute in Spain; and have their own church and their own priests.

The jewellers' shops in Algiers are full of rudely-fashioned representations in silver of human eyes, noses, arms, legs, and ears, and these I used to take at first as being in some way connected with the Mahometan superstition of the evil eye; but in reality they are votive offerings, and their chief purchasers are Spaniards, who devoutly hang them up on the altars of favourite saints, in gratitude for their recovery from deafness, toothache, chilblains, ophthalmia, or otherwise, as the case may be. For the rest, these Algerine Spaniards, usually emigrants from Carthagena and Valencia, are peaceable citizens enough, and give the government but little trouble. They are honest, industrious, and eminently temperate—bread, garlic, tobacco, and cold water being their principal articles of diet. They occasionally indulge in stabbing affrays, when arrears of ill-feeling, arising from bygone cock-fighting and card-playing disputes, are cleared up; but as a rule the use of the knife is strictly confined to the family circle. Pepe has it out with and then the thing is hushed up, and the swarthy gentle- who is taken to the hospital with a punctured wound h the fifth rib is reported to have accidentally slipped upon an open knife as he was cutting the rind of a of cheese. They don't run mucks, and they seldom stab the gendarmes. They are inveterate gamblers and finished cock-fighters.

The Maltese sailors, of whom there are usually a numerous tribe in Algiers belonging to the speronares in port, are likewise

enthusiastic admirers of the "gallimachia;" but the Spaniards,
to cull a locution from the pit, "fight shy" of the brown islanders.
Your Maltese, not to mince matters, is a drunken, quarrelsome
dog, fearfully vindictive, as lazy as a duke's hall-porter, and a
great rogue.   Rows are rare at Algerian cock-fights; but if ever
a difficulty occurs, and the police are called in, the Maltese are
sure to be at the bottom of it.

Cafés, breweries with gardens attached, and dancing-saloons, are
plentiful in the neighbourhood of Algiers.   As the road grows
crowded and more crowded with soldiers and sailors, with French
workmen in blouses and French farm-labourers in striped nightcaps and sabots; with German artisans with their blonde beards,
belted tunics, and meerschaums; with little grisettes and Norman
bonnes with their high white caps; with grave, dusky Spaniards
in their round jackets, bright sashes, pork-pie hats, clubbed hair,
and earrings; with Greek and Italian sailors, and fishermen from
the Balearic Isles, all mingled pell-mell; with the Jews in their
gorgeous habiliments, clean white stockings, snowy turbans, and
shiny shoes; with the Jewish women with high conical head-
dresses of golden filigree, and long falling veils of lace, and
jewelled breastplates, and robes of velvet and rich brocade; with
Arabs in white burnouses and flapping slippers, who stalk grimly
onward, looking neither to the right nor to the left; with Berbers
and Kabyles swathed in the most astonishing wrap-rascals of
camel's hair, and goat's hair, and cowskin; with fez-capped, barefooted, and more than half bare-backed Arab boys, shrieking out
scraps of broken French; with Zouaves so bronzed and so barbaric
in appearance as to make one doubt whether they have not tu
Mussulmans for good and all; with sellers of fruit, and sh
and dates, and sweetstuff, and cigars, and lucifer-matches
begin at last to wonder whether the days of the Crusades have
returned, and whether this motley crowd, belonging to all nations
and jabbering all dialects, is not part of the enormous host
whilom encamped at Jaffa or Ascalon.   Surely the Duke of
Bethlehem or the Marquis of Jericho must be somewhere hereabouts.   Surely Richard of England must have patched up a

truce with the Sultan Saladin, and the camp-followers of the Christian and the Saracen army must be making merry together. No; this is only an ordinary Algerine Sunday. It is the Christian Sunday, remember; but it is worthy of remark that the Hebrews who had their Sabbath yesterday, and the Mahometans who had theirs the day before, do not evince the slightest disinclination to take an extra holiday on the real or Nazarene one.

The Café de l'Ancienne Kiosque was rather a tumble-down place of entertainment, and might have been easily mistaken for one of the inferior "guinguettes" outside the barriers, whither, in olden times, ere Paris, both outside and inside its barriers, had grown to be the dearest city in the world, one used to repair to drink "petit bleu" at eight sous the litre. The different nationalities were enjoying themselves, each after its peculiar fashion, at the Ancienne Kiosque. The burnoused Arabs were gravely squatting on the benches outside, paying a trifle, I suppose, to the proprietor of the café for that privilege; for they brought their own tobacco, and partook of no other refreshment. A noisy group of Frenchmen were wrangling over a "pyramid" game of billiards—the once green cloth of the table tinted dun-gray from long use and many absinthe stains, and grown as full of rents as poor Robin's jerkin. At the side-tables some sailors were drinking drams. Sailors are cosmopolitans in that respect. The Germans had a back yard to themselves, where they were playing ninepins and wallowing in drouthy draughts of "bière de Mars." The cockpit was at the extremity of a long garden, originally laid out in the French or sham classical style, but where the indigenous and spiky cactus had long since had it all its own way, carrying things before it literally with a high hand, and driving out the modest plants of Europe with sticks and staves and sharp-pointed knives. Next to the horse-armoury at the Tower, a grove of cactus is about the most formidable array of lethal-like weapons I know.

We paid a franc apiece and were admitted into a square barn-like apartment, the walls whitewashed and the roof supported by heavy beams. Within this quadrangle had been constructed a

theatre, properly so called, consisting of twenty rows of seats
disposed one over the other in circles, and gradually widening in
diameter as they ascended. You entered this theatre by means of
ladders and trap-doors, of which there might have been half a
dozen in the different grades of seats ; and I may best explain my
meaning by saying that the outside of the structure looked, from
the floor of the barn, like a gigantic wooden funnel. The neck of
the funnel was the cockpit itself.

We climbed up to the highest range of seats, and getting as
close as we could to the two gendarmes who represented authority,
looked curiously around and beneath. There was little fear of
disturbance, however. The "roughs" were not present that
Sunday morning ; indeed, we heard subsequently that it was
Saint Somebody's day—a Maltese saint—and that the brown
islanders were protracting their devotions at their own church.
The Spaniards, who had all doubtless attended mass before eleven
a.m., were the chief occupants of the theatre ; and into it were
crammed, tight as herrings in a barrel, at least two hundred and
fifty amateurs. Turn where you would, were visible the swarthy
faces, bright black eyes, closely-cropped whiskers, upper lips and
chins blue from constant shaving, ear-lobes decorated with rings
of gold, hair in clubs, in queues, in nets, and in bags, pork-pie or
soft felt hats with rosettes, round shaggy jackets, loose necker-
chiefs, and curiously-worked gaiters or embroidered slippers, so
distinctive of the children of sunny Spain.

They were all smoking. On such solemn occasions as bull-
fights and cock-fights the papelito or paper roll is accounted puerile
and jejune, and the genuine weed or Puro enjoyed. Such Puros
as were in a state of combustion here were probably not of
Algerine or three-a-penny species. They were big, black, odorous,
and probably smuggled from the Peninsula. The company had
obviously taken a good deal of garlic with their morning meal ;
and if you will again be pleased to recollect that the month was
May and the country Africa, I need not enter into any details
concerning the somewhat powerful aroma which issued from the
two hundred and fifty amateurs. But a better behaved, a quieter

audience, I never saw. It is a pity they had not something worthier than a cock-fight at which to display their good behaviour.

I am so ignorant of the technology of cock-fighting as to be unaware of the precise meaning of a "main;" but we saw five different battles between five brace of birds. They were, for the most part, as game as game could be. One only—it was the third fight—a red long-legged fellow, "El rubio," as he was called in the betting, showed, figuratively speaking, the white feather. He essayed to run away from his adversary, and even to scale the walls of the pit; whereat there were dull murmurs among the auditory, and cries of "Fuera!—fuera el rubio"—"Out with him!" His owner very speedily put an end to the growing discontent by jumping into the pit, seizing the recreant gladiator, wringing his neck, and stamping upon him. He then handed over a handful of dollars, his loss on the event, to the owner of the opposition bird, and philosophically lighting a fresh Puro, regained his seat, and betted throughout the next fight on a white bird with a gray gorget.

Cockpit Royal! As I gazed on the fierce struggle I could not but recall the mild Wordsworth's mellifluous description of Chanticleer under pacific circumstance:

> "Sweetly ferocious round his native walks,
> Pride of his sister-wives, the monarch stalks;
> Spur-clad his nervous feet, and firm his tread,
> A crest of purple tips the warrior's head;
> Bright sparks his black and rolling eyeball hurls,
> Afar his tail he closes and unfurls.
> On tiptoe rear'd, he strains his clarion throat,
> Threaten'd by faintly answering forms remote.
> Again with his shrill voice the mountain rings,
> While, flapp'd with conscious pride, resound his wings."

Are not the numbers melodious? Is not the description charming? Was there ever a prettier amplification of cock-a-doodle-do-o-o-o? But here he was—the "monarch" "sweetly ferocious"—with a vengeance. I have heard ere now the term "pitted against each other," and I know not what may have been formerly the practice in cock-fighting England; but in this Algerine pit there did not seem to be any need to excite the combatants for the fray. The two owners stepped into the arena, each with his bird in his hand. Solemn declarations were made and written down as to the ages and prior performances of the champions. Weights and scales were then produced, and the birds were duly weighed. The appointed judges subjected them to a minute examination. Their spurs and beaks were then rubbed with the half of a lemon ; they were put down at opposite corners of the pit ; and the owners, bowing to each other, went to their places.

Not a cry, not a gesture, was used to excite the birds to the attack. There was a quiet walk round the pit ; then a few sidelong looks, a careful mutual examination of the opposite party's general build and make-up ; then a rush, a rise on the wings, another, another ; then it seemed as though a small feather-bed had been suddenly ripped up and the plumes scattered in all directions. Such a furious clapper-clawing, such a tooth-and-nail exhibition of gameness ! But not a crow was heard. Not a cry, not a gasp even, of pain. The loudest sound audible was the rustling of feathers. Then the rivals would emerge from the downy cloud, stalk round the pit again, and eye and take stock of each other as before. Then would come rush number two, and another rise and another furious clapper-clawing. And so on, round after round, for perhaps an hour.

This volume not being *Bell's Life in London*, I am absolved from chronicling the minutiæ of the various rounds. In the first fight I may remark that one of the birds, a black one, was defeated early. Time was called ; he could not come up to it ; he consequently lost the fight, and was put out of his misery, but not contumeliously, by his owner. The victor expired just as he was being handed over the barrier to his triumphant proprietor. The next duel was between a little gray fiend of a bird and a gaunt white creature of most doleful mien. How handicapping is managed in the Algerian Cockpit Royal I do not know ; but there was evidently a great disparity in bottom and bone between these two. The pluck, however, of the gaunt white creature was indomitable. He grew rather wild after about eighteen minutes' clapper-clawing, and staggered rather than walked round the pit: the little gray fiend strutting by his side, and ever and anon whispering in his ear, so it seemed, like an importunate bore; but in reality finding out fresh tender parts about the unhappy creature's head wherein to progue him with his sharp beak.

It was very horrible to see this gaunt white creature *gradually turn first a streaky and then a complete crimson* with the blood he lost. It was more horrible when both his eyes were gone, and blind and "groggy," but undismayed, he still went reeling about, occasionally closing with his enemy and clawing him. At last, in the twentieth round, I think, the little gray fiend coolly went up to the luckless white knight, looked in his face as though he were laughing in it, and with one trenchant blow of his beak cut the poor wretch's throat. I am sure by the blood that spurted out that the great artery had been severed. The white cock balanced himself for a moment on one leg, then threw back his head, gave one smothered "cluck," and as sharply as a human hand can be turned round from the position of supination to that of pronation, fell over dead, and turned his toes up. So may you have seen in the shambles a bullock stricken by the slaughterer's poleaxe. One stupid moment motionless he stands, as though all unconscious that his skull is cleft in twain and that his brains lie bare. But anon the quicksilver current or dissolution searches every vein and plumbs every nerve. The giant frame trembles, the legs give way, and the great beast topples over into so much beef.

Can any extenuation for the manifest cruelty of this sport be found in the fact that the birds in Spanish pits wear only their natural horny pedal protuberances or spurs? This, like everything else, is a moot point. The uninitiated generally jump at the conclusion that a fight with steel or silver spurs is much more barbarous than one without. These sharpened glaives, they argue, inflict the most hideous gashes. On the other side, it may be shown that when spurs are used the fight is over much

sooner ; and that spurs, besides, give an equality in weapons to
the combatants.   A bird may be of the same weight and age as
his opponent, but much overmatched by him in adroitness and
endurance ; yet it will often happen that when apparently at the
last gasp, the bird who is getting the worst of it may turn the
tables by driving his spur into his enemy's brain.

To others I leave the task of drawing a moral from the tale
I have told.   As I went to the cock-fight, and it was Sunday,
I am, so far as moralising is concerned, out of court.

XII.

MAURESQUES.

HAT was the name of the Frenchman who translated the "Arabian Nights" in the middle of the last century? It began with a G, I think. Well, Algiers is that gentleman's translation, in stone, and plaster, and whitewash, and glaring pigments. The Place du Gouvernement might be the principal square of a French provincial town of the first class. There are big hotels, cafés, counting-houses, and shops; the names are French, the green blinds are French, the merchandise is French. You may buy Paris chocolate, and pectoral paste, and pills, and sham jewellery, and crinolines. You may dine "à la carte" or "au prix fixe;" you may buy the latest "scrofulous French novel" at the bookstalls, and read the same etiolated little newspapers, with their timid murmurings of news a fortnight old, and their leading article devoted to a puff on a corn-cutter or a juggler fresh come to town.

In a word, you are in a little Paris. The "*pst!*" of the consumer sounds shrilly through the air, and the "*v'là M'sr!*" of the garçon is audibly responsive. The itinerant musicians of Gaul, the wheezy flute, the rachitic fiddle, and the harp dying of atrophy, strum and tootle feeble music at the street corner; the commissionnaire slumbers on his truck in the sun; the shoeblack plies his trade; the bonne parades the same elaborately-laced babies; the little girls in Hessian boots and frilled trousers go through competitive exhibitions with skipping ropes; a real French poodle, shaven and shorn, crosses your path; groups of red-trousered soldiers lounge by, their mouths agape

and their hands thrust in their pockets; the roguish little
milliner flits past with her bandbox; the tremendous officier
supérieur, aiguilletted and epauletted, strolls out of the café
where he has been breakfasting, picking his teeth; the orderly
trots by with his leathern satchel on his hip; the gamin makes
faces at you, flees behind a corner if you threaten him with
your cane, and, when you are at a convenient distance, flings
a stone at you; the snowy-vested, white-capped cook emerges
into the morning and leans against the door-jamb to inhale the
fresh air, all hot and hot though it be, until it is time for
him to dive into his burning tomb of pots and pans again.

Adolphe, in curly-brimmed hat and turn-down collar pre-
posterously vandyked, and cravat in a gigantic true-lover's-knot,
leers under the bonnet of Madame, the spouse of the employé of
the administration, taking her walks abroad attired in the height
of Parisian fashion to cheapen leathery artichokes and skinny
chickens in the market; whilst Jules is humming " Rien n'est
sacré pour un Sapeur," and puffing his halfpenny cigar as
superbly as though it were a half-crown Embajador.   Wan
children press you to buy cigar-lights and three-sous bunches of
flowers; bright in the sun glitter the gilded signs of the photographers and the dentists—two branches of industry which
appear at present to absorb the most energetic of French
faculties; there is a distant sound of trumpeting and drumming;
the calèche-drivers are asleep on their boxes, as usual; and
cropping up like poppies in a cornfield are the red ribbons of
the Legion.   So plentiful, indeed, are these glorified button-
holes, that you begin to wonder how many people there are
in the French empire who are *not* decorated.   Surely this is
Paris, or Lyons, or Bordeaux, or at least Boulogne or
Dieppe!

No; you are in Africa; this indeed is Algiers; and the
" Arabian Nights" are all round you.   There goes the Sultana
Scheherazade.   The Sultana in walking costume resembles a
clothes-bag bifurcated, or say a pair of well-inflated pillows,
surmounted by a bolster and covered with a mosquito curtain.

The Sultana may be one of the wives of a wealthy Moresco, or she may be a washerwoman. She is a Mauresque, and her outdoor costume is invariable. It consists of a pair of very baggy galligaskins, precisely that kind of Turkish trousers which Mandane wears in the opera of "Artaxerxes." These —the shintiyan of the Turkish women—are of plain white muslin; above is a quantity of semi-diaphanous drapery, which I cannot attempt to describe; and over all is thrown a long robe, or feminine toga, of very fine white linen or gauze, called a "haik." Sometimes another haik of a somewhat stouter material is worn over the first. This drapery does not fall in graceful folds, but is drawn close to the form, and the general composition of the pillow-case legs and bolster body is, in the entire effect, droll.

The feet and ankles are bare, and from the hue of those extremities the Algerine expert is, I suppose, enabled to judge whether the veiled lady is dark or fair. Of course, I only presumed to look at the Sultana Scheherazade's supporters for the purpose of verifying the fact that her feet are thrust into wide shoes called "sebabath," which, again, are encased in looser slippers of yellow morocco, the papouches or babouches. Looking at these slippers, I could not, however, avoid regarding that which the slippers covered; and I must admit that the greatest part of the flesh I peeped at was very dusky indeed. The upper class of Mauresques, however, are said to be as fair as Europeans.

You can see nothing of the Sultana Scheherazade's face but her eyes. The upper haik comes well down over her temples; then you have a pair of big, black, sloe-like orbs, the lids so prolonged that they almost meet, or are darkened at least with kohl till they seem to join. The rest of the face is hidden by a handkerchief tied tightly behind. Some Arab ladies are said coquettishly to make use, as a veil, of a handkerchief so very transparent that their features can be perfectly well discerned beneath; but with the vast majority of the sultanas I have seen the gauze mask has been a reality and the concealment effectual.

L

I don't wonder at this veil, answering to the Turkish yashmak, having been through so many centuries so obstinately retained. It may be regarded as a beautiful dispensation of Providence for promoting outdoor equality among the ladies. A pretty woman may let the passers-by know, even through her veil, that she is comely ; but an ugly woman is, by the merciful interposition of the knotted handkerchief, enabled altogether to hide her ill-favouredness. Once veiled and packed and pinned together, the Mauresques enjoy entire liberty out of doors. No jealously-curtained "arabas" convey them ; no hideous eunuchs—ushers of a perpetual seminary for grown-up young ladies—hurry them along, forbidding them to look to the right or the left. Let me hasten to admit that in point of tidiness and cleanliness the Mauresques offer a very favourable contrast to the dignified and dirty male child of the desert. Haik, veil, and unmentionables are alike spotless and snowy. Sometimes the clothes-bag is portly, and suggests a stout mamma beneath—a suggestion strengthened by a pursuivant tribe of children, all, down to little-girl toddlekins of four or five (so at least to judge from their stature), as closely veiled as their elders. Altogether the "get-up" of a Mauresque *en promenade* is livelier and smarter than that of a Turkish woman, whose veil is horribly ugly, who wears instead of the haik a pillow-case of black silk, and whose trousers hang in ugly folds over her loose and slovenly boots of untanned leather. There is a spick-and-span, just-home-from-the-wash look about these Moorish ladies very refreshing to view ; but their *ensemble* is, nevertheless, as I have hinted, funny.

If you are in the penseroso mood, you may picture to yourself that all the feminine tombs in the great cemetery of Mustapha have disgorged their tenants, and that they, or their pallid ghosts rather, are wandering about in the sunshine, vainly seeking for the Janissaries of the good old times, and wondering how the Dey could think of allowing so many Christians to be at large without shackles on their shins and burdens on their backs. Or, still in ghostly frame of mind, you may liken them to the phantom nuns who serenade Robert le Diable. Very much like these sainted apparitions did the white Mauresques look, gliding through the dim arcades of the Rue Bab-Azzoun. Or, if the allegro suit you better, you may fancy yourself gazing on the corps de ballet in "Giselle," and that the airy creatures are but "Wilis," with their ballet-skirts tucked lightly round them. Or, to one of ruder vision, they may appear like those five-and-thirty boarders at the ladies' school where Mr. Pickwick went to prevent the elopement, in their bed-gowns. Take them, however, as you will, and granting the grotesqueness of their trim, and you shall not divest them of an indefinable but omnipresent perfume of the East—of the dreamy, vaporous, sensuous land of mystery and sorcery and jealousy and intrigue. I abandon for good the bifurcated clothes-bag, the double pillow-case similes. At night, albeit the gas contends with the moon's rays, each pair of baggy pantaloons becomes a novel in two volumes.

The shops are full of cartes de visite of Arab and Jewish ladies, not only veiled, but with uncovered countenances—not only smothered in the haik, but arrayed in all the picturesque splendour of Oriental costume. Whence have these photographers obtained their models ? Have they been permitted to enter the penetralia of the Moresco houses ? Has the camera become one of the lights of the harem ? I trow not. The models, I apprehend, have been selected from the Rikat, or naughty tribe—numerous enough here, as everywhere else. In these photographs you may see, at least, the lay figure dressed in the gorgeous attire of the Mauresque at home. The baggy trousers, drawn tight about the ankles, are replaced by the serroual, or, wide drawers of silk, or china crape, and reaching only mid-leg. The inmost garment is of finest gauze ; the feet are in slippers of velvet embroidered with gold ; the hair, plaited in long tresses, is knotted behind the head, and descends almost to the ground ; the head-dress is a dainty little skull-cap or chachia of velvet, thick with gold and seed pearls, and attached by golden cords beneath the chin. The upper garment is the rlila, or jacket of brocaded silk, beneath which are one or more vests of

gay colours, ornamented with innumerable sugar-loaf buttons.
Round the waist is swathed the fouta, or many-folded sash of
striped silk.   Add rings and earrings, often of diamonds and
emeralds very clumsily cut ; necklaces with side rows of fine
pearls strung on common string ; bracelets for the arms, called
" m'saïs," and bangles for the ankles termed " m'kaïs," and the
Mauresque in her carte de visite or indoor costume is complete.
Stay ; she sometimes wears a kind of upper jerkin called a
" djabadoli," curiously filigreed with gold.

A knowing Frenchman of long Algerine experience tells me
that you may see the Mauresques in all this bravery of dress, and
in actual reality of visage, if you will only remain at your window
for an hour every evening before sunset, armed with a powerful
opera-glass.   Then, sweeping the horizon of houses, you may espy
the beauteous she-Moors, gorgeous as the Queen of Sheba, come
forth on the flat roofs of those old tenements in the upper town
which have escaped the ruthless progress of French improvements.
Simple she-Moors !   Like the ostrich which is said to hide its
head in the sand—but doesn't do anything of the sort—and
fancies itself invisible to the hunter, the confiding Mauresques
imagine that nobody can see them when, glowing in silk, and
velvet, and gold, and fine linen, they take their evening walk upon
the house-top.   Another informant tells me that scarcely an evening passes without his seeing the unveiled Moorish women crawling
over the tiles, very much after the fashion of cats, from roof to
roof, from house to house, and often from street to street; for in the
old quarters of the town the thoroughfares are, as a rule, consider-
ably narrower than Middle Temple Lane or old Cranbourne Alley,
or one of those queer back streets at Venice, and each storey pro-
jects so much above the other that at the summit they touch.

Shinning over the tiles is the orthodox way of paying evening
visits.   The tiles are the stairs, the flat roofs the drawing-rooms.
It is precisely the same at Mexico, where the " azoteas " are the
great sunset rendezvous.   Sky Parlour is where the Mauresque
woman most enjoys herself.   Thither she comes to gossip with
her neighbours, to sing, to eat sweetmeats, to hang out her linen,

to beat her carpets and her children. Life in a Moorish town would be dreary indeed without the house-top. The house-top! For how many thousands of years have these unchangeable races been walking on the house-top! And the sheet that was let down before the eyes of the visionary : what was that but the old canvas curtain they rig here every night on their roof to temper the sea breeze and afford shade from the latest fierceness of the sun's rays.

This Moorish woman's dress which I have figured bit by bit from a bundle of photographs might have been copied almost verbatim from Lady Mary Wortley Montagu's description of the dress of a Turkish lady in the seraglio a hundred and fifty years ago; and for centuries, perhaps, ere that, no fashions in the harem had changed. Staunch old Conservatism walks Algiers as proudly as of yore, and, for all the improvements of the innovating Franks, they cannot improve it out of the land which they occupy, but have not conquered.

The position of the Mahometan woman in Algeria is theoretically much preferable to that of her sex in Tunis or Morocco. The strictly equitable nature of the French rule forbids her being treated with harshness or sold into slavery ; but practically she is not much better off than in other Oriental countries. She is the victim of a stupid and brutalising social code, founded on and bound up in a religion whose theory is pure, but whose practice is barbarous. She is either contemned or maltreated : a toy to the rich, a beast of burden to the poor. When a child is born to a Moorish woman, she cries, if it be a boy, " it is a blessing ;" if it be a girl, " it is a curse." Directly she comes into the world she is baptised in the name of Fatma, which is that of the mother of the Prophet. A week afterwards another name is given to her. The choice of appellatives lies between Aïcha, Bedra, Djohar, Halima, Hasuria, Khredoudga, Khreira, Meriem, Mimi, Mouni, Rosa, Safia, Yamina, Zina, and Zohra. Some of these names seem to have a characteristic sound. Wouldn't you like to fall in love with a young lady named Mouni ; and can't you fancy being blessed with a mother-in-law by the name of Khredoudga ?

If the Moorish girl's parents are poor they will regard her only as an incubus. Her mother was probably married at ten or twelve years of age; she ages early; and each accession of maternal cares is to her only a renewed warning that she is no longer fair to look upon. As for the father, it is as much as he knows that he has a daughter till some one buys her of him in marriage. The poor girl grows up to be beaten, overworked, and despised : a Cinderella without a fairy godmother, but with sisters as miserable as herself. The rich girl is neglected by her mother, and is relegated to a corner of the harem and the care of an old negress. When she is old enough to be sold, she is married. She is profoundly ignorant, of course, very fond of sweetstuff, very fond of the bath, very fond of flowers, very fond of smoking cigarettes. In the street she ogles you with her big eyes, and if there be anything peculiar in your appearance, points a henna-stained finger and giggles shrilly. Beyond these characteristics, which may be gotten by heart in the course of half an hour's stay in Algiers, I question whether a European, not being a hakim or physician, would know much more of the Mauresques if he dwelt in the country for forty years.

This state of life is no doubt very pitiable. The government can do little to ameliorate it. They have guaranteed to the natives the possession of the civil law—which is the Koran—and the social code and the civil law are one. They might as well decree that the Mahometan women should go unveiled, or that the Arabs should leave off their burnouses, as interfere with the domestic arrangements of the Moorish gynecæum. A benevolent French lady residing in Algiers has of late years endeavoured to do that which the admirable Miss Whateley attempted in Cairo, though on a purely secular basis. She has established a school where nearly a hundred little Mussulman girls, from four to ten years of age, receive a very good education; and I am told that the progress made by some of these young Paynims in geography, arithmetic, and history—besides the more feminine accomplishments of needlework and flower-painting—would have done no discredit to a ladies' college in Europe. But the civilisation given to these poor little creatures is perforce superficial. The lower classes are glad enough to send their children to this school, for the teaching is gratuitous, and the parents are even encouraged by bribes to send them ; but the half-educated girl goes back to all the dreariness and all the drudgery of Oriental life. She is married and becomes a mother when she should still be learning her lessons ; and she very soon forgets the few she has learnt. The wives of the very rich Morescoes are said never to leave the house save to visit the holy koubbas to pray that they may have men-children, and to propitiate the Marabouts with gifts. It is an animal kind of existence altogether ; but can be no more altered or mended than the Koran. In the cities, it is true, there is a class of Mauresques who go out to the brasseries and cafés chantant at night in garments and bonnets fresh from Paris. *Elles valent ce que valent leurs sœurs* at Paris, and everywhere else.

XIII.

SAMBO AND FATHMA.

OU have doubtless been told that the reason why the free negro gets on so badly in America is because he is despised and looked down upon on account of his colour—because no road of social advancement is open to him—because, through the cruelty and injustice of his white brethren, he is plunged in an abyss of degradation as bad as, if not worse than, involuntary servitude with its accompaniment of cotton-picking and the cowhide. You have been told that with education and equal political and social rights the free negro will in process of time rise to the level of the white man. Some amiable fanatics, moreover, go so far as to maintain that Sambo is in all respects about thirty-five per cent. better than his fair-skinned brother.

Well, the free-nigger experiment has been tried by the French in Algiers, not dogmatically, but almost unconsciously, for nearly forty years. Sambo in Algeria is held by authority to be as good as any other man. The Europeans, the Arabs, the Jews, and the negroes all enjoy equal rights. The Moors often marry their negresses. The French have not the slightest prejudice against the negro on account of his ebony skin. They never have had. Among the ladies Sambo is even popular. He is "un beau noir." The Zouave walks arm-in-arm with the Turco; negroes and negresses ride in the same omnibuses and carriages as white men; and there seem to be as many negroes in Algiers—full-blooded black niggers—in comparison with the population as in any considerable city of the Northern States of America. I am

quite certain that if a deserving colonist were recommended for
the cross of the Legion of Honour, the decoration would not be
withheld from him on the ground that he had a black face. I
don't think the community would offer the slightest objection to
a negro sub-prefect or a negro commissary of police. Why
should they ? The negro is a French subject, and all Frenchmen
are equal before the law.

Thus, without civil disabilities, without the stigma of belonging
to an abhorred and contemned race, one might imagine that
enfranchised Sambo would have done something for himself by
this time. The State provides gratuitous education for all races,
classes, and creeds ; and there is plenty of work, and money to be
made, for those who are sober and industrious. The end of all
which is that Sambo goes to sleep in the sun, waking up to refect
himself with "abundant pumpkin," or plenteous plantains—you
may buy a bunch of them for twopence—and devouring preferably
another man's pumpkin to his own. He does a little fishing—that
avocation affording him plenty of time to swing his legs over a
bank, crooning forth songs of the "tam-tam" kind, and taking
short dozes between the bites ; he does a little gardening ; he
peddles a few baskets, calabashes, and bead rosaries, and higglos
also fowls and eggs. This is all.

He works, perhaps, two days a week. He is very Catholic in
his creed, keeping with much scrupulosity, and as the closest of
holidays, the Mahometan Sabbath, which is Friday, the Jewish,
which is Saturday, and the Christian, which is Sunday, with very
likely a little Saint Monday of his own. And whenever there is
the slightest excuse for an extra festival, he begs or steals an old
cocked-hat and a pair of worsted epaulettes to surmount his
turban or his shoulders withal ; he sticks spangles and tinsel over
his caftan, and with Pompey, and Quashie, and Quimbo, his
brethren, he perambulates the streets, thumping the tam-tam,
clanging the castanets, howling the chants of his country, and
demanding sous. In the whole of Algiers there is not a single
reputable negro shopkeeper or artisan. You never see the negroes,
now that they are free, carrying heavy burdens or doing any kind

of arduous manual labour ; that they leave to the Arabs. Sambo
prefers to loaf and " slosh around."

The negro women officiate as shampooers in the Moorish baths,
as peripatetic bakers of galettes or pancakes, as nurses, prostitutes
and sorceresses. On the first Monday after the feast of the
Nissam they have a grand Obeah festival at the Ain-el-Abiad (the
White Fountain), distant about three miles from Algiers on the
sea-shore. Then they have their Derdebas, or private festivals,
in their own particular quarter near the Kasbah or citadel of
Algiers, in the streets of Darfour and Kattaroudjil. There, in
their beastly dens, the women throw off the striped blue mantles
in which they muffle themselves abroad, and appear in every
variety of barbarous finery. The tam-tam and karakob, or castanets, then come into play, and the women go through those dances
of which it is enough to say that they resemble the orgies of the
Ghawahzee and Almé of Egypt or the Nautch girls of India
dipped in a vat of lampblack.

There are always low-class Arab touters hanging about the
hotels to entice tourists into putting down so many francs a head
to get up a Derdeba in the Kattaroudjil. If you decline to
witness the disgusting gambols of a "dignity ball," they will
offer to organise a Mauresque fandango for you, " chez Fathma."
Fathma is the Ninon de l'Enclos of Algiers. She does not belie
her name, and is enormously fat. She is supposed to be very rich,
and to carry most of her wealth in gold and jewels about her
person. She goes about as closely veiled as though she were a
respectable woman ; but you may know her, the adepts say, by
her wearing scarlet stockings. Of course she has rivals and
imitators who also wear red stockings, and would fain make
believe that they are each and all of them the real Fathma.
Anonyma, Synonyma, it does not matter much. A pair of red
stockings in one country, and a paletot made by Poole, with a
phaeton and a pair of piebald ponies, in the other, and see to what
a common tune the world wags.

Fathma at Algiers is a personage. She has been sent for, it is
rumoured, by great people, to palaces, to be paraded as the most

perfect—that is to say, the fattest—specimen of a Mauresque extant, although her non-admirers declare that she is not a Mauresque at all, but the offspring of a negress and a Biskri. She boasts of gold chains and diamond rings, given to her by the illustrious ones of the earth. She is the only veiled woman who has been known to enter a European café, and every morning, about eleven, you may see her sipping her "demi-tasse" at a particular marble table, her bracelets, chains, and ouches glinting through the thin folds of her haik, and exhibiting her red stockings with conscious superiority to a throng of whispering admirers. She is a shrewd jade, and Jules and Adolphe think she is an Odalisque—a sultana. She is only a Mauritanian Doll Common.

Fathma never condescends to give a ball unless a minimum sum of one hundred and twenty-five francs is brought to her as a peace-offering by one of the low-class Arab touters. These balls, or ballets, or nautches, which are as stupid as they are revolting, serve, however, one useful purpose. Without the facilities offered by these balls you would not see on the walls of the Royal Academy or the Water-colour Societies those brilliant representations of "The Light of the Hhareem," or "Moorish Maidens Dancing," or "An Eastern Lady playing on the Mandolin," or "Life in the Seraglio," which seem to argue so amazingly intimate an acquaintance with the inmost penetralia of Oriental life. Fathma and her colleagues in Algiers, as in Tunis, as in Stamboul, as in Cairo, are lay figures-in-ordinary to the worshipful guild of painters in oil and water colours. The meanest Moorish women, not being of the "Rikat" sisterhood, would disdain to sit to an artist as a model. A few photographs for backgrounds, a few visits to the Bazaars, and a good stock of odds and ends of wearing apparel and frippery from the curiosity-shops, and the painter may go to work. Of putting a real Moorish lady from nature on canvas he has about as much chance as of drawing the portrait of the late Queen of Sheba from the life.

In connection with these balls gotten up by greedy adventurers for the hoodwinking of ingenuous Europeans—young Harry Foker, travelling in the East after having been jilted by Blanche

Amory, is passionately fond of seeing "a real Moorish fandango, sir, by Jove"—and returning to my old friend Sambo, I must not omit to mention the Issaoua, or fire-eaters, who are supposed to be a religious sect, but are in reality only so many swindlers and impostors. They are negroes, and profess to swallow live coals, to lick bars of red-hot iron, to devour scorpions, the rind of the prickly pear—which is certainly very tough eating, let alone the prickles—ashes, chalk, and clay, always with a pious intent, and for the greater glory of Allah. The red-hot poker and live-coal swallowing are clever tricks, which the late lamented Ramo Samee might have explained, and which I have seen before now performed at country fairs in England; but as for the natural capacity of the negro for gobbling up earth, there is no reason to doubt it. The parliamentary blue-books will tell you that the frightful disease common in the West India Islands, and called "Le mal d'estomac," was brought on by the invincible propensity of the blacks for gorging clay; and "dirt-eating" was one of the recognised offences punishable by the slave laws of Jamaica.

An Issaoua is, as I have hinted, a swindle. The sole object of the fervid religionists is to extract the greatest possible number of twenty-franc pieces from the visitor. They will begin their performances and then suddenly stop, declaring that the police are at the door, but that if ten francs more be advanced, they will eat a peck more dirt and a bushel more prickly pear. Then the poker cannot be heated under an additional fifteen francs, or swallowed without an extra twenty. In short, it is a continual round of "Twopence more, and up goes the donkey."

There is another ceremony among the Algerine negroes, more closely connected with the rites of Obeah, but which is also made to serve the purposes of cheating and extortion. On Wednesday morning in every week, on the road from the faubourg of Bab-el-Oued to St. Eugène—which last is distant about four miles from Algiers—you may meet groups of Moorish women and children, on foot or on muleback, followed by servants carrying live fowls under their arms. They halt on the sea-shore, at a spot called Sebâ-Aïoun, the Seven Fountains. Here the good and the evil

AN ISSAOUA EXHIBITION IN ALGERIA.

Page 172

genii of the Mussulmans are to be invoked and exorcised. The good genii are white, green, blue, and yellow ; the bad ones are red, black, and brown. The exorcisers are all negresses, who, when they conjure, tell fortunes, or sell love-philters, are called " guezzanates."

The audience being grouped on their haunches round one of the fountains, the performances commence. An old black woman lights a fire under a brazen incense burner, on which are some grains of benzoin. The person who wishes to propitiate the genii inhales the vapour of the gum. Then the old black woman takes the fowls prepared for sacrifice, cuts their throats half through, and throws them on to the sand. If these unhappy birds, partly slaughtered, half flying and half staggering, can contrive to drag themselves as far as the sea, the sacrifice has been propitious—the sick person will be cured or the dearly-cherished wish fulfilled. On the contrary, if the fowl dies at once under the knife, the genius invoked is displeased, and the whole thing has to be done over again. It need scarcely be said that the sable sorceress contrives to make a good many failures ere a half-killed fowl reaches the briny ocean, and that the abortive sacrifices are her perquisites.

Sometimes a sheep is sacrificed instead of a fowl, and on very grand occasions—that is to say, when the touters can beat up a sufficient number of sight-seers from the hotels in Algiers—a bullock is slaughtered. In this case, however, a buck negro officiates as sacrificing priest, and the bullock is allowed to expire on the sand without being expected to put out to sea, like Jupiter running away with Europa. There is a great deal of manoeuvring of the "twopence more, and up goes the donkey" order before the act is accomplished. The bull is either too sacred, or not sacred enough ; he has been smitten by the evil eye—*your* eye, it may be ; the priest has been warned in a dream not to slay him ; will you give twenty, fifteen, ten, five francs more to see him slain ? and so on in a *diminuendo*. Finally it is urged that " the police are coming," which is the most impudent lie of all ; the sacrificial bullock being actually provided at the cost and charges of a paternal government, which, under the erroneous but good-natured impression that the bestial and fraudulent mummeries of the Sebâ-Aïoun are really religious observances, generously makes the nigger sorcerers a periodical present of a bullock from the commissariat stores.

Now, won't this tempt you, lady and gentleman tourists, to come to Algeria! Think of

> "The priest who slew the slayer
> And shall himself be slain."

Think of the Bull-Sacrifice at the Seven Fountains—Flamens and augurs, and all within eighty hours' journey from Charing Cross. "The priest who slew the slayer" may be seen all alive and grinning, with an old gendarme's cocked-hat on his woolly cocoa-nut pate and a pair of cast-off dress boots with red morocco tops on his spindle-shanks. It would be unjust too severely to blame the French authorities for thus subsidising Obeah to the extent of a rather skinny bullock. For many years the British Government in India greased the wheels of the Car of Juggernaut at an enormous expense.

XIV.

OLD SPAIN IN AFRICA.

CCORDING to the historian El Bekri, the actual city of Oran dates from the year 297, when a certain Mohammed-ben-Abi-Aoun came over from Spain with a band of Andalusian fishermen, and patched up a sufficiently amicable alliance with the Beni-Mosguen, the original holders of the soil. The neighbouring tribes burnt and sacked the place, or were repulsed from it for four or five centuries or so—the only light thrown on the "dark ages" being that of internecine conflagrations—then, in 1086, the Almoravides conquered all this part of Africa. The Almoravides were succeeded by the Almohades, and these again by the Merinides; until, in the middle of the fifteenth century, there came to Oran a refugee from his revolted subjects, the famous Muley Mohammed, surnamed the Lop-sided, King of Granada.

At this period the historians declare Oran to have been, as the Yankees say, "quite a place." Elephants' teeth and ostrich feathers, tanned hides, gold-dust, negro slaves, and corn were the staple of exports, and made the Oranese very rich. They excelled also in the manufacture of rich stuffs and weapons of war. The Venetians, the Genoese, the Marseillais, and the Catalans came in great numbers to trade with them, bringing looking-glasses, silks and velvets, and hardware in exchange. Alvarez Gomez says that in 1437 there were six thousand houses in Oran, many splendid mosques, colleges as learned as those at Cordova and Seville, quays cumbered with merchandise, and the most sumptuous "stews" or baths in the world. Unfortunately, wealth seems to have brought luxury, luxury excess, and excess the most alarming depravity; since we find a holy man named Sidi-Mahomed-el-Haouari lifting up his voice in this epoch against the city, and crying out, "Oran, city of innumerable adulteries, the stranger shall enter into thy gates and abide there until the day of meeting and of dispersion;" by which is meant the day of judgment.

El-Haouari died in 1439, and, seventy years afterwards, his ominous prediction was fulfilled by the capture of Oran by the Spaniards. The expedition which subdued it was a sort of fragmentary tail-piece to the Crusades. In 1506, Ferdinand of Spain, Emmanuel of Portugal, and Harry of England entered into a compact to Christianise all heathendom by force of arms; but they soon fell out among themselves, and then Emmanuel and Ferdinand had to go to the assistance of his Holiness the Pope, who, not for the first time in history, had fallen out with the Eldest Son of the Church in France. An edifying spectacle: the mediæval Pontiff. He was either cursing Christendom all round, or blessing some prince with a view to persuade him to batter another prince's brains out.

But Cardinal Ximenes, the King-Cardinal of Spain, had set his heart upon a crusade of some kind, and persuaded Ferdinand to fit out an expedition to the African Main. The Spaniards knew little of the geography of the country, and contemplated a landing at the little town of Honein, on the frontiers of Morocco. Then they were told that Mers-el-Kebir was the richest point on the coast; for plunder, as well as proselytism, was part of Ximenes' plan. Then the Spanish treasury—likewise not for the first time in history—was found to be empty. But the Cardinal, in his religious and filibustering zeal, agreed with his sovereign to pay for the crusade out of his own pocket. Finally, Mers-el-Kebir was attacked and captured, and General Don Gonzales de Ayora wrote home, quite in the Spanish fashion, "We have conquered half Africa." And the Desert of Sahara, and the country of the Touaregs, and that great white patch upon the map, the Region of the Utterly Unknown! Oh, thou most wall-eyed Don!

Then occurred once more an abhorrent vacuum in the exchequer of the most Catholic King, but the indomitable Ximenes came to the rescue again. An army of fifteen thousand men sailed from Carthagena for Mers-el-Kebir. His Eminence himself accompanied the crusaders, performed high mass on the shore, and headed the troops, crucifix in hand. So many millions of the children of humanity have in all ages been smitten to death by those who arrogate to themselves a peculiar property in the symbol of our salvation, that I wonder it has never occurred to ingenious small-arms manufacturers to contrive crucifixes with spring-bayonets in the arms, or to cast cross-shaped rifle-bullets. They might hurt as sorely as conical ones.

The Spaniards marched upon Oran, and took it with but the loss of thirty men. The new era was at once inaugurated by the pitiless massacre of eight thousand Muslim prisoners. Public buildings and private houses were alike sacked, and the treasures accumulated in Oran by three centuries of industrious trade and half a century of piracy on the high seas were divided among the Christian officers and soldiers. The great filibuster X. was himself too highly placed and too proud to enrich himself by vulgar booty. He took nothing but a few Arabic manuscripts and rare objects, which he presented on his return to Spain, to the Cathedral of Toledo and the Convent of San Ildefonso at Madrid. Before Ximenes went away, however, he ordered all the fortifications to be rebuilt, and the Tribunal of the Holy Inquisition to be established.

The Spaniards kept possession of the place for two centuries; but in 1708 the Regency of Algiers, profiting by the distracted state of the Peninsula, in which the War of the Succession was then raging, sent Moustafa-bou-Chelar'em, Bey of Maskara, to besiege Oran. He besieged it accordingly; the city fell, and the Turkish janissaries ruled in the place of the captains-general of Philip V. But Oran was still to be a challenge cup. The Peace of Utrecht having been signed, the King of Spain began to make preparations for the recovery of Oran, and a few years afterwards wrested it from the Turks. The new lease of Spanish rule lasted from 1732 to 1790, when came the great earthquake and the

M

final evacuation by the Spaniards. The Turks, once more masters of the city, strove to rebuild it *à la Turque*—that is to say, in a pleasing intermixture of strong castles and blind alleys full of mud hovels; but this style of architecture was equally disgusting to the tasteful Moors and to the Spaniards who remained behind.

The Turks governed by means of a Bey, a Khralifa or Finance Minister, and two Aghas. The scheme of administration was of the simplest. The Bey ordered a certain sum to be raised by way of revenue. The Khralifa, with the assistance of the Aghas, proceeded to squeeze it out of the natives. He got it out of their backs, their stomachs, or the soles of their feet, to all which parts of the body the great persuader, the bastinado, was indifferently applied. He got it out of their fingers by means of thumbscrews and lighted matches, and out of their heads by the skilful super-position on their skulls of nightcaps of heated copper. When the money was raised the Bey took as much of it as he chose, and the Khralifa and the Aghas stole as much of it as they dared. The remainder was carried by the Khralifa to Algiers as tribute to the Dey. If the sum was not sufficient, his Highness caused the financier to be soundly beaten. Sometimes he had him bowstrung —as, according to Voltaire, Admiral Byng was shot, "pour encourager les autres." So that everything was very nice and comfortable.

The natives of the province of Oran are not at all grateful to the French for having put an end to this state of things. When have you found Orientals grateful to Europeans for having given them an " administration " in lieu of an out-and-out despotism? Perhaps the natives thought that an occasional dose of the bastinado assisted the circulation of the blood and helped to kill the fleas. It is certain that when a Bey or a Khralifa vexed them too sorely, some one managed to strangle him for the public good, and the new broom, or Bey, swept clean for awhile. In 1830, the French, not having any quarrel with the Government of Oran, were constrained for a period to let them alone. Then Marshal Clausel assigned the city to Sidi-Ahmed, Bey of Tunis, who was to pay to France an annual tribute of a million of francs. Sidi-Ahmed sent his Khralifa, Kheir Eddin, to Oran, but the natives would not obey him; the French Government refused to ratify the convention between the Marshal and the Bey of Tunis, . and in the end, almost in their own despite, the French had to annex the province. Among the French governors who have ruled here you may find the famous names of Delmichels, Létang, Lamoricière, Cavaignac, Pélissier, Montauban, Martimprey, and Walsin-Esterhazy.

There are no Turks in Oran now, and but very few Koulouilis or sons of Turks. The noise and bustle of the French system has been too much for these sleepy Orientals. They have gone to Tunis or to Morocco, where they can still enjoy the privilege of having their heads chopped off comfortably, or of dozing cross-legged, with their chibouks between their lips, on their carpets, and, as they count their beads, thanking Allah that they have escaped decapitation yet another day. Hope deferred maketh the heart sick; but, in certain phases of the human mind, postponed disaster maketh the heart glad. " Petit bonhomme vit encore ! " Mayor Bailly used to say, rubbing his hands, every morning that his name did *not* appear in the executioner's list. It appeared there at length, and they guillotined him; but to the last moment he who is holding on to life even by the skin of his teeth may comfort himself with the hope that the Deluge, or the Millennium, or an earthquake may come to avert his doom.

The Moors of Oran are very much fairer than their brethren at Algiers. You may even see red and auburn beards among them. This is explained on the ground that they are not Moors of Mauritania, or Morocco proper, but descendants of the Moriscoes of Spain, who fled there before the conquering arms of Ferdinand and Isabella. They rarely wear the domino-like burnouse of the Bedouin, the flowing white garment which conceals the whole costume, however rich it be, but go clad in a comfortable though somewhat sombre splendour. The well-to-do Moors at Oran all wear shoes and stockings, and, save that they are more given to corpulence and are less demonstrative in their manner, are nowadays, and to an unpractised eye, scarcely to be distinguished from the Jews.

These Israelites are certainly, next to the Arabs, the most interesting and the most picturesque of the inhabitants of Algeria, and to keep them in the background would be to suppress the most glowing tints of the picture which spreads itself before the tourist. At Oran, so far as costume goes, there are Jews and Jews. There are the Old Jews, who cannot forget days when the Turks forced them to wear a peculiar and degrading dress, and who from habit still adhere to the dark Levite robe, the black turban, and the loose trousers with stocking-feet attached thrust into yellow slippers, which is still the distinguishing garb of the Jews of Morocco. To these must be added the Jews of the interior, who come to Oran on business and who wear the haik or over-burnouse, but with a bandage of camel's hair dyed black round the head. To these again must be added the affluent Hebrew merchants, bankers, and shopkeepers, who adopt the Moorish dress in all its details, save that they are rather partial on the Sabbath to shoes with heels and of patent leather. Their turbans are of the whitest and amplest, and curiously crimped in diagonal lines to the folds. Finally, there are the young Jews, who of late years have shown a predilection for the European style of dress.

I had the advantage of the society of one of these young gentlemen for three days and a half in a diligence, and it was very amusing to mark the supreme contempt with which he was regarded by two other Jews in the diligence, respectable old parties with full beards, enormous turbans, voluminous sashes, and baggy knickerbockers. This young dandy was evidently very ill at ease in his new clothes. He had a tall shiny hat, which was always tumbling off; he had shaved his chin, and preserved only a tiny moustache, and he was continually putting his hand to his lips to make sure that he had not swallowed it; he evidently did not know what to do with his legs, which were imprisoned in the newest Parisian pantaloons of the most violent stripe. Watching the two elders, with their handsome caftans of purple cloth with sugar-loaf buttons of gold, their rich sashes and roomy nether garments, I could not help thinking of the story of the old Turk at Cairo, who, passing a European exquisite lounging from Shepherd's Hotel, plucked his little boy by the wrist, and said, "My son, if you do not obey the commands of Allah and the Prophet, you will come some day to look *like that*."

I am not treading, I hope, on anybody's toes by hinting that in an Eastern country my young Hebrew friend would have acted wisely in sticking to the Eastern garb. The French have had the common sense to acknowledge its utility in this climate by adopting the old Janissary dress into the uniform of their Zouaves and Spahis. Even the European civilian wears the caban, or short white Algerian jerkin, the veil for the head and neck or nuquière, and the roomiest of shoes in lieu of tight boots. The Jews, moreover, are foolish to pine over the tailor's goose fripperies of Paris, for the Eastern costume becomes them admirably. They, every tourist must have remarked, are the handsomest people, both in face and figure, in all Algeria; tall and muscular, and shapely in form, with regular Roman features; with beards, black, glossy, and flowing, and with complexions not sallow as the town Arabs, or dusky red like the Bedouins, but clear and fair. As a rule they are pale—probably from incessant smoking; for the women, who are comely, but not nearly so handsome as the men, are ruddy to sanguineousness. I can conscientiously say that, out of that regiment of our Horse Guards who are said to be recruited exclusively from a Dacio-Roman colony settled since the year One in the county of Durham, I have never seen finer men than the Algerine Jews. Their children are exquisitely beautiful, but, in the majority of cases, of Saxon fairness. Their hair darkens as they age.

Indeed, the striking comeliness of the Hebrew community in Algeria presents more than one curious ethnological problem. One of the surest effects of slavery—so, at least, it has been usually assumed—is the degradation of the physical as well as the moral status of its victims. In Poland and Lithuania they will tell you that the abject appearance of the dreadful Israelites—who hang about the posting-houses and entreat you to buy tea,

tobacco, almanacs, and even brandy—is due to the miserable
social obloquy which for centuries has been their lot. Whence
arises another problem: Why do they swarm most densely in the
countries where they are most scandalously treated? In Constantinople, where they have always been reviled and spit upon,
they have always abounded ; whereas in the United States, where
they have never laboured under any civil disabilities, they are
rarely to be found.

But the Jews of Algeria, it is certain, show no signs of having
been either morally or physically degraded by the long ordeal of
contumely and maltreatment they have undergone at the hands
of the Turks — the rudest, the most bigoted, and the most
intolerant of all the Mahometan races. Indeed, the Jews make
no very grievous complaints of hardships inflicted on them by the
Moors. There is much even now in the sedentary Moors of
Africa to remind the student of what he has read of the mild,
polished, learned, and ingenious Moriscoes of Spain ; and there
are many old Spaniards who maintain that the Moors and Jews
are substantially of the same stock—that they are brothers in
blood, though not in creed, thus bearing out Mr. Disraeli's idea
of the Mosaic Arab. When Granada fell, and the Arab dominion
in Spain was destroyed by Ferdinand and Isabella, Moors and
Jews were involved in a common ruin, and shared in many
instances a common exile. They lived without any serious moles-
tation from their Mahometan neighbours on the African littoral
for many years ; but it was when the Turks subjugated the
country that their sufferings began. It was the children of
Osman, and the ruffianly soldadoes of the Porte, the cruel and
fanatical Jenitcheri or Janissaries, who were their real persecutors.

They became the Djifa-ben-Djifa—carrion and the sons of
carrion. They were confined to a particular quarter, like the
Ghetto at Rome, which is now represented at Oran by the suburb
called La Blanca. At six o'clock at night they were bound to be
indoors. If they wished to remain abroad after sunset, they were
compelled to ask permission of the police, who gave them a strip
of bull's-hide, by which they might be known if met by the patrol

going the rounds. If the night was dark, instead of carrying a lantern like the Moors, the unhappy Israelites were expected to carry a lighted candle, which the merest puff of wind might extinguish. Every time they passed the Kasba, or citadel, they were required to fall on their knees, and then withdraw rapidly, the head bent and averted. They were mercilessly beaten for the slightest offence, and—as there was until the other day in Morocco—a female officer of justice was appointed, whose special duty it was to flog Jewesses. They were bound to wait with their pitchers at the fountain for the last turn—that is, until every blackguard little Arab boy or smutty negress had filled his or her jar. If a Jew insulted a Mussulman, he was put to death. If a Mussulman killed a Jew, he only paid a certain fine ; if a Janissary slew one, he was only mulct in a pound and a half of tobacco. For offences which in a Turk would have been visited only with the bastinado the Jew was burnt alive. These oppressed people could not leave the Regency without giving enormous bail for their return. In addition to the innumerable extortions practised on them on the slightest pretext, they were bound to pay a heavy weekly tribute, which every Thursday evening, before sunset, the chief or king of the Jews—for these bondmen were allowed a king—bore himself to the Kasba. And, finally, if driven to desperation by these tortures, the Jew wished to apostatise, he was obliged as a preliminary measure, and with a fiendish refinement of insult, to turn Christian before he could become a Mussulman. I have dwelt on these facts with thus much particularity for the reason that the Jews of Morocco—in whose cause Sir Moses Montefiore so nobly exerted himself—were, in the year 1865, very little better off than their brethren in Algeria in the days of the Janissaries.

And yet, amid all this intolerable misery, degradation, and oppression, the Algerian Jews throve. That they gathered wealth is no matter for wonder ; they have enriched themselves in all countries. It is, however, their having kept their good looks and gallant bearing that excites astonishment. Their vitality under so many cruel wrongs must have been prodigious. We have been

too much accustomed in Europe to study only the Shylock type
of the Jew—the sallow, cowering, browbeaten Hebrew, in his
dingy gabardine and badge of sufferance.   Go to Algeria—and I
think every traveller will bear me out—and you will see the
robust and bellicose-looking Jew, as you read of him in the
Book of Maccabees, the Jew of martial mien and haughty port ;
aye, and the Jewess, tall and stern, and well-knit as she who slew
Holofernes in the night.

Alignation and Cæsareanism and earthquakes and conquest
and reconquests notwithstanding, Oran is still much more a
Spanish than a French town.   Two hundred and fifty years of
Castilian rule are not so easily shaken off.   The Château Neuf
and the new or French town rise in an amphitheatre to the east
of the bay, and are encroaching more and more every day on the
Moorish and Jewish sections ; but the lower town is half Spanish
and half Maltese.   The most indelible traces of the Spanish occupation are, however, in the long lines of bristling forts with which
the town is girt about, and which make of Oran a kind of
Mediterranean Cronstadt.   One French writer, struck with the
solidity of all these bastions, ravelins, curtains, redoubts, and
demilunes—a solidity which has defied earthquakes and can-
nonadings without number—qualifies them as "an orgie of
masonry, a debouch of stone and lime."   They were all built,
the histories say, by convicts.   The Spaniards were capital task-
masters : witness the colossal paved roads they made in Mexico,
and which forty years of civil war have been powerless to destroy.
Nor do their public works, at Oran at least, seem to have been
very expensive, for at the eastern end of the Kasba may still be
read this remarkable inscription :

EN EL ANO 1589

SIN COSTAR A SO MAGESTAD

MAS QUE EL VALOR DE LAS MADERAS

HIZO ESTA OBRA

DON PEDRO DE PADILLA SO CAPITAN GENERAL

Y JUSTICIA MAYOR DE ESTAS PLAZAS

POR SO DILIGENCIA Y BUENOS MEDIOS.

"In the year of our Lord 1589, Don Pedro de Padilla, Captain-

General and Grand Justiciary of these parts, caused this edifice to be constructed, without any other expense to his Majesty than the cost of the wood employed for scaffolding." The convicts got the stone from the quarries, and then they built the Kasba. This inscription is, to say the least, edifying. Only fancy an analogous one on the breakwater at Cherbourg, or on a draw-bridge at Portsmouth!

Oran was for years the great bagnio or penitentiary of Spain. Thither the corregidors sent Guzman de Alfarache and Lazarillo de Tormes, rogues both, to mind their morals and build forts. And yet, according to some accounts, the rascals had not such a bad time of it in Africa. The Kasba must have taken a good many years to build, or the convicts must have persuaded the Arabs to do their work for them. There was a garrison of seven thousand men, and about an equal number of puridarios, or felons. Of Spanish inhabitants there were about three thousand. Between the soldiers, the convicts, and the townspeople there reigned the most charming *entente cordiale*. The soldiers let the thieves do pretty well as they liked, and when there was a captain-general who turned rusty and talked of the cat-o'-nine-tails, the rogues took themselves off gaily to Morocco, where to this day there are whole towns peopled by their descendants.

The Spanish Government were in the habit of banishing to Oran such hidalgos and caballeros as were in disgrace for political and other reasons. Many of these exiles had plenty of money, and Oran became one of the most jovial, most rollicking, and wickedest places it is possible to imagine. It gained the sou-briquet of " La Corte Chica "—the Little Court. Night and day there was nothing but balls, collations, and festivities, wine-quaffing, cigarette-smoking, guitar-strumming, bull-baiting, love-making, and cock-fighting. It was a "presidario" of pleasure ; but every now and then the Arabs or the Turks would come thundering at the gates, and there would be a bloody fight by way of diversion,

XV.

KING PIPPIN'S PALACE.

DEEPLY regret that it should be my duty to sound the alarm, but I am constrained to state my fears that there is something the matter with our old and, generally, esteemed friend the Dwarf. I don't meet him in society, that is to say, at the fairs, as I was wont to do ; and although I do not overlook the fact that I have ceased to attend fairs, and that indeed there are very few fairs of the old kind left to frequent, it is difficult to avoid the unpleasant conviction that dwarfs as a race are dying out. Very recently, in his strange, eloquent romance, " L'Homme qui rit," M. Victor Hugo has told us that the pigmy, preferably monstrous and deformed, whose pictured semblance is to be found in so many works of the old Italian and German masters, was to most intents and purposes a manufactured article.

That mysterious association of the " Comprachicos," of whom M. Hugo has told us so many strange things, pursued among their varied branches of industry the art of fabricating hunch-backed, abdominous, hydrocephalous, and spindle-shanked dwarfs for the European market : the purchasers being the princes, potentates, and wealthy nobles of the Continent. The Comprachicos would seem to have borrowed the mystery of dwarf-making from the Chinese, who had an agreeable way of putting a young child into a pot of arbitrary form from which the top and bottom had been knocked out, and in the sides of which were two holes through which the juvenile patient's arms protruded. The merry consequence was that young master's body, if he did not die during the process, grew to be of the shape of the pot; and so far as the torso went, the order of amateurs for a spherical dwarf, or an oval dwarf, or a hexagonal dwarf, or a dwarf with knobs on his chest or an "egg-and-tongue" pattern on his shoulders, could be executed with promptitude and dispatch.*

But we have another informant, of perhaps greater weight and authority, who has told us in what manner dwarfs, and bandy and rickety and crooked-spined children, can be manufactured without the aid either of the Comprachicos or of the Chinese potters. The learned and amiable Cheselden has dwelt minutely in his "Anatomy" on the wickedly cruel and barbarous folly which marked the system of nursing babies in his time, and has shown how the practice of tightly swaddling and unskilfully carrying infants was calculated to cripple and deform their limbs and to stunt their growth. We have grown wonderfully wiser since Cheselden's time, although I have heard some cynics mutter that the custom of growing children in pipkins could not have been more detrimental to health or to the symmetry of the human form than is the modern fashion of tight-lacing.

Be all this as it may, I still hold that the dwarf — well, the kind of dwarf who can be seen for a penny at a fair—continues, as the French say, "to make himself desired." Surely his falling

* Setting M. Hugo's wild myth of the Comprachicos entirely on one side, most students of the social history of England are aware that the custom of kidnapping children (generally to be sold as slaves in the West Indies or the American plantations) was frightfully prevalent in this country in the seventeenth and during the early part of the eighteenth century, and that Bristol was dishonourably distinguished as the port whence the greater number of the hapless victims were dispatched beyond sea. And it is a very curious circumstance, which appears to have been overlooked by Lord Macaulay in his notice of Jeffries, that the infamous judge, shortly before the Bloody Assize, went down to Bristol and delivered to the grand jury at the assizes a most eloquent and indignant charge, overflowing with sentiments of humanity, bearing on the practice of kidnapping children for the plantations—a practice which his lordship roundly accused the Corporation of Bristol of actively aiding and abetting for their own advantage and gain. Jeffries' charge is preserved in the library of the British Museum, and is as edifying to read as the sentimental ballad, "What is Love?" by Mr. Thomas Paine, or as would be an Essay upon Cruelty to Animals, with proposals for the suppression thereof, by the late Emperor Nero.

off must be due to the surcease of the manufacture. Old manufactured dwarfs are as difficult to light upon as Mortlake tapestry
or Chelsea china, simply, I suppose, because tapestry is no longer
woven at Mortlake, and Chelsea produces no more porcelain ware.
To an amateur of dwarfs it is positively distressing to read the
numerous detailed accounts which the historians have left us of
bygone troglodytes. Passing by such world-famous manikins as
Sir Jeffery Hudson and Count Borulawski, where can one hope in
this degenerate age to light on a Madame Teresia, better known
by the designation of the Corsican Fairy, who came to London in
1773, being then thirty years of age, thirty-four inches high,
and weighing twenty-six pounds? "She possessed much
vivacity and spirit, could speak Italian and French with
fluency, and gave the most inquisitive mind an agreeable
entertainment."

England has produced a rival to Madame Teresia in Miss
Anne Shepherd, who was three feet ten inches in height, and
was married, in Charles the First's time, to Richard Gibson, Esq.,
page of the backstairs to his majesty, and a distinguished
miniature painter. Mr. Gibson was just forty-six inches high,
and he and his bride were painted "in whole length" by Sir
Peter Lely. The little couple are said to have had nine children,
who all attained the usual standard of mankind; and three of
the boys, according to the chronicles of the backstairs, enlisted
in the Life Guards.

But what are even your Hudsons and your Gibsons, your
Corsican Fairies and your Anne Shepherds, to the dwarfs of
antiquity? Where am I to look for a parallel to the homunculus
who flourished in Egypt in the time of the Emperor Theodosius,
and who was so small of body that he resembled a partridge, yet
had all the functions of a man and would sing tunably? Mark
Antony is said to have owned a dwarf called Sisyphus who was
not of the full height of two feet, and was yet of a lively wit.
Had this Sisyphus been doomed to roll a stone it must surely have
been no bigger than a schoolboy's marble. Ravisius—who was
Ravisius?—narrates that Augustus Cæsar exhibited in his plays

one Lucius, a young man born of honest parents, who was twenty-three inches high, and weighed seventeen pounds, yet had he a strong voice. In the time of Jamblichus, also, lived Alypius of Alexandria, a most excellent logician and a famous philosopher, but so small in body that he hardly exceeded a cubit, or one foot five inches and a half in height.

Finally, Carden tells us—but who believes Carden ?—that he saw a man of full age in Italy not above a cubit high, and who was carried about in a parrot's cage. " This," remarks Wanley, in his " Wonders of the Little World," " would have passed my belief had I not been told by a gentleman of a clear reputation that he saw a man at Sienna about two years since not exceeding the same stature. A Frenchman he was, of the county of Limo-sin, with a formal beard, who was likewise shown in a cage for money, at the end whereof was a little hatch into which he retired, and when the assembly was full came forth and played on an instrument." The very thing we have all seen at the fairs, sub-stituting the simulacrum of a three-storied house for a cage, and not forgetting the modern improvements of the diminutive inmate ringing a bell and firing a pistol out of the first-floor window !

And after banqueting on these bygone dwarfs, who were scholars and gentlemen as well as monstrosities—for was not Alypius, cited above, a famous logician and philosopher ? and did not Richard Gibson, Esq., teach Queen Anne the art of drawing, and proceed on a special mission to Holland to impart artistic instruction to the Princess of Orange ?—after dwelling on the dwarfs who formed part of the retinue of William of Normandy when he invaded England, and who held the bridle of the Emperor Otho's horse ; after remembering the dwarfs whom Dominichino and Rafaelle, Velasquez and Paul Veronese have introduced in their pictures ; after this rich enjoyment of dwarfish record I am thrown back on General Tom Thumb. I grant the General and the Commodore and their ladykind a decent meed of acknowledgment. I confess them calm, self-possessed, well-bred, and innocuous ; but I have no heart to attend their " levées." Nutt, in the caricature of a naval

uniform, does not speak to my heart ; I have no ambition to see
Thumb travestied as the late Emperor Napoleon—that conqueror
could on occasion cause himself to appear even smaller than
Thumb—nor am I desirous of purchasing photographic *cartes de
visite* of Minnie Warren. *My* dwarf is the gorgeously attired
little pagod of the middle ages ; the dwarf who pops out of a
pie at a court banquet ; the dwarf who runs between the court-
jester's legs and trips him up ; the dwarf of the king of Brobdingnag, who is jealous of Gulliver, and souses his rival in a bowl
of cream, and gets soundly whipped for his pains. Or, in default
of this pigmy, give me back the dwarf of my youth in his sham
three-storied house with his tinkling bell and sounding pistol.

It is not to be, I presume. These many years past I have
moodily disbursed in divers parts of the world sundry francs, lire,
guilders, florins, thalers, reals, dollars, piastres, and marks-banco
for the sight of dwarfs ; but they (Thumb and his company
included) have failed to come up to my standard of dwarfish
excellence. Did you ever meet with anything or anybody that
could come up to that same standard ? Man never is, but always
to be blest ; still, although my dreams of dwarfs have not as yet
been fully realised, I have been able to enjoy the next best thing to
fulfilment. I call to mind perhaps the wonderfullest dwarf's house
existing on the surface of this crazy globe. It is a house in the
construction and the furniture of which many thousands of
pounds were expended, and it was built by a king for his son.
It is for this reason that I have called the diminutive mansion
"The Palace of King Pippin."

King Pippin's Palace is in Spain, and has been shamefully
neglected by English tourists in that interesting country. For
my part, I think that it would be a great advantage to picturesque
literature if the Alhambra and the Alcazar, the Bay of Cadiz and
the Rock of Gibraltar, the Sierra Morena and the Mezquita of
Cordova, the Cathedral of Burgos and the Bridge of Toledo,
could be eliminated altogether from Spanish topography. By
these means travellers in Spain would have a little more leisure to
attend to a number of *cosas de España* which are at present

passed by almost without notice. Among them is this incomparable dwarf's house of mine. You will observe that I have excluded the Escorial from the catalogue of places which English sight-seers in the Peninsula might do well for a time to forget. The Real Monasterio de San Lorenzo must needs be visited, for King Pippin's Palace is a dependency of that extraordinary pile.

Few tourists have the courage to admit, in print at least, that this palace-monastery or monastery-palace of the Escorial is a gigantic bore. When it was my lot to visit it my weariness began even before I had entered its halls ; for in the railway carriage which conveyed our party from Madrid to the "Gridiron station" there was a fidgety little Andalusian, a maker of guitar-strings, I think he was, at Utrera, who was continually rebounding on the cushions like a parched pea in a fire-shovel, and crying out to us, "El edificio, caballeros, donde está el edificio ?" It was his first visit to the northern provinces of his native country, and he was burning to see the *edificio*. To him evidently there was but one edifice in the world, and that was the Escorial. When at last he caught sight of its sullen façades, its stunted dome and blue-slate roofs, the little Andalusian fell into a kind of ecstasy, and protruded so much of his body out of the carriage-window that I expected him every moment to disappear altogether. To my surprise, however, when the train drew up at the station he did not alight, but murmuring the conventional "Pues, señores, echemos un cigarito," "Well, gentlemen, let us make a little cigar," calmly rolled up a tube of paper with tobacco, lit it, and adding, "Vamos al Norte," subsided into sleep, and, the train aiding, pursued his journey to the Pyrenees, or Paris, or the North Pole, or wheresoever else he was bound. He was clearly a philosopher. He had seen *el edificio* from afar off. Was not that enough ? I daresay when he went back to Utrera he talked guide-book by the page to his friends, and minutely described all the marvels of the interior of the palace. I rarely think of the little Andalusian without recalling Sheridan's remark to his son Tom about the coal-pits : " Can't you *say* you've been down ? "

The "edifice" itself is really and without exaggeration a bore.

The good pictures have all been taken away to swell the attrác-
tions of the Real Museo at Madrid ; the jolly monks have been
driven out and replaced by a few meagre, atrabilious-looking,
shovel-hatted seminarists (even these, since the last political earthquake in Spain, may have disappeared) ; and it is with extreme
difficulty that you can persuade the custodes to show you the
embroidered vestments in the sacristy or the illuminated manuscripts in the library. The guardians of every public- building
in Spain have a settled conviction that all foreign travellers are
Frenchmen, who, following the notable example of Marshals Soult
and Victor in the Peninsular War, are bent on stealing something.
Moreover, the inspection of embroidered copes, dalmatics, and
chasubles soon palls on sight-seers who are not crazy on the
subject of Ritualism ; and as for being trotted through a vast
library when you have no time to read the books, all I can say is
that in this respect I prefer a bookstall in Gray's Inn Lane, with
free access to the " twopenny box," to the library of the Escorial,
to the Bibliothèque (ex-)Impériale, the Bodleian, Sion College,
and the library of St. Mark to boot.

The exterior of the Escorial, again, is absolutely hideous ; its
grim granite walls, pierced with innumerable eyelet-holes, with
green shutters, remind the spectator of the Wellington Barracks,
Colney Hatch Lunatic Asylum, and the Great Northern Hotel at
King's Cross. The internal decorations principally consist of
huge, sprawling, wall-and-ceiling frescoes by Luca Giordano,
surnamed "Luca fa Presto," or Luke in a Hurry. This Luke
the Labourer has stuck innumerable saints, seraphs, and other
celestial personages upon the plaster. He executed his apotheoses
by the yard, for which he was paid according to a fixed tariff, a
reduction, I suppose, being made for clouds ; and the result of his
work is about as interesting as that of Sir James Thornhill in the
Painted Hall of Greenwich Hospital. Almost an entire day must
be spent if you wish to see the Escorial thoroughly, and you grow
at last fretful and peevish well-nigh to distraction at the jargon
of the guides, with their monotonous statistics of the eleven
thousand windows of the place, the two thousand and two feet of

its area, the sixty-three fountains, the twelve cloisters, the sixteen *patios* or courtyards, the eighty staircases, and so forth.

As for the relics preserved of that nasty old man Philip the Second, his greasy hat, his walking-stick, his shabby elbow-chair, the board he used to rest his gouty leg on, they never moved me. There is something beautifully and pathetically interesting in the minutest trifle which remains to remind us of Mary Queen of Scots. Did you ever see her watch, in the shape of a death's-head, the works in the brain-pan, and the dial enamelled on the base of the jaw? But who would care about a personal memento of Bloody Queen Mary? She was our countrywoman, but most of us wish to forget her bad individuality utterly. Should we care anything more about her Spanish husband?

To complete the lugubrious impressions which gather round you in this museum of cruelty, superstition, and madness, you are taken to an appalling sepulchre underground: a circular vault, called, absurdly enough, the "Pantheon," where on ranges of marble shelves are sarcophagi containing the ashes of all the kings and queens who have afflicted Spain since the time of Charles the Fifth. The bonehouse is rendered all the more hideous by the fact of its being ornamented in the most garishly theatrical manner with porphyry and verde antique, with green and yellow jasper, with bronze gilt bas-reliefs and carvings in variegated marble, and other gimcracks. There is an old English locution which laughs at the man who would put a brass knocker on a pigsty-door. Is such an architect worthier of ridicule than he who paints and gilds and tricks-up a charnel-house to the similitude of a play-house? As, with a guttering wax-taper in your hand, you ascend the staircase leading from the Pantheon into daylight and the world again, your guide whispers to you that to the right is another and ghastlier Golgotha, where the junior scions of Spanish royalty are buried, or rather where their coffins lie huddled together pell-mell. The polite name for this place, which might excite the indignation of "graveyard" Walker (he put a stop to intramural interments in England, and got no thanks for his pains) is the "Pantheon of the Infantes." The

N

common people call it, with much more brevity and infinitely more eloquence, *El Pudridero*, the "rotting-place." The best guide-book you can take with you to this portion of the Escorial is Jeremy Taylor's sermon on death.

Once out of the Escorial, "Luke's iron crown"—I mean the crown of Luca fa Presto's ponderous heroes—is at once removed from your brow, on which it has been pressing with the deadest of weights. Once rid of the Pantheon and the stone staircases and the slimy cloisters, and you feel inclined to chirrup, almost. The gardens are handsome, although shockingly out of repair ; but bleak as is the site, swept by the almost ceaseless mountain blasts of the Guadarrama range, it is something to be rid of Luca fa Presto, and Philip the Second, and St. Lawrence and his gridiron, and all their gloomy company. You breathe again ; and down in the village yonder there is a not bad inn called the Biscaina, where they cook very decent omelettes and where the wine is drinkable. But before you think of dining you must see King Pippin's Palace.

This is the "Casita del Principe de abajo," the "little house of the prince on the heights," and was built by Juan de Villa-nueva for Charles the Fourth, when heir-apparent. The only circumstances, perhaps, under which a king of Spain can be contemplated with complacency are those of childhood. In Madrid I used always to have a sneaking kindness for the infantes and infantas—"los niños de España"—who with their nurses and governesses, and their escort of dragoons and lancers, used to be driven every afternoon, in their gilt coaches drawn by fat mules, through the Puerta del Sol to the Retiro. The guard at the Palace of the Gobernacion would turn out, the trumpets would be flourished bravely as "los niños" went by.

Poor little urchins ! In the pictures of Don Diego Velas-quez, the "niños," in their little ruffs and kirtles and farthin-gales, or their little starched doublets and trunk-hose, with their chubby peachy cheeks, their ruddy lips and great melting black eyes, look irresistibly fascinating. Ah ! my infantes and infantas of Don Diego, why did you not remain for aye at the toddlekins' stage? why did you grow up to be tyrants and madmen and bigots and imbeciles, and no better than you should have been? This Carlos the Fourth, for instance, for whom King Pippin's Palace was built, made an exceedingly bad end of it. He was the king who was led by the nose by a worthless wife, and a more worthless favourite, Godoy, who was called "Prince of the Peace," and who lived to be quite forgotten and to die in a garret in Paris. Carlos the Fourth was the idiot who allowed Napoleon to kidnap him. He was the father of the execrable Ferdinand the Seventh, the betrayer of his country, the restorer of the Inquisition, and the embroiderer of petticoats for the Virgin.

King, or rather Prince Pippin, Charles the Third's son, is represented in a very curious style of portraiture in one of the apartments of the Escorial itself, a suite fitted up by his father in anti-monastic style, that is to say, in the worst kind of Louis Quinze rococo. The king employed the famous Goya to make a series of designs to be afterwards woven on a large scale in tapestry; and Goya consequently produced some cartoons which, with their reproductions in loom-work, may be regarded as the burlesque antipodes to the immortal patterns which Rafaelle set the weavers of Arras. In one of the Goya hangings you see the juvenile members of the royal family at their sports, attended by a select number of young scions of the *sangre azul.* .At what do you think they are playing? at *bull-fighting :* a game very popular among the blackguard little street-boys of Madrid to this day. One boy plays *Bos.* He has merely to pop a cloth over his head, holding two sticks passing through holes in the cloth at obtuse angles to his head, to represent the horns of the animal. The "picadores" are children pickaback, who with canes for lances tilt at the bull. The "chulos" trail their jackets, the "bandarilleros" fling wreathed hoopsticks for darts, in admirable caricature of the real bloodthirsty game you see in the bull-ring. Prince Pippin of course is the "matador," the slayer. He stands alone, superb and magnanimous, intrepidity in his mien, fire in his eye, and a real little Toledo rapier in his hand. Will the bull dare to run at the heir-apparent of the throne of Spain and the Indies? *Quien sabe?* Train up a child in the way he should go; and a youth of bull-fighting is a fit preparative for a manhood of cruelty and an old age of bigoted superstition.

It is somewhat difficult to give an idea of the precise size of Pippin's Palace. Mr. Ford, who speaks of the entire structure with ineffable contempt, says that it is "just too small to live in, and too large to wear on a watch-chain;" but I maintain that the Casita del Principe is quite big enough to be the country residence of Thumb, or Nutt, or Miss Warren, or Gibson, or Hudson, or Anne Shepherd, or Madame Teresia, or Wybrand Lolkes the Dutch dwarf; a wonderful little fellow with a head like a dolphin's, no perceptible trunk, and two little spindle-shanks like the legs of a skeleton clock. There should properly be a statue cast from the Manneken at Brussels in the vestibule of the Casita; but, if I recollect aright, the only object of sculpture in the hall is a life-size cast of the Apollo Belvedere, whose head of course touches the palatial ceiling. Could that inanimate effigy stand on tiptoe, he would assuredly send the first floor flying; and could he perform but one vertical leap, he would have the roof off the palace in the twinkling of a bedpost. There is a tiny grand staircase, which (from dolorous experience) I know to be somewhat of a tight fit for a stout tourist; and to increase the exquisite grotesqueness of the whole affair, the walls are panelled in green and yellow jasper and porphyry, and there are verde-antique columns and scagliola pilasters, and bas-reliefs in gilt bronze on every side, just as there are in the horrible tomb-house hard by. There are dozens of rooms in King Pippin's Palace: dining-rooms, audience-chambers, council-chambers, bedrooms, libraries, ante-chambers, boudoirs, guard-rooms, and ball-rooms, the dimensions of which vary between those of so many store-cupboards and so many mid-shipmen's sea-chests.

But the pearl, the cream, the consummation of the crack-brained joke is that the furniture does not in any way harmonise with the proportions of the building. The house is a baby one, but the furniture is grown up. The chairs and tables are suited for the accommodation of adults of full growth. The walls are hung with life-size portraits of the Spanish Bourbons. The busts, statuettes, French clocks, chandeliers, china gimcracks, and ivory baubles are precisely such as you might see in a palace inhabited by grown-up kings and princes. The whole place is a pippin into which a crazy king has endeavoured to cram the contents of a pumpkin ; and but for the high sense I entertain of the obligations of decorum, and the indelicacy of wounding the susceptibilities of foreigners, I might, had the proper appliances been at hand, have wound up my inspection of the Palace of King Pippin by ringing a shrill peal on a hand-bell, or firing a pistol out of the first-floor window.

XVI.

Form-Sickness.

HERE is a mysterious disease which the doctors find difficult of diagnosis, and from which foreign conscripts are said to suffer. They call it nostalgia, or *le mal du pays*—in plainer English, home-sickness. We have all read how the band-masters of the Swiss regiments in the French service were forbidden to play the "Ranz des Vaches," lest the pensive children of the mountains, inspired by the national melody, should run home too quickly to their cows— that is to say, desert. That dogs will pine and fret to death for love of the masters they have lost is an ascertained fact; and I have been told that the intelligent and graceful animal, the South American llama, if you beat, or overload, or even insult him, will, after one glance of tearful reproach from his fine eyes and one meek wail of expostulation, literally lay himself down and die. Hence the legend that the bât-men, ere they load a llama, cover his head with a poncho, or a grego, or other drapery, in order that his susceptibilities may not be wounded by a sight of the burden he is to endure: a pretty conceit vilely transposed into English in a story about a cab-horse whose eyes were bandaged by his driver lest he should be ashamed of the shabbiness of the fare who paid but sixpence for less than a mile's drive. I was never south of the Isthmus, and never saw a llama save in connection with an overcoat on a cheap tailor's show-card; but I am given to understand that what I have related is strictly true.

If the lower animals, then, be subject to nostalgia, and if they be as easily killed by moral as by physical ailments, why should humanity be made of sterner stuff? After all there may be such things as broken hearts. With regard to home-sickness, however, I hold that generally that malady is caused less by absence from home than by the deprivations of the comforts and enjoyments which home affords. Scotchmen and Irishmen are to be found all over the world, and get on pretty well wherever they are ; but a Scot without porridge to sup, or an Irishman without butter-milk to drink at breakfast, is always more or less miserable. The Englishman, accustomed to command, to compel, and to trample difficulties under his feet, carries his home-divinities with him, and has no sooner set up his tent in Kedar than he establishes one sup-plementary booth for making up prescriptions in accordance with the ritual of the London Pharmacopœia, another for the sale of pickles, pale ale, and green tea, and a third for the circulation of tracts intended to convert the foreigners among whom he is to abide.

He suffers less perhaps from home-sickness than any other wanderer on the face of the earth, since he sternly refuses to look upon his retirement from his own country as anything but a temporary exile ; he demands incessant postal communication with home, or he will fill the English newspapers with the most vehement complaints ; he will often—through the same news-papers—carry on controversies, political or religious, with adver-saries ten thousand miles away ; and after an absence from England of twenty years, he will suddenly turn up at a railway meeting, or in the chair at a public dinner ; bully the board ; move the previous question ; or, in proposing the toast of the evening, quote the statistics of the Cow-cross Infirmary for Calves, as though he had never been out of Middlesex. In short, he no more actually expatriates himself than does an *attaché* to an English embassy abroad, who packs up Pall Mall in his portmanteau, parts his hair down the middle, and carries a slender umbrella—never under any circumstances unfurled—in the streets of Teheran.

But are you aware that there is another form of nostalgia which afflicts only Europeans, and, so far as I know, is felt only in one part of the world ? Its symptoms have not hitherto been described, and I may christen it Form-sickness. I should wish to have Mr. Ruskin, Mr. Tom Taylor, and Mr. Beresford Hope on the medical board to which I submitted my views on this disease, for it is one architecturally and æsthetically occult. Form-sickness begins to attack you after you have resided some time—say a couple of months—in the United States of America. Its attacks are more acutely felt in the North than in the South; for in the last-named parts of the Union there are fig and orange trees, and wild jungles and cane brake—some of the elements of FORM, in fact. It is the monotony of Form, and its deficiencies in certain conditions—that is to say, curvature, irregularity, and light and shade—that make you sick in the North. I believe that half the discomfort and the uneasiness which many educated Englishmen experience from a protracted residence in the States springs from the outrage offered to their eye in the shape of perpetual flat surfaces, straight vistas, and violent contrasts of colour.

There are no middle tints in an American landscape. In winter, it is white and blue; in spring, blue and green; in summer, blue and brown; in autumn, all the colours of the rainbow, but without a single neutral tint. The magnificent October hues of the foliage on the Hudson and in Vermont simply dazzle and confound you. You would give the world for an instant of repose—for a gray tower, a broken wall, a morsel of dun thatch. The immensity of the area of vision is too much for a single spectator. Don't you remember how Banvard's gigantic panorama of the Mississippi used to make us first wonder and then yawn? Banvard is everywhere in the States; and so enormous is the scale of the scenery in this colossal theatre, that the sparse *dramatis personæ* are all but invisible.

An English landscape painter would scarcely dream of producing a picture, even of cabinet size, without a group of peasants, or children, or a cow or two, or a horse, or at least a flock of geese, in some part of the work. You shall hardly look half a dozen times out of the window of a carriage of an express train in England, without seeing something that is Alive. In America, the desolation of Emptiness pervades even

the longest settled and the most thickly populated States.
How should it be otherwise? How should you wonder at it
when, as in a score of instances, not more people than inhabit
Hertfordshire are scattered over a territory as large as France?
One of the first things that struck me when I saw the admirable works of the American landscape painters—of such men
as Church and Kensett, Bierstadt and Hart—was the absence
of animal life from their scenes. They seemed to have been
making sketches of the earth before the birth of Adam.

This vacuous vastness is one of the provocatives of Form-
sickness. To the European, and especially to the Englishman,
a country without plenty of people, pigs, poultry, haystacks,
barns, and cottages, is as intolerable as the stage of the Grand
Opera would be if it remained a whole evening with a sumptuously set scene displayed, but without a single actor. New
England is the region in which perhaps the accessories of life
are most closely concentrated; but even in New England you
traverse wastes into which it appears to you that the whole of
Old England might be dropped with no more chance of being
found again than has a needle in a pottle of hay. But it is
when you come to dwell in towns that Form-sickness gets its
firmest grip of you. In a city of three or four hundred thousand inhabitants, you see nothing but mere flat surfaces, straight
lines, right angles, parallel rows of boards, and perpendicular
palings. The very trees lining the streets are as straight as
walking-sticks. Straight rows of rails cut up the roadway of
the straight streets. The hotels are marble packing-cases,
uniformly square, and pierced with many quadrangular windows;
the railway cars and street omnibuses are exact oblongs; and
to crown all, the national flag is ruled in parallel crimson
stripes, with a blue quadrangle in one corner, sown with stars
in parallel rows.

Philadelphia, from its rectangularity, has been called the
"chess-board city;" Washington has been laid out on a plan
quite as distressingly geometrical; and nine-tenths of the other
towns and villages are built on gridiron lines. There are some

crooked streets in Boston, and that is why Europeans usually show a preference for Boston over other Northern American cities; while in the lower part of New York a few of the thoroughfares are narrow, and deviate a little from the inexorable straight line. In most cases there is no relaxation of the cord of tension. There are no corners, nooks, archways, alleys; no refuges, in fact, for light and shade. In the State of Virginia there is one of the largest natural arches in the world; but in American architecture a curved vault is one of the rarest of structures. The very bridges are on piers without arches. Signboards and trade effigies, it is true, project from the houses, but always at right angles.

This rigidity of outline makes its mark on the nomenclature and on the manners of the people. The names of the streets are taken from the letters of the alphabet and the numerals in the "Ready Reckoner." I have lived in G Street. I have lived in West-Fourteenth, between Fifth and Sixth Avenues. Mathematical calculation is the basis of daily life. You are fed at the hotels at stated hours; and the doors of the dining-room are kept locked until within a moment of the gong's sounding. At some *tables d'hôte* fifty negro waiters stand mute and immobile behind the chairs of two hundred and fifty guests; and at a given signal uncover, with the precision of clock-work, one hundred dishes. These are not matters of fancy; they are matters of fact. Routine pursues you everywhere: from the theatre to the church; from the fancy fair to the public meeting. In the meanest village inn, as in the most palatial hotel, there is a traveller's book, in which you are bound to enter your name. You may assume an alias; but you must be Mr. Somebody. You cannot be, as in England, the "stout party in Number Six," or the "tall gent in the Sun." You must shake hands with every one to whom you are introduced; you must drink when you are asked, and then ask the asker to drink—though I am bound to say that this strictly mathematical custom has, owing to the piteous protests of Europeans, somewhat declined of late.

If you enter a barber's shop to be shaved, a negro hands you a check bearing a number, and you must await your turn. When your turn arrives, you must sit in a certain position in a velvet-covered *fauteuil* with high legs, and must put your feet up on a stool on a level therewith. The barber shaves you, not as *you* like, but as *he* likes ; powders you, strains a napkin over your countenance ; sponges you ; shampoos you ; pours bay rum and eau-de-Cologne on your head ; greases, combs you out ; and "fixes" you generally. The first time I was ever under the hands of an American tonsor, I rose as soon as he had laid down his razor, and made a move in the direction of the washhand basin. He stared at me as though I had gone mad. "Hold on !" he cried, in an authoritative accent. "Hold on ! Guess I'll have to wash you up." That I should be "washed up" or "fixed," was in accordance with the mathematical code.

This all but utter absence of variety of form, of divergence of detail, of play of light and shade, is productive in the end of that petulant and discontented frame of mind, of that soreness of spirit, with which so many tourists who have visited the Great Republic have come at last to regard its civilisation. As a rule, the coarser the traveller's organisation—the less he cares about art or literature—the better he will get on in America. I met a fellow-countryman once, the son of an English earl, at one of the biggest, most mathematical, and most comfortless of the New York hotels, who told me that he should be very well content to live there for ten years. "Why," he said, "you can have five meals a day if you like." This is the kind of traveller— the robust, hardy, strong-stomached youth, fresh from a public school, who goes to America, and does not grumble.

But do you take, not a travelled Englishman, but a travelled American—one who has been long in Europe, and has appreciated the artistic glories of the Continent, and you will discover that he finds it almost impossible to live in his own country, or "board" at an American hotel. Every continental city has its colony of refined Americans, good patriots and staunch republicans, but who are absolutely afraid to go back to their native land. They dread the mathematical system. Those who, for their families' or their interests' sake, are compelled to abide in the States, live at hotels conducted, not on the American, but on the European system—that is to say, where they can dine, breakfast, or sup, not as the landlord likes, but as they themselves like. Those who are wealthy shut themselves up in country houses, or splendid town mansions, surrounded by books, and pictures, and statues, and tapestry, and coins from Europe, until their existence is almost ignored by their countrymen. In no country in the world are so many men of shining talents, of noble mind, of refined taste, buried alive as in the United States.

That which I call the "Mathematical System" is only another name for a very stringent and offensive social tyranny; and did we not remember that humanity is one mass of inconsistencies and contradictions, it would be difficult to understand how this social despotism could be made compatible with the existence of an amount of political liberty never before equalled in this world. Until 1861, the American citizen was wholly and entirely free; and now that the only pretext for the curtailment of his liberties has disappeared, he will enter upon, it is to be hoped, a fresh lease of freedom, as whole and unrestricted as of yore. How far the social despotism spoken of has extended would be almost incredible to those who have not resided in America. "Whatever you do," said an American to me on the first day of my landing in the States, "don't live in a boarding-house where you are to be treated as one of the family. They'll worry you to death by wanting to take care of your morals."

To have one's morals taken care of is a very excellent thing; but as a rule you prefer to place the curatorship thereof in the hands of your parents and guardians, or of your ghostly director, or, being of mature age, of yourself. "Taking care of morals" is apt to degenerate into petty impertinence and espionage. One of the most eminent of living sculptors in New York told me that for many years he experienced the greatest difficulty in pursuing the studies incidental to, and indeed essential to, his attaining excellence in his profession, owing to the persistent care taken of his morals by the lady who officiated as house-keeper in the chambers where he lived. It must be premised that these chambers formed part of a building specially erected for the accommodation of artists, and with a view to their professional requirements. Our sculptor had frequent need of the assistance of female models, and the "Janitress," as the lady housekeeper was called, had a virtuously indignant objection to young persons who posed as Venuses or Hebes, in the costume of the mythological period, for a dollar an hour. She could only be induced by the threat of dismissal from the proprietor of the studio building to grant admission to the models at all; even then she would await their exit at her lodge gate, and abuse them as they came downstairs. Much more acclimatised to models was the good sister of William Etty, who used to seek out his Venuses for him; but a transition state of feeling was that of the wife of Nollekens, the sculptor, who, whenever her husband had a professional sitter, and the day was very cold, used to burst into the studio with a basin in her hand, crying: "You nasty, good-for-nothing hussey! here's some hot mutton broth for you."

To recapitulate a little. Form-sickness is the unsatisfied yearning for those broken lines, irregular forms, and infinite gradations of colour—reacting as those conditions of form invariably do on the manners and characteristics of the people—which are only to be met with in very old countries. However expensively and elegantly dressed a man may be, he is apt to feel uncomfortable in a brand-new hat, a brand-new coat and trowsers, and brand-new boots and gloves; and I believe that if he were compelled to put on a brand-new suit every morning, he would hang himself before a month was over, and send his abhorred garments to Madame Tussaud's, to swell the wardrobe in the Chamber of Horrors. The sensation of entire novelty is one inseparable from the outward aspect of America. You can smell the paint and varnish; the glue is hardly dry.

The reasons for this are very obvious. American civilisation

is an independent and self-reliant entity. It has no connections,
or ties, or foregatherings with any predecessors on its own soil.
It is not the heir of long-entailed patrimony. It is, like Rudolph
of Hapsburg, the first of its race. It has slain and taken
possession. In Great Britain we have yet Stonehenge and some
cairns and cromlechs to remind us of the ancient Britons' acts;
but in the settled parts of the United States, apart from the
Indian names of some towns and rivers, there remains not the
remotest vestige to recall the existence of the former possessors
of the soil. There are yet outlying districts, millions of acres
square, where Red Indians hunt, and fight, and steal, and scalp;
but American civilisation marches up, kills or deports them—
at all events, entirely "improves them" off the face of the
land. They leave no trace behind; and the brand-new civilisation starts up in a night, like a mushroom. Where yesterday
was a wigwam, to-day is a Doric meeting-house, also a bank
and a grand pianoforte; where yesterday the medicine-man
muttered his incantations, to-morrow an advertising corn-cutter
opens his shop; and in place of a squaw, embroidering moccasins,
and cudgelled by the drunken brave, her spouse, we have a
tight-laced young lady with a chignon and a hooped skirt,
taking academical degrees, and talking shrilly about Woman's
Rights.*

A few years since, the trapper and pioneer race formed a
transition stage between the cessation of barbarism and the
advent of civilisation. The pioneer was a simple-minded man;
and so soon as a clearing grew too civilised for him, he would
shoulder his hatchet and rifle, and move farther out into the
wilds. I have heard of one whose signal for departure was the
setting up of a printing press in his settlement. "Those darned
newspapers," he remarked, "made one's cattle stray so." But
railway extension, and the organisation in the Atlantic cities of
enormous caravans of emigrants, are gradually thinning the
ranks of the pioneers. In a few years, Natty Bumppo, Leather-

---

* And I wish that she would talk more shrilly still, all over the world
until those Rights are granted.

stocking, the Deerslayer, the Pathfinder, will be legendary. Civilisation moves now *en masse*. There is scarcely any advanced guard. Few skirmishers are thrown out. The main body swoops down on the place to be occupied, and civilises it in one decided charge.

It may be advantageous to compare such a sudden substitution of a settled community for a howling wilderness with the slow and tentative growth of our home surroundings. European civilisation resembles the church of St. Eustache at Paris, in whose exterior Gothic niches and pinnacles, Byzantine arches, Corinthian columns, Composite cornices, and Renaissance doorways, are all jumbled together. Every canon of architectural taste is violated, but the parts still cohere ; a very solid façade still rears its head ; and at a certain distance its appearance is not inharmonious. At Cologne, in Germany, they will point out to you an ancient building, here a bit of Lombard, here a morsel of florid Gothic, here some unmistakable Italian, and here ten feet of genuine old Roman wall. There are many Christian churches in Italy whose walls are supported by columns taken from Pagan temples.

The entire system, physical as well as moral, has been the result of growth upon growth, of gradual intercalation and emendation, of perpetual cobbling and piercing and patching ; and although at last, like Sir John Cutler's silk stockings, which his maid darned so often with worsted that no part of the original fabric remained, the ancient foundations may have become all but invisible, they are still latent, and give solidity to the superstructure. We look upon the edifice, indeed, as we would on something that has taken root—that has something to rest upon. We regard it as we would that hoary old dome of St. Peter's at Rome. We know how long it took to build, and we trust that it will endure for ever. The brand-new civilisation we are apt to look at more in the light of a balloon. It is very astonishing. We wonder how ever it contrived to rise so high, and how long it will be before it comes down again ; and we earnestly hope that it will not burst.

It is not necessary to avow any kind of partisan predilection for one phase of civilisation as against another. It is sufficient to note the fact, that Europeans the least prejudiced, and the most ardent admirers of the political institutions of the United States, very soon grow fretful and uneasy there, and are unable to deny when they come back that the country is not an elegant or a comfortable one to look upon. I attribute this solely to æsthetic causes. I do not believe that Englishmen grumble at America because the people are given to expectoration, or "guessing," or "calculating," or trivialities of that kind. Continental Europeans expectorate quite as freely as the Americans; and for rude cross-questioning of strangers, I will back a German against the most inquisitive of New Englanders. It is in the eye that the mischief lies. It is the brand-new mathematical outline of Columbia that drives the Englishman into Form-sickness, and ultimately to the disparagement and misrepresentation of a very noble country.

In many little matters of detail American manners differ from ours ; but in the aggregate we are still one family. Americans speak our language—frequently with far greater purity and felicity of expression than we ourselves do—they read our books, and we are very often glad and proud to read theirs. They have a common inheritance with us in the historic memories we most prize. If they would only round off their corners a little ! If they would only give us a few crescents and ovals in lieu of "blocks !" If they would only remember that the circle as well as the rectangle is a figure in mathematics, and that the curvilinear is, after all, the Line of Beauty !

XVII.

CUAGNAWAGHA.

CUAGNAWAGHA! Cuagnawagha! it is but a word. I may plead at least that it is fertile in vowels, and has not the spiky *chevaux de frise* appearance, when written down, which Polish and Hungarian and others of the Sclavonic family (those quadrilaterals of orthography) present. To me, even Cuagnawagha looks pretty in black and white. I have adopted the spelling accepted by those who rule over Cuagnawagha, and are neighbours to it; but the Cuagnawaghians themselves are not much given to reading or writing.

Cuagnawagha! Cuagnawagha! will you agree in the premiss that there are certain words—the names of things and places, and sometimes, but very rarely, of men—the bare sound of which will haunt you? That they should do so is not always the result of the associations they recall. Windermere is close to Patterdale; yet the first is a name that haunts you, and is full of a soft and mysterious beauty. Patterdale is one of the loveliest spots in Europe, but its sound is harsh, severe, and ugly.

In all human probability I shall never more behold Cuagnawagha—on this side the grave, at least. On the other we may all see sights that shall astonish us. I was never in Cuagnawagha but once in my life; I only passed fifty minutes within its confines; I was thoroughly disappointed in all that I had come to see; yet Cuagnawagha, its name and itself, have haunted me from the day on which I first beheld it until this, and in my dreariest moments its dear name sweeps

o

like soft music over the chords of my heart and lights up
the dim old Vauxhall of my twilight with thrice fifty thousand additional lamps.

I do not know why. I have seen the lions of the world,
their manes and their tails, and have heard them roar. I
can gaze upon the ocean without addressing it as Vast, and
Interminable, and Blue, and without bidding it Róll on—a
request which, on my part or any one else's, I hold to be one
of surplusage, if not grossly impertinent. I have lost most
of my enthusiasm about great rivers. I wait for the Ganges
and the Indus, the Euphrates and the Amazon; but I have
seen the Guadalquivir, the Ebro, the Tagus, the Rhône, the
Rhine, the Mincio, and the Danube; but I am of opinion
that the Thames at Ditton, in that priceless half-hour between
your ordering the stewed eels and the cutlets to follow and
the arrival of the banquet itself, is brighter and more shining
than any other river which I might have asked, again impertinently, to " flow on."

The lions and the rivers, the cataract and the Alpine passes,
are apt, indeed, to pall upon you when they are seen, not
from choice but from necessity ; and goodness gracious ! how
many miles would I willingly travel, and with peas in my
shoes, to get out of the way of an Old Master or a connoisseur given to talking about one ! I almost blush to recall
the irreverent terms in which I heard one of her Majesty's
Messengers allude, the other day, to that sublime chain of
mountains the exploration of which has been undertaken by
an association of Climbing-boys, and whose peaks, passes, and
glaciers are so fascinating to our landscape painters that they
seem to be quite unaware of the existence of any more sublime mountain scenery in the world. The Queen's Messenger
called the sublime chain those " something " Alps. So might
you, if you had to carry a bag across them twenty times a
year, in hail, rain, or sunshine.

But Cuagnawagha has not lost one iota of its primeval charms
to me. My love for it is as fresh as—what shall I say ?—as

your love for the face you always love : for the face which, like
that of Queen Victoria on the postage-stamps, never grows
older. As it was in 1840 so it is in 1872, only younger and
fresher and prettier (to you) ; so was it when your life began,
so is it now you are a man, so may it be when you grow old.
And I am sure, had Wordsworth ever seen Cuagnawagha, he
would have written as melodiously about it as he has written
of Grasmere or Dungeonghyll.

Cuagnawagha is only an unpretending little Indian village on
the bank of the River St. Lawrence, over against the French
village of La Chine, one of the earliest settlements of the Jesuit
missionaries in Canada (and so called by them in affectionate
reference to the labours of which the " Lettres Edifiantes et
Curieuses " are a record). It is some six miles' drive from the
thriving and populous city of Montreal.

This is not, perhaps, the first time you have been told that
there are no more genial and hospitable folks in British North
America (where capital punishment will never be abolished, so
far as killing with kindness is concerned) than the inhabitants
of Montreal. The Canadians generally labour under a notion—
not an entirely mistaken one, perhaps—that their brethren of
the Old Country do not hold them in sufficient estimation ; that
the glare and bustle and sensational whirligig life of the United
States offer greater attractions to English tourists who cross
the Atlantic than the solid, steady, sober-sided existence of the
British provinces. They have an idea that an Englishman
travelling in the States gets rid of Canada at an early stage in
his journey, or just looks in upon it at the fag-end thereof, and
that the real centres of his curiosity are in the cities of the
Atlantic seaboard.

The " Kenucks " and the " Blue noses " and the other provincials murmur at this, but always in a placable and good-
humoured manner. " At least," says Canada, " the better half
of Niagara belongs to us. At least, the Falls of Montmorency
are equal to those of Gennessee ; at least, the St. Lawrence is
not inferior to the Ohio, and the Thousand Islands beat Boston

Harbour. There is not on the whole North American continent a city so picturesque as Quebec ; and if you are curious about redskins, we can show you plenty of Indians—fat, copper-coloured, prosperous, and happy, instead of the gaunt, dwarfed, half-starved wretches who are being 'improved' off the face of the earth by the restless Yankees."

These grievances, however, do not prevent the Montrealese from pressing the heartiest of welcomes on every stranger who comes within their gates. It is enough for them that he *is* a stranger, and they immediately take him in. He is asked out, systematically and stubbornly, to dinner. If he pleads previous engagements, he is asked whether Monday week or Tuesday fortnight will suit him ; and the dinner comes due, and must be met, like a bill. The Amphitryons who cannot bag him for a dinner are fain to secure him for breakfasts or suppers or lunches. Then they drive him out in trotting-waggons in summer and sleighs in winter ; they take him to the club and to the "rink ;" they wrap him up, as in buffalo-robes, with kind offices and generous deeds. When I say that my experiences of Montreal hospitality, on the last occasion of my visit to the Royal Town, included the gift of a roll of Canada homespun sufficient to make a couple of travelling suits, and the loan of a railway-car, combining sitting-room, bedrooms, smoking-rooms, and kitchen, in which I travelled at my ease many hundreds of miles, you will be enabled to infer that the people of Montreal are not in the habit of doing things by halves, and that when they say they are glad to see you, they mean it.

Hospitality has generally its price ; and I have known more than one country where the price exacted was slightly beyond the value of the article itself ; but the terms on which kindness is obtainable in Montreal are not very onerous. You are not expected to praise everything you see, to make flowing speeches, or to write a book declaring Lower Canada in general, and Montreal in particular, to be the grandest and most glorious country and city in the universe. Nor are you absolutely required to furnish the album of every young lady fresh from boarding-school, or *at* boarding-school, with autographs and *cartes-de-visite*, or to write scraps of poetry of your own composition (not to exceed thirty lines) on little bits of parti-coloured silk, to be returned post-paid to localities a thousand miles away, there to be sewn into patchwork counterpanes. Nor are you asked for opinions on the abstract questions of Woman's Rights, Moral Suasion, or International Law.

You are only expected to eat a great deal, to pass the bottle, to go round the Mountain, to go through the Tube, and to visit Cuagnawagha. There are always plenty of kind friends, with knives, forks, bottles, carriages, and horses, to enable you to accomplish the first three feats. For the performance of the fourth every assistance will be rendered you by the courteous officials of the Grand Trunk Railway of Canada; and the Victoria Bridge at Montreal is, in its way, quite as great a wonder of the world as the Falls of Niagara. When you have dispatched that tremendous piece of engineering—when you have not only ridden through the tube on a locomotive, but walked through it and inspected the identical rivet driven into the iron by the Prince of Wales, the last of I know not how many millions—you have done all that is required of you in Montreal, with the exception of visiting Cuagnawagha.

The name strikes you at once. What is it? where is it? you eagerly inquire. It is an Indian village, you are told, easily accessible. The best way is by road to La Chine, where you can obtain a canoe and be ferried across to the village itself. The very word "canoe" sets you all agog to go. Sunday, your counsellors continue, is the best day for a visit to Cuagnawagha. The squaws are then in their best dresses, and the papooses or children are neat and clean, for the inspection of visitors. It was on a Saturday afternoon that I made an appointment with a hospitable friend to start for Cuagnawagha at noon on the morrow. All night I dreamt about it. A radiant chaos filled my sleep of moccasins and wampum-belts, of wigwams

and medicine-men, of war-paint and calumets, of tomahawks
and scalps, of fire-water and unburied hatchets, of gallant
braves and beauteous squaws, of the Council Fire and the
Happy Hunting-grounds.

Sunday morning dawned. It was a Canadian summer Sunday,
which is perhaps saying enough ; but our open carriage had a
hood, and the day, though warm, was so beautiful that we felt
it would have been a sin to remain at home. Perforce, however,
so fierce was the glare of the sun, we lingered in the cool shades
of the St. Lawrence Hall Hotel until two in the afternoon. To
broil in Canada was with me a new sensation, for on the occasion
of my last visit to Montreal the thermometer had been at a
whole flight of stairs below zero, and my tour round the Mountain
accomplished in a sleigh, with such a jingling accompaniment of
bells as might have been envied by the celebrated female traveller
to Banbury Cross. But why did she not attach the bells to the
cock-horse instead of to her toes ?

There are but two changes of the seasons at Montreal, but
they are pantomimic in their suddenness. I could scarcely
believe that the Mr. Hogan who suggested iced sangaree or a
trifle in the way of a cobbler, ere we started for Cuagnawagha,
was the same obliging host who, the last time I started from St.
Lawrence Hall, had lent me the skin (seemingly) of a mega-
therium to wrap myself in, with a mighty fur cap, and a pair of
sealskin gloves like unto leviathan his paws, and had whispered
that half-way round the mountain there were some excellent
hot " whiskey skins " to be obtained.

The drive to La Chine was not very interesting. Few drives
in North America, save where the scenery is mountainous, can
be said to possess much interest, picturesquely speaking. The
farming is all doubtless in strict accordance with the precepts of
Jethro Tull, great-grandfather of Anglo-Saxon husbandry ; but
to the European eye it looks shiftless and slovenly. The fields
are too large (which would scarcely be a fault in the eye of a
farmer) ; there are ugly posts and rails in lieu of hedges, and the
trees are few. Gentlemen's houses, parks, and pleasaunces you

never expect to see. Add to this an all-pervading dust powdering the vegetation with the monotonous livery of Midge the miller, and those chronic Canadian nuisances, abundant turnpike-gates. There were plenty of cattle about, however, well bred and full of flesh, and the cottages along the road, although mainly of wood, had a substantial and satisfied appearance, as though they belonged to country folks who ate meat every day. I am inclined to think that meat twice, if not three times a day, would be nearer the mark, as the habitual dietary of the Canadian peasant or farmer, for they are both one here. Given a country where the babes and sucklings clamour for beefsteak at breakfast :—should not that country be a happy one ?

There was the usual confusion of French and English nomenclature, and of Protestant and Romanist places of worship, and of people of Saxon and Celtic race along the road ; but, as seems happily the case in Canada, the Gaul and the Saxon, the follower of Peter and the disciple of Martin, seemed to get on pretty well together. Fenianism was in an ugly embryo state when I was in Canada. It had scarcely got beyond its first fœtal squalling in its cradle in Chicago ; and the Canadian Paddy, so far as I had any experience of him, was a jovial, easy-going mortal, civil to the Saxon, obedient to his rule, and passably contented with plenty of work and high wages. I am inclined to hope, and even to believe, that the outburst of Fenianism—now grown from a fretful wail to a frantic howl—notwithstanding, the kind of Paddy (the contented one) I have mentioned is still in a majority in Lower Canada. What he may be in the West I am rather chary of opining. On this present Sunday he was evidently, so far as his patronage of French and English public-houses went, wholly free from prejudice. "The Queen's Arms" and "Les Armes d'Angleterre" were all one to him. I could not help thinking, as we saw these hybrid taverns, that half-and-half should properly be the only beverage sold there ; and when I passed a knot of scarlet-coated British guardsmen issuing from a

wayside hostel, I fancied an international version of the old
nursery rhyme :

> " Qui est là ?
> A grenadier.
> Où est votre argent?
> I forgot.
> Allez-vous-en, ivrogne ! "

Conversations closely resembling the above were certainly
audible from time to time when the Guards were in Canada.
Happy was it when they were content to demand a "pot of
beer" in lieu of the atrocious "white eye" and the abominable "fixed bayonets"—the cheap whiskey or cheap hell-
fire of Canada. Not that the guardsman was given in any
marked degree to misbehave himself. He did not get tipsier,
or with greater frequency, than his cousin of the Line does in
Gibraltar. He was much more sober in Canada than he is
generally in London. The Guards were deservedly popular with
the people of Montreal, and went home "as fit as fiddles."
Many obtained their discharge while in America, and married
and settled in the province.

They must have been quick about their sweethearting ; but
next to a sailor's, is there anything shorter than a soldier's
courtship ? Three Sundays might be given as a fair average.
Let us take a virtuously inclined corporal. A regiment, we
will say, disembarks on a Saturday night ; on the first Sunday
afternoon you will meet your virtuously inclined corporal walking down Notre-Dame Street with a young lady in a three-
dollar shawl and a two-dollar bonnet. The next Sunday, if
you happened to be passing down Bonaventure Street, you
might catch a glimpse of the virtuously inclined corporal taking
tea with the entire family of his *innamorata;* cutting the
bread-and-butter, carving the ham, nursing the married sister's
baby, or handing the old grandsire a light for his pipe. And
on Sunday number three you heard that Corporal Smith had
got leave to be married to a "Kenuck."

How do they manage it, these wonderful military men ?
What inflammatory quality is there in their scarlet coats to

set maidens' hearts ablaze so ? How many weary months, years perhaps, did it take you to win the present Mrs. Bene-dick ? Mind, I can't help thinking that if civilians would adopt the short sharp mode of military courtship, the girls would meet them half-way. I heard of a train breaking down once on the Camden and Amboy Railroad, and before a fresh locomotive could be brought to its assistance no less than three offers of marriage were made and accepted among the passen-gers. And did you ever hear of a courtship more expeditious than that of the mystic William Blake, *pictor ignotus ?* He had had some great trouble. "I pity you, William," remarked a young lady. "Then I am sure I love you with all my heart," quoth William Blake; and they went off and got married at once. But if she had not added the endearing "William" to the expres-sion of pity, that young lady might never have become Mrs. Blake.

There was not much to remind one of the Celestial Empire at the clean little village of La Chine. It was nearly all French. The hotel or tavern was, as usual, half and half. The little sanded parlour was decorated with portraits of Queen Victoria and the late Duke of Wellington, side by side with a Madonna and Child, and his Grace the Archbishop of Quebec in full canonicals; and the *Montreal Herald* lay on the table cheek-by-jowl with *L'Echo du Canada.* A French servant-maid brought us some English beer; and on our expressing a desire to hire a canoe, the Scotch landlord hailed two boatmen, one of whom was an Indian and the other an Irishman, to "pole" us across to Cuagnawagha. It only wanted a raven and a cage and the celebrated professor of Trafalgar Square, to make the exhibition of the Happy Family complete.*

We crossed the magnificent river, at this point far enough from the La Chine Rapids to be lying calm in the sun like one sheet of burnished gold. There was no awning to the canoe, and a Venetian gondola would perhaps have been preferable as a

---

* The Happy Family was composed of cats, rats, mice, an owl, a raven, canaries and other singing birds, all of which were exhibited together in a large cage in front of the National Gallery.

conveyance; but there was something after all in riding lightly on the bosom of the famous St. Lawrence in a real canoe of birch bark, with a real Red Indian at the stern. I will say nothing of the Irishman at the prow, for he rather detracted from the romance of the thing. A Canadian *voyageur* now, softly murmuring "La Complainte de Cadieux," or chanting in lugubrious tones the fearful history of Marie Joseph Corriveau and the iron cage of Quebec : such an oarsman would have left nothing to be desired. You must get on to the Ottawa river ere you can catch your *voyageur*. The Irishman and the Indian did not attempt the "Row, Brothers, Row," or any other variety of the Canadian boat-song. It was worth coming a good many miles, however, to hear the Irishman endeavour to make himself understood in the French tongue by the redskin, and that noble savage, not to be behindhand in courtesy, endeavouring to talk English to the Irishman. I must not omit to mention that the noble savage wore a pea-jacket and a billy-cock hat, and informed us that in addition to the skill and dexterity with which he feathered his oar, or rather his pole, he was "one dam good pilot."

As the opposite shore was approached the navigation became somewhat difficult, and the channel rather a matter to be faintly hoped for than confidently fixed upon. Several times we were, as I thought, within an inch of being "snagged," the "snags" in this case not being trunks of trees, as on the Mississippi, but sharp-pointed fragments of rock. However, the Indian successfully guided us through the watery labyrinth, and in some degree justified his claim to the title of "one dam good pilot." There were more rocky fragments on the bank; indeed, the littoral of the St. Lawrence opposite La Chine might remind the Eastern traveller of the shores of Arabia Petræa; and the quarter-of-a-mile walk or so lying between the river and the village was, to one of the visitors to Cuagnawagha, of a gouty constitution, and to another with tight boots, and to third with bunions and an irritable temper, agonising.

We brought up at last in a long straggling street, or rather lane, of hovels built of loose stones and planks nailed together in apparently as loose a fashion. Here and there perhaps a little mud had been used to finish off the corners, or stick on the chimney-pots ; but looseness was the prevailing characteristic of the street architecture. When I call these dwellings hovels, I use the word in no offensive sense. They were hovels in construction, but exceedingly clean and abundantly furnished. The doors and windows were all wide open, and the domestic arrangements of the inhabitants of Cuagnawagha were almost as fully exposed to public gaze as those of a doll's-house in Mr. Cremer's London shop-windows. As the majority of the houses comprised only one room, the publicity given to the domesticity of the place may be more easily understood. They were, as I have hinted, supplied with abundant chattels. I saw more than one four-post bedstead, several easy-chairs, and any number of profusely ornamented tea-trays.

Next to these the most fertile product of Cuagnawagha appeared to be babies. I could not at first make out what had become of the children of medium growth, nor of the seven-year olds up to the ten-year olds ; but I learnt subsequently that the elder ones were at church and the younger at play in the cemetery. In Cuagnawagha itself the babies ruled the roast. They were very fat—of a rich oily fatness indeed, and in the ridiculous swaddling-bands in which they were enveloped, looked not unlike very little sucking-pigs seen through reddish-brown spectacles. But all the babies I saw were, I am pleased to say, immaculately clean. Those who had any hair had it of a lustrous raven hue, such as Horace Vernet has put on the head of the baby Napoleon in that exquisite vignette where the hero is depicted naked, and one hour old, sprawling on a fragment of tapestry. Their black eyes, too, had a merry twinkle ; and altogether their coppery hue was not unpleasing, and they were the nicest babies I had seen for many a long month.

In Cuagnawagha a baby is called a " papoose ; " and a solemn rite, the performance of which is exacted from all strangers, is that the papooses should be kissed. I had been warned in Montreal that the maternal squaws of Cuagnawagha were sometimes actuated by mercenary motives in offering their babies to the caresses of tourists ; and that the request, "Anglis, kiss papoose," was not unfrequently followed by another, "Give little quarter"—meaning twenty-five cents. I took a provision of small money with me—the newest and brightest I could procure ; but the mothers of Cuagnawagha were that day in no mercenary mood. At least they did not actually beg for money. They clapped their hands for joy, and the papoose crowed in unison whenever we did present them with a backshish ; so that on the whole in this lane full of copper-coloured babies we had our money's worth and more.

We would no sooner halt at an open threshold than cheery voices in an amazing jargon of French and English invited us to walk in. If we hesitated about intruding, the inevitable papoose, tightly swaddled and strapped on to a board, like a diminutive Egyptian mummy, was handed to us through the window. A gipsy woman of felonious tendencies might have made a fortune in ten minutes' perambulation of Cuagnawagha by running off with the papooses thus offered on trust ; only, as the gipsies are said to steal only Nazarene children, and the Red Indians themselves are by some ethnologists supposed to be of kin with the gipsies, those Zingarini persons might not have cared perhaps about stealing their own flesh and blood.

I was given to understand afterwards that these Indians of Cuagnawagha were a very industrious and well-to-do community. The men hunted and fished, and were boatmen and river pilots ; the women stayed at home, took care of the papooses, and filled up their time by making baskets and creels, and embroidering those exquisite moccasins, slippers, pouches, fans, wampam-belts, and other articles of bead and feather-work which are so much in request in the fancy bazaars of Montreal and Quebec, and for which the retail dealers charge such exorbitant prices. The squaws of Cuagna-wagha have certain market days for the disposal of their manufactures. On these occasions they are conveyed by their lords in canoes of birch-bark across the river, and may be seen, with their black hair abundantly oiled and their persons spruced up in infinite Indian finery, gliding from shop to shop in the most frequented streets of Montreal, in strange contrast to the European costumes around them. I did not hear that the Indians of Cuagnawagha, male or female, were much given to the consumption of fire-water, or to quarrelling or pilfering, or to the other generic weaknesses of the noble savage when in a state of free nobility and nastiness. I did not see any liquor-shop in the place.

The domestic affairs of the village are administered by a chief—John or Peter, or Big Bellows or Bear's Paw, was, I think, his name; but it does not matter now—who was reported to have done uncommonly well in the fur trade, and to be worth many dollars. I had the honour of an interview with this Sachem, who was sitting, after the manner of his subjects, at his open door, in a Windsor chair, and smoking the calumet of peace—an ordinary tobacco-pipe, containing, as I was led to infer from the odour, bird's-eye. He was old, and immensely fat, but very affable. He showed me a pair of the most beautifully embroidered moccasins I had ever beheld. Not to mince the matter, they served as coverings to his own stout legs and feet; but nothing could exceed the courteous manner in which he cocked up his bead-worked limbs on the window-sill, and allowed me narrowly to inspect, and even to smooth and pat them. The Sachem's house was so full of chattels that it looked like a broker's shop; and the name of his tea-trays was legion. He wore on his breast, and was evidently exceedingly proud of, a silver medal bearing the effigy of King George the Fourth, and had, so far as I could make out, served at some remote period in the local militia. He had the usual twin engravings over his mantle-piece—the Madonna and the Queen of England, and was a staunch Conservative and a devout Roman Catholic.

So I left him, never to behold him more, in this semi-ignored corner of the world, so close to civilisation and yet so far from it. He was sitting under his own vine and his

own fig-tree ; and who was there to make him afraid ? Not
the British Government, surely, whose rule over these honest
folks is mild and equitable and protective ; not the Pope of
Rome, assuredly.   In Lower Canada the Roman Catholic
religion seems to have lost the terrifying character which it
is apt to assume elsewhere.   The priest neither bullies nor
teases nor grinds the faces of his parishioners.   He is their
master ; for he is lawyer, arbitrator, journalist, schoolmaster,
letter-writer, match-maker, guide, philosopher, and friend, all
in one ; but his spiriting seems to be done with infinite
gentleness, and he is certainly beloved by a population who,
but for his quietly paternal despotism, would very likely be
drunken and savage and profligate, and not peaceable and
affectionate and docile.

At one extremity of the village street there was a church, a bare
structure of considerable antiquity, highly whitewashed.   The
irregular area before this edifice seemed to be the general trysting-
place of the young squaws and the young braves of Cuagnawagha,
who were sweethearting after the manner of young squaws and
young braves the whole world over.   The braves, I am sorry to
say, had repudiated the slightest approach to Indian costume, and
in the round blue jackets and glazed hats which they mostly
affected, had somewhat of a sailor-like appearance.   They were
pure redskins, however, and half-castes were rare.   Now a Red
Indian in a blue jacket and a round glazed hat sounds rather
anomalous and incongruous.   Where were the feathers and the
war-paint and the tattooing ?   Not at Cuagnawagha, certainly.
You must go much farther west if you wish to see the noble
savage in his full native splendour and squalor ; and even in the
wildest districts the Indian rarely fails to supply himself with
a European outfit whenever he has an opportunity to do so.

I remember a hard-hearted but withal very amusing speculator
from down East telling me of a gambling transaction he had had
with an Indian somewhere in the territory of Colorado.   "The
cuss," he observed, " had been tradin' hosses, and bought a lot of
store clothes.   There he was, in a stove-pipe hat, a satin vest and

a coat and pants most handsome. We took drinks, and I kinder froze to him till I had him comfortable over draw-poker in the verandah of the Cummin's House. Sir, in the course of three hours and three quarters I won of that Ingin all the money he'd got from tradin' hosses, and all his clothes, from the crown of his hat to the soles of his boots. Sir, it was very hot ; and, lawful sakes ! it was a sight to see that Ingin, a child of Adam and as bare as a robin, a walking away solemn, perspirin' with rage in the rays of the setting sun, and *looking like a hot roast turkey*." The hot roast turkeys of Cuagnawagha had not yet been plucked of their feathers by speculators from down East, direct lineal descendants of the cunning man of Pyquag, who questioned Anthony Van Corlcar the trumpeter out of his horse.

But O ! the squaws of Cuagnawagha. The elder squaws were unutterably hideous ; so they prudently stayed at home and minded the papooses. The younger squaws were here, philandering. Such mellow brunettes did I see with nature's pure carmine mantling upon their dusky cheeks. Such lustrous blue-black tresses. Such liquid, lingering, longing eyes. If their foreheads had not been quite so low, and the chiselling of their mouths not quite so square, many of these girls would have been positively beautiful. Their figures in early youth are very shapely and graceful, and their gait a strictly "gliding". motion, as already noted. A lady of our party admitted that they walked prettily, but that they turned their toes in. Another critic discovered that they walked on tiptoe in consequence of the wretched condition of the pavement. I could only notice that they glided, that their ankles were faultless, and that they were exquisitely shod. Moccasins they may have worn on week-days ; this Sabbath their pretty feet were arrayed in brodequins and bottines of varnished and bronzed leather, of soft kid, and even of bright-coloured silk and satin. Otherwise there was little European in their costume.

Crinoline had not yet invaded Cuagnawagha. There was an upper garment, which was the inner garment—the innermost garment, in fact—snowy white, leaving the arms bare, but very maidenly and modest. This was all they had for bib, or tucker, or bodice. Then came a petticoat falling in straight heavy folds, and decorated round the bottom with three or four rows of ribbons, the whole offering a close resemblance to the garment known in operatic wardrobes as the "Amina skirt." Over all, and covering the head, was a long mantle, in shape somewhat like a priest's cope—a square of fine broadcloth, of yellow, of red, or of black, and adorned with curious patchwork embroidery. The lady critic above mentioned complained that they went about with drawing-room table-covers over their heads; but what will not lady critics say? Such were the squaws of Cuagnawagha. Their necklaces and armlets of beads, "their ribbons, chains, and ouches," I need not dwell upon. As for their manner of receiving the addresses of the young braves, it was remarkably like that which on previous occasions I have observed in Kensington Gardens, in many private parlours and on some staircases.

We were turning our faces towards the shore again, when there issued from one of the hovels a procession which we could not choose but follow. It was the funeral train of a little child. As at a Turkish funeral, the assistants came along at the double quick, but not jostling and hallooing as the Turks, or at least the Arabs, do. The men were first, absolutely running, but with that grave, concentrated expression in their faces of which only Indians and Breton peasants seem masters. Then came a squad of squaws; and then, alone, the mother of the dead child, bearing in her own arms—whose could be better?—the tiny corpse, which was in a species of wicker pie-dish, adorned with innumerable streamers of rainbow-hued ribbon and strips of cloth. A bevy of dusky children, capering but silent, brought up the rear.

We followed this curious train into the church, and I went up into a rickety gallery and looked down on the coffin of the poor little papoose stranded in the midst of a big bier in the chancel, like a pincushion in a brewer's vat. The priest came, with his cross-bearer and his acolytes and tapers and holy water, and the service for the dead was chanted; but in the midst of a timid quavering of the "Dies Iræ" there burst from the hitherto silent assemblage a prolonged and harrowing wail. It rings in my ears even now; and I can see the Indian women on their knees on the church pavement, rocking themselves to and fro and howling dismally. It was savagery asserting itself. It was as the voice of the wild animal in the depths of the forest, mourning for her cubs.

We followed the train again, away from the church and to the cemetery, and saw the papoose comfortably stowed away, gay-ribboned pall and all, in a quiet corner where the grass grew tall. Sleep soundly, O papoose; thou art well out of a troublous world. Then we came back to the shore and took boat and sped across the great river, and saw the last of Cuagnawagha. And many and many a time in far-distant lands have I recalled the rocky shore, the fat old chief, the gliding squaws, and the dead papoose with its rainbow pall.

XVIII.

STALLS.

T may not have occurred to you, amæne reader, to trouble yourself much concerning the Philosophy of Stalls, if haply you have ever thought it worth your while to inquire whether there was anything philosophical connected with a stall at all. To my mind there is, and much. To me a stall typifies in an intense degree the quality of selfishness. I draw a direct alliance between a stall and celibacy. I hold the possession of a stall to be linked with the ideas of independence, of isolation from and superiority to the rest of mankind. In a stall, properly so termed, you cannot put two people. The stalled ox is alone, and may look with infinite contempt on the poor sheep huddled together in a fold ; the cobbler who lived in his stall, which served him for kitchen and parlour and all, was, I will go bail, a bachelor. Robinson Crusoe for a very long time occupied a stall, and was monarch of all he surveyed. When Man Friday came, the recluse began to yearn to mingle with the world again. Diogenes in his tub perfectly fulfils the idea of an egotist. From his tub-stall he could witness at leisure the entire grand opera of Corinth.

I have heard of a royal duke—one of the past generation of royal dukes : burly, bluff princes in blue coats and brass buttons, who said everything twice over, drank hard, swore a good deal, and were immensely popular at the Crown and Anchor and the Thatched House Taverns—who, being in Windsor one Sunday afternoon, thought he would like to attend divine service in St. George's Chapel. Of course he was a Knight of the Garter, and had his stall in the old Gothic fane, with his casque and banner above, and a brass plate let in to the oaken carving, recording what a high, mighty, and puissant prince he was. The chapel happened to be very crowded, and as H.R.H. essayed to pass through the throng towards his niche in the choir, a verger whispered him deferentially that a distinguished foreign visitor, his Decrepitude the Grand Duke of Pfenningwurst-Schinken-braten, had been popped into the place of the English duke. " Don't care a rush—a rush," quoth H.R.H., poking his walking-cane into the spine of a plebeian in front of him. " Want to get to my stall—my stall." And from it, I suppose, he eventually succeeded in ousting the intruder from Germany. Was not H.R.H. in the right ? His stall was his vine and his fig-tree, and who was there to make him afraid ?

So much for stalls in the abstract. Practically, a stall may be defined as a place of occupation, in relative degrees, of a canon, a chorister, a cow, a cobbler, or a connoisseur. To study stalls most profitably in their ecclesiastical or monastic aspect, you should go to Flanders or to Spain. In the grand old cathedrals in those countries the traveller has always free access to the choir, and can take his surfeit of contemplation of the stalls. They will be found to the observant mind replete with human interest. They may be peopled with priests. Pursy pre-bendaries, dozing the doze of the just, and dreaming placidly, perchance, of good fat capon and clotted cream, while the brawny choirmen at the lecterns are thundering from huge oak-bound and brass-clamped folios, on the parchment pages of which corpulent minims and breves flounder over crimson lines ; pale, preoccupied priests, fretfully crimping the folds of their surplices and enviously eyeing my Lord Archbishop yonder, awfully enthroned, with his great mitre on his head and his emerald ring glancing on the plump white hand which he complacently spreads over the carved arm of his chair of state. Will they ever come to sit in that chair ? those pale, preoccupied men may be think-ing. Will they ever wear a mitre and hold out their hands for an obedient flock to kiss ? . Or will dignity and power and wealth fall to the lot of those drowsy prebendaries ?

More absorbing even in interest than the stalls in the choir of
a cathedral are those in a convent chapel. The reason is, I
suppose, that a monk has always been to me a mystery. A nun
I can more easily understand, for the monastic state in its best
and purest acceptation is a dream or an ecstasy ; and there
are vast numbers of women who pass their whole lives in a
dreamy and ecstatic frame of mind, and in a species of unob-
trusive hysterics. But the monk, with his manhood and his
great strong frame and the fire of ambition lambent in his eye,
and his lips firm-set in volition, always puzzles me. Continental
physicians will tell you that in every monastery there will be
found a certain proportion of mad monks—friars who have
strange lunes, and hear voices while they are sweeping out the
chapel or extinguishing the altar-candles, and to whom the saints
and angels in the pictures on the walls are living and breathing
personages.

I remember a dwarfish Cappuccino at Rome once executing
a kind of holy hornpipe before Guido's famous painting of the
Archangel vanquishing the Demon, and, as he jigged, taunting
the fiend on the canvas on the low estate to which he had
fallen, and derisively bidding him to use his claws and fangs.
Nor do I think that I was ever more terrified in my life than
by the behaviour of a gaunt young friar in the Catacombs of
San Sebastiano, who, opposite the empty tomb of a renowned
martyr, suddenly took to waving his taper above his head and
to abusing the Twelve Cæsars. He was our guide, and I feared
the candle would go out, and trembled to think what would
become of us, lost in Necropolis. But mad monks, or dreamy or
ecstatic monks, are sufficiently rare, it is to be surmised. Most
of the wearers of the cowl and sandals with whom I have made
acquaintance seemed to be perfectly well aware of what they
were about ; and a spirit of shrewd and pungent humour and
drollery is not by any means an uncommon characteristic of male
inmates of the cloister.

As for a Knight of the Garter in his stall, I regard him
simply as an awful being. Understand that, to strike one with

sufficient awe, he should be, not in plain dress, but in the "full fig" of his most noble order : a costume more imposing than the full uniform of the captain of a man-o'-war ; and *that*, backed by the man-o'-war herself in the offing, can be warranted to send any black king on the west coast of Africa into fits. But a K.G. with his garter on, with his sweeping velvet robe, with his collar and his George, with his tassels and badges and bows of ribbons, next to Solomon in all his glory is the most sumptuous sight I can conceive. The very stall he sits in is historical ; a knight of his own name occupied it three hundred years ago. It bears brazen chronicle of the doughtiest barons that ever lived.

What should one do to get made a K.G. and to earn the privilege of sitting in such a stall ? Would the genius of Shakespeare or Dante, would the learning of Boyle or Milton, would the imagination of a Tennyson, the graphic powers of a Millais, the researches of a Faraday—would even the giant intellect of a Brougham, help a man in the climbing upward to that stall ? Not much, I fancy. Its occupancy is to be obtained only by one process, ridiculously simple, yet to be mastered only by very few children of humanity. " Vous vous êtes donné la peine de naître," says Figaro to Count Almaviva, in the play. To be K.G.'d you must take the trouble to be . born of the K.G. caste.

But envy, avaunt ! Social fate is not without its compensations, and there are stalls and stalls. Lend me a guinea, and for a whole evening, from eight to nearly midnight, I can sit supreme in a stall, solitary, grand, absolute ; for who shall dare to turn me out ? The stall is mine, to have and to hold corporeally until the curtain has fallen on the last tableau of the ballet, and (in imagination at least) I can hang my banner and my casque over my stall and deem myself a high, mighty, and puissant prince. As the process put into practice might interfere with the comfort of the patrons of the Royal Italian Opera, I content myself with hanging my overcoat over the back of my stall and placing my collapsible Gibus beneath it.

I notice a large party of beautiful dames and damsels in a box
on the pit tier, who, I am vain enough to think, are intently
inspecting me through their opera-glasses. I plume myself. I
pull down my wristbands, I smooth my shirt-front and caress
the bows of my cravat. I turn the favourite facet of my
diamond ring well on to the box on the pit tier. If you are
the sun, shall you not shine? I am taken, I fondly hope, for
one of the Upper Ten.

I am aware, from eyesight acquaintance with the aristocracy,
that my neighbour on the right, with the purple wig, the
varnished pumps, and the ear-trump, is Field-Marshal Lord
Viscount Dumdum, that great Indian hero; and that the yellow-
faced little man on my left, with the yellow ribbon at his button-
hole, is the Troglodyte ambassador. Behind me is Sir Hercules
Hoof, of the Second Life-Guards. In front of me is the broad
back—I wish in respect to the back that it wasn't quite so
broad—of Mr. Bargebeam, Q.C. How are that family in the
pit tier to know that I am not a nobleman, a diplomatist, a
guardsman, or a queen's counsel? I am clean. I had my
hair dyed the day before yesterday. My boots are polished;
my neckcloth is starched stiff; my stall is as big as anybody
else's. How is beauty in the boxes to tell that I came in
(failing to borrow one-pound-one) with an order?

The playhouse stall is a thoroughly modern innovation; and
even the pit of the Italian theatres of the Renaissance was
destitute of seats. When Sterne first visited the opera in Paris
the groundlings stood to witness the performance, and sentinels
with fixed bayonets were posted to appease tumults, as in the
well-known case quoted in the "Sentimental Journey," when
the irate dwarf threatened to cut off the pigtail of the tall
German. I am old enough to remember when the pittites in
the Scala at Milan stood. You paid, I think, an Austrian
florin—one-and-eightpence—for bare admission to the house,
and then you took your chance of lighting upon some lady who
would invite you to a seat in her box; or some bachelor
acquaintance who, having had enough of the performance, would

surrender to you his reserved seat near the orchestra for the rest of the evening.

Seated pits have always been common in our English theatres, owing to the strong determination of the people to make themselves comfortable whenever it was possible to do so ; and these reserved seats of the Scala were the beginning of the exclusive seats we call stalls. They are not older than the era of the dominion of the Austrians in Lombardy, after the downfall of Napoleon the First. There were many Milanese nobles not wealthy enough to take boxes for the season, and too proud to sponge on their friends every evening for a back seat in a "palco," and too patriotic to mingle in the standing-up area with the Austrian officers, who, according to garrison regulations, were admitted to the Scala at the reduced price of ninepence halfpenny. So the manager of the Scala hit upon the crafty device of dividing the rows of benches near the orchestra into compartments, each wide enough to accommodate a single person, and the seats of which could be turned up as in the choir of a cathedral. Moreover, these seats were neatly fitted with hasps and padlocks, so that the subscriber could lock up his seat when, between the acts, he strolled into the *café* for refreshment. Perhaps he was absent from Milan during the whole operatic season ; and if he did not choose to lend the key of his stall to a friend of the right political way of thinking, the seat remained inexorably closed.

The system had a triple charm : First, the subscriber could revel to the fullest extent in the indulgence of that dog-in-the-manger-like selfishness which I have held to be inseparably connected with stall-holding ; next, he could baffle the knavish boxkeepers, with whom in an Italian theatre you can always drive an immoral bargain, and by a trifling bribe secure a better seat than that for which you have originally paid ; finally, he could obviate the possibility of his stall being contaminated by the sedentary presence of any Austrian general of high rank who happened to be an amateur of legs. High-handed as were the proceedings of the Tedeschi in Italy, they were wisely reluctant to interfere with the social habits of the people.

Just before the great French Revolution it became the fashion to place arm-chairs close to the orchestra of the Academy of Music, for the use of noble visitors who came down from their boxes to take a closer survey of the *coryphées ;* but these were *fauteuils* at large ; they were few in number, and could be shifted from place to place at will. Veritable stalls are those which, albeit they are fitted with arm-rests, are still immovably screwed to the floor ; and such stalls, old playgoers will bear me out, are things of very recent introduction in our theatres. The pit of Her Majesty's Theatre was once the resort of the grandest dandies in London. Going over the new structure the other day, I observed that the pit proper had been almost entirely suppressed, and that stalls monopolised seven-tenths of the sitting-room of the ground area.

In English theatres a similar monopoly has been from year to year gradually gaining strength. The most rubbishing little houses have now numerous rows of stalls, from which bonnets are of course banished ; and the pit is being quietly elbowed out of existence. "The third row of the pit" was once a kind of bench of judgment—I don't say of justice—on which those tremendous dispensers of dramatic fame and fortune, the critics, sat. Our papas and mammas did not despise the pit of Old Drury ; and I have heard tell of a lady of title who paid to the pit to see Master Betty, and who took with her a bag of sandwiches and some sherry in a bottle. I think I heard tell that she lost her shoe in the crowd before the doors were opened.

Should this remarkable extension of the stall system be considered as a blessing or an evil ? Has it not tended to the vast increase of selfishness, superciliousness, and the pride of place ? Dear sir, if I were a Professor of Paradoxes, I might tell you that the more selfish, the more supercilious, and the prouder of our places we are, the likelier will be the attainment of universal happiness. I might whisper to you that virtue is only selfishness in a sublime degree. But I am a professor of nothing, and I dread paradoxes—having had a relative once who was afflicted with them, and died. So I go back to stalls.

The stalled ox, and the stalled cows in the byres of Brock, in Holland, with their tails tied up to rings in the rafters, I leave to their devices, for my talk is of men and not of beasts. But lovingly do I glance at the cobbler in his stall—a merry man with twinkling eyes, a blue-black mazard, and somewhat of a copper nose, for ever cuddling his lapstone, smoothing his leather with sounding thwacks, drawing out his waxed string, working and singing, and bandying repartee with the butchers' boys and the fishwives passing his hutch. I would Mr. Longfellow had sung of that cobbler ; for as many tuneful things could be said about Crispin as about the Village Blacksmith. That he has been left unsung, I mourn sincerely ; for times change and types of humanity vanish, and I am beginning to miss that cobbler. Metropolitan improvements are unfavourable to him ; our pride and vanity militate against him ; for somehow we don't care about seeing our boots mended in public nowadays. In old times the cobbler's stall was permitted to nestle in the basement of mansions almost aristocratic in their respectability ; but at present no architect would dream of building a new cobbler's stall in a new house, and the old ones are fast disappearing. Crispin has risen in the world. He has taken a shop, and " repairs ladies' and gentlemen's boots and shoes with punctuality and dispatch."

The term "stall," as applied to the board on trestles, or supported perchance by a decayed washing-tub, laid out with apples, sweetstuff, or oysters, and presided over by an old Irishwoman with a stringless black bonnet flattened down on a mobcap, I consider a misnomer. It lacks the idea of exclusive possession which should attach to a stall. The apple, or sweetstuff, or oyster woman is but a tenant-at-will. She has no fee simple. She may be harried by the police, and petitioned against by churlish shopkeeping neighbours jealous of her poor outdoor traffic. Drunken roysterers may overturn her frail structure ; a reckless hansom cabdriver may bring her to irretrievable crash and ruin ; rival apple-women may compete with her at the opposite street corners ; and passing costermongers with strong-wheeled barrows may gird at her and disparage her wares. 'Tis not a stall at which she sits, but a stand, a mere thing of tolerance and sufferance : here to-day and gone to-morrow, if the proud man chooses despitefully to use poor Biddy.

But once give me sitting-room in a cathedral stall, and, by cock and pye, I will not budge! You may threaten to dis-establish and disendow me, but I will carry my stall about with me, as old gentlemen at the seaside carry their camp-stools. And if at last, by means of a measure forced on an unwilling nation by ministers more abandoned in their principles, sir, than Sejanus, Empson, Dudley, Polignac, Peyronnet, or the late Sir Robert Walpole, you declare that my stall must be abolished, you shall compensate me for its loss at a rate as rich as though I had always had it clamped with gold and stuffed with bank notes.

235

XIX.

Wretchedville.

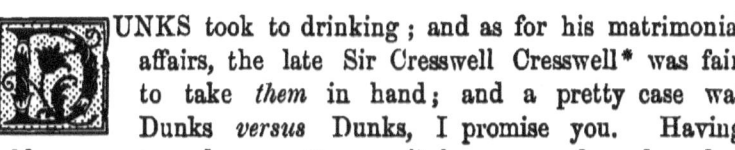UNKS took to drinking; and as for his matrimonial affairs, the late Sir Cresswell Cresswell* was fain to take *them* in hand; and a pretty case was Dunks *versus* Dunks, I promise you. Having sold or mortgaged every "carcass" he possessed, and undermined his own with strong liquors, Dunks went into the Bankruptcy Court, and soon afterwards died of a severe attack of rum-and-water, and trade-assignee on the brain—a wholly-ruined and still-uncertificated trader. It was a sad end for a man who had once served the office of churchwarden and driven his own chaise-cart—who had banked · with the London and County—and whose brother-in-law's uncle was reputed to be the proprietor of a New River share; but the mills of the gods grind small, and Dunks, to my thinking, only met in his decadence with his deserts.

When I spoke of "carcasses" just now, I did not intend to imply that Dunks was a wholesale butcher. *His* carcasses were of bricks and mortar, and of his own making. Dunks was a builder. He took the contract once for the Doleful Hill Lunatic Asylum, by which he did so well—notwithstanding the complaints of the architect in respect to the bricks—that he was enabled to build a large number of semi-detached villas, and a still larger quantity of "carcasses," as a speculation of his own. Had he been prudent—had common sense or even common decency been his guide—he might have made

* A former well-known judge of the Divorce Court.

a fortune and been living at this day in his own house at South Kensington, six stories high, and with a belvedere at one end, like the Eddystone lighthouse. His wife might have had a box at the Opera in lieu of that sad witness-box at the Divorce Court; and his sons might be enjoying a college education instead of being (as I know is the case with Tom) a waiter at a chop-house in Pope's Head Alley, or suffering every kind of hardship and privation (which I am afraid is Phil's mournful lot) as cabin-boy to that well-known disciplinarian, Captain Roper, of the ship *Anne and Sarah Cobbum* of Great Grimsby. This misguided Dunks might have become rich, respected, and a member of the Metropolitan Board of Works. Instead of this—flying in the face of his reason and experience, of which he should have had a fair share, seeing that he weighed nearly seventeen stone—he went and built Wretchedville. And then, forsooth, the man wondered that he was ruined.

The ground, to begin with, was the very worst in the whole county. It was an ugly, polygonal plot, shelving down from the higher road that leads from Sobbington to Doleful Hill: a clay soil, of course, but in very bad repute for the making of bricks. Indeed, the clay did not seem to be fit for anything save to stick to the boot-soles of people who were incautious enough to walk over it. When any rain fell, it remained here for about seven days after the adjoining ground had dried up. Then the clay resolved itself into a solution of a dark-red colour, and the spot assumed the aspect of a field of gore. When it was not clayey it was marshy; and the neighbours had long since christened the place "Ague Hole." Dunks in his frenzy, and with the Vale of Health at Hampstead in his eye, wanted to call it "Pleasant Hollow;" but the ground landlord, or rather landlady, Miss Goole (she went melancholy mad, left half her fortune to the Doleful Hill Asylum, and the will is still the subject of a nice little litigation in Chancery)—Miss Goole, I say, who granted Dunks his building lease, insisted that the group of tenements he intended to erect should be called

Wretchedville. Her aunt had been a Miss Wretched, of Ashby-de-la-Zouch.

And Wretchedville the place remains to this day. Dunks did his best, or rather his worst, with it. He proposed to drain the ground; the result of which was that water made its appearance in places where it had not appeared before. He laid out a declivitous road branching downwards from the highway and leading nowhere save to the reservoir of the West Howlington Gasworks; and a nice terminus to the vista did this monstrous iron tub make. He spent all his own money, and as much of other people's as he could possibly borrow, on Wretchedville, and then, as I have hinted, Bacchus and he became inseparable companions, and he continued to "wreathe the rosy bowl" and "quaff the maddening wine-cup," the two ordinarily assuming the guise of rum-and-water, cold, till he woke up one morning in the Messenger's Office in Basinghall Street, waiting for his protection.

Swamper, the great buyer-up of carcasses, was a secured creditor, and came into possession of Wretchedville; but Swamper is the world-known contractor, whose dealings with the Bucharest Improvements, and the Herzegovina Baths and Washhouses Company have been made lately the subject of such lively public comment. He is generally oscillating between his offices in Great George Street, Westminster, and the Danubian provinces, and has had little time to attend to Wretchedville. He has been heard to express an opinion that the place—the confounded hole, he calls it—will "turn up trumps" some day; and, indeed, plans for a new county prison on a remarkably eligible site between Doleful Hill and Sobbington have been hanging up for some time, neatly framed and glazed, in his office. Meanwhile the Wretchedville rents are receivable by Messrs. Flimsy and Quinsy, auctioneers, valuers, and estate agents, of Chancery Lane; and Swamper's affairs being, as I am given to understand, in somewhat evil trim, it is not unlikely that Wretchedville ere long will fall into fresh hands. And I don't envy the man into whose hands it falls.

How I came to be acquainted with Wretchedville was in this wise. I was in quest last autumn of a nice quiet place within a convenient distance of town where I could finish an epic poem—or stay, was it a five-act drama ?—on which I had been long engaged, and where I could be secure from the annoyance of organ-grinders and of reverend gentlemen leaving little subscription-books one day and calling for them the next—I should like to know what difference there is between them and the people who leave the packets of steel pens, and the patent lamp-globe protector, and Bullinger's "History of the Inquisition," under the special patronage of the Archbishop of Tobago, to be continued in monthly parts—together with the people who want your autograph, and others who want money, and things of that kind. I pined for a place where one could be very snug, and where one's friends didn't drop in "just to look you up, old fellow;"· and where the post didn't come in too often. So I packed up a bag of needments, and availing myself of a mid-day train on the Great Domdaniel Railway, alighted haphazard at a station.

It turned out to be Sobbington. I saw at a glance that Sobbington was too fashionable, not to say stuck-up, for me. The Waltz from "Faust" was pianofortetically audible from at least half a dozen semi-detached windows; and this, combined with some painful variations on "Take, then, the Sabre," and a cursory glance into a stationer's shop and fancy warehouse where two stern mammas of low-church aspect were purchasing the back numbers of "The New Pugwell Square Pulpit," and three young ladies were telegraphically inquiring, behind their parent's backs, of the young person at the counter whether any letters had been left for them, sufficed to accelerate my departure from Sobbington. The next station on the road, I was told, was Doleful Hill, and then came Deadwood Junction. I thought I would take a little walk and see what the open and what the covert yielded.

I left my bag with a moody porter at the Sobbington station and trudged along the road which had been indicated to me as leading to Doleful Hill. It happened to be a very splendid afternoon. There were patches of golden gorse and purple heather skirting those parts of the road in which the semi-detached villa eruption had not yet broken out ; the distant hills were delicately blue, and the mellow sun was distilling his rays into diamonds and rubies on the roof of a wondrous Palace of Glass, which does duty in these parts, as Vesuvius does duty in Naples, as a pervading presence. At Portici and at Torre del Greco, at Sobbington or at Doleful Hill, turn whithersoever you will, the mountain seems close upon you always.

It is true that I was a little dashed when I encountered an organ-grinder lugubriously winding " Slap, bang, here we are again ! " off his brazen reel, and looking anything but a jolly dog. Organ-grinding was contrary to the code I had laid down to govern my retirement. But the autumnal sun shone very genially on this child of the sunny South—who had possibly come from the bleakest part of Piedmont ; his smile was of the sunniest likewise, and there was a roguish twinkle in his black eyes ; and though his cheeks were brown, his teeth were of the whitest. So, as I gave him pence, I determined inwardly that I would tolerate at least one organ-grinder if he came near where I lived. It is true that I had not the remotest idea of where I was going to live.

I walked onwards and onwards, admiring the pied cows in the far-off pastures—cows the white specks on whose hides occurred so artistically that one might have thought that the scenic arrangement of the landscape had been intrusted to Mr. Birket Foster.

Anon I saw coming towards me a butcher-boy in his cart, drawn by a fast-trotting pony. It was a light high spring-cart, very natty and shiny, with the names and addresses of the proprietors, Messrs. Hock, Butchers to the Royal Family, West Deadwood—which of the princes or princesses resided at West Deadwood, I wonder ?—emblazoned on the panels. The butcher-boy shone, too, with a suety sheen. The joints which formed his cargo were of the hue of which an English girl's cheeks should be—pure red and white. And the good sun shone upon all. The equipage came rattling along at a high trot, the butcher squaring his arms and whistling—I could *see* him whistle from afar off. I asked him, when he neared me, how far it might be to Doleful Hill.

"Good two mile," quoth the butcher-boy, pulling up. "Steady, you warmint!" This was to the trotting pony. "But," he continued, "you'll have to pass Wretchedville first. Lays in a 'ole a little to the left, 'arf a mile on.'"

"Wretchedville," thought I; what an odd name! "What sort of a place is it?" I inquired.

"Well," replied the butcher-boy; "it's a lively place, a werry lively place. I should say it was lively enough to make a cricket burst himself for spite: it's so uncommon lively." And with this enigmatical deliverance the butcher-boy relapsed into a whistle of the utmost shrillness, and rattled away towards Sobbington.

I wish that it had not been quite so golden an afternoon. A little dulness, a few clouds in the sky, might have acted as a caveat against Wretchedville. But I plodded on and on, finding all things looking beautiful in that autumn glow. I came positively on a gipsy encampment; blanket tent; donkey tethered to a cart-wheel; brown man in a wide-awake hammering at a tin pot; brown woman with a yellow kerchief, sitting cross-legged, mending brown man's pantaloons; brown little brats of Egypt swarming across the road and holding out their burnt-sienna hands for largesse, and the regular gipsy's kettle swinging from the crossed sticks over a fire of stolen furze. Farmer Somebody's poultry simmering in the pot, no doubt. Family linen—somebody else's linen yesterday—drying on an adjacent bush. Who says that the picturesque is dead? The days of Sir Roger de Coverley had come again. So I went on and on admiring, and down the declivitous road into Wretchedville and to destruction.

Were there any apartments "to let"? Of course there were. The very first house I came to was as regards the parlour-window nearly blocked up by a placard treating of "Apartments

Furnished." Am I right in describing it as the parlour-window? I scarcely know ; for the front door, with which it was on a level, was approached by such a very steep flight of steps that when you stood on the topmost grade it seemed as though, with a very slight effort, you could have peeped in at the bedroom window, or touched one of the chimney-pots ; while as concerns the basement, the front kitchen—I beg pardon, the breakfast parlour—appeared to be a good way above the level of the street.

The space in the first-floor window not occupied by the placard was filled by a monstrous group of wax fruit, the lemons as big as pumpkins and the leaves of an unnaturally vivid green. The window below—it was a single-windowed front—served merely as a frame for the half-length portrait of a lady in a cap, ringlets, and a colossal cameo brooch. The eyes of this portrait were fixed upon me ; and before almost I had lifted a very small light knocker, decorated, so far as I could make out, with the cast-iron effigy of a desponding ape, and had struck this against a door which, to judge from the amount of percussion produced, was composed of bristol-board highly varnished, the portal itself flew open and the portrait of the basement appeared in the flesh. Indeed, it was the same portrait. Downstairs it had been Mrs. Primpris looking out into the Wretchedville Road for lodgers. Upstairs it was Mrs. Primpris letting her lodgings and glorying in the act.

She didn't ask for any references. She didn't hasten to inform me that there were no children or any other lodgers. She didn't look doubtful when I told her that the whole of my luggage consisted of a black bag which I had left at the Sobbington station. She seemed rather pleased than otherwise at the idea of the bag, and said that her Alfred should step round for it. She didn't object to smoking ; and she at once invested me with the Order of the Latch-key—a latch-key at Wretchedville, ha ! ha ! She further held me with her glittering eye, and I listened like a two years' child while she let me the lodgings for a fortnight certain. Perhaps it was less her eye that dazed me than her cameo, on which there was, in high relief and on a ground the hue of a pig's

Q

liver, the effigy of a young woman with a straight nose and a round chin and a quantity of snakes in her hair. I don't think that cameo came from Rome. I think it came from Tottenham Court Road.

She had converted me into a single gentleman lodger of quiet and retired habits—or was I a widower of independent means seeking a home in a cheerful family?—so suddenly that I beheld all things as in a dream. Thinking, perchance, that the first stone of that monumental edifice, the bill, could not be laid too quickly, she immediately provided me with tea. There was a little cottage-loaf, so hard, round, shiny, and compact, that I experienced a well-nigh uncontrollable desire to fling it up to the ceiling to ascertain whether it would chip off any portion of a preposterous rosette in stucco in the centre, representing a sunflower, surrounded by cabbage-leaves. This terrible ornament was, by the way, one of the chief sources of my misery at Wretchedville. I was continually apprehensive that it would tumble down bodily on the table. In addition to the cottage-loaf there was a pretentious teapot, which, had it been of sterling silver, would have been worth fifty guineas, but which, in its ghastly gleaming, said plainly "Sheffield" and "imposture." There was a piece of butter in a "shape" like a diminutive haystack, and with a cow sprawling on the top in unctuous plasticity. It was a pallid kind of butter, from which with difficulty you shaved off adipocerous scales, which would not be persuaded to adhere to the bread, but flew off at tangents and went rolling about an intolerably large tea-tray, on whose papier-mâché surface was depicted the death of Captain Hedley Vicars. The Crimean sky was inlaid with mother-of-pearl, and the gallant captain's face was highly enriched with blue-and-crimson foil-paper.

As for the tea, I don't think I ever tasted such a peculiar mixture. Did you ever sip warm catsup sweetened with borax? *That* might have been something like it. And what was that sediment, strongly resembling the sand at Great Yarmouth, at the bottom of the cup? I sat down to my meal, however, and made as much play with the cottage-loaf as I could. Had the loaf

been varnished ? It smelt and looked as though it had undergone
that process. Everything in the house smelt of varnish. I was
uncomfortably conscious, too, during my repast—one side of the
room being all window—that I was performing the part of a
" Portrait of the Gentleman in the first floor," and that as such I
was "sitting" to Mrs. Lucknow at Number Twelve opposite—I
know her name was Lucknow, for a brass plate on the door said
so—whose own half-length effigy was visible in her breakfast-
parlour window, glowering at me reproachfully because I had not
taken her first floor, in the window of which was, not a group of
wax fruit, but a sham alabaster vase full of artificial flowers.
Every window in Wretchedville exhibited one or other of these
ornaments, and it was from their contemplation that I began to
understand how it was that the "fancy-goods" trade in the
Minories and Houndsditch throve so well. They made things
there to be purchased by the housekeepers of Wretchedville.

The presence of Mrs. Lucknow at the glass case over the way
was becoming unbearable, when the unpleasant vision was shut
out by the appearance of Mrs. Primpris's Alfred, who with his
sister Selina had been sent to Sobbington for my bag. Alfred
was a boy with a taste for art. In the daytime he was continually
copying the head of a Greek person (sex uncertain) in a helmet,
who reminded you equally of a hairdresser's dummy in plaster
and of a fireman of the Fire Brigade. He used to bring studies
of this person, in white, red, and black chalk, to me, and expect
that I would reward him for his proficiency with threepenny-
pieces "to buy india-rubber ;" and then Mrs. Primpris would be
sure to be lurking outside the door and audibly expressing her
wish that some good, kind gentleman would get Alfred into the
Blue Coat School, which she appeared to look upon as a kind of
eleemosynary institution in connection with the Royal Academy
of Arts. I can't help suspecting, from sundry private conversations I had with Alfred, that he entertained a profound detestation
for the plaster person in the helmet and for the Fine Arts generally ; but, as he logically observed, he was "kep at it," and "it
was no use hollerin'."

As for Alfred's sister Selina, all I can remember of her is that
one leg of her tucked calico trousers was always two inches and a
half longer than the other, and that for a girl of thirteen she had
the most alarmingly sharp shoulder-blades I ever saw.   I always
used to think when I saw these osseous angularities, oscillating
like the beams of a marine engine, that the next time her piston-
rod-like arms moved, the scapulæ must come through her frock.
Mrs. Primpris was a disciplinarian, and whenever I heard Selina
plaintively yelping in the kitchen, I felt tolerably certain that
Mrs. Primpris was correcting her on her shoulder-blades with
a shoe.

The shades of evening fell, and Mrs. Primpris brought me in a
monstrous paraffin lamp, the flame of which wouldn't do anything
but lick the glass chimney till it had smoked it to the hue proper
to observe eclipses by, and then splutter into extinction, emitting a
charnel-house-like odour.   After that we tried a couple of com-
posites (six to the pound) in green glass candlesticks.   I asked
Mrs. Primpris if she could send me up a book to read, and she
favoured me, *per* Alfred and Selina, with her whole library, consisting of the Asylum Press Almanac for 1860 ; two odd volumes
of the Calcutta Directory ; the Brewer and Distiller's Assistant ;
Julia de Crespigny, or a Winter in London ; Dunoyer's French
Idioms ; and the Reverend Mr. Huntington's Bank of Faith.

I took out my cigar-case after this and began to smoke ; and
then I heard Mrs. Primpris coughing and a number of doors being
thrown wide open.   Upon this I concluded that I would go to
bed.   My sleeping apartment—the first-floor back—was a perfect
cube.   One side was window overlooking a strip of clay soil
hemmed in between brick walls.   There were no tombstones yet,
but if it wasn't a cemetery, why, when I opened the window to get
rid of the odour of the varnish, did it smell like one ?   The
opposite side of the cube was composed of a chest of drawers.   I
am not impertinently curious by nature, but, as I was the first-
floor lodger, I thought myself entitled to open the top long drawer
with a view to the bestowal therein of the contents of my black
bag.   The drawer was not empty ; but that which it held made

me very nervous. I suppose the weird figure I saw stretched out there with pink arms and legs sprouting from a shroud of silver paper, a quantity of ghastly auburn curls, and two blue glass eyes unnaturally gleaming in the midst of a mask of salmon-coloured wax, was Selina's best doll ; the present, perhaps, of her uncle, who was, haply, a Calcutta director, or an Asylum Press Almanac maker, or a brewer and distiller, or a cashier in the Bank of Faith. I shut the drawer again hurriedly, and that doll in its silver paper cerecloth haunted me all night.

The third side of my bedroom consisted of chimney—the coldest, hardest, brightest-looking fireplace I ever saw out of Hampton Court Palace guardroom. The fourth side was door. I forget into which corner was hitched a washhand stand. The ceiling was mainly stucco rosette, of the pattern of the one in my sitting-room. Among the crazes which came over me at this time was one to the effect that this bedroom was a cabin on board ship, and that if the ship should happen to lurch or roll in the trough of the sea, I must infallibly tumble out of the door or the window, or into the drawer where the doll was—unless the drawer and the doll came out to me—or up the chimney. I think that I murmured " Steady " as I clomb into bed.

My couch—an "Arabian " one, Mrs. Primpris said proudly— seemingly consisted of the Logan, or celebrated rocking-stone of Cornwall, loosely covered with bleached canvas, under which was certain loose foreign matter, but whether composed of flocculi of wool or of the halves of kidney potatoes I am not in a position to state. At all events I awoke in the morning veined all over like a scagliola column. I never knew, too, before, that any blankets were ever manufactured in Yorkshire, or elsewhere, so remarkably small and thin as the two seeming flannel pocket-hand-kerchiefs with blue-and-crimson edging, which formed part of Mrs. Primpris's Arabian bed-furniture. Nor had I hitherto been aware, as I was when I lay with that window at my feet, that the moon was so very large. The orb of night seemed to tumble on me, flat, until I felt as though I were lying in a cold frying-pan. It was a " watery moon," I have reason to think ; for when I

awoke the next morning, much battered with visionary conflicts
with the doll, I found that it was raining cats and dogs.

"The rain," the poet tells us, "it raineth every day." It
rained most prosaically all that day at Wretchedville, and the next,
and from Monday morning till Saturday night, and then until the
middle of the next week. Dear me! dear me! how wretched I
was! I hasten to declare that I have no kind of complaint to
make against Mrs. Primpris. Not a flea was felt in her house.
The cleanliness of the villa was so scrupulous as to be distressing.
It smelt of soap and scrubbing-brush like a Refuge. Mrs. Primpris was strictly honest, even to the extent of inquiring what I
would like to have done with the fat of cold mutton-chops, and
sending me up antediluvian crusts, the remnants of last week's
cottage-loaves, with which I would play moodily at knock-'em-
downs, using the pepper-caster as a pin. I have nothing to say
against Alfred's fondness for art. India-rubber, to be sure, is
apter to smear than to obliterate drawings in chalk ; but a threepenny piece is not much, and you cannot too early encourage the
imitative faculties. And again, if Selina did require correction, I
am not prepared to deny that a shoe may be the best implement
and the bladebones the most fitting portion of the human anatomy
for such an exercitation.

I merely say that I was wretched at Wretchedville, and that
Mrs. Primpris's apartments very much aggravated my misery.
The usual objections taken to a lodging-house are to the effect
that the furniture is dingy, the cooking execrable, the servant a
slattern, and the landlady either a crocodile or a tigress. Now
my indictment against my Wretchedville apartments simply
amounts to this: that everything was too new. Never were
there such staring paper-hangings, such gaudily printed druggets
for carpets, such blazing hearthrugs—one representing the Dog
of Montargis seizing the murderer of the Forest of Bondy—such
gleaming fire-irons, and such remarkably shiny looking-glasses,
with gilt halters for frames. The crockery was new, and the
glue in the chairs and tables was scarcely dry. The new veneer
peeled off the new chiffonier. The roller-blinds to the windows

were so new that they wouldn't work. The new stair-carpeting used to dazzle my eyes so, that I was always tripping myself up; the new oil-cloth in the hall smelt like the Trinity House repository for new buoys; and Mrs. Primpris was always full-dressed, cameo brooch and all, by nine o'clock in the morning. She confessed once or twice during my stay that her house was not quite "seasoned." It was not even seasoned to sound. Every time the kitchen-fire was poked you heard the sound in the sitting-room. As to perfumes, whenever the lid of the copper in the washhouse was raised, the first-floor lodger was aware of the fact. I knew by the simple evidence of my olfactory organs what Mrs. Primpris had for dinner every day. Pork, accompanied by some green esculent, boiled, predominated.

When my fortnight's tenancy had expired—I never went outside the house until I left it for good—and my epic poem, or whatever it was, had more or less been completed, I returned to London, and had a rare bilious attack. The doctor said it was painter's colic; I said at the time it was disappointed ambition, for the booksellers had looked very coldly on my poetical proposals, and the managers to a man had refused to read my play; but at this present writing I believe the sole cause of my malady to have been Wretchedville. I hope they will pull down the villas and build the jail there soon, and that the rascal convicts will be as wretched as I was.

XX.

NOBODY ABROAD.

ARLY in the present century, that is to say, in the month of October, 1801, it occurred to Mr. Nobody to visit the famous city of Paris. According to the Republican calendar, which then obtained among our neighbours, the month was not October and the year was not 1801. The month was Brumaire and the year was Ten of the Republic one and indivisible. But Mr. Nobody being an Englishman, the non-republican computation of time and season may be adopted. I call my traveller Mr. Nobody because I have not the slightest idea who he was, whence he came, or whither—when he returned from his Parisian tour—he went. He was certainly not Tom Paine, but I am not prepared to assert that he might not have been the author of Junius, taking a shady and secretive holiday, according to his inscrutable wont.

Mr. Nobody wrote a book about his travels, entitled "A Rough Sketch of Modern Paris," and he caused it to be published anonymously in a thin octavo by a bookseller in St. Paul's Churchyard. He did not even favour the public with his initials, or with three asterisks, or with a Greek or Roman pseudonym. At the end of four pages of preface he signs himself "The Author," which, in default of any other explanation, is, to say the least, baffling. To increase the bewilderment of posterity, the work of this occult traveller takes the form of a series of letters addressed to a friend, who is qualified as "My Dear Sir;" but who "My Dear Sir" was is unknown to Everybody except Nobody. At the conclusion of each of his letters Mr. Nobody observes, "As soon as I have anything to communicate, I shall write again. In the meantime I take my leave, and am, &c." What are you to do with an author who persists in saying that he is et cetera ?

Mr. Nobody, however, is not to be neglected, for two reasons ; the first, that he has drawn a very curious and interesting picture of Paris as it appeared to an Englishman during the brief peace, or rather truce, of Amiens ; the second that, his obstinate anonymity notwithstanding, Mr. Nobody's pages are fruitful of internal evidence that he must have been Somebody, and somebody of note, too. He had a wife who shared his pleasures and his hardships. He was on visiting terms with his Britannic Majesty's ambassador in Paris, and was presented at the Tuileries. Mrs. Nobody even dined there. Finally, he took his own carriage abroad with him, and his letters of credit on his bankers were illimitable.

On the twenty-sixth of October he left the York House at Dover and embarked on board a neutral vessel, which he was compelled to hire, no English packet-boat being yet permitted to enter a French port. After a smooth and pleasant passage of four hours, Mr. Nobody found himself at Calais. As soon as the vessel entered the port, two Custom-house officers in military uniform came on board, and took down the names of the passengers. One of them retired to make his report to the municipality of Calais, while the other remained on board to prevent any of the passengers from landing. While the French *douanier* was on shore, Calais pier was crowded by spectators, the greater part of whom were military men. They seemed to derive great gratification from staring at the English ladies, and from examining the body of Mr. Nobody's carriage, which was hung on the deck of the ship ; while Mr. N. himself was equally entertained with the great *moustaches*—the italics are his own—of the grenadiers, the wooden shoes of the peasants, and the close caps of the grisettes.

The *douanier* returning on board, Mr. Nobody and suite were permitted to touch the territory of the Republic, and, escorted by a guard of *bourgeois*, desperately ragged as to uniform, were marched from the quay to the Custom-house, from the Custom-

house to the mayor, and from the mayor to the Commissary of
Police. At each of these offices, examinations—oral, impedi-
mental, and personal—were made. Mr. Nobody was fain not only
to surrender his passport but also his pocket-book and letters.
The last-named were returned on the following day. These little
police amenities coming to an end about seven p.m., Mr. Nobody
was then free to sit down to an excellent dinner at the celebrated
hotel formerly kept by Dessein, now succeeded by his nephew
Quillacq—a very respectable man, who met Mr. N. at landing, and
with the utmost civility and attention took care of his carriage
and baggage. The Unknown wished to set out on the following
morning for Paris, but, according to respectable M. Quillacq, that
was a simple impossibility ; for although the Unmentioned had
brought with him a passport in due form from M. de Talleyrand,
countersigned by M. Otto, the French minister in London, and
backed by his Britannic Majesty's own gracious licence to travel
in foreign parts, it was necessary to have all these documents
exchanged for a *laissez-passer* from the mayor of Calais.

Mr. N. accordingly passed the whole of the next day in Calais,
and on Wednesday morning, accompanied by " Mrs. ——," he
left Calais with post-horses. Why won't he call her his Araminta
or his Sophonisba ? Betsy Jane, even, would be preferable to this
colourless " Mrs. ——." The roads were very bad, particularly
near Boulogne ; the posting charges were moderate—six livres, or
five shillings, a stage of five miles ; say a shilling a mile. How
much is first-class fare by the Great Northern of France ? About
twopence-halfpenny.

Montreuil, where the travellers were to sleep, was not reached
until sunset. Here was found excellent accommodation " at the
inn celebrated by Sterne." The Reverend Mr. Yorick seems to
have been the Murray of the eighteenth century and the beginning of the present one, and it is astonishing that his publishers
did not put forth an advertising edition of the "Sentimental
Journey." At Montreuil, Mr. N. (the rogue !), in true Yorick-
like spirit, noticed " the smiling attentions of two very pretty girls
who acted as waiters." He omits to state whether Mrs. ——

noticed their smiling attention. The next day, through a fine country and bad roads, Amiens was reached. The cultivation by the wayside was good ; the peasants were well clad ; the beggars were numerous. The waiters, postboys, and landlords were everywhere remarkably civil, and expressed their joy at seeing "Milords Anglais " once more among them. Can Mr. Nobody have been a nobleman, and Mrs. —— only a shallow delusion veiling an actual ladyship ?

His Lordship—I mean his Nonentity—remarked that the lower classes were more respectful than before the Revolution. The reason appeared to him obvious. The old nobility treated their inferiors with jocular familiarity—the familiarity which, it may be, bordered on contempt—and the inferiors, mere thralls and bondsmen as they were, took trifling verbal liberties with their lords. Did not something akin to this prevail in Scotland during the last century, and is it not very well illustrated in Dean Ramsay's story of the Scotch lord who picks up a farthing in the sight of a beggar ? " Earl ! " cries out the gaberlunzie man, "gie us the siller." " Na, na," replies his lordship, pocketing the coin, " fin' a baubee for yoursel', puir bodie." When the social gulf between classes is unfathomable, do we not sometimes affect to shake hands across it ? But when we stand foot to foot—" mensch zu mensch," as Schiller as it—on the same earth, do we not often feel inclined to shake our fists in each other's faces ? " The loss of their rank," observes Mr. Nobody, " has compelled the higher classes to command respect by a distance of manner, which has of course produced a similar course of conduct in the persons beneath them." But for that merciless date—1801—one would think that Mr. Nobody had travelled in the State of Virginia since the abolition of slavery. The planters are no longer hail fellow well met with their serfs, and enfranchised Sambo no longer addresses the white man as " Mas'r," but as " Sa." Liberty is a wonderful teacher of etiquette.

At Amiens the Unknown drove to the Hôtel d'Angleterre, where he was magnificently and miserably lodged. The windows and doors declined to keep out the wind and rain ; the fires were

bad and the supper was worse ; nor was the final touch of
extravagant charges wanting. The journey was resumed on
Friday morning ; the beauty of the country and the badness of
the roads increasing at every step. At length the weary travellers
clattered into Chantilly, found a comfortable bed, and on Saturday
morning visited the " magnificent ruins " of the Palace of Chantilly. The superb edifice of the stables only remained intact.
The Government of the First Consul had forbidden the sale of
these buildings, and the mistress of the inn told Mr. Nobody,
with tears in her eyes, that had Napoleon been at the head of
affairs only six months sooner, the palace also would have been
rescued from destruction.

A little way out of Chantilly a fine paved road commenced,
extending to Paris, which city Mr. Nobody reached at two p.m.
on Saturday. He had been three and a half days and three
nights on the road. At the Paris barrier passports were asked
for, but were at once and civilly returned. " Carriages," Mr. N.
adds, " are no longer stopped, as formerly, in every town, to be
searched for contraband goods ; but turnpikes are numerous and
expensive." On entering Paris the travellers drove to several
hotels before they could procure accommodation, and such as they
at last found was wretched. Many of the hotels had been stripped
during the Revolution, and had not been refurnished ; and the
few remaining in proper gear were crowded by foreigners, who
since the peace had flocked hither in vast numbers from every
country in the world. Mr. Nobody very strongly advises persons
intending to visit Paris to write some days beforehand to their
correspondents if they desire to be comfortably lodged on their
arrival. The Mysterious Man was not, however, disheartened by
the badness of the inn. So soon as he had changed his attire he
hastened to call on M. Perregaux, his banker, who, notwithstanding his recent promotion to the rank of senator, was as civil and
obliging as ever. Mr. Nobody *must* have been Somebody. See
how civil everybody was to him !

I have been an unconscionable time bringing this shadowy friend
of mine from Calais to Paris ; but I hold this record of his

experiences to be somewhat of the nature of a text on which a
lay sermon might be preached, to the great edification of modern,
fretful, and grumbling travellers. "Young sir," I would say,
were it my business to preach—the which, happily, it is not—
"modern young British tourist, take account of the four days'
sufferings of Mr. Nobody and Mrs. Dash, and learn patience and
contentment. Some eighty hours did they pass in hideous discomfort on dolorous roads or in unseemly hostelries. Much were
they baited anent passports ; much were they exercised in consequence of the stiff-neckedness of that proud man the mayor of
Calais. How many times, for aught we know, may not their
linch-pins have disappeared, their traces snapped, their axles
parted ? Who shall say but that their postilions, although civil,
smelt fearfully of garlic, and (especially during the stages between
Beauvais and St. Denis) became partially overcome by brandy ?
St. Denis has always been notorious for the worst brandy in
Europe. And the dust ! And the beggars ! But for the
'smiling attentions' of those two pretty waiter girls at Montreuil, I tremble to think what might have been the temper of
Mr. Nobody when he found himself at last in Paris. Thus he
of 1801.

"This is how your grandpapa, your uncle William, went to
Paris ; but how fares it with you, my young friend ? You
designed, say on Friday afternoon last, to take three days'
holiday. You would have a 'run over to Paris,' you said. You
dined at six p.m. on Friday at the Junior Juvenal Club, Pall Mall.
You smoked your habitual cigar ; you played your usual game of
billiards after dinner. It was many minutes after eight when you
found yourself, with a single dressing bag for luggage, at Charing
Cross terminus. You took a 'first-class return' for Paris, for
which you paid, probably, much less than Mr. Nobody disbursed
for the passage of himself and his high-hung carriage (to say
nothing of Mrs. Dash) from Dover to Calais. A couple of hours
of the express train's fury brought you that Friday night to
Dover—brought you to the Admiralty pier, to the very verge and
brink of the much-sounding sea, and bundling you, so to speak,

down some slippery steps, sent you staggering on board a taut little steamer, which, having gorged certain mail bags, proceeded to fight her way through the biggest waves. In two hours afterwards you were at Calais. No passports, no botheration with municipalities, commissaires, or stiff-necked mayors awaited you. Another express train waited for you, giving you time to dispatch a comfortable supper ; and by seven o'clock on Saturday morning you were in Paris.

"You went to the Porte St. Martin on Saturday night and to Mabille afterwards. On Sunday I hope you went to church, and perhaps you went to Versailles. On Monday you had a good deal of Boulevard shopping to get through for your sisters or for the Mrs. Dash of the future ; and after a comfortable five o'clock dinner at the Café Riche in the afternoon, you found yourself shortly after seven p.m. at the Chemin de Fer du Nord, and by six o'clock on Tuesday morning you were back again at Charing Cross or at Victoria. Arrived there, you had yet a florin and a fifty centime piece left of the change for a ten-pound note. And yet you murmur and grumble. You have spoken heresy against the harbour-master of Dover. You have hurled bitter words at the directors of the South Eastern Railway Company, and have made mock of the London, Chatham, and Dover. Thrice have you threatened to write to *The Times*. Once did you propose to 'punch' the head of an obnoxious waiter at the Calais buffet." To this purport I could say a great deal if I preached sermons.

My esteemed friend Mr. Nobody abode in Paris for full six months ; but the amount of sight-seeing he went through was so vast, and his account thereof is so minute, that for reasons of space I do not dare to follow him from each Parisian pillar to its corresponding post. I can only briefly note that he attended a sitting of the legislative body in the *ci-devant* Palais Bourbon, and that he paid five francs for admission to the gallery. Drums and fifes announced the approach of the legislators, and a guard of honour, consisting of an entire regiment, escorted them. The president having taken the chair, more drums and fifes proclaimed the arrival of three counsellors of state bearing a message from the government. These high republican functionaries were preceded by ushers wearing Spanish hats with tricoloured plumes ; the counsellors themselves were dressed in scarlet cloth, richly embroidered. They ascended the tribune, read their message, and made three separate speeches on the subject of honour, glory, and France ; whereafter the legislative body, with loud cries of " Vive le Premier Consul ! " " Vive Madame Bonaparte ! " separated. It was the last day of the session.

Abating the scarlet coats and the Spanish hats of the huissiers, the break-up of a parliamentary session in 1801 must have very closely resembled that which we see in the French Corps Législatif in 1869. Mr. Nobody went away much pleased, especially with the admiration bestowed by his neighbours in the gallery on Lord Cornwallis, who was present among the Corps Diplomatique, and for whom Mr. Nobody seems himself to have entertained an affection bordering on adoration. " Yes, yes," cried an enthusiastic republican near him, " that tall man is Milord Cornwallis. He has a fine figure. He looks like a military man. He has served in the army. Is it not true, sir ? Look at that little man near him. What a difference ! What a mean appearance ! "

Mr. Nobody was in one aspect an exceptional Englishman. He appears to have been imbued with a sincere admiration for the talents of Napoleon Bonaparte, and even to have had some liking for the personal character of that individual. " My dear sir," he writes to that nameless friend of his on the sixth of December, "my curiosity is at length gratified. I have seen Bonaparte. You will readily conceive how much pleasure I felt to-day in beholding for the first time this extraordinary man, on whose exertions the fate of France, and in many respects that of Europe, may be said to depend." Mr. N. was fortunate enough to obtain places in the apartments of Duroc, governor of the Tuileries, from which he witnessed a review in the Carrousel. The Consular, soon to become the Imperial, Guard were inspected by the Master of France, than in the thirty-third year of his age. He was mounted on a white charger. As he passed several times before Mr. Nobody's window, that Impalpability had ample

leisûre to observe him ; and it appears to me that the portrait he
has drawn of the First Consul, then in the full flush of his fame,
undarkened by D'Enghien's murder, Pichegru's imputed end, and
Josephine's divorce, is sufficient to rescue Mr. Nobody's notes
from oblivion.

"His complexion," writes the Unknown, "is remarkably
sallow ; his countenance expressive, but stern ; his figure lithe,
but well made ; and his whole person, like the mind which it
contains, singular and remarkable. If I were compelled to
compare him to any one, I should name Kemble the actor.
Though Bonaparte is less in size, and less handsome than that
respectable performer, yet, in the construction of the features
and the general expression, there is a strong resemblance. The
picture of Bonaparte at the review, exhibited some time back in
Piccadilly,* and the bust in Sèvres china, which is very common
in Paris, and has probably become equally so in London " (it was
soon to be superseded by Gillray's monstrous caricatures of the
Corsican Ogre), " are the best likenesses I have seen. As to his
dress, he wore the grand costume of his office, that is to say, a
scarlet velvet coat, profusely embroidered with gold. To this he
had added leather breeches, jockey boots, and a little plain
cocked-hat, the only ornament to which was a national cockade.
His hair, unpowdered, was cut close to his neck."

Now this (excuse the anachronism) is a perfect photograph,
and might serve as a guide to any English artist desirous of
emulating as a Napoleographer the achievements of Meissonier
or Gerome. We have had from English painters Napoleon in
blue, in green, in a gray greatcoat, in his purple coronation
robes, even in the striped nankeen suit of his exile on the Rock.
But the great enemy of England in scarlet ! the vanquished of
Waterloo in a red coat ! But for Mr. Nobody's testimony I
should just as soon have imagined George the Third with a

* This picture was by Carle Vernet, the father of Horace,. and was
exhibited at Fores's—ancestor of the present well-known printseller. At
Fores's, just eight years previously, had been on view an engraving of the
execution of Louis the Sixteenth, by Isaac Cruikshank (father of our
George), and a "working model" of the guillotine.

Phrygian cap over his wig, or the Right Honourable William Pitt weathering the storm as a sans-culotte.

Again did Mr. Nobody see the Corsican, and at his own house —in the audience hall of the Tuileries. Mr. Jackson was minister plenipotentiary from England prior to Lord Whitworth's coming; and to Mr. Jackson did Mr. Nobody apply to obtain presentation at the court of the First Consul. His name —*what* was his name?—being accordingly sent in to Citizen Talleyrand, three years afterwards to be Prince of Beneventum, minister of foreign affairs, Mr. N. drove to the Tuileries at three o'clock in the afternoon, and was ushered into a small apartment on the ground floor, called the Saloon of the Ambassadors, where the foreign ministers and their respective countrymen waited until Napoleon was ready to receive them. Chocolate, sherbet, and liqueurs in abundance having been handed around—a hint for St. James's Palace—the doors, after an hour's interval, were thrown open, and the guests ascended the grand staircase, which was lined by grenadiers with their arms grounded.

Passing through four or five rooms, in each of which was an officer's guard who saluted the strangers, the *cortége* came into the presence chamber. Here stood Bonaparte, between Cambacérès, the second, and Lebrun, the third consul. The triumvirs were all in full fig of scarlet velvet and gold. The generals, senators, and counsellors of state who surrounded Napoleon made way for the foreigners, and a circle was immediately formed, the nationalities ranging themselves behind their proper ministers. The Austrian ambassador stood on the right of the First Consul; next to him Mr. Jackson; then Count Lucchesini, the Prussian minister; and next to him the Hereditary Prince of Orange, who was to be presented that day, and who was not to meet Napoleon again until Waterloo. In compliment to the Dutch prince, Napoleon, contrary to his practice, began the audience on his side the circle. He spoke some time to the son of the deposed Stadtholder, and seemed anxious to make his awkward and extraordinary situation as little painful to him as possible. According

R

to Mr. Nobody, the Napoleonic blandishments were lost on his Batavian highness, who was sulky and silent.

In passing each foreign minister, the First Consul received the individuals of each respective nation with the greatest ease and dignity. Where had he learnt all this ease and dignity, this young soldier of thirty-two? From the goatherds of Corsica? From the snuffy old priests who were his tutors at Brienne? From the bombardiers at Toulon? In the camps of Italy? From the Sphinx in Egypt? From Talma the actor, who, when the conqueror was poor, had often given him the dinner he lacked? When it came to Mr. Jackson's turn, sixteen English were presented. After he had spoken to five or six of their number, Napoleon remarked, "with a smile which is peculiarly his own, and which changes a countenance usually stern into one of great mildness : 'I am delighted to see here so many English. I hope our union may be of long continuance. We are the two most powerful and most civilised nations in Europe. We should unite to cultivate the arts and sciences and letters; in short, to improve the happiness of human nature.'" In about two years after this interview Englishmen and Frenchmen were cultivating the arts and sciences and doing their best to improve the happiness of human nature by cutting each other's throats in very considerable numbers. Did Napoleon really mean what he said? Was he really anxious to be our friend, if we would only let him? Or was he then, and all times, a prodigious Humbug?

Mrs. Dash was to have her share in the hospitalities of the Tuileries. Returning home from viewing the sights one afternoon at half-past four o'clock, Mr. N. found a messenger who was the bearer of an invitation to Mrs. Dash, asking her to dinner that very day at five. The lady dressed in haste and drove to the palace. She returned enraptured. The entertainment was elegant ; the sight superb. More than two hundred persons sat down to dinner in a splendid apartment. The company consisted, besides Napoleon's family, of the ministers, the ambassadors, several generals, senators, and other constituted authorities. There were only fifteen ladies present. All the English ladies who had been presented to Madame Bonaparte were asked ; but only two of their number remained in Paris. The dinner was served entirely on gold and silver plate and Sèvres china, the latter bearing the letter B on every dish ; the central plateau was covered with moss, out of which arose innumerable natural flowers, the odour of which perfumed the whole room. The First Consul and Madame Bona- parte conversed very affably with those around them. The servants were numerous, splendidly dressed, and highly attentive, and the dinner lasted more than two hours.

Seven years ago the lord of this sumptuous feast had been glad to pick up the crumbs from an actor's table, and vegetated in a garret in Paris, had haunted the antechambers of the war minister in vain, had revolved plans of offering his sword to the Grand Turk if he could only procure a new pair of boots wherein to make his voyage to Constantinople. O the ups and downs of fortune ! The First Consul was fated to invite few more Englishmen to dinner. But he was doomed to dine with us, not as a host, but as an unwilling guest. I can picture him in the cabin of the *North-umberland*, rising wearily from heavy joints to avoid heavier drinking, and the admiral and his officers scowling at him because he wouldn't stop and take t'other bottle. "The General," pointedly remarked Sir George Cockburn once when his captive rose from the table and fled from port and sherry, "has evidently not studied politeness in the school of Lord Chesterfield." The poor temperate Italian, to whose pale cheek a single glass of champagne would 'bring a flush ! Yet Mr. Nobody thought him dignity and politeness itself; and my private opinion is that Mr. Nobody knew what was what.

XXI.

SHOCKING!

HE other day, being at Seville, at the inn dinner of the Fonda de Paris, I saw an English lady thrown into great perturbation by the conduct of a Frenchman, her neighbour, who having finished his plate of soup, and the "puchero" being somewhat tardy in making its appearance, drew forth a leathern case and a box of wax matches, and having bitten the end off a very big and bad cigar, proceeded to light and smoke it. I do not think a Spaniard of any class, to the lowest, would have done this thing. Although smoking is common enough at Spanish dinner-tables, when only men or natives are present, the innate good breeding of a caballero would at once cause him to respect the presence of a lady and a stranger ; and he would as soon think of kindling, unbidden, a weed before her, as of omitting to cast himself (metaphorically) at her feet when he took his leave.

Moreover, the Frenchman was wrong even in his manner of smoking. To consume a cigar at meal-times is not even *un costumbre del pais*—a custom of the country. It is the rather a stupid solecism. Between soup and "puchero," or fish and roast, you may just venture on a cigarito—a dainty roll of tobacco and tissue paper. Any other form of fumigation ere the repast be over is ill-mannered. The Gaul, however, thought no doubt that to puff at one of the hideous lettuce-leaf sausages of the Régie Impériale at dinner-time was precisely *the* thing to do in Spain. He smoked at Seville, just as on a hot day in an English coffee-room he would have ordered turtle-soup, a beefsteak, "well-bleeding," and a pot of porter-beer. I only wonder that he did not come down

to dinner at the Fonda de Paris in full bull-fighter's costume—
green satin breeches, pink silk stockings and his hair in a net, or
strumming a guitar, or clacking a pair of castanets. Indeed, he
grinned complacently as he pulled at the abominable brand, and
looked round the table as though for approval. The Spaniards
preserved a very grave aspect, and Don Sandero M'Gillicuddy,
late of Buenos Ayres, my neighbour, whispered to me that he
thought the Frenchman "vera rude."

As for the English lady, she was furious. She gathered up her
skirts, grated away her chair, turned her left scapula full on the
offending Frenchman, and I have no doubt wrote by the next post
to Mr. John Murray, of Albemarle Street, indignantly to ask why
English readers of the "Handbook" were not warned against the
prevalence of this atrocious practice at Spanish dinner-tables.
In fact, she did everything but quit the hospitable board. In
remaining she showed wisdom, for Spain is not a country where
you can afford to trifle with your meals. You had best gather
your rosebuds while you may, and help yourself to the *puchero*
whenever you have a chance. Ages may pass ere you get
anything to eat again.

The Frenchman was not abashed by this palpable expression of
distaste on the part of his fair neighbour. I had an over-the-
way acquaintance with him, and glancing in my direction, he
simply gave a deprecatory shrug, and murmured, "*Ah! c'est
comme ça.* Shocking !" It never entered the honest fellow's head
that he had been wanting in courtesy to the entire company, but
he jumped at the conclusion that the demoiselle Anglaise was a
faultless monster of prudery, and that the inhalation of tobacco-
smoke at dinner-time, the employment of a fork as a toothpick,
the exhibition of ten thousand photographed "legs of the ballet"
in the shop windows, and frequent reference to the anonymous
or Bois de Boulogne world in conversation, were, to her and
her sex and nation generally, things abhorrent, criminal, and
" shocking." .

The French, who never get hold of an apt notion or a true
expression without wearing it threadbare and worrying it to

death, and have even traditional jests against this country which
are transmitted from caricaturist to caricaturist and from father
to son, have built up the "faultless monster" to which I alluded
above, and persist in believing that it is the ordinary type of the
travelling Englishwoman.   Oddly enough, while their ladies—
and all other continental ladies—have borrowed from ours the
quaint and becoming hat, the coloured petticoats and stockings,
and the high-heeled boots which of late years have made feminine
juvenility so coquettish and so fascinating, no French draughtsman, no French word-painter, ever depicts the English young
lady save as a tall, rigid, and angular female—comely of face if
you will, but standing bolt upright as a lifeguardsman, with her
arms pendant and her eyes demurely cast down. ' She always
wears a straw bonnet of the coal-scuttle form, or an enormous flap
hat with a green veil.   Her hands, encased in beaver gloves, and
her feet, which are in sandalled shoes, are very large.   She
usually carries a capacious reticule, in variegated straw, of a bold
chessboard pattern.   She seldom wears any crinoline, and her
hair is arranged in long ringlets most deliciously drooping.   She
seldom opens her mouth but to ejaculate " Shocking ! "

It is absolutely astounding to find so accurate an observer and
so graphic a narrator as Monsieur Théophile Gautier falling into
this dull and false conventionalism in his charming book on
Spain.   He is describing Gibraltar, and is very particular in the
pourtrayal of such a " Mees Anglaise " as I have sketched above.
The fidelity of the portrait will of course be fully appreciated by
all British officers who have mounted guard over the Pillars of
Hercules.   The ladies of the garrison at Gibraltar are not, it is
true, so numerous as they might be.   Calpe is not a popular .
station with military females.   There is no native society beyond
the families of the " Rock scorpions," who are usually dealers in
mixed pickles and Allsopp's pale ale, and a few Spaniards who
earn a remunerative but immoral livelihood by coining bad
dollars and smuggling Manchester cottons and Bremen cigars
through San Roque ; and unfortunately, to ladies of a theological
turn, one of the chief charms of a sojourn in a foreign garrison is

here lacking. There is nobody to convert in Gibraltar but the Jews, and as it takes about a thousand pounds sterling to turn a Hebrew into a Christian—and a very indifferent Christian at that, for you have to set him up in business and provide for his relations to the third and fourth generation—missionary enterprise, to say the least, languishes.

With all these drawbacks, I am told that English female society at the Rock is charming ; that their costume, their features, and their manners are alike sprightly and vivacious, and that the "girls of Gib," as regards that rapidity and entrain which are so pleasingly characteristic of modern life, are only second to the far-famed merry maidens of Montreal, whose scarlet knickerbockers and twinkling feet, disporting on the glassy surface of the Victoria "Rink," have led captive so many old British grenadiers. When a maiden of Montreal is unusually rapid—what is termed "fast" in this country—they say she is "two forty on a plank road," two minutes and forty seconds being the time in which a Canadian trotter will be backed to get over a mile of deal-boarded track.

Now, whatever could Monsieur Gautier have been thinking of so to libel the ladies of Gibraltar ? They slow ! They angular ! They "*avec la demarche d'un grenadier !*" They addicted to the national ejaculation of "Shocking !" That old oak, however, of prejudice is so very firmly rooted that generations perhaps will pass away ere foreigners begin to perceive that the stiff, reserved, puritanical Englishman or Englishwoman, if they still indeed exist and travel on the Continent, have for sons and daughters ingenuous youths who in volatile vivacity are not disposed to yield the palm to young France, and gaily attired maidens, frolicsome, not to say frisky, in their demeanour. It is curious that the French, ordinarily so keen of perception and so shrewd in social dissection, should not by this time have discovered some other and really existent types of English tourists, male and female, to supply the place of the obsolete and well-nigh mythical "Mees" with her long ringlets, her green veil, her large hands and feet, and her figure full of awkward and ungainly angles. And may not the British Baronet, with his top-boots and his bull-dog and

his hoarse cries for his servant " Jhon," and his perpetual thirst
for "grogs," be reckoned among the extinct animals ?

I was reading only yesterday, in the *chronique* of one of the
minor Parisian journals, a couple of anecdotes most eloquent of
the false medium through which we are still viewed by the lively
Gaul. In the first the scene is laid at the Grand Hôtel. An
Englishman is reading *The Times* and smoking a cigar. It is a
step in advance, perhaps, that the Briton should have come to a
cabana instead of pulling at a prodigiously long pipe. The Englishman happens to drop some hot ashes on the skirt of his coat.
" Monsieur, monsieur !" cries a Frenchman sitting by, "take care,
you are on fire !" "Well, sir," replies the Briton, indignant at
being addressed by a person to whom he has not been formally
introduced, "what is that to you ? You have been on fire twenty
minutes, and I never mentioned the fact." I refrain from giving
the wonderful Anglo-French jargon in which the Englishman's
reply is framed.

The second anecdote is equally choice. An English nobleman
is " enjoying his *villeggiatura* at Naples "—by which, I suppose,
is meant that he is betting on the chances of a proximate eruption
of Mount Vesuvius—when his faithful steward, Williams Johnson,
arrives in hot haste from England. "Well, Williams," asks the
nobleman, "what is the matter ?" "If you please, milor, your
carriage-horses have dropped down dead." "Of what did they
die ?" "Of fatigue. They had to carry so much water to help
put out the fire." "What fire ?" "That of your lordship's
country house, which was burnt down on the day of the funeral."
"What funeral ?" "That of your lordship's mother, who died of
grief on hearing that the lawsuit on which your lordship's fortune
depended had been decided against you." Charming anecdotes
are these, are they not ? The gentleman who popped them into
his column of chit-chat gave them as being of perfect authenticity
and quite recent occurrence, and signed his name at the bottom ;
and yet I think I have read two stories very closely resembling
them in the admired collection of Monsieur Joseph Miller.

The Englishman who is the hero of cock-and-bull stories, and the English lady who is always veiling her face with her fan and exclaiming "Shocking !" are so dear to the French and the general continental heart that we must look for at least another half century of railways, telegraphs, illustrated newspapers, and international colleges before the mythical period passes away and the reign of substantial realism begins. I remember at the sumptuous Opera House at Genoa seeing a ballet called the "Grateful Baboon," in which there was an English general who wore a swallow-tail coat with lapels, Hessian boots with tassels, a pigtail, colossal bell-pull epaulettes, and a shirt-frill like unto that of Mr. Boatswain Chucks. The audience accepted him quite as a matter of course as the ordinary and recognised type of an English military officer of high rank ; and then I remembered that during our great war with France, Genoa had been once occupied by an English force under Lord William Bentinck, and that his lordship had probably passed bodily into the album of costumes of the Teatro Carlo Felice, and remained there unchangeable for fifty years.

In like manner the Americans, irritated, many years since, by the strictures of Mrs. Trollope, and stung to the quick by her sneers at the national peculiarities of "calculating" and spitting, thought they could throw the taunt back in our teeth by assuming that we were a nation of cockneys, hopelessly given to misplacing our H's. I had no sooner put down the lively *chronique* containing the Joe Millerisms than I took up a copy of the *New York Times*, a paper of very high character and respectability, and whose editor, Mr. Henry Raymond, one of the most distinguished of living American politicians, is doing good service to the Republic by striving—almost alone, unhappily—to stem the tide of the intolerance and tyranny of the dominant faction. In a leading article of the *New York Times* I read that when the British Lion was reproached with his blockade-running sins and other violations of neutrality during the war, the hypocritical beast turned up his "cotton-coloured eyes" and whimpered, "Thou cannot say Hi did it."

The gentleman who wrote the leader doubtless thought he had

hit us hard with that "Hi." He would have shot nearer the bull's-
eye had he asked why Lord Russell is always "obleged" instead
of obliged, and why the noble proprietor of Knowsley is Lord
"Derby" to one set of politicians and Lord "Darby" to another.
But these little niceties of criticism seem to escape our neighbours.
The imputation of cockneyism is a bit of mud that will stick. The
Americans have made up their minds that we are "halways
waunting the walour of hour harms," and "hexulting hover hour
'appiness hunder the 'ouse of 'Anover." No disclaimers on our part
will cause them to abandon their position. Nor in this case, nor
in that of "Shocking," do we lie open, I venture to think, to
accusations of a *tu quoque* nature.

We caricature our neighbours more closely and observantly
than they do us. We have found out long since that the Yankee
is not invariably a sallow man in a broad-brimmed straw hat and
a suit of striped nankeen, who sits all day in a rocking-chair with
his feet on the mantelpiece, sucking mint julep through a straw.
We know the circumstances under which he *will* put his feet up,
and the seasons most favourable to the consumption of juleps.
We have even ceased to draw him as he really was frequently
visible, some twenty years since, as a cadaverous straight-haired
individual, clean-shaved, in a black tail-coat and pantaloons, a
black satin waistcoat, and a fluffy hat stuck on the back of his
head and the integument of his left cheek much distended by a
plug of tobacco.

The English painter of manners takes the modern American as
he finds him : a tremendous dandy, rather "loud" in make-up,
fiercely moustached and bearded, ringed and chained to the eyes,
and, on the continent of Europe at least, quoting Rafaelles and
Titians, Canovas and Thorwaldsens, as confidently as he would
discourse of quartz or petroleum in Wall Street. We know that
he has long ceased to "calculate" or "reckon," and that it is
much, now, if he "guesses" or "expects." Not long ago, at
Venice, an old English traveller was telling me of an American
family with whom he had travelled from Florence to Bologna.
One of the young ladies of the party, it seems, did not approve of

the railway accommodation, and addressed the Italian guard in this wise : " My Christian friend, is this a first-class kyar or a cattle-waggon ? " At a subsequent stage of the journey the eldest gentleman of the group had remarked : "Say, if any of you gals bought frames at Florence, I can supply you with a lot o' picturs I got at Rome, cheap."

"They were model Yankees," the old English traveller chuckled, as he told me the story. "Not at all," I made bold to answer ; " they were very exceptional Yankees indeed. They were probably shoddy people of the lowest class, rapidly enriched, and who had rushed off to Europe to air their new jewellery and their vulgarity." Nine-tenths of the Americans one meets travelling abroad nowa- days are well-informed and intelligent persons, often more fully appreciative of the beauties of art than middle-class English tourists. The American's ambition extends to everything, in the heavens above and on the earth beneath, and in the waters under the earth. If he doesn't appreciate Italian pictures, his wife and daughters will, so that at least there shall be a decent amount of connoisseurship in the family ; whereas to the middle-class English foreign picture galleries are usually an intolerable bore ; and Paterfamilias very probably labours besides under a vague and secretly uneasy feeling that it does not become a man with less than twenty thousand a year and a handle to his name to talk of Rafaelles and Titians.

There may be vulgar pretenders among the Americans whom one meets roving through the churches and galleries of the Continent—among what nation are vulgarity and pretence not to be found ?—but take them for all in all, the love and appreciation for high art, although its very elements are of yesterday's intro- duction, are more generally discriminated in the United States than in England. The amazing development of photography, and the consequent circulation of the noblest examples of art at very cheap rates, together with the American mania for travelling, are the leading causes of their precocious proficiency in studies in which our middle classes are as yet but timid and bungling beginners.

It is true that they have not yet learnt to discriminate between Englishmen whose speech is that of educated gentlemen and those who put their H's in the wrong place. Perhaps their ears are at fault. There are none so deaf as those who will not hear. But I adhere to my position, that we are able to jot down their little changes of manners more accurately than they are able to do ours. We do not wear our jokes against them threadbare, or worry their foibles to death after the French fashion. Pennsylvania repudiation was a good jest in its day, made all the more bitter by being almost wholly destitute of foundation in truth ; but no one could help laughing at Sydney Smith's denunciations of the "men in drab," and his comically vindictive wish to cut up a Quaker and apportion him, buttonless coat, broad-brimmed hat and all, among the defrauded bondholders.

When it was discovered that Pennsylvania paid her obligations the jokes about pails of whitewash grew stale, and we abandoned them for good. So it was with the great sea-serpent. For years the English newspapers used to have their weekly quota of examples of American exaggeration and longbowism. We used to read about the cow which, being left out on a frosty night, never afterwards gave anything but ice-creams ; about the man who was so tall that he had to climb up a ladder to take his hat off ; about the discontented clock down east which struck work instead of the hours. These jokes too have now become stale, and barely suffice to gain a giggle from the sixpenny seats when emitted by the comic singer at a music-hall. Sarcasms anent American brag and bunkum have not quite died out from English conversation and English journalism, for unfortunately the newest file of American papers are full of evidence that bunkum and brag are on the other side of the Atlantic as current as ever.

How is it that, when foreigners wish to quiz us, however good-humouredly, they always date their witticisms from the morrow of the battle of Waterloo? The English began to be habitual travellers in the autumn of 1815. To us who know, or fancy that we know ourselves, the changes which have taken place in our manners and customs since that period are marvellous ; but

to foreigners we seem to be precisely the same people who came
rushing to Paris when the allies were in the Palais Royal, and
have since overrun every nook and corner of Europe. We know
what we were like in '15 ; we had been bereft for twelve years
of the French fashions. It was only once in some months or
so that a Paris bonnet or the design for a Paris dress was
furtively conveyed to us from Nantes or Hamburg in a smuggling lugger. Of the French language and of French literature
we were almost entirely ignorant. To be a fluent French
scholar was to be put down either as a diplomatist or a spy ;
and not all diplomatists could speak French. We had not
learned to waltz ; and foreigners invited to the houses of English
residents in Paris used to turn up their eyes at our barbarous
country dances and hoidenish Sir Roger de Coverley. We
knew no soup but turtle and pea ; no made dishes but Irish stew
and liver-and-bacon ; no wines but port and sherry ; claret gave
us the colic ; champagne was only found at the tables of
princes. We used to drink hot brandy-and-water in the morning. We used to get drunk after dinner. We had no soda-
water. We had no cigars, and smoking a pipe was an amusement in which few persons besides ship captains, hackney-
coachmen, and the Reverend Dr. Parr, indulged. Our girls
were bread-and-butter romps ; our boys were coarse and often
profligate hobbledehoys whose idea of " life" was to drink
punch at the Finish and beat the watch. Our fathers and
mothers were staid and prim and somewhat sulky, and carried
with them everywhere a bigoted hatred of popery and a wither-
ing contempt of foreigners. This is what we were like in 1815 ;
and in '15 I can easily understand that the angular young
woman in the coal-scuttle bonnet and the " green veil," who
was always crying " Shocking!" was as possible a personage as
the baronet in top-boots who continually swore at " Jhon," his
jockey, and roared for fresh grogs.

But can it be that we have not changed since the morrow of
Waterloo ? If we are to believe our critics, we are the self-same
folk. It seems to me that we have let our beards and moustaches

grow, and have become the most hirsute people in Europe ; but a
Charivari Englishman, or a Gustave Doré Englishman, or a
Bouffes Parisiens Englishman, is always the same simpering
creature, with smooth upper and under lip and bushy whiskers.
Types must be preserved, you may argue. As a simpering and
whiskered creature the Englishman is best known abroad, and
foreigners have as much right to preserve him intact as we have
to preserve our traditional John Bull. But may I be allowed to
point out that a type may become so worn and blunted as to be
no longer worth printing from ? For instance, there is the
Frenchman in a cocked-hat and a pigtail and high-heeled shoes,
and with a little fiddle protruding from his hinder pocket. That
Frenchman's name was Johnny Crapaud. His diet was frogs.
His profession was to teach dancing. One Englishman could
always thrash three Johnny Crapauds. We have broken up that
type for old metal ; and it has been melted again and recast into
something more nearly approaching the actual Crapaud.

Let me see : how many years is it since the lamented John
Leech drew that droll cartoon in *Punch* entitled "Foreign Affairs" ?
It must be a quarter of a century at least. He delineated the
Frenchman of his day to the life : the Frenchman of the old
Quadrant and Fricourt's and Dubourg's, and the stuffy little pass-
port-office in Poland Street. That Frenchman—long haired,
dirty, smouchy, greasy—has passed away. Before he died, Mr.
Leech found out the new types : the fat yet dapper "Mossoos"
with the large shirt-fronts and the dwarfed hats who engage a
barouche and a *valet de place* at Pagliano's, and go for "a
promenade to Richmond." And had Mr. Leech's life been prolonged he would have discovered the still later type of Frenchman
—the Parisian of the Lower Empire, the Frenchman of the
Jockey Club and the Courses de Vincennes—the Frenchman who
has his clothes made by Mr. Poole, or by the most renowned
Parisian imitator of the artist of Saville Row, who reads *Le Sport*
and goes upon le Tourff, and rides in his "bromm" and eats his
"laounch," and if he could only be cured of the habit of riding
like a miller's sack and sitting outside a café on the Boulevards

would pass muster very well for a twin-brother of our exquisites of the Raleigh and Pratt's.

It is all of no use, however, I fear. For good old true-blue Toryism and a determined hatred to new-fangled ways, socially speaking, you must go abroad, and especially to France. In prose and verse, in books and newspapers, in lithographs and etchings and terra-cotta statuettes, the traditional Englishman and the traditional Englishwoman will continue to appear as something quite different from that which they really are. In the halcyon day when it is discovered that we are no more " perfidious " than our neighbours, and that in the way of greedy rapacity for the petty profits of trade the French are ten times more of a nation of shopkeepers than we are—then, but not till then, it may be acknowledged that the English female's anatomy is not made up exclusively of right angles, and that the first word in an English-woman's vocabulary is not always " Shocking ! "

XXII.

THE HOTEL CHAOS.

O say that Chaos is come again is a tolerably common locution for expressing an excessive amount of confusion; but there need not be the slightest fear of the return of the Hotel Chaos. It can *never* come again. It was too rich of its kind, too peculiar, too overwhelming in its characteristics, to bear repetition. Among chaotic things it was unique, and on the whole it may be esteemed a matter for congratulation that there never could have been by any possibility but one Hotel Chaos, and that in all human probability there never will be another. There are limits even to disorder, and the acutest ravings of mania must have their turn. The Hotel Chaos was the maddest hostelry ever known or ever dreamt of. It did its work; it reached its consummation; it burst; and it can be no more restored to its pristine shape than can one of those paper bags which schoolboys inflate with their breath until the bags are as plump as a balloon ready to start, and then, with smart concussion from the palms of their hands, rend into irremediable fragments.

I never enjoyed the felicity of a bed at the Hotel Chaos; which, to have been consistent, should have been fitted up, in the way of sleeping accommodation, with padded rooms, frequented by laundresses bringing home nothing but strait-waistcoats as clean linen from the wash. A room at the Hotel Chaos! Bless you, such a thing was an infinity of cuts above me, and was meat for my masters—marshals of France, grand provosts, and similar grandees. I don't think they took in anybody lower in rank than a deputy-assistant commissary-general, and it is not probable that I shall ever attain a grade so exalted. There had been, to be sure, a few modest civilians, despicable creatures, with not so much as a sol'-tary ribbon of the Legion of Honour among them, who had been fortunate enough to obtain apartments at the Chaos before the hotel went hopelessly and stark-staringly mad ; and as these contemptible creatures (who were mainly Englishmen) were content to pay about seventy-five per cent. more for their board and lodging than the grandees were willing to disburse, the landlord—a covetous rogue with but scant patriotism in him—was naturally reluctant to turn these ignoble but lucrative customers into the street.

Ere long, however, a dashing member of the staff of Field-Marshal Bombastes Furioso was heard to ask the proprietor how long it would be before he put "*tout ce tas de pékins à la porte*"— before he expelled all those cads of civilians ; and so shortly afterwards the proprietor—really much against the grain, I am willing to believe—began to grow insolent to the civilian cads, and to hint that their rooms were required for *Messieurs les Militaires ;* that General Fusbos couldn't wait any longer, that Colonel Grosventre must really be accommodated, and that Milord Smith, Count Thompson, and Sir Brown must find lodgings elsewhere. Smith, Brown, and Thompson, quiet souls, well aware that in wartime the toga must cede to the tunic, meekly withdrew from the foul and wretched garrets where for sums varying from ten to fifteen francs a day they had been suffered to hide their degraded heads ; but, although ostracised from the upper rooms, they were by no means free, financially, from the exaction of the Hotel Chaos. It was one of the myriad humours of this bedlamite establishment that your bill, if you didn't stop in the house, had a tendency to grow longer than had been its custom when you did stop.

But how was a bill possible at all ? you may ask. Thus. The Hotel Chaos was the only place in the maniacal city of Moriah where you could get a decent breakfast or dinner, and where tolerable coffee, liquors, and cigars could be obtained. Moreover, as the chief madmen of Moriah were always congregated at the

Chaos, and as in its *salle à manger* and its courtyard all that was notable and worth studying in the way of hallucination, foaming at the mouth, homicidal mania, epilepsy, demoniacal possession, hysteria, melancholia, kleptomania, hypochondriasis, dipsomania and midsummer madness, was sure to be visible and audible at all hours of the day and night; as within its walls there was a perpetual narration of tales told by idiots, full of sound and fury, signifying nothing; of visions so wild and fantastic that Ossian read tamely and Emmanuel Swedenborg flatly afterwards; and of lies so grandiose and so impudent that Marco Polo or Sir John Mandeville might have sickened with envy to hear them—you were perforce impelled to make of the Hotel Chaos a common news-room, exchange, and lounge. You breakfasted and dined at the *table d'hôte;* you smoked and took your *demi-tasse*, or your seltzer-and-something, on the terrace overlooking the courtyard— shaking sometimes in your shoes, miserable civilian cads as you were, at the knowledge of the close propinquity of Marshal Bombastes and General Fusbos, and sometimes of a plumed and embroidered aide-de-camp of the great Emperor Artaxomines himself.

Thus, you "used" the Hotel Chaos, although you had no bed there, and you were always heavily in debt to the waiter. If you wanted to pay him for your dinner he had no change·; and when you had no change—and nothing to change, perchance, for ready money was apt to run wofully short in the mad city of Moriah— he was sure to present a bill exhibiting a fabulous back score of breakfasts, dinners, *demi-tasses*, and *petits verres*, and impetuously demanded payment. If you demurred, he threatened you with the grand provost. He knew you to be a miserable cad of a civilian, only fed upon sufferance, incessantly watched and followed about by the gendarmerie and by police-agents in plain clothes, and he also knew that the propriety of your expulsion altogether from Moriah was debated every day by some of the grandees in cocked-hats and epaulettes. The best thing to do was to conciliate the waiter with humble and obsequious phrases, and, giving him silver money for himself, promise to pay the bill—usually a mere schedule of fictitious items—that afternoon. Under those circumstances you were tolerably safe ; for in five minutes the head-waiter usually forgot all about you. He had dunned somebody else successfully, or the still small voice of conscience had deterred him from making another attempt to fleece you ; or—which is the likeliest hypothesis of all—his intermittent fit of madness had come on and he had gone upstairs to tear his hair and claw his flesh and gnaw the bedclothes and howl till he was hoarse, according to the afternoon custom of the men of Moriah.

Moriah, I may take occasion to observe, lest I should get benighted in the maze of allegory, was, in sane parlance, the fortified city of Metz, the headquarters, at the end of the month of July, 1870, of the Army of the Rhine, of the Imperial Guard of France, and of the Emperor Napoleon the Third, who, with his young son the Prince Imperial, his cousin Prince Napoleon, a brilliant staff, and a sumptuous following, were lodged at the Hotel of the Prefecture. Marshals Le Bœuf and Bazaine, General de Saint Sauveur (the grand provost), General Soleil, commanding the artillery of the Guard, and a glittering mob of generals, colonels, and aides-de-camp of the Guard, the Staff, and the Line, were at the Hotel Chaos.

But be it borne in mind that when I speak of the Chaotic Inn, my statement must be taken with a slight reservation or allowance. You may be horror-stricken at the confession that there were two Hotels Chaos in Metz, and that to this day I cannot remember with exactitude which was which. They were in the same street, the Grande Rue Colneyhatchi, I think, exactly opposite one another : each with a courtyard, each with a terrace, each with head-waiters who presented you with extortionate bills, each full of marshals, generals, colonels, and aides-de-camp : in fact, as like unto one another as two peas, or the two Dromios, or Hippocrates' Twins. One, I am inclined to think—but Reason totters on her throne—was called the Grand Hôtel de Metz. The other—but my brain burns with volcanic fierceness when I strive to recall it—was known as the Grand

Hôtel de l'Europe.   It is my firm conviction that, for the major portion of the edibles and potables I consumed at the Grand Hôtel de Metz, I paid the waiter at the Grand Hôtel de l'Europe, and *vice versâ*.   It did not matter much then, for there was a solidarity of insanity between them, and both were integral parts—if any integrity could be in that which was normally and essentially disintegration—of the Hotel Chaos. It matters less now, since, for aught we know, both hotels have been burnt to the ground or shattered by bomb-shells, and nothing remains within the huge earth-works of Metz but charred beams and crumbling brickwork and dust and ashes. Perhaps the head-waiters at the two caravansaries—I have heard that a fierce mutual hatred existed between them—have eaten one another.

Let me strive to embody some fleeting memories of that demented time.   There is breakfast.   We that were English in Metz, a feeble folk, continuously snubbed by the military authorities and harassed by the police, and pursuing an arduous vocation under all manner of slights, discouragement, and obstacles, usually made a rendezvous to breakfast together at the same time—about half-past ten.   There was canny Mr. M'Inkhorn, from the Land o' Cakes, special correspondent of the *Bannockburn Journal and Peck o' Maut Advertiser*, who in the performance of his duties as a war-scribe was chronically perturbed in mind by the thought that he had left unfinished in North Britain a series of statistical articles on the Sanitary Condition of Glen M'Whiskey.   There was Mr. Mercutio, once gallant and gay, now elderly and portly, who was called Philosopher Mercutio in early life, and wrote that celebrated work on the Rationale of the Categorical Imperative as Correlative to the Everlasting Affirmation of Negation, and who now laughed and gossiped and drank kirschwasser all day long, and wrote war-letters to a High Tory evening paper all night. He had brought his son with him, an ingenuous youth in a gray tweed suit, who was his sire's guide, philosopher, and friend ; who controlled him gently in the matter of kirschwasser, was the

ARREST OF NEWSPAPER CORRESPONDENTS AT METZ.

profoundest cynic and the shrewdest observer for his age I ever
met with, and who otherwise, from sunrise to sunset, did nothing
with an assiduity which was perfectly astonishing. There was
mild-eyed Mr. Sumph, of Balliol, who indited those fiery letters
from Abyssinia during the campaign, and had a special faculty
while in Metz for getting arrested as a Prussian spy.

There were a brace of quiet, harmless, industrious artists
belonging to English illustrated newspapers, pilgrims of. the
pencil, who had wandered, in discharge of their functions, to
the Crimea, to Italy, to India, to China, to the Isthmus of
Suez, and to the banks of the Chickahominy, and who were
now, in fear and trembling, making notes in their sketch-books
of the most salient madnesses of Metz susceptible of pictorial
treatment. And especially there was Mr. O'Goggerdan of the
Avalanche, a small man, but of a most heroic stomach and of
venturesomeness astounding. He had been, they said, a colonel of
American Federal cavalry, a Confederate bushwhacker, a Mexican
guerillero, a Spanish contrabandista, a Garibaldino, one of the
Milia di Marsala of course, a Fenian centre, and a Pontifical
Zouave. He was Dugald Dalgetty combined with Luca fa
Presto ; doubling the rapier of the practised swordsman with
the pen of the ready-writer. A wind blowing from Fleet Street,
London, had brought these strangely assorted people together :
the elder, the philosopher, the Oxford fellow, the painter, the
soldier of fortune, were all bent on achieving the same task,
and were all occasionally partakers of that misery which makes
us acquainted with such very strange bedfellows.

When the customary salutations of the morning were over,
when we had inquired whether any of our number had been
arrested as spies during the preceding evening, and when we had
striven to ascertain whether there were any news from the front—
it was just after Saarbrück—and when we had, as usual, been
baffled in our attempt, we fell to discussing a very substantial
breakfast *à la fourchette,* to which dropped in, between eleven and
noon, group after group of artists in the great drama of which the
first scene had as yet been but ill played. It is possible that I

may be rather understating than overstating the fact when I assume that three-fourths of the French people we used to meet every morning at breakfast, and who as a rule treated us with infinite scorn and contumely—it is true that as civilian cads we had no business there, and should have been hiding our heads in squalid *auberges* suited to our degree—are by this time dead and buried or scattered to the four winds of heaven : in exile, in captivity, or in other ruinous and irremediable dispersion.*

Of the mere bald aspects and trite humours of a French garrison town, with which most of us who have made even a week's trip to the Continent must be familiar, I should be ashamed to treat ; and Metz in ordinary times had been, I doubt it not, as dull and trite a place as its hundred-and-one congeners among French garrisons. A great deal of drumming and a great deal of bugling ; much swaggering about streets and leering under feminine bonnets on the part of portly captains and wasp-waisted lieutenants, and of shiftlessly dawdling and futile pavement beating on the part of gaby-faced soldiers, not over-clean, and with an inch and a half of coarse cotton shirt visible between the hem of their undress jackets and the waistband of their red pantaloons ; much moustache-twisting, tin-canful-of-soup carrying, absinthe-tippling, and halfpenny-cigar smoking : these were the most salient features of French military life, and they were as well known to the majority of educated Englishmen as the manners and customs of the metropolitan police.

But when Metz went mad with the war fever early in August, 1870, her military guise underwent a development so extensive and so exceptional that the spectator of many strange scenes in many strange countries may be warranted in sketching the things he saw without being open to the charge of telling a thrice-told tale. To our breakfast table at the Hotel Chaos came officers— few of them below the rank of captain—from every branch of the French military service. The Imperial Guard were the most numerously represented ; for at Metz were the imperial head-

* This paper was written in November, 1870.

quarters, and the Cent Gardes mounted sentry at the Prefecture. Their lieutenant did not condescend to breakfast with us; but he frequently deigned to take coffee and kirsch on the terrace. I see him now, a sky-blue giant—I mean that his tunic was sky-blue— with a fat, foolish face. For the rest he was all epaulettes, and jack-boots, and buckskins, and aiguillettes, and buttons, and sword and sash, and splendour generally. I used to reckon him up, and calculate that at the lowest valuation he could not be bought, as he stood, for less than a hundred and fifty pounds. His boots alone must have been worth three-pounds-ten. I used, I own, to envy him. To what surprising stroke of good luck did he owe his commission in the cream of the Prætorians; in the Golden Guard of Cæsar? Had he been born to greatness? had he achieved it? or had greatness been thrust upon him in con- sequence of his breadth of chest and length of limb? What a position! Here was a fortunate youth, obviously not more than five-and-twenty years of age, who was privileged to mount guard on Cæsar's staircase and before the curtains of the alcoves of the Empress. He had been at all the grand Tuileries balls, at the state ceremonies in the great Hall of the Louvre, at the imperial hunts at Fontainebleau and Compiegne. The faces of half the kings in Europe must have been familiar to him; and as for princes, princesses, senators, members of the Institute and Grand Croix of the Legion of Honour, they must have been to his sated vision the smallest of small deer.

Yet here was this ambrosial creature—this happy combination of the Apollo Belvedere and Shaw the Life Guardsman—for I am sure that he was as brave as he was beautiful—sipping his coffee and kirsch, and smoking his cigar, as though he had been an ordinary mortal. And—no; my olfactory nerves did not deceive me : the cigar was a halfpenny one, a veritable *petit Bordeaux* of the Régie. What has become of that gay and gallant Colossus by this time? It is some satisfaction to have the conviction that his corpse is not entombed in some dreadful trench in the blood- drenched fields of Alsace or Lorraine, for the Cent Gardes did not fight. After Sedan, the corps being abolished by a hard-

hearted republican government, these sumptuous but expensive
Janissaries retired into private life.

By the way, what became of the real Turkish Janissaries?
They were not all massacred by the Sultan Mahmoud; some few
escaped. What became of those Mamelukes who were not cut to
pieces by the troops of Mehemet Ali? What would become of
our Beefeaters if a cruel House of Commons declined to vote the
miscellaneous estimate necessary for their support? What becomes of the supernumeraries when the Italian Opera-house closes
—the men with the large flat faces, sphinx-like in their impassi-
bility, the large hands, the larger feet, and the legs on which the
"tights" are always in loose wrinkles, and which are frequently
bandy? There is a strange faculty of absorption and engulfment
in life. There are whole races of people who seem to "duck
under," as it were, and remain quietly and comfortably submarine,
while the great ocean overhead moans and struggles or is lashed
to frenzy in infinite surges.

Some of these days, perchance, I shall meet a marker at billiards
or a "putter-up" in a bowling alley, an assistant at a hairdresser's or a model in a life school, who may casually mention
the fact that once upon a time he was a Cent Garde. Why not?
I met a Knight of Malta in Spain, who was travelling in dry
sherries; and I have heard of an ex-Dominican monk who at
present follows the lively profession of clown to a circus. I
have been aware of a baronet who earned his living as a
photographer, and an unfrocked archdeacon who sold corn and
coals on commission.

They say that in the Prussian army every commissioned officer
below the rank of major is bound to perform every day, in
addition to his military duties and ere he can think of recreation,
a given task of serious study, precisely as though he were a
schoolboy. He must draw up some map, plan, or elevation, solve
some problem in military mathematics, make an abridgment or an
analysis of a portion of some technical work, or write some
"theme" upon a given subject—say the causes of the Seven
Years' War, the commissariat system of the Tenth Legion, or the

amount of historical truth in the story of the battle of the Lake Regillus. To the enforcement of such an unbending course of mental as well as physical discipline the Prussian army may owe no inconsiderable portion of the success which has lately attended its operations in the field.

Looking back upon the Hotel Chaos, and the huge camp of which it was the centre, I cannot help thinking that a little daily schooling after the Prussian manner would have done the paladins of Gaul an immensity of good. An hour's history, an hour's geography, an hour's mathematics a day would have been scarcely felt by the multitude of officers who, their slight regimental duties at an end, were privileged, or rather condemned, for the remainder of the twenty-four hours, to do nothing but eat, drink, smoke, dawdle about the courtyard and the streets, and babble. Of female society, to refine or to amuse them, there was none; for the burgesses of Metz, a prudent race, so soon as ever the vanguard of the Grand Army appeared in sight, had locked up all their daughters, and seemingly sent all their pretty servant-maids home to their mothers. With a bright exception or two, the womanhood of Metz were about as engaging in aspect as Sycorax, mother of Caliban.

There was a large and handsome theatre, but the company had been dispersed, and old ladies and little schoolgirls sat in the stalls and on the stage all day long scraping lint. The two billiard-tables in the place had speedily collapsed. Of one, the Third Chasseurs cut the cloth with their cues, and declining to pay for the damage, the proprietor closed the entire concern in a huff. I think some of the tables must have been let out as beds; at all events, the sound of the clicking of balls grew fainter every day, while that of babbling grew louder. It was the babbling that drove the Grand Army mad. It was the infinite babble that brought about Chaos. Of golden silence there was none; of silvery speech, little. It was the age of bronze and brass swagger and braggadocio, mouthed by copper captains and smock-faced sous-lieutenants, who but a fortnight before had been schoolboys at St. Cyr. It would have been better for them to be at school still. Poor lads, I see them now, with their brand-new uniforms which they were never tired of admiring when they could get near a mirror; the fresh lace glittering on collar and cuffs; the buttons scarce freed from the tissue-paper in which they had been wrapped; the first sheen upon the sword-scabbard; the varnish hardly dry on the belts, and in their bright boyish eyes the first exultation born of independence, of the consciousness of being men—of the rapture of the coming strife.

Poor lads! poor lads! I hear their loose and idle talk, their vain boastings, their complacent disparagement of the Prussians, " *mangeurs de choucroute*," forsooth, whom they were going to " eat" without pepper or salt. One might have fancied Maffeo Orsini and the rest gaily defying Donna Lucrezia at Venice. But what said that Borgia woman in the end? " You gave me a ball at Venice, I return it by a supper at Ferrara ;" and then the lugubrious chant arose, " Nisi Dominus ædificat Domum," and the seven monks with the seven coffins appeared in the doorway of the brilliant banqueting-chamber. The answer to the defiance at Metz was at Wissembourg, at Woerth, and in the bloody shambles below Sedan. When I think upon these lads now it is as though I had been down to a charnel-house and lived among corpses; and were I to meet one of the babblers of the Hotel Chaos in the street, I should take him for a ghost.

Babbling, continual babbling, made the warriors dry; and it is not libellous, I trust, to hint that the army at Metz, ere the first tidings of discomfiture came, had grown to be—for Frenchmen, who in old times had a repute for temperance—a drunken army. Absinthe, kirsch, and cognac tippling went on all day and nearly all night at the Chaos, and the dissipation engendered by sheer idleness among the officers was not slow to spread among the rank and file, who in their cups not only babbled but brawled. For the rest, there was Chaos outside as well as inside the hotels. The tradespeople of the town were doing a roaring business. Wholesale traders could sell as much meat, flour, wine, and forage to the government as ever they could supply; and retail vendors could scarcely keep pace with the demand for flannel shirts, potted meats, sardines, sausages, razors, and other cutlery; railway-rugs, mattresses, canteens, pipes, cigar-cases, and other camp luxuries and campaigning comforts. The officers had all received their "*entrée en campagne*"—a donation of so many hundred francs, allotted at the commencement of war—and were never tired of shopping. They bought everything, except books. The courtyard of the Chaos used to be littered with packing-cases, kegs, sacks, packages, and tin cans, the private stores of the Grand Army.

Vividly do I remember a most dashing turn-out belonging to General Soleil, of the artillery—a break, with the general's name and titles conspicuously painted on it, and which was as handsome as ever paint and varnish, wheels of a bright scarlet, electro-silvered lamps and fittings, could make it. Every afternoon the general, with a select party of epauletted and decorated friends, used to take a drive about the town in this imposing vehicle, to which were attached four splendid gray Percheron horses, with harness of untanned leather. And then, a change of headquarters being imminent, the break took in cargo for active service. Truffled goose-liver pies from Strasbourg, andouillettes from Troyes, pigs' feet from Sainte Menehould, green chartreuse and dry curaçoa, fine champagne cognac, Huntley and Palmer's biscuits, Allsopp's pale ale—the capacity of the break had stomach for all these goodies, to say nothing of boxes of cigars in such numbers that, as you passed the break, you caught ambrosial whiffs, reminding you equally of the cedars of Lebanon and Mr. Carrera's tobacco-shop. I wonder who ate and drank all these dainties? Prince Frederick Charles, Bismarck the omnivorous, or Hans Göbbell, full private in the Uhlans?

And so they went on in their madness, growing madder every day, and doing scarcely anything, as it subsequently turned out, to put the Grand Army in real fighting trim. The noise and hub-bub, the babbling and boasting of the Chaos, became at last so intolerable that I was fain to wander away far from the revellers, far from the great Carnival of Insanity—down by the river banks, anywhere out of Bedlam where there was some stillness and peace.

Very often, late at night, I have crossed the bridge and paced the broad esplanade before the Prefecture. A great silken banner floated over the roof; two voltigeurs of the guard stood sentry by the gateway. From time to time dusty couriers would gallop up to the portals. Dragoon horses were picketed to the railings, and officers and orderlies would emerge and mount and spur away in hottest haste. Cæsar was there, Cæsar and the chiefs of the legions. Mine eyes were wont to sweep the long lines of windows, and wonder which of the brilliantly-lit rooms could be his. That upper chamber, perhaps, where the light burned so steadily and so late. There, I thought, at least were sanity, sagacity, foresight, and a wise prescience of possible disaster. In that upper chamber was the cold, calm, long-headed, imperturbable man who, nineteen years before, on the night when he made that *coup d'état* which gave him an empire, had sat with his feet on the fender in his room at the Elysée, slowly puffing his cigarette, and to all the remonstrances and the objections of the timid and the half-hearted, had given for answer, "Let my orders be executed!"

Nineteen years ago! It seemed but yesterday since I had stood in the Faubourg St. Honoré, looking at the brightly illumined windows of the Elysée, and wondering which was the room of Louis Napoleon Bonaparte. He was the same man, no doubt, now, at Metz, as in the days when he put down liberty, equality, and fraternity by means of musketry—the same cold, calm, resolute Thinker and Doer, who wanted only his "orders executed." I had seen him twice at the railway-station and in the cathedral of Metz. He was not, they said, in very good health, and walked feebly. But he had always been somewhat shaky as regards the lower limbs. The mind was still of crystal, the will of iron, no doubt.

Error, delusion, and that which may be termed the "deadest of sells" generally! There must have been ten thousand times more Chaos, more hallucination, delusion, and delirium in that room at the Prefecture in August, 1870, than at the Hotel Chaos itself. Now the Prussians have got into Metz, I may pay another visit to the mad city and the madder hotels. But I shall go in disguise, with green spectacles and a false nose ; for Metz must be in a frightful state of impecuniosity by this time, and, pricked by the javelins of scarcity, the waiters may make such fearful demands on me for bygone—and fictitious—scores, that a life's earnings might not suffice to discharge the prodigious bill. They would expect me to pay the debts of the dead ; and how many of the lunatics who babbled in the courtyard must be by this time cold and silent !

XXIII.

POSTE RESTANTE.

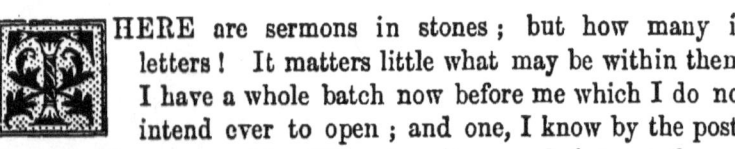

HERE are sermons in stones; but how many in letters! It matters little what may be within them. I have a whole batch now before me which I do not intend ever to open; and one, I know by the postmark, is fifteen years old. There is quite enough interest for me in their envelopes and their superscriptions, in their crests and stamps, in the blots and the scratches they have picked up on their way. For a letter can, no more than a man, get through the world without some rubs, often of the hardest. Here is a dainty little pink thing of an envelope, longer than it is broad—a flimsy brick from the Temple of Love, shot away as rubbish long ago. It is directed in the beautifulest little Italian hand—so small that the effigy of Her Most Gracious Majesty on the stamp might be, by comparison, the portrait of the sovereign of Brobdingnag. But woe is me, that careless postman! The little letter, ere ever it reached me, tumbled into the mud. Dun brown splashes deface its fair outside. The mud is dry as dust now, but not dustier or drier than the memories which the envelope awakens.

Those droll dogs of friends you knew once were addicted to sending you "comic" envelopes through the post—monstrous caricatures of yourself, or themselves, sketched in pen and ink— waggish quatrains in the corner addressed to the postman, or to Mary the housemaid who took the letters in. They fondly hoped, the facetious ones, that the letter-carrier would crack his sides, that Mary would grin her broadest grin, at the sight of their funny letters. But Mary and the postman did nothing of the kind. Once in a way, perhaps, the hardworked servant of the

G.P.O. who handed in the "comic" missive would observe, "He must be a rum 'un as sent *this*;" but the remark was made more in grim disparagement than in humorous appreciation. As for Mary, she would still farther turn up that nasal organ for which nature had already done a good deal in the way of elevation, and would remark, "*I* wonder people isn't above such trumperies!" Mary knew and revered the sanctity of the post.

Did you ever study the outsides of servants' letters? When the housemaid has a military sweetheart he is generally in the pedestrian branch of the service, and his hand being as yet more accustomed to the plough than to the pen, he induces a smart sergeant to address his letters for him. The non-commissioned officer's stiff, up-and-down, orderly-room hand is not to be mistaken. He is very gallant to the housemaid. He always calls her "Miss" Mary Hobbs; but, on the other hand, he never omits to add a due recognition of yourself in the "At William Penn's, Esq." I have even known a sergeant ascend to the regions of "Et cetera, et cetera, et cetera," and a flourish. Mary's old father, the ex-butcher, does not waste any vain compliments upon her or upon you. "Mary Hobbs, housemaid at Mr. Penn's." He is a courteous old gentleman, nevertheless: and if Mary shows you her letter, which she does sometimes in pardonable pride at the proficiency of her papa, who, "although he was never no schollard and going on for seventy-three, is as upright as a May-pole," you will rarely fail to discover in the postscript that he has sent his "duty" to you.

But, I repeat, I have had enough in my time of the insides of letters, and I intend to write no more letters, and to read as few as ever I possibly can. With the aid of a poker, a good wide fire-place, and a box of matches, I got rid recently of a huge mass of old letters. It was the brightest of blazes, and you would have been astonished by the diminutiveness of the pile of sooty ashes which remained in the grate after that bonfire. Yet have you not seen in the little frescoed pigeon-holes of the Roman Columbaria that a vase not much bigger than a gallipot will hold all that is mortal of one who was once senator, pro-consul, prætor—what you please? The ashes of a lifetime's letters will not more than fill a dustpan.

Dismissing the letters themselves, relegating them all to fiery death behind those bars, I linger over the envelopes; I dwell upon the postmarks, I long to be in the distant lands to which those marks refer. There is vast room for speculation in the address of a letter, for in the mass of handwritings you have seen, many have been forgotten. In the letter itself your curiosity is at once appeased, for you turn to the signature mechanically, and ten to one, if the letter be an old one, to read it gives you a sharp pang. Burn the letters, then; keep to the envelopes. Especially scan those which have been directed to you at hotels abroad. In very rare instances does the memory of a foreign hotel remind you of aught but pleasant things. You lived your life. The bills were heavy, but they were paid. You enjoyed.

How good the pickled herrings were at the Oude-Doelen at the Hague! What a famous four-poster they put you into at the Old Bible in Amsterdam! Could anything be better than the *table d'hôte* at the Hôtel d'Angleterre at Berlin—save perhaps that at the Hôtel de Russie close by, and that other Russie at Frankfort? That Drei Mohren at Augsburg was a good house too. What a cellar! what imperial tokay! 'Tis true that the waiter at Basle swindled you in the matter of the Bremen cigars, which he declared to be Havanas; but was not that little mishap amply atoned for at the Schweizer Hof, Lucerne, six hours afterwards? The Schweizer Hof! Dear me! how happy you were, idling about all day long, peering at Mount Pilate, or watching, with never-ending interest, the tiny boats on the bosom of the great blue lake!

Here is an envelope directed to you at Cernobbio; another at the Villa d'Este; another at Bellaggio, on the Lake of Como. Here come Salò and Desenzano, on the Lake of Garda. Ah! a villanous hostelry the last; but with what exultation you hurried back through Brescia to the clean and comfortable Hotel Cavour at Milan! You were rather short of money, perhaps, when you arrived in the capital of Lombardy. Your stock of circular notes was growing small. No cash awaited you at the Albergo Cavour —nay, nor letters either. But there would be letters for you, it was certain, at the Poste Restante. Quick, *portière, un broum*— Milanese for brougham, and not very wide of the mark. You hasten to the Poste Restante. There the letters await you; there is the stack of circular notes. Yes, and here among your envelopes at home is the banker's letter of advice, enumerating a hundred cities where he has agents who will gladly cash your notes at the current rate of exchange, deducting neither agio nor discount.

The postage and the reception of a letter in foreign countries —notably the less civilised—are events accompanied by circumstances generally curious and occasionally terrifying. I never saw a Chinese postman, but I can picture him as a kind of embodied bamboo, who presents you with your packet of correspondence with some preposterous ceremonial, or uses some outrageously hyperbolical locution to inform you that your letter is insufficiently stamped. As for the Russian Empire, I can vouch personally for the whole postal system of that tremendous dominion being, sixteen years ago, environed with a network of strange observances. The prepayment of a letter from St. Petersburg to England involved the attendance at at least three separate departments of the imperial post-office, and the administration of at least one bribe to a dingy official with a stand-up collar to his napless tail-coat, and the symbolical buttons of the *Tchinn* on the band of his cap. As those who have ever made acquaintance with the stage doorkeepers of theatres in any part of the world are aware that those functionaries are generally eating something from a basin (preferably yellow), so those who have ever been constrained to do business with a Russian government clerk of the lower grades will remember that, conspicuous by the side of the blotting-pad (under which you slipped the rouble notes when you bribed him), there was always a soddened blue pocket-handerchief, the which rolled up into a ball, or twisted into a thong, or waved wide like a piratical flag, served him alternately as a sign of content,

T

a gesture of refusal, or an emblem of defiance. You couldn't prepay your letter without this azure semaphore being put through the whole of its paces; unless, indeed, previous to attending the post-office, you took the precaution of requesting some mercantile friend to affix the stamp of his firm to your envelope. Then the official pocket-handkerchief assumed permanently the spherical or satisfied stage, and you had, moreover, the satisfaction of knowing that the stamp of the firm might stand you in good stead as an Eastern firman, and that in all probability your letter would not be opened and read as a preliminary to its being dispatched to its destination.

So much for sending a letter, on which you seldom failed (purely through official oversight, of course) to be overcharged. There were two ways of receiving a letter, both equally remarkable. I used to live in a thoroughfare called the Cadetten-Linie, in the island of Wassili-Ostrow. It was about three times longer than that Upper Wigmore Street to which Sydney Smith declared that there was no end. When any English friend had sufficiently mastered the mysteries of Russian topographology as to write Cadetten-Linie and Wassili-Ostrow correctly, I got my letter. This was but seldom. It was delivered at the hotel where I resided in a manner which reminded me vaguely but persistently of the spectacle of Timour the Tartar and of the Hetman Platoff leading a pulk of Cossacks over the boundless steppes of the Ukraine. The postman was one of the fiercest little men, with one of the fiercest and largest cocked-hats, I ever saw. His face was yellow in the bony and livid in the fleshy parts; and the huge moustache lying on his upper lip looked liked a leech bound to suck away at him for evermore for some misdeeds of the Promethean kind.

This Russian postman: don't let me forget his sword, with its rusty leather scabbard and its brazen hilt, which seemed designed, like Hudibras's, to hold bread and cheese; and not omitting, again, the half dozen little tin-pot crosses and medals attached by dirty scraps of parti-coloured ribbon to his breast; for this brave had "served," and only failed to obtain a com-

mission because he was not "born." This attaché of St.
Sergius-le-Grand, if that highly-respectable saint can be accepted
as a Muscovite equivalent for our St. Martin of Aldersgate, used
to come clattering down the Cadetten-Linie on a shaggy little
pony, scattering the pigeons and confounding the vagrant curs.

You know the tremendous stir at a review, when a chief,
for no earthly purpose that I know of save to display his horsemanship and to put himself and his charger out of breath, sets
off at a tearing gallop from one extremity of the line to the
other : the cock feathers in the hats of his staff flying out
behind them like foam from the driving waters.

Well, the furious charge of a general on Plumstead Marshes
was something like the pace of the Russian postman. If he
had had many letters to deliver on his way he would have
been compelled to modify the ardour of his wild career; but
it always seemed to me that nineteen-twentieths of the Cadetten-
Linie were taken up by dead walls painted a glaring yellow,
and that the remaining twentieth was occupied by the house
where I resided. It was a very impressive spectacle to see him
bring up the little pony short before the gate of the hotel,
dismount, look proudly around, caress the ever-sucking leech
on his lip—as for twisting. the ends of it, the vampire would
never have permitted such a liberty—and beckon to some passing
Ivan Ivanovitch, with a ragged beard and caftan, to hold his
steed, or, in default of any prowling Ivan being in the way, attach
his pony's bridle to the palisades. It was a grand sound to hear
him thundering—he was a little man, but he *did* thunder—up the
stone stairs, the brass tip of his sword scabbard bumping against
his spurs, and his spurs clanking against the stones, and the
gloves hanging from a steel ring in his belt playing rub-a-dub-
dub on the leather pouch which held his letters for delivery—*my*
letters, my newspapers, when they hadn't been confiscated—with
all the interesting paragraphs neatly daubed out with black paint
by the censor. And when this martial postman handed you a
letter, you treated him to liquor and gave him copecks.

All this kind of thing is altered by this time in Russia. I have

seen the lowest order of police functionary—and the martial
postman was first cousin to a *polizei*—seize Ivan Ivanovitch, if he
offended him, by his ragged head and beat him with his sword-
belt about the mouth until he made it bleed. Whereas in these
degenerate days I am told a Russian gentleman who wears
epaulettes or a sword, is not allowed so much as to pull a
droschky-driver's ears, or kick him in the small of the back, if
he turns to the left instead of the right. Decidedly the times
are as much out of joint as a broken marionette.

I have no doubt either that the transaction of prepaying a
letter has been very much simplified since the period in which I
visited Russia. The Poste Restante also has of course been
sweepingly reformed. Brooms were not used in Russia in my
time save for the purpose of thrashing Ivan Ivanovitch. The
St. Petersburg Poste Restante in 1856 was one of the oddest
institutions imaginable. It was a prudent course to take your
landlord or some Russian friend with you to vouch for your
respectability. In any case you were bound to produce your
passport, or rather your "permission to sojourn," which had been
granted to you—on your paying for it—when the police at Count
Orloff's had sequestrated your Foreign Office passport. When
divers functionaries—all of the type of him with the blotting-pad
and the blue pocket-handkerchief—were quite satisfied that you
were not a forger of rouble-notes, or an incendiary, or an agent
for the sale of M. Herzen's *Kolokol*, their suspicions gave way to
the most unbounded confidence. You were ushered into a large
room ; a sack of letters from every quarter of the globe was
bundled out upon the table ; and you were politely invited to try
if you could make out anything that looked as though it belonged
to you. I am afraid that, as a rule, I did *not* obtain the property
to which I was entitled, and somebody else had helped himself to
that which belonged to me. I wonder who got my letters and
read them, or are they still mouldering in the Petropolitan Poste
Restante ?

Poste Restante ! Poste Restante ! I scan envelope after
envelope. I know the Poste Restante in New York, with its

struggling, striving crowd of German and Irish emigrants, craving for news from the dear ones at home. In connection with this department of the American postal service I may mention that in the great Atlantic cities they have an admirable practice of issuing periodically alphabetical lists of persons for whom letters have arrived by the European mails "to be left till called for," or whose addresses cannot be discovered. The latter cases are very numerous ; letters addressed "Franz Hermann, New York," or "My Cousin Biddy in Amerikey," not being uncommon.

I roam from pillar to post, always "Restante ; " and ten years slip away and I come upon an envelope inscribed "Poste Restante, Madrid." There is another name for this traveller's convenience in Spanish, but I have forgotten it. Otherwise "Poste Restante" belongs to the universal language. Everybody knows what it means. The Madrileña Poste Restante is, like most other things of Spain, a marvel and a mystery. You reach the post-office itself by a dirty little street called, if I remember aright, the Calle de las Carretas, one of the thoroughfares branching from that Castilian Seven Dials, the Puerta del Sol. The entrance to the office is in a dingy little alley, lined with those agreeable blackened stone walls, relieved by dungeon-like barred windows, common in the cities of northern Spain. Opposite the post-office door cower a few little book-stalls, where you may buy cheap stationery ; and there, in a little hutch, in aspect between a sentry-box and a cobbler's-stall, used to sit a public scribe, who for the consideration of a few reals would indite petitions for such supplicants as deemed that their prayers would be more readily listened to by authority if they were couched in words of four syllables, and written in fat round characters, with flourishes or *parafos* to all the terminals. The scribe also would write love-letters for love-lorn swains of either sex whose education had been neglected.

I don't think I ever knew such a black, dirty, and decayed staircase as that of the Madrid post-office, save perhaps that of the Mont de Piété, Paris. You ascended, so it seemed, several flights, meeting on the way male and female phantoms, shrouded in cloaks or in mantillas. The mingled odour of tobacco smoke,

of garlic, and of Spain—for Spain has its peculiar though inde-
scribable odour—was wonderful. The odds were rather against
you, when you visited the Poste Restante, that the occasion might
be a feast or a fast day of moment. In either case the office
opened late and closed early ; and the hour selected for your own
application was usually the wrong one. If the postal machine
were in gear, you pushed aside a green baize door and entered a
long low apartment, with a vaulted roof of stone. Stuck against
the whitewashed walls were huge placards covered with names
more or less illegible. Knots of soldiers in undress stood calmly
contemplating those lists. I don't think a tithe of the starers
expected any letters ; it was only another way of passing the
time. A group of shovel-hatted priests would be gravely scanning
another list ; a party of black-hooded women would be gossiping
before a third ; and everybody would be smoking.

You wandered into another vaulted room, and there you found
your own series of lists—those of the *estrangeros.* In the way of
reading those lists madness lay. The schedules belonging to
several months hung side by side. There were names repeated
thrice over, names written in different coloured inks, names crossed
out, names blotted, names altered, names jobbed at with a penknife so as to be indecipherable, by some contemplative spirit in
a sportive mood. The arrangement of names was alphabetical,
but arbitrary. Sometimes the alphabet began at A and sometimes
at T. The system of indexing was equally mysterious. I will
suppose your name to be Septimus Terminus Optimus Penn. To
this patronymic and prefixes your correspondent in England has
foolishly added the complimentary Esquire. Under those circumstances the best thing you could do was to look for yourself under
the head of "Esquire." Failing in unearthing yourself, then you
might try Optimus and Terminus, and so up to Penn.

When you found yourself a number was affixed to you. At one
extremity of the apartment was a grating, and behind that grating
sat an old gentleman in a striped dressing-gown and a black velvet
skull-cap. If you can imagine a very tame and sleepy tiger at
the Zoological Gardens smoking a cigarito, and with bundles of

letters and newspapers in lieu of shin bones of beef to eat, you may realise the idea of that old gentleman in his cage at the Poste Restante behind the Puerta del Sol. You spake him kindly and called him *Caballero*. He bowed profoundly and returned your compliment. Then you told him your number and handed your passport through the bars. He looked at the number and he looked at the passport. Then he kindled another cigarito ; then in a pre-occupied manner he began the perusal of a leading article in the *Epoca* of that morning. Then after a season, remembering you, he arose, offered you a thousand apologies, and went away out of the cage altogether, retiring into some back den—whether to look for your letters or to drink his chocolate, or to offer his orisons to San Jago de Compostella, is uncertain.

By this time there were generally two or three free and independent Britons clamouring at the bars—the Briton who threatened to write to *The Times ;* the Briton who declared that he should place the whole matter in the hands of the British ambassador ; and the persistent Briton who simply clung to the grate, or battered at the doortrap with an umbrella, crying " Hi ! Mossoo ! Donnez-moi mon lettre. Larrup, Milk Street, Cheapside, à Londres. Donnez-moi. Look alive, will you ?" At last the old gentleman returned, lighted another cigarito, and began to look for your letters. For whose letters is he looking now, I wonder, and where ?

Poste Restante ! Poste Restante ! It has rested for me close to the Roman Pantheon and under the shadow of that blood-stained sacrificial stone by the great Cathedral of Mexico. Poste Restante ! How many times have I journeyed towards it with fluttering pulse and a sinking in my throat—how many times have I come from it with my pocket full of dollars or my eyes full of tears: tears that were sometimes of joy and sometimes—but not often—of sorrow ! The Poste Restante has been to me these many years a smooth and a kind post, on the whole.

XXIV.

THE IDLE LAKE.

E who is acquainted with the Idle Lake should be thoroughly versed in the topography of mythical localities—should be familiar with the Bower of Bliss, the House of Fame, and the Cave of Despair; with Doubting Castle, Vanity Fair, and the Valley of the Shadow; with the Debatable Land and the Islands of the Blest; with Armida's Garden, and that fearfully beautiful Arbour of Proserpine, where nothing but that which was noxious grew. All these legendary regions should strengthen in the beholder the love and wonderment which, as a confirmed lotus-eater, an inveterate truant, and an incorrigible sluggard, he should feel for the Idle Lake.

It is situated—anywhere; and why not in Fairyland? Why should I not chronicle its bearings thus? Once upon a time a certain Sir Cymochles, a mailed knight, certainly, who had the privilege of the *entrée* at Arthur's Court on levée days, whatever the privilege of the *entrée* may mean, but otherwise of no very bright repute, was wandering up and down "miscellaneously" (a common practice in Faëry), accompanied by one Atin, a person of unquestionably bad character, and in quest of another chivalrous person, hight Sir Guyon, with the wicked intent him to kill and slay. Sir Cymochles, on this felonious errand bent, chanced to come to a river, and, moored by the bank thereof, what should he discern but a little "gondelay," or gondola, spick and span, shining like a new pin, and so trimly bedecked with boughs and cunningly woven arbours that the tiny cabin at the stern looked like a floating forest. In this delightful wherry there sat a lady

fair to see, gaily dressed, and with a quantity of wild flowers in
her hair. She was seemingly of a frivolous and irreverent tem-
perament, and (the legends say) sat in the gondola grinning like a
Cheshire cat. When she ceased to grin she giggled or hummed
a refrain from some idle ditty.

Now Sir Cymochles was desirous of passing to the other side of
the river, and he asked the giggling lady if she would give him a
cast across. Said the lady, tittering, "As welcome, Sir Knight,
as the flowers in May;" but she was not so ready to oblige Atin :
stoutly, indeed, refusing him boat-room. Possibly she doubted
his capacity to trim the boat properly; or haply she thought that
he could not pay the ferry fee. So Atin was, like Lord Ullin in
the ballad, "left lamenting" on the shore, and Sir Cymochles,
with the grinning lady, went on a rare cruise. Away slid the
shallow ship, "more swift than swallows skim the liquid sky;"
but the behaviour of the merry mariner on the voyage was, I
regret to say, most improper. She possessed a whole store-house
of droll anecdotes, and while she told them she laughed till the
tears rolled down her pretty naughty face. It is certain that she
"chaffed" Sir Cymochles, and I am very much afraid that she
tickled him; but he was rather pleased than otherwise with "her
light behaviour and loose dalliance." Her name, she said, was
Phædria. The inland sea, from which the river ran, and on
whose bosom the gondelay was floating, was named, she remarked,
the Idle Lake.

How the pair came at last to an island, waste and void, that
floated in the midst of that great lake; how the laughing lady
conducted the bemused knight to a chosen plot of fertile land,
"amongst wide oases set, like a little nest;" how in that painted
oasis there was "no tree whose branches did not bravely spring,
no branch on which a fine bird did not sit;" how she fed his eyes
and senses with false delights; how she led him to a shady vale
and laid him down on a grassy plain; how he—O, idiotic knight !
—took off his helmet and laid his disarmed head in her lap;
how she, as he sunk into slumber, lulled him with a wondrously
beautiful love-lay, in which she sang of "the lily, lady of the

flow'ring field," and of "the fleur de lys, her lovely paramour;"
how subsequently, steeping with strong narcotics the eyelids of
that bamboozled knight, she left him snoring and hied her to
her gondelay again; and how eventually she, plying at the
Wapping Old Stairs of Faëry, like a jolly, wicked young water-
woman as she was, picked up Sir Guyon, and him inveigled to
the Idle Island in that Idle Lake; and how there was a terrific
broadsword combat of two about that "ladye debonnaire"—are
not all these things written in the chronicle of the land which
never was—in the "Faërie Queene" of Edmund Spenser? If you
be wise, you will take the marvellous poem with you as your
only travelling companion the next time you journey to the Idle
Lake.

I am not habitually idle. I cannot afford to be. Highly as I
appreciate the delight of doing nothing, of lying in bed and
being fed with a spoon, or of eating peaches from the wall with
my hands in my pockets, like Thomson, I am yet constrained as
a rule to work for a certain number of hours in the course of
every day or night, in order to obtain a certain quantity of household bread. I have been wandering these many years past in a
wilderness of work, not unrelieved, however, by occasional oases.
I remember them all, and dwell on the remembrance of them with
infinite delight; even as that stolid wretch in hodden gray,
tramping the treadmill's intolerable stairs, may dwell upon that soft
and happy Sybarite time he passed after he was so lucky as to
find the gentleman's gold watch and chain in the gentleman's
pocket, and before he was "wanted" by the myrmidons of a
justice which would take no denial, and stigmatised his treasure-
trove as plunder and his lucky find as an act of larceny. A jovial
time he had; all tripe and dominoes, and shag tobacco and warm
ale. It was an oasis in his desert life of walking about in search
of something to steal; and although there are poets and
philosophers who maintain that the memory of happier days is a
sorrow's crown of sorrow, I have always been of a contrary
opinion; holding that as hope springs eternal in the human
breast, a man is seldom so miserable but that, if he has been

already happy, he cherishes the aspiration of being happy again. He may be conjuring up visions of future tripe and warm ale, more succulent and more stimulating than ever: that tramping man in hodden gray.

I am mindful of an oasis in Hampshire and of one in Surrey; of a lotus-garden (where I over-ate myself once) in an island in the Adriatic, and of a Valley of Poppies in North Africa. I know a bank in Andalusia on which I have reclined, pleasantly yawning, and drawing idle diagrams with my walking-stick in the sands of time at my feet. I know a cascade, far, far up in the mountains of Mexico, among the silver mines, the silvery plashing of whose down-come rings in the ear of my soul now, drowning the actual and prosaic lapping of the water "coming in" at Number Nine, next door. I am braced up tight between the shafts, blinkers block my eyes, and a cruel bit chafes my mouth, while those tearing wheels behind me seem pressing on my heels and ever and anon the smacking whip of the driver scathes my sides; but do you think I forget the paddock in which I kicked up my heels, or, resting my nose on the top of the fence, calmly contemplated the hacks on the highway, bridled and bitted, pursued by wheels, and quivering under the whipcord? Do you think that I forget the Idle Lake?

I had been to the wars when I came upon it. It was an ugly war in which I was concerned, a desultory, unsatisfactory, semi-guerilla warfare in the Italian Tyrol. Our commander was a famous Hero, but his troops were, to use the American expression, "a little mixed," and I am afraid that in several of the encounters in which we were engaged we ran away. We got scarcely anything to eat, and we slept more frequently in the open air than under a roof. It was a campaign performed by snatches and interspersed with armistices; and now and again I used to come down out of the mountains, ragged, dirty, hungry, demoralised, and "exceeding fierce," and journey to Milan for letters, money, and clean linen, to have a warm bath and enjoy a little civilisation. I am afraid that the guests at the Hotel Cavour, in the capital of Lombardy, formed anything but a favourable opinion of my manners;

still, if I did nearly swallow my spoon as well as my soup, and occasionally seize a mutton cutlet by the shank and gnaw it wolfishly, where was the harm ? It was so long since I had had a decent dinner ; nor did I know, when I got back to the mountains, when I might get another.

It was on one of these expeditions to Milan that Eugenius Mildman and I struck up a friendship. He was as mild as his name : a beaming, pious, gushing, amiable creature, as innocent as a lamb, as brave as a lion—I marked his conduct once in a battle, from which, with the prudence of a non-combatant camp-follower, I timeously retreated—and as affectionate as a young gazelle. I wish they would keep such exemplary Englishman as Mildman's race in England ; but the good fellows have a strange fancy for wasting their sweetness on the desert air of foreign countries; they do good at Florence and blush to find it fame at Malaga ; they act the part of the Man of Ross in Norway, and their right hand knoweth not what their left hand doeth at Smyrna ; they enrich Thebes and beautify Tadmor in the Wilderness ; and with deplorable frequency, and in the prime of life, they die of low fever at Damascus. Mildman was just the kind of charitable soul to die at Damascus, universally regretted, yet with a life wasted, somehow, in good deeds, done at the wrong time, in the wrong place, for the benefit of the wrong kind of people.

He was beautifully purposeless when I met him ; was undecided as to whether he should publish a series of translations from the Sarmatian anthology in aid of the Polish emigration, or raise a loan in furtherance of public (denominational) education in the republic of Guatimozin. Meanwhile he had been fighting a little with Garibaldi. I need scarcely add that he was a spiritualist and a homœopathist, and that he occasionally spoke, not in the strongest terms of censure, of the community of Oneida Creek, the Agapemone, the followers of Johanna Southcote, and the Unknown Tongues. It was a toss-up, I used to warn Mildman, between La Trappe and Colney Hatch for him. "Do something practical," I used to say to Mildman. "Pay a premium to a stockbroker and spend a year in his office. Article yourself to a sharp solicitor.

Enlist in the Sappers and Miners. You have plenty of money :
take chambers in St. James's, and discount bills at sixty per cent.
Make a voyage to Pernambuco before the mast. Go in for the
realities." But he wouldn't ; and I am afraid that he will die at
Damascus, universally regretted, and that his courier will run away
with his dressing-case and his circular notes.

I shall be ever grateful to Eugenius Mildman, for he made me
acquainted with the Idle Lake. It was during one of my expeditions to Milan, and broiling summer weather. The Scala was
closed ; and at the Canobbiana (the operatic succursal to the
grander theatre) the tenor had a wooden leg, the *prima donna
assoluta* was fifty-three years of age, and the *prima ballerina* was
slightly humped in the back and was endowed with but a single
eye ; so, as you may imagine, the Canobbiana entertainments did
not draw very crowded audiences. The garden of the usually
pleasant Caffè Cova, where we dined (chiefly on macaroni and
fried intestines) *al fresco*, had become a nuisance, owing to the
continual presence of noisy patriots, smoking bad " Cavours," and
screeching about the incapacity of General de la Marmora and the
shameful tergiversation of the Emperor Napoleon the Third in the
matter of the Dominio Veneto. The caricatures in the *Spirito
Folletto* were wofully stupid, and altogether Milan had become
socially uninhabitable.

Mildman and I determined to start on a ramble. We got to
Chiavenna, and so by Vico Soprano to St. Moritz. Thence,
hiring a little *calescino*, a picturesque kind of one-horse chaise, we
made Samaden, and for three weeks or so dodged in and out of
the minor Alpine passes—the Bernina, the Tonale, and so forth —
taking to mule-back when the roads were impracticable for the
calescino, and coming out into the Tyrol at last somewhere near
Storo, where we rejoined our famous Hero and his red-shirted
army. After another skirmish or so—we called them battles—
there was another armistice, and back I came to Milan, but this
time alone. I shook hands with Mildman, and the last I saw of
him was his slender figure bestriding a mule in a mountain gorge,
and in the setting sun. He was departing in quest of windmills

to charge or forlorn Dulcineas to rescue ; he was bound for
Damascus or the *ewigkeit*. What do I know about it ? Farewell,
excellent Quixotic man.

But I went back to Mediolanum ; and for the next eight weeks
I was continually running backwards and forwards to the Idle
Lake. I had grown to love it. I loved even the quaint old
Lombard town from which the lake derives, not its sobriquet, but
its real name. There are two of the dirtiest and dearest hotels in
Northern Italy in that town ; yet I was fond of them both.
There are as many evil smells in the town as in Cologne ; yet the
imperfect drainage and the too apparent presence of decaying
animal and vegetable matter in the market-place did not affect
me. Was I not on the shore of the great, calm, blue lake, with
the blue sky above and the blue mountains in the distance, and
the whole glorious landscape shot with threads of gold by the
much-embroidering sun ?

I had made the acquaintance of a Milanese banker who had a
charming villa on the opposite side of the lake, say at Silva Sel-
vaggia. He had a pretty yacht, in which many a time we made
voyages on the idle expanse, voyages which reminded me of the
cruise of Sir Cymochles. My host was an enthusiastic fresh-
water sailor, so much so that the lake boatman used to call him
" *Il Signore della Vela*." He was perpetually splicing his main-
brace and reefing his topsail. Sail ! we did nothing but sail : that
is to say, when we were not breakfasting, or dining, or smoking, or
drinking *asti spumante*, or dozing, or playing with a large French
poodle that was rated on the books of the yacht, and I think did
more work than any of the crew (one man, very like Fra Diavolo
in a check shirt, and without shoes and stockings, and a boy who
played the guitar), for he was incessantly racing from the bow to
the stern and barking at the passing boats. We spent at least
eight hours out of the twenty-four on the water ; and when there
was a dead calm we lay to and went to sleep. At breakfast time
the *Perseveranza*, the chief journal of Lombardy, came to hand,
and our hostess would read out the telegrams for our edification
After that we bade the *Perseveranza* go hang, and strolled down

towards the yacht. I never read anything, I never wrote anything, I never thought of anything while I was floating on the
Idle Lake, save what a capital thing it would be to be idle
for ever.

In our boating excursions we frequently landed at different
points on the lake and called upon people. They were always
glad to see us and to entertain us with fruit, wine, cigars, sonatas
on the pianoforte (if there were ladies present), and perfectly idle
conversation. I never yet learnt the " nice conduct of a clouded
cane ;" but I think that I acquired during my sojourn on the Idle
Lake the art of twirling a fan and of cutting paper. Had I
stayed long enough I might have learned to whistle : that grand
accomplishment of the perfect idler. By degrees I became
conscious that my visiting acquaintance was extending among
a very remarkable set of people ; and that nearly everybody
occupying the dainty palazzi and trim little villages nestling
among the vines and oranges and olives of the Idle Lake was
somebody.

It will be no violation of confidence, I hope, and no ungrateful
requital of hospitality, to hint that at Bella Riviera to the north-
east was situated the charming country house of Madame la
Princesse Hatzoff, the consort, indeed, of the well-known General
Adjutant and Grand Chamberlain to his Imperial Majesty the Tsar
of All the Russias. M. le Prince resides on his extensive estates
in the government of Tamboff. Some say that he is sojourning
in a yet remoter government, that of Tobolsk in Siberia, where he
is occupied in mining pursuits, in the way of rolling quartz stone
in the wheelbarrow to which he, as a life convict, is chained. The
Princess Hatzoff passes her winters either in Paris or Florence, her
springs in England, her autumns at Homburg or Baden, and her
summers on the Idle Lake. She is enormously rich, although M.
le Prince, during their brief wedded life, did his best to squander
the splendid fortune she brought him. She is growing old now ;
her clustering ringlets—she was renowned for her ringlets—are
silvery white ; her shoulders are arched, and her hands tremble
ominously as she holds her cards at piquet ; but her complexion is

still exquisitely clear, and she is not indebted to art for the roses on her cheeks.   Her feet are deliciously small and shapely, and she is fond of exhibiting them, in their open-worked silk stockings, and their coquettish little slippers with the high heels and the pink rosettes.

Forty years ago you used to see waxen models, coloured to the life, of those feet (with the adjoining ankles), ay, and of those half-paralysed hands, in the shops of the Palais Royal and Regent Street, and the Great Moskaia at Petersburg.   Forty years ago her portraits, in half a hundred costumes and a whole hundred attitudes, were to be found in every printseller's window in Europe. Forty years ago she was not Madame la Princesse Hatzoff, but Mademoiselle Marie Fragioli,* the most famous opera-dancer of her age.   The world has quite forgotten her, but I doubt whether she has as completely forgotten the world : nay, I fancy that in her sumptuous retreat she sometimes rages, and is wretched at the thought that age, decrepitude, and her exalted rank compel her to wear long clothes, and that in the airiest of draperies she can no longer spring forward to the footlights, night after night, to be deafened by applause and pelted with bouquets, and to find afterwards at the stage-door more bouquets, with diamond bracelets for holders, and reams of billet-doux on pink note-paper.

Those triumphs for her are all over.   They are enjoyed by sylphs as fair, as nimble, and as caressed as she has been ; and when she reads of their successes in the newspapers a bitter sickness comes across her.   What artificer likes to reflect upon his loss of competency in his art ?   Are retired ambassadors, are generals hopelessly on half-pay, are superannuated statesmen, or the headmasters of public schools, who have retired on handsome pensions, so very happy, think you ?   Not so, perchance.   Ambition survives capacity very often.   The diplomatist clings to his dispatch-bag, the soldier to his bâton of command, the minister to his red box, the pedant to his rod, the actor to his sock and buskin or his comic mask, long after the verdict of superfluity has been delivered ; long after the dread fiat of inefficiency has gone forth—the fiat

* Mademoiselle Marie Taglioni.

proclaiming that the bellows are burned, that the lead is consumed of the fire, and that the founder worketh in vain.

All round the coasts of the Idle Lake there were retired celebrities. The district was a kind of prosperous Patmos, a St. Helena tenanted by voluntary exiles, a jovial Cave of Adullam. Here vegetated an enriched director of promenade concerts; there enjoyed his sumptuous *otium* the ex-proprietor of dwarfs and giants, of learned pigs and industrious fleas; and in yonder Swiss châlet lived a lion-tamer, much famed on the Idle Lake for his proficiency in breeding rabbits. Millionaire patentees of cough lozenges, bronchitic wafers, anti-asthmatical cigarettes, universal pills, and Good Samaritan ointments, abounded on the Lake; together with a group of wealthy veteran tenors, baritones, and bassi, several Parisian restaurateurs and café keepers who had realised large fortunes, a contractor of one of the Rhine watering-place gambling tables, many affluent linendrapers and court milliners, and an English ex-butcher from Bond Street, as rich as Crœsus. All who were out of debt and had nothing to grumble at seemed to have gathered themselves together on these shores, leading a tranquil, dozy, dawdling kind of existence, so that you might have imagined them to be partakers before their time of the delights of some Eastern elysium, and to be absorbed in the perpetual contemplation of Buddha.

But my days of relaxation on the banks of the Idle Lake came with that autumn to an end ; and away I went into the *ewigkeit*, always into the *ewigkeit*, to be tossed about in more wars and rumours of wars, and rebellions and revolutions. For years I have not set eyes upon the Idle Lake; but I often dream of it, and puzzle myself to determine whether it is situated somewhere between the Lake of Garda and the Lake of Como. But that there is such a Lake, and that it is gloriously Idle, I am very certain.

XXV.

EMPTY BOXES.

HIS will be, I know, but a beggarly account. There are few things in the world so hopelessly dreary to look upon as are empty boxes. It is a truism to say that you can get nothing out of them. A full box may be picturesque, poetical. It may be Pandora's box or one of Portia's caskets. It may be the Iron Chest or Somebody's Luggage. It may be that notable trunk in which the mysterious Spanish Hidalgo, to whom Gil Blas was valet, kept his pistoles. It may be the coffer, gorged of millions, of the Wandering Jew. It may be Autolycus' box, crammed with "ribbons, chains, and ouches," or it may be the chest with the spring-lock immortalised in the story of Ginevra and the ballad of the Mistletoe-bough, or it may be the cowskin trunk in which Richard Cromwell kept the "lives and fortunes of the people of England"—in the shape of the addresses presented to him by the English municipalities when he was Lord Protector of the Commonwealth—or it may be the inscrutable sea-chest astride which Washington Irving's Dutchman went to sea in a storm. In short, a box with anything in it will furnish a plot for a melodrama or a novel, inspire poets and painters, awaken cupidity, excite ambition, fan the flame of love.

With what wistful eyes have I scanned the great iron safe in a City counting-house! With what rapture have I gazed on a lady's jewel-box—the tiny casket with a patent lock, steel beneath, russia leather above—and pictured the dainty gems within: their lustre prisoned in coffins of morocco lined with

white satin ! Nor without a pleasant trembling—a hope not
unmingled with fear—have . I beheld the cash-box which Mr.
Elzevir, of Ludgate Hill, has produced from his drawer, when,
my account being audited, he has been persuaded to draw a
cheque in my favour. Sweet cash-box, full of cheques, crisp
bank-notes, gold and silver, and sometimes of acceptances at
three months and I O U's !—I say that I have trembled, for
it has been just within the bounds of possibility that Mr. Elzevir,
a sudden spasm of hardness coming over his heart, might push
his cash-box back into the drawer, double-lock it, and suddenly
remembering that my account was overdrawn, button up his
pantaloons and dismiss me chequeless. Or how would it be
if, opening the cash-box, Mr. Elzevir discovered that his cheque-
book was worn to the last stump, and begged me to call the
day after to-morrow ?

If this paper were to be devoted to the topic of boxes that were
full, you should see that I had plenty to say and to spare. The
account of the work-box of a woman would fill a page at least. I
could expatiate till you were tired on a schoolboy's play-trunk,
with its hidden hoard of slate-pencil and its inevitable substratum
of contraband goods—say gunpowder, silkworms, cayenne pepper,
or the "Adventures of Robin Hood ;" and I am sure I could
pen several columns on the subject of a box to me the most
curious of all—the key-box ; the locked-up receptacle . for
things which lock up others, the wheel without the wheel, the
keeper of the keepers. It is on empty boxes, however, that I
am at present intent.

Empty boxes! Take that symmetrical sarcophagus of cedar
which, a month since, held one hundred choice Havanas. They,
the *flor fina* of Colorado Claros, are all smoked out ; you have not
even preserved their ashes, which, mingled with camphorated
chalk, are said to make an excellent tooth-powder, or, ground
with poppy oil, will afford for the use of the painter a varied
series of delicate grays. Old Isaac Ostade so utilised the
ashes of his pipe ; but had he been aware of Havanas he
would have given us pictures even more pearly in tone than

those which he has left for the astonishment and delight of mankind.*

The empty cigar-box makes you sad. You must have injured your constitution to an appreciable degree by smoking, say fifty out of that century of Colorado Claros. You have lately discovered that your cousin Tom, on whom you pressed a handful of your choicest cigars when you left him at Gravesend, on his way to Bombay, is a humbug. It was owing to your cruel and brutal persistence in smoking the last of your cigars in the Blue Boudoir, thereby disturbing the afternoon nap of the Italian greyhound, and causing that intolerable little beast to sneeze thrice, that you had last Thursday a few words with the partner of your joys and woes, and afterwards looked out in the *Court Directory* the private address of the judge who sits in divorce and matrimonial causes, and has power to loose and to bind. Worse than all, you have a running account with Messrs. Lope de Vega and Co., cigar merchants of Bond Street, W., and the hundred Colorado Claros, all smoked out, remain to be paid for.

If empty boxes yield anything, the harvest is but one of regrets. The scholar who bade Albertus Magnus raise the devil for him, found dashed in his face an empty purse ; and if you would conjure up the ghosts of dead hopes and the phantom of the love that is no more, and the skeleton ribs, black and rotten, of the Ship of Ambition, aboard which you vowed to ride into the Port of Fame and seize the Golden Fleece—if you would lift the veil, and recall

---

* Much has been talked in modern times about the "lost secrets" of the Venetian painters ; and Messrs. Winsor and Newton have been worried to death by artists to produce new blues, new crimsons, and new yellows, by means of which the gorgeous hues of Titian and Giorgione might be rivalled. But the tints most thoroughly lost or mislaid are, to my mind, the pearly gray tints of the Dutchmen. Very few modern painters seem to be aware that gray may be, and should be, a cunning compound of all colours, and not mere black and white, with a seasoning of lake, or indigo, or ochre, to make it cold or warm. The finest grays, perhaps, in modern art are those of M. Abel de Pujol, in the imitation of bas-reliefs on the covered roof of the Paris Bourse. Those who have closely examined them may have noticed that in the shadows there are great splashes of positive colour, bright vermilion, chrome, and cobalt, which, at the distance of the ordinary spectator from the picture, give pearliness and transparency to the whole.

the agony, and survey the wilderness of desolation and the valley of dry bones, I would advise you to plunge into the contemplation of empty boxes. " The late Miss Craggs's Estate." Such an inscription on a japanned tin box, in a lawyer's office near Cavendish Square, once meant to me a thousand pounds. The box was full. I saw a will, trust-deeds, dividend-warrants, through its tin sides. I walked round the house that held the box, in my dreams, and woke up in terror, thinking that thieves had stolen it, and longed for the day when I should be twenty-one and find a swift stockbroker and sell my money out. It never did anybody any good. It is lost in the fastnesses of the Neilgherry Hills; it is at the bottom of the river Rhine ; it is in Kensal Green.

I shudder now to think that I may meet some day in Ship Yard or Brokers' Row an empty box, the japanning half worn off the tin, and the late Miss Craggs's Estate grinning out of the shadows made by piles of second-hand office furniture. I do not think I could bear that sight. I should buy the box, and scrape out all remembrance of Miss Craggs, and melt up the japanned tin to an unrecognisable lump. Saddest of empty boxes ; and O the vanity of youth untoward, ever spleeny, ever froward ! What a school might be built, what a house bought, what a neat little purse made against the laying of the first stone of the Asylum for Decayed Turncocks by H.R.H. the Prince of Wales, what a capital venture made to the Spanish Main, with a thousand pounds ! Depend upon it, the Prodigal Son had an empty box, and sat upon it the while he tended swine and fed on draff and husks. .

Saddest of empty boxes ? No, not *the* saddest. There are boxes whose aspect is even more melancholy. Kicked about in yards, despised as the vilest rubbish, are the boxes which once held the sparkling *chefs-d'œuvre* of Mumm and Roederer, and the Widow Clicquot. Who cares for an empty champagne-box ! An empty egg-box is stouter. The empty box which has contained bottles of Warren's blacking will afford a firmer rostrum from which Stump Orator may address his dupes. It is not generally known that the haut pas of the thrones from which theatrical kings and queens issue their decrees, and witness the evolutions of the

occasional ballet, are often built up from egg-boxes. Champagne-
boxes would be too fragile. This is the end, then, of all your
frothing, and popping, and spuming forth effervescent delight.
A bottle, if it be not cracked, may serve again. Shot, or a wire
besom, may cleanse its interior. It may be degraded to serve as
a candlestick for a tallow dip, but it may be washed and purified,
re-filled, re-corked, re-wired, re-wrapped in pink paper, re-exported, to make the name of the Widow Clicquot famous to the
ends of the earth. But its empty box will never serve again.
Rough deals are cheap, and can be easily nailed together, and
daubed with mystic trades-marks and legends, as " Fragile,"
" With care," " This side upward," and a portrait of a full (not
empty) bottle.

Writers who set up for cynics are very apt to talk of the
skeleton closet which is said—although I do not believe anything
of the sort—to form part of the architectural arrangements of
every modern house. At least, I do not believe in the solitary
skeleton—the one bony osteological " boguey "—hanging to a nail
in one particular cupboard, of which only the master—if it be not
the mistress—of the establishment keeps the key. But if you
will mount to an apartment at the top of the house—an apartment which is open to all, cook, butler, and housemaid, and
whither the children often repair for the purpose of playing at
Wild Beasts, or at Shops—you may find, not one, but twenty
skeletons, in the shape of empty boxes. There are the portmanteaus, long since bulged into uselessness ; the bullock-trunks
of the lieutenant who died in India ; the bonnet-boxes of the girl
who bloomed into a woman and is now a widow ; the carpet-bag
you used to carry on those rare fishing excursions to Walton-on-
Thames ; the little, fat, black valise which was your companion
during that notable week you stayed at the country-house of the
Lord Viscount Toombsley—the only lord you ever knew—and he
cut you dead in the Burlington Arcade last Wednesday was a week.

Pleasant journeys, joyous outings, trips to Paris, runs to the
Rhine, wedding tours, jolly friends, pretty girls, merry meetings :
the spectres of all these linger about the empty boxes. Look at

the luggage-labels. You can hear the pat of the paste-brush, and see the red-faced porter trundling the luggage along the platform. You are off by the express. A guard has winked at you. He feels that you want a locked-up *coupé*, that you mean to smoke, and that he will have half-a-crown. You are off for Paris. You are off for Switzerland. You are off for the East. Empty boxes! I have one, the bare sight of the luggage-labels on which fills me with sorrow, with remorse, with bitter shame. "Liverpool," "Manchester," "Boston," "Niagara," "Madrid," "Riga," "Cronstadt," "Wien," "Seville," "Frankfort," "Homburg," "Venezia," "Paris," "Maçon," "Milan"—it is a Bradshaw cut up into strips and stuck hap-hazard all over the lid and sides. I thank the prudent porters who have striven to tear off some of the labels. I am spared the remembrance of some. This empty box has held my gala clothes, my dearest books, my choicest photographs, my rarest bits of bric-à-brac, and "the soul of the licentiate Pedro Garcia." And what has come of it all, beyond forty and odd years, an augmenting stomach, a damaged liver, and a confused consciousness that one has made rather a mess of it, and had better have stayed at home?

But we will endeavour to be cheerful, if you please, Cheerful! How *can* cheerfulness be extracted from empty boxes: far less when I am about to conduct you to the dullest and gloomiest of all the boxes in the empty world. Silent rolls the songless gondolier, and sullen plash his oar-blades on the waters of the back-slum canal. I am going to see the mournfullest sight in Venice. At the prow crouches the hotel guide. He too looks sad, although he is in my service to-day; for I have told him that to-morrow I shall have no need for his services. I have "done" all the lions of Venice twice over; and Venice is in a state of siege, and I am the only tourist in the desolate city; and my guide has been half-starving for weeks, and will wholly starve, I fear, when he has spent the last two florins I purpose to bestow upon him. For charity begins at home; and few travellers care to grant weekly pensions to hotel guides out of work, who are always bores, and often rascals.

The oars continue dully to plash ; and the gondolier—who has
not had a fare for a week—only breaks the sickening silence by
his lugubrious cry of warning when he turns a corner. There
was a time when I went a gondoliering with the pleasantest of
poodles at the prow ;* but darker and darker days have set in
for Venice ; and things have gone from bad to worse, and the
city has faded into a cemetery. Whither are we bound ? To the
magnificent palace which has been turned into the governmental
pawn-shop, and through whose windows, now close barred, but
whose balconies were once hung with rich tapestries, and over
whose sills fair ladies smiled, mountains of unredeemed pledges
in ghostly bundles palely loom ? Not thither. To the deserted
halls of the great Pesoro Palace, now converted into an old-
curiosity shop, rented by a Jew from Geneva ? Not thither. To
the empty arsenal, with its shipless basins and ropeless rope-
walks—the arsenal where Dante once saw the pitch and tar
boiling in huge caldrons that reminded him of the Stygian Lake ?
No ; not thither. Nor to the island of Murano, where the huge
mirrors and crystal chandeliers of Venice were once made, but
where now there is only a paltry manufactory of toy beads. Nor
to picture-gallery, nor church, nor cabinet of mosaics. We are
only on our way to see some empty boxes.

A dreadful beggar-man, by his father's side a leper, by his
mother's a hunchback, and himself an idiot ; a creature whose
rags are so intimate with his flesh that the tatters might be strips
of unwashed epidermis—this specimen of the Republic in Ruins
with a long hook draws our gondola to the landing-place, holds
out his shrivelled arm to help me to shore, cringing low as he
begs an obilus for the sake of the Madonna, and is grateful for
the farthing which I give him. (For, as all day long the beggars
of Venice buzz about you, and you are bound to relieve, say, one
in ten, you will find that a soldo, or farthing, at a time will make
before midnight a considerable vacuum in your pocket.) We
mount some slimy steps, and pass under a colonnade, whose

* See the volume "Dutch Pictures, and Pictures done with a Quill,"
p. 224.

stones are damp and green, and recall those of a dead-house by the waterside. Between each pair of columns hangs a huge lamp, some faded gilding clinging to its iron work, and its top crowned with the battered effigy of a phœnix. "Those lamps," whispers the guide, "have not been lighted for seven years." We stand before an old wooden door, the knocker and the keyhole red with rust, the huge-headed nails which once studded it half gone, the holes left black and meaningless, like the sockets of dead eyes. Paint it must have had, this door, in the bygone; but mildew has picked the pigment away, and streaks and smears of oozy moisture laugh grimly at what the painter's brush may have effected years ago.

This was once a stage door. Hither the pets of the ballet came tripping to rehearsal, with wreaths of artificial flowers in their reticules, and practising shoes under their arms. Here the servitors of the Venetian nobility left perfumed billets. Here the great *prima donna*, Assoluta di Cartello, landed from her own splendid gondola, and perhaps condescended to be assisted to shore by the *primo tenore*. Where once her stately feet trod, is now only the brackish sea-slime. We knock at the door, and after awhile a Judas-wicket opens, and through the grating peers a wrinkled old parchment face, with a few white bristles on the chin, which Balthazar Denner might have painted. A piping voice inquires our will. I answer that I wish to see the empty boxes, and I softly slap some loose florins in my pocket. The Judas-trap closes; but anon the door itself is opened, and a little old man, who might have been a junior clerk in an office close to the Rialto when Shylock did business there—who, as a specimen of Venice Preserved—seemingly in a solution of garlic—is highly respectable, no doubt, but who is assuredly the nastiest old man I have set eyes upon during many a long day's march—entreats me, with many bows and complimentary adjurations, to enter.

We cross a vestibule—the stage-doorkeeper's den—and see the rusty nails whence once hung the keys of the dressing-rooms, and the places of the racks where the perfumed billets once rested. It is inexpressibly dingy, and smells of lamp-oil a hundred years old.

The nasty old man has kindled a rush-light, and, by ·its pale glimmer, guides us up a damp stone staircase. Then we go down some stone steps, then mount again, then pass through a narrow corridor. I remember that, some months ago, a guide as old and as nasty led me up and down the stone staircases in the palace of the Escorial. He was a sexton, and took me to the sepulchre where the kings and queens of Spain are buried in stone boxes resting on shelves, and where there are yet some empty boxes waiting for the kings and queens of Spain that are to die.

We emerge into a dim area, and stand on the stage of an enormous theatre. The sconces of the footlights seem to mark the boundaries of another world, and all beyond them yawns the dark vasty gulf of pit. From a window in the topmost gallery darts, sharp and clear, one transverse ray of light, and I am enabled to make out at last five tiers of boxes, all perfectly empty. The woodwork of the stage is half decayed. There are as many inequalities on its surface as in the mosaic pavement of St. Mark's church. Can this rotten and grimy expanse, whose stiffened traps might be the "drops" on which doomed wretches stand, the ropes round their necks secured to the timbers of the flies above, be the same boards on which Ellsler, Cerrito, Taglioni, have danced, in the midst of a sea of gas, and a shower of bouquets and a storm of plaudits? Can this be the place where Billington and Catalani, Pasta and Malibran, have sung? Yes; look behind you; piled pell-mell against the stark damp walls, rigid and faded, like the mummies of Titans, are the "flats" and "wings" and set pieces of the place. There are Norma's altar and Amina's bridge and Zerlina's bedroom and Don Giovanni's villa, and Ninus's tomb and Marta's spinning-wheel, and the supper-table of Lucrezia Borgia.

I follow the nasty old man up and down more dark staircases and through more dark corridors, and now he unlocks a door, and I stumble into a kind of cell, which, the rushlight being held up and waved around, turns out to be a proscenium box, with a frescoed ceiling and walls brave with mirrors and damask hangings. I have nearly broken my shin over an antique fauteuil once splendid in carving, gilding, and velvet, but which, on inspection, turns out to have but three legs; and my foot is caught, to my almost overthrow, in one of the holes of a once gorgeous Turkey carpet. As we pass from the box, the nasty old man holds his rushlight to the central panel of the door, and there I see a flourishing coat of arms, with as many quarterings as there were in the scutcheon of the Princess Cunegonde, beloved of Candide. But marked with the stigmata of desolation is all that heraldry. The blazonry has faded, or has turned from sable and gules to grubbiness. I cannot make out the motto beneath, but it should be "Resurgam," seeing how remarkably like the whole affair is to the hatchments set up by cheap undertakers, who strive to persuade the natives of Soho or Tottenham Court Road in far-off London to allow them to conduct their funerals, by heraldically hinting in their windows that they have already buried half Boyle's Court Guide.

This proscenium box, and the next, and the next, all round, from the P.S. to the O.P. side, pertain to the proudest families of the Venetian nobility. The house, indeed, belongs to a proprietary, and three-fourths of the shareholders are Venetian nobles. On many box doors are their spectral achievements of arms and their antique titles. Tier above tier, vasty gulf of pit, stately crush-room with mirrors yet uncracked, and settees of velvet, and ceiling of fresco, and flooring of gesso, but all obscure and faded; corridor and lobby, and ante-chamber and grand staircase and vestibule are haunted by pallid spectres, calling themselves Foscari and Falier, Grimani and Contarini, Pesaro and Grani, Papadopoulo and Nani-Mocenigo.

I return to the stage and peer into the cavern of shadows, sharp sected by that transverse ray from the topmost gallery, when, all at once, the empty boxes fill! Yes; there they are, fair women and brave men, in veils, and lace, and silk, and satin, and broidered stuffs, with swords, and fans, and flashing gems. The great theatre is lighted *a giorno*. The huge chandelier blazes up with countless crystals in the midst of a frescoed firmament; and then the orchestra fills too, and I see the conductor, white-gloved,

waving his batôn. I hear the loud bassoon, and the crash of the
cymbals, and the scraping of many fiddles. The footlights flash
up like the demon lights in the "Freyschütz." A vision in gauze
and silk and artificial flowers bounds by me. It is Marie Taglioni.
Why not? The Queen of Dance is alive still, and it would do
her old bones good to come and foot a final jig in this place. For
this is the famous Opera House of La Fenice. Yonder, in his box
of state, is the King of Italy. Around him are the nobility and
the beauty, not alone of Venice, but of his whole magnificent
kingdom—There's no such thing ; at least, not yet. There is
nothing but darkness, and desolation, and empty boxes.

If I can find e'er a ghost to tenant the state box it will be a
phantom in a white coat—the Cavaliere Toggenburg, indeed
Luogotenente, or civil governor of Venice, representing the
Austrian Kaiser. I see this ghost of Toggenburg continually
squabbling with the noble shareholders of La Fenice, worrying
and baiting them ; and they, it must be owned, rendering him as
good as he gives ; for the Italians are eminently skilled in the art
of ingeniously tormenting, and these fifty years past the Venetians,
if they have groaned under tyranny, and suffered misery from the
presence of the stranger, have at least succeeded in making their
masters desperately uncomfortable. Sir John Falstaff declined to
march through Coventry with his ragged regiment ; but I could
tell of a penance far more disagreeable—to be in command of a
regiment not at all ragged, but beautifully made up, and then to
be sent to Coventry, and quartered in Coventry, and forced to stop
in Coventry, year after year, to be cut, shunned, loathed, scowled
upon, scorned, when, at the bottom of their hearts, your command
is really a very jolly regiment, fond of waltzing, and good cheer,
and blithesome company. Cavaliere Toggenburg wishes La Fenice
to be opened in order that everybody may enjoy themselves, and
that his tight-waisted, white-coated officers may flirt with the
Venetian ladies, and listen to the opera for fourpence-halfpenny,
according to the tariff made and provided in dear old unsophisti-
cated Deutschland.

But the noble shareholders of La Fenice snarl "No!" If they open the theatre at all, it shall be to hang it with black crape, and light it with corpse candles, and intone a mortuary mass there, for Venice, laid out on the Lagoons so cold and stark. "Come," cries Toggenburg, "let bygones be bygones. Here are fifty thousand florins as a subvention from my government. Engage an energetic impresario and a first-rate troupe. Let us have plenty of masked balls next carnival, and the Austrian Hymn, with full chorus, on the Kaiser's birthday !" The noble shareholders will have none of Toggenburg's money. At the last carnival ball given here, there were but six maskers, and this forlorn half-dozen were dressed and paid by the police. From 1859—the year of hoped-for liberation, but, as it turned out, the year of the renewal of the lease of Venetian slavery —unto the year 1866 La Fenice has been entirely closed, and the spider has woven his web, and the flea has gone to sleep for want of somebody to bite, in these empty boxes.

Empty, but not perchance, for ever. Ere these lines shall be printed, it is to be hoped and believed that the emptiness of La Fenice will have become a thing of the past—that the splendid house will be really lighted *a giorno*—that a substantial King of Italy will sit in the state-box and listen, not to the Austrian Kaiser's, but to his own national hymn—and that the boxes of this historical theatre will be full to overflowing of the noblest blood, the brightest beauty, the keenest intellect, and the soundest worth of the peninsula.

NOTE.—The Canticle of Simeon can now be sung, as regards these "Empty Boxes." In November, 1866, I went to a masquerade at the Fenice Theatre. Victor Emmanuel, King of Italy, sat in the state-box listening to the shouts of "Italia Una" and "Venezia Libera" ringing through the house. They only wanted ROME in '66. They have got *that* now.

XXVI.

The Surrender of Venice.

T six o'clock on the morning of October 18th, 1866, the Austrian dominion in Venice ended, so far as human prescience can foresee, for ever. The last bands of German soldiers who, by a blundering policy, had been permitted to linger in the barracks and the public buildings, and whose continued presence was a source of legitimate irritation to the Venetians, packed up their needments and slunk away during the night of the 16th. I do not remember to have witnessed a spectacle more melancholy, and at the same time more suggestive, than that which I saw the following midnight under the colonnade of St. Mark's Place. A young Austrian officer—a captain—had got his route. There was a war-steamer waiting for him somewhere, to take him to the land of the Teuton; but he did not know exactly where she lay. He was wandering in a pitiably desultory manner about the "sotto portici," two orderlies following him in obsequious but uncertain obedience; one bearing on his brawny shoulders the captain's portmanteau, the other laden with his shako, his holsters, and his sword-case. The poor young gentleman was evidently lost in Venice. He no longer recognised the capital whose inhabitants he had so long trampled under foot. In vain, by dint of his eye-glass did he strive to discern one friendly face of whose possessor he might ask the way to a place where he could take oars and go away for good.

"Retributive justice, O captain," I thought; and I daresay that my thoughts were echoed, unconsciously, by a good many Venetians. "Retributive justice! The poisoned chalice is at last come unto your own lips! Within these last few days the handwriting has come out on the wall, and the fingers of a man's hand have written, as in sand, that the Medes and Persians are at Mestre, waiting to cross the railway-bridge, which you vainly threatened to blow up with gunpowder, and that your kingdom is given to another."

I know that there is nothing meaner nor shabbier than to exult over a fallen enemy. I know that the Austrians have many good and estimable points. I know that it is through the default of their own stupid and headstrong Government that they have lost the fairest province upon which God's sun ever shone ; and yet I confess that I did not feel at all sorry when I saw the Austrian captain wandering about like a strayed puppy under the "sotto portici." My thoughts carried me back just four months, minus three days. I remembered that then I had had to bend the neck and hinge the knee to the Archduke Albert for permission to leave Venetia, and was repulsed from the outer rooms of the Austrian Hauptmann, his aide-de-camp, who was wolfing beef and cabbage at Verona, at eight o'clock in the morning. He told me to "wait down-stairs," did he ? until he chose to consider my petition to be allowed to quit the "Austrian Empire." Aha! it is the aide-de-camp, now, who has to "wait down-stairs" in the cold, and is of less account than the meanest creature on the Canareggio.

This is, I am aware, very unchristian and very uncharitable ; but it is human nature; and if you will be good enough to multiply by five thousand the feelings of annoyance I suffered through this temporary slight in the citadel of Verona, and add to the product a long-accumulated score of hatred and disgust, you may form some idea of the sentiment entertained by the Venetians for the ousted Government by which they had been, for so many years, bullied, outraged, and oppressed.

I was at Florian's until very late on the night of the 17th, and at the Specchi until later, and at Quadri's, and, indeed, wherever there was a chance of seeing Venetian life on the Eve of Liberation; but up to the time I went to bed, which was at a

most unholy hour, there were Austrian officers about. Wrapped
in their gray gaberdines, their *lorgnons* faithful to their mild blue
eyes, their sabres still clanking, their spurs still jingling on the
pavement, their white teeth, blonde whiskers, and fresh complexions still gleaming in the gas, they continued, until the night
was very old, to vindicate their claims to be the best "set-up,"
most soldier-like, and most gentlemanly-looking officers in Europe.
Somehow or another, between the time I retired to rest and the
time I got up again, they all disappeared.

There is a vague and mysterious period during the small hours,
so Mr. Frederick Greenwood tells us in his beautiful "Essay
without End," during which all kinds of curious things are done
—during which the Palpable fades into the Impalpable—and sick
men preferably die, and infants elect to live. It must have been
in this shadowy time that the Tedeschi went away, to return, I
hope, no more. It was a great astonishment, a vast relief, to
walk forth on to the Piazzetta in the bright October sun, and find
that there were no more Croats under the arcade of the Palazzo
Ducale. The Cancellate, that grim range of dungeon-bars, which
screened the colonnade, and behind which the Austrian drums and
the Austrian banner, the hated "Schwarz-gelb," used to rest ;
behind which the Austrian bayonets used to be piled ; behind
which the Austrian soldiers used to squat on their benches,
puffing at their meerschaums, and contemplating the Imperiale
e Reale Zecca opposite with a stale and accustomed look ; behind
which, in fine, were ranged those six-pounders whose trail was so
terrific, and which were to blow the Venetians into peelings of
onions if they dared to misbehave themselves—the Cancellate,
those most obnoxious of iron railings, were gone. They had been
torn up bodily by a suddenly enfranchised people. Gondoliers,
Garibaldini, beggars even, had lent a hand to wrench those prison
stockades from their sockets. Even strangers and chance visitors,
yielding to an impulse of enthusiasm, had rushed forward to help
unroot the ugly signs of Austrian rule.

Was there not, as historians tell us, a turbaned Turk among
the fierce French patriots who assaulted the Bastille ? He could

have known nothing about *lettres de cachet*, or Latude, or the Man with the Iron Mask, that muslin-kerchiefed Moslem ; yet, when the time came, he tucked up his sleeves, and went to work. with a will to pull down that horrible old castle of the devil.

The Cancellate were the last outward and visible signs that remained of the Austrian rule in Venice. The double eagle had disappeared some days since from the ensigns of the tobacconists. The Imperial " I " had been divorced from the Royal " R " on the façades of the Police and Post-Office. The Venetian National Guard had been suffered to stand sentry at that grand Paviglione behind the Palazzo Reale which, of old time, was only allowed to be tenanted when Majesty itself, or at least an Austrian Archduke, was resident in Venice. The Arsenal, the Mint, the Tobacco-factory, the Finances, the Monte di Pietà, had been given up. But to the guard-house under the Ducal Palace, with its unsightly Wombwell's-show-like Cancellate, the Tedeschi stuck until the very last moment. When they gave up that they gave up everything.

At six o'clock on the morning of the 18th, General Alemann, whilom military governor of the city and fortress, bade a long farewell to Venice. It was time for him, like Prospero in "The Tempest," to break his staff, burn his book, and abjure his magic. A war-steamer waited for him, too ; but it was a bright and beautiful morning, and he knew full well where to find her. He came from under the Piazzetta porch of the royal palace as the clock struck six, rosy, clean-shaven, alert, and smiling, in that familiar sky-blue tunic, and with that well-remembered diamond cross on his brave old breast I had seen so often in the hot, hopeless nights on the Molo, when Alemann trotted about monarch of all he surveyed, but very likely wishing most devoutly that any monarchy rather than the unthankful Venetian one was his to survey. Early as was the time of his embarkation the Piazzetta was thronged. There were there a motley crowd : " barcaruoli," fishermen, bargees, blackguards—the raff and scum of Venice, indeed, mingled with the early-rising toilers.

It was a grand opportunity, a fine occasion whereon to hoot and yell and screech, and mob a deposed ruler who had no longer

x

any bayonets at his back. I rejoice to say that as the ex-
governor stepped into his gondola there arose from the ragged
and rough multitude a great, hearty, honest "Evviva!" Yes,
they cheered him lustily. *He* had never done them any harm,
and had always striven to do them good. The valiant and loyal
little old gentleman had at first only raised his cocked-hat in
military punctilio, but when he heard that sounding shout of
"Good-bye, and God be with you!" he took out his white
handkerchief and waved it cheerily in acknowledgment of the
salute. Austrian generals are but mortals after all, and who
shall say that he did not afterwards convey the cambric to his
eyes, to stanch the witness of "unfamiliar brine?" Good-bye,
brave and trim little captain, ever ready in the forefront of the
battle, but ever kind and gentle and courteous. The Venetians
are good haters; but they will long keep a pleasant corner in
their hearts for "Guglielmo Barone di Alemann."

The Venetian population, I opine, would not have preserved
a demeanour quite so placable had any of the minor agents of
Austrian tyranny ventured upon a public departure. I verily
believe that they would have torn Toggenburg* to pieces. That
"indegno cavaliere," as Masetto called Don Giovanni, was wise
enough to steal away many weeks previously to Verona, and
thence across the Brenner into Austria. He did not care about
exchanging adieux with the Veneziani. They might have been
apt to remember that the Cavaliere Toggenburg's favourite
amusement was to go down to the railway-station, and gloat over
the convoys of political prisoners arriving, handcuffed, from
every part of Venetia, on their way to the Spielburg.

Other subordinate despots in Venice did not retreat so timeously as did Toggenburg. Rats will desert a sinking ship, but
there are always some rats who will remain until the leak assumes
alarming proportions. It was difficult to make the German
'polizzotti," understand that their presence had become an abom-
nation in a free Italian Town, and the Italian National Guard

* The Cavaliere Toggenburg was civil governor of Venice up to within a
short time of the surrender of the city.

had hard work in rescuing the Austrian gendarmes and detectives from the effects of patriotic indignation. The private policemen were only hooted and pelted ; but the crowd on several occasions evinced a lively desire to have the heart's blood of the police captains and commissaries who were wont to domineer over them.

One Ramponi, for instance, who had been a terrible tyrant in his time, was within an inch of being murdered. The crowd discovered him (pretty much as George Lord Jeffreys was discovered looking out of the window of an ale-house at Wapping) in some obscure caffè of the Canareggio. I am sure.I don't know what he was doing there. The miserable man had perhaps a monomania for espionage, and was prowling about, even after his power had departed, in the hope of "taking up" somebody. The mob were down upon him at once ; he was dragged from his lurking-place, hustled, spat upon, half-stripped, and brought into dangerous propinquity with a canal, when the National Guard, arriving in force, rescued him from the fate which threatened him. For safety they conveyed him, for awhile, to the nearest guard-house, and then put him on board a gondola, and transported him to the railway-station, advising him, if he valued his own skin, to leave Venice by the very next train. The man put forth a piteous plea to be allowed to see his wife and children before he left ; upon which the commandant of the National Guard observed to him that he must forego that indulgence. "You might remember, Signor Ramponi," he added, " that when you arrested the Venetians at dead of night, and put them on board the steamers which conveyed them to imprisonment or exile, you were not in the habit of asking them whether they wished to bid farewell to their wives and families."

All Venice had learnt by heart the official programme put forth by the Congregazione Municipale of Venice as to the order of proceedings to be observed on the momentous 18th of October. The Austrians, it was stated, would have entirely evacuated the city by daybreak. The formal surrender of the keys by the Austrian General Möring to the French General Lebœuf, and by him to the Italian General Revel, would then take place. At nine o'clock precisely, amidst a salvo of artillery the Italian banner would be hoisted from the three tall masts in the Piazzo San Marco, which in bygone days bore the symbols of the dominion of the Most Serene Republic over Venice, Cyprus, and the Morea. At ten a corps of five thousand Italian troops, under the command of General Medici, would arrive from the mainland at the railway-terminus, and would enter the city in three different bodies and by three different routes ; one body embarking in barges, and proceeding straight along the Canal Grande to the Piazzetta ; another coming round also by water, by the channel of the Zattare ; the third crossing and recrossing the two iron bridges, and marching through the streets—not one of which is wider than old Cranbourn Alley—to St. Mark's.

The hoisting of the Italian standard was a brief but most impressive ceremony. From earliest dawn St. Mark's Place had been thronged ; indeed, I have no doubt that many hundreds of patriots had been bivouacking at Florian's, or among the benches of the " sotto portici," all night. I am not prepared to state that the Piazza, by nine o'clock in the morning, was full, because it is to me a matter of extreme uncertainty whether any number of human beings congregated together, short of the number who were dispersed at the Tower of Babel, would be sufficient to fill St. Mark's Place. It is like the harbour of Halifax, Nova Scotia, which is said to be big enough to hold all the navies of the world, but opening out of which is a supplementary harbour, capable of holding any number of additional navies. So has the Piazza its supplementary port in the shape of the Piazzetta.

St. Mark's itself was all alive. The platform above the façade was black with humanity, who did everything but bestride those immortal horses of St. Mark, which came from Corinth, which have been at Byzantium, which have been at Paris, which have been at Vienna, which may go to St. Petersburg or to New York, for aught we know, before this Human Comedy is finished, but which I was pleased to look upon this morning, preserving, even in their grimmest and bronziest aspect, a jocose and Astley's-like

look, and unmurmuringly performing their eternal trot. Those
marvellous semi-circular fringes to St. Mark's frontage, surmounted by sculptured crockets, which Mr. Ruskin has eloquently
but fantastically compared to the twisted and petrified foam of
the sea, were on the present occasion obscured by adventurous
climbers. The balconies and loggie of the Ducal Palace were one
mass of life; and I am sorry to say that the Venetian *gamins*
had been permitted to invade the tiny courtyard of the exquisite
Loggetta at the foot of the Campanile, and to climb over the
beautiful bronze gates, the which to see is at once to conceive the
desire of committing robbery in a dwelling-house, by carrying
them off to England.

Nine o'clock strikes from the Torre dell' Orologio. With the
last chime you see something like a fractured rainbow battling
with the air. Then three great masses of colour spring up, droop,
hang, raise themselves again, develop, and at last flame out broad
and triumphant against the blue. It is done. A band strikes up.
The multitude give a cry of joy that is almost a sob. The cannon
thunders from San Giorgio Maggiore, now an Italian fortress.
From the three great masts streams out the standard of twenty-
five millions of human souls who are "united and equal." The
cannon thunder again. At the Hôtel de la Ville, General Möring
has exchanged the last protocol with General Lebœuf. The
Surrender of Venice is accomplished, and Italy is free " from
the Alps to the Adriatic." Will it last?

After this, although the month be October, all is midsummer
madness. Venice goes clean out of her mind. Venice is stark
staring mad as I sit down to pen these lines. Venice will be
suffering, I have no doubt, from acute mania when I take this
letter to the post, and will not recover her sanity for many moons
to come. I had taken the precaution to engage a two-oared
gondola for the entire day, and to stipulate with the chief boatman
that a very large Italian flag should be displayed at the stern. I
hurried back from St. Mark's Place to the Hotel Victoria, where
my bark was to be in waiting; but, during even the brief
period of my absence, Venice had become transformed. Flags by

hundreds, flags by thousands, flags by myriads, had cropped up and out from every housetop, from every eave, from every waterspout, from every lamp-iron, from every bourne-stone, from every railing, from every window, from every balcony, from every door, from every hole, from every corner in this city which is full of holes and corners. "La città era imbandierata ;" that is to say, everybody who possessed a morsel of red, white, and green was displaying it. The "stoffe colorate," against which the Austrian police director used to fulminate, had at last asserted themselves.

The scene on the Grand Canal was astounding. The municipality had entreated the citizens to confine the manifestation of their enthusiasm on this particular day to flags and streamers, and to reserve the more gorgeous and more peculiarly Venetian display of tapestry, carpets, and window-curtains hung out of the windows, for the occasion of the arrival of the King of Italy ; but popular enthusiasm had been deaf to the voice of the municipality, and the woven wealth that is within Venetian palaces had to a great extent run o'er. The spectacle of a "house out of windows" was performed a hundred times a minute on the Grand Canal. Out came the Brussels and the Aubussons, the Kidderminsters and the printed druggets ; out came hearthrugs and damask-curtains, all mingled with wondrous tapestries of the sixteenth century— the *chefs-d'œuvre*, it may be, of the looms of Courtray and Arras. Next to the display of textile fabrics was the lavish exposure or pocket-handkerchiefs. Everybody seemed to have at least three, not to apply to their legitimate use, but to wave in a frantically patriotic manner.

I have somewhere read that when Catherine Malcolm, a horrible old woman who murdered a gentleman in the Temple in the reign of Queen Anne, was executed at the Middle Temple-gate, the crowd in Fleet Street was so great that an industrious tradesman who sold hot mutton-pies by retail walked, without stumbling, over the close-packed heads of the multitude from where is now the shop of Messrs. Butterworth, the law booksellers, to the corner of Chancery Lane, where he disposed of a hot "twopenny" to a gentleman from Lincoln's-inn, who had adventitiously hailed him. Without vouching for the historical truth of this anecdote, I am perfectly willing to take my affidavit before any sworn commissioner appointed for that purpose, that I could have walked dryfooted, at noon on this instant 18th of October, over any part of the Grand Canal between the railway-station and Santa Maria della Salute.

The great waterway was paved with boats. There were gondolas everywhere ; and the few interstices which presented themselves were filled with skiffs and barges. It was an enormous and glowing parterre of pleasure-boats, of banners and streamers, of gay costumes, of gondoliers in new apparel, of flowers and bright carpets. There were public gondolas and private gondolas ; there were men, there were women, there were children, there were soldiers and sailors ; there were brown-cowled monks peeping from the casements of convents ; there was a great kaleidoscopic jumble of life and noise, and movement and colour, and light and shade, and reflection and refraction ; there was the Tohubohu of the Hebrews ; there was a pictorial come-and-go, a mingling and a massing, a surging and weltering of chromatic caprice, there was a sea of gold and purple glory such as the Venetian painter Canaletto never imagined, such as the Venetian painter Guard, never realised, such as the Englishmen Joseph Turner and John Ruskin, with all their magic power of pen and pencil, with all their bright poetic insight, never approached, such as no human limner, no human scribe, can ever hope completely to portray.

I saw it—dulled and hardened as I have been to shows and sights all over the world—I saw it, and felt inclined to cry because I knew that I could never convey one-tenth part of the immensity of its real aspect to you in England. I see it now, clear and distinct in my mind, as the faces of those who are dead, and who come to me in my dreams ; and I am ashamed of my impotence to translate into language the ideas of which my heart is full—I am ashamed to blunder over that which at its very best must be a lame and halting narrative of a sight which I shall never behold again.

In the midst of this tremendous sea of happy holiday people, laughing and shouting and embracing, came, slow and stately, half a dozen great galleys, decked with flags, brave in draperies, full from stem to stern of Italian soldiers. As the clock struck. noon the guests of the day marched out of the railway-station, and down its noble staircase into the barks appointed to receive them. There is the clash of martial music. There is Garibaldi's Hymn. There is the Royal Anthem. There is the "grido di guerra." Now comes, swan-like, a great Argo, laden with National Guards. Then follow the Carabinieri, the picked men, the boldest, bravest of Italians, the "bene meriti dell' armata," the only police force perhaps in Europe who are not unpopular. Like doves from a thousand arks, the white handkerchiefs of the women in the balconies fly out to greet these good, solid men. Now come the Bersaglieri, bronzed and saucy-looking, but eminently serviceable. To these succeed many boats full of Italian infantry, and gondolas conveying officers of all arms in full uniform. The pace at which the flotilla moves is but a snail's one ; but it is all too rapid for the spectators, who cannot dwell too long or too lovingly on the soldiers, who, to them, represent their restoration to national existence, and their deliverance from a cruel and galling servitude.

We crept ahead and got into a fresh crowd of gondolas ; but eventually landing at the Molo, crossed the Piazzetta to the Clock Tower, where I was fortunate enough to have secured a front place at a first-floor window. Thence at my leisure I saw the disembarkation of the troops, their march past the Ducal Palace, and heard the frantic acclamations by which they were greeted by the crowd. And then, I am constrained to say, it being close on four o'clock in the afternoon—we had been three hours and a half coming from the terminus to the Molo—and remembering that the post for England went out at eight, I left the Venetians together in their glory, and diving dexterously through a labyrinth of by-lanes, returned to mine inn, there to set down so much as time would allow me of what I had seen on this most memorable day.

XXVII.

EVE IN ST. MARK.

N her charming life of her witty father, Lady Holland tells us that when the Canon of St. Paul's was old and infirm, he was wont, on fine mornings, to bid his domestics " throw open the shutters and glorify the room." By which the Rev. Sydney Smith simply meant that his servants should let in the sun. Under the sun he had beheld, in his long life, much madness and folly ; but he loved to look upon the luminary, and to warm his good old face in it, and to be thankful for sunshine, until the end. The sun is the patrimony of age ; all, save the blind, can bask in its rays when all other wealth is spent, and even Blind Tobias can feel its warmth.

" Vieux vagabond, le soleil est à moi," cries Béranger's worn-out mendicant, from his ditch. So Mirabeau, writhing on his bed of death, and vainly striving to stifle agony with spiced meats and fiery wines, bade them open the window, that he might gaze upon the sun—if not the Deity Himself, at least his cousin-german. So Jean Jacques, at Ermenonville, in the evening of *his* career of miserable glory—poor, neglected, half-poisoned may be—bade Thérèse unfasten the window-latch, that he might fill his soul for the last time with the rays of " the Master of the World ; the only master who is adored without flattery, and without greed of temporal reward." For you get nothing by toadying the Sun. It is a matter of mathematical calculation as we were once assured on illustrious authority, that he will rise to-morrow morning ; and the chances are ten millions to one in favour of humanity that he will so rise. But it is a matter of certainty as mathematical that he is not to be propitiated by odes or won to the side of gentility by corporation addresses ; that he will shine with impartial munificence upon David's enemies, as upon David himself ; and that, if he intends to veil his face, not all the psalms, supplications, or adjurations in the world can conjure his clouds away.

There is a certain time in the afternoon, at the autumnal season, when a certain part of the basilica of St. Mark—the most gorgeous, but the darkest church in Europe—is "glorified" by the sun. Worshippers there are in St. Mark's at all hours ; but at about ten minutes to five every afternoon, when the weather is fine, a number of loungers are sure to drop into the church to see the apsis behind the high altar "glorified." The contrast which they come to see is all the more striking, as by four o'clock three-fourths of the basilica have become a gloomy wilderness, through which you might wander long ere you discovered that all around you rose columns of porphyry and malachite and verd-antique, panels glowing with gold and gems, pavements dazzling in vermiculato and mosaic work.

Lost in umbrageous dimness are the sumptuous Baptistery, the jewel-crowded chapel of the Madonna de' Mascoli, the two fanciful *pale* that flank the high altar ; nay, even the famous Icone Bisantina and the stately baldacchino have but a pale and uncertain glimmer. From between the intercolumniations of the windows sweep down great dark shadows, so thick that they seem well-nigh palpable, and you fear to stumble over them, as though they were half-hung draperies left there by undertakers' men who were preparing to hang St. Mark's in black for the obsequies of Day, but who had knocked off from work to lounge out into the Piazza and see the sunset.

I should counsel you to keep your eyes bent downwards till the proper moment or to relieve them amidst the shadows. The change you are about to see will be all the stronger. As the chimes from the Torre dell' Orologio strike the three-quarters, do you, standing right in front of the rood-screen, look up boldly towards the east. As boldly as you may ; but the strongest vision will but feebly withstand the astonishing spectacle you will witness. At this moment the sun is in the west, on a level with the centre of the façade, added by Eugène Beauharnais to the Palazzo Reale. Using that façade as a fulcrum, the master-Archimedes, sends a gigantic lever of sun-ray slanting across the entire Piazza. The ray rushes through the central window, just tips the summits of the Evangelists' statues on the rood-loft, touches the topmost grating of the altar-screen, and ends in the apsis or semicircular recess behind the altar.

I called it a lever. It is surely one which should lift the whole world up to Faith. The great recess is all at once in a blaze. Looking out of the darkness you might fancy the high altar to be on fire. Understand that this apsis is wholly covered with golden mosaic, and that in its centre is a colossal figure of the Redeemer. This golden alcove of glory, this inexhaustible treasure chamber, this stupendous shrine glittering and trembling in its abundance of radiance, fills you at first with unspeakable awe and veneration. You do not wonder that the poor people who come here to pray, and who are crouching humbly in the tenebrous nave, muttering their orisons, should accept in this a sure and visible symbol of their salvation—that, abject, poverty-stricken, oppressed, ragged, and hungry, they should swathe their souls in those golden cerements, anointed to them with blessed balm—that, after a toilsome day and scant pay, these weary water-carriers, and flower girls and gondoliers, and fishermen, should find in the contemplation of the glorified shrine, peace, consolation, and hope. It is very edifying, subsequently, to reflect that the glorification of the apsis is, after all, only the result of mathematical calculation—that the architects of the church knew full well that at a certain hour, at a certain time of the year, the sun would send a most mathematical ray through the great west window to the eastern extremity of the church. So they covered the eastern extremity of the church with a rich ground of gold mosaic to be lit up by the sun's rays, accordingly.

I have watched this grand sight many and many a time, early and late ; for I need scarcely say that it is not always at a quarter to five p.m. that Phœbus-Archimedes chooses to use the centre

of Eugène Beauharnais' façade as a fulcrum for his lever. I
have watched the apsis turn into golden glory in the darkest days
of Venice, when the oppressor's hand was upon her throat with
a clutch which, in human likelihood, would never be relaxed—
when nearly all hope of her deliverance and her resuscitation had
been abandoned by a generation worn out and heartsick with
continued disappointment. The great door of St. Mark's, leading
to the vestibule where the story of the Creation and the Fall
and the Deluge are told, in mosaic, with such quaint yet touching
naïveté, is always open. To keep the radiating heat out in
summer and the radiating cold out in winter, a mighty veil
hangs before the sumptuous tabernacle. Towards sunset this
curtain is drawn aside and looped up, to admit some cheerfulness
into a church which always stands in need of daylight. Often
and often, standing beneath the great cross pendent from the
central cupola, and which on festival days becomes a cross of a
thousand lamps—often and often, waiting for the sun's time to
come and for the apsis to be " glorified," have I turned my face
towards the great entrance-portal and looked far through the
vestibule across St. Mark's Place, all blank and deserted, like
some vast, calm, shipless sea which had been turned to stone.

St. Mark's given up to utter emptiness, is more oppressive in
its loneliness than the Crystal Palace on a wet Sunday afternoon
when there are no shareholders about—than even the reading-
room of the British Museum when the last book-worm has been
politely persuaded to depart, and the last hardworked attendant
has wheeled the last truckload of books along the gilded galleries.
And I have seen St. Mark's in broad daylight *quite empty*. This
has generally been the time when the Austrian band had finished
playing—when the hotel-bells had summoned the few foreign
visitors to the tables-d'hôte, and when the fewer Venetians who
chose to walk abroad had retired to sip lemonade and murmur
discontent in the "sotto portici" of the Procuratie, and in
Florian's or the Specchi's shady groves. They hang secular veils
between the columns before the caffès to keep out extreme heat
and extreme cold, as they do at St. Mark's, and these draperies

ST. MARK'S PLACE, VENICE.

have contributed still further to increase the desolation of the Place.

Once I remember seeing a solitary poodle with the whole of the Piazza San Marco to himself. I saw a kindred bow-wow once in the middle of the Admiralty Square, at St. Petersburg, by moonlight. The Russian dog squatted down on his haunches, and, lifting his head towards the moon, howled at it dismally. The Venetian poodle trotted about the deserted stones of St. Mark's, worn to glossy smoothness by so many millions of human footsteps. He trotted to the three tall masts which stood all of a row in front of St. Mark's, bannerless. He sniffed at Alessandro Leopardi's bronze bases, as though to inquire what had become of the three gonfalons of the Republic—of Venice, Cyprus, and the Morea. He did not howl, or seem to lament that, like Ichabod, his glory had departed. He fell, instead, into a merry mood, and happening to remember that he had a tail, began an exciting chase after that caudal appendage, gambolling in unseemly and unpatriotic gyrations, as though all were going as merrily as a marriage bell—as though Marino Faliero's head had never rolled upon the scaffold, and the two Foscari had never lived—as though the Most Serene Republic had never come to grief and shame, and the Austrian eagle, cruellest of birds, had not clawed out the eyes of the Lion of St. Mark. An inconsequent poodle ; but he had the whole of the Piazza to himself.

Now yesterday I looked through the great entrance-portal, and all was changed. The vast expanse was full of human movement. It was as though a whole federation of ant-hills had spumed forth their teeming commonwealths upon one vast marble slab. I emerged into the Place, and I strove to look upon the strange and unaccustomed spectacle, first from the enthusiastic, next from the morose point of view. Regarding it from the first the sight was glorious. It made one's heart leap for joy. Gone, for ever, were the Austrian sentries from before the Zecca and the royal palace. Gone were the detestable patrols, whose bayonets were continually, morally speaking, prying over your shoulders, or poking into your loins. There were no more gray-coated, bandy-

legged Croats sulking or grinning behind the hideous bars of the
Cancellate, like hyænas in their dens.   That aggressive standard
of black and yellow was furled for ever.   Those two murderous
field-pieces had ceased to point menacingly across the Piazzetta.
They had been unlimbered for good, and packed, with other
rubbishing marine-stores, on board an Austrian Lloyd's bound
for Trieste.   The two monstrous gilt eagles that used to flap
their domineering wings from twin pedestals in the palace-garden
had taken away their four ugly heads to other eyries.   The Austrian military band had uttered their last toot, and migrated to
more congenial orchestras.   There were no more white-tunicked
or sky-blue-coated Tedeschi to loll over the tables at Quadri's,
or promenade up and down the Piazza with their much-bedizened
Frauen, eyeing the Venetians, half with a scowl of hatred, half
with a sneer of supercilious contempt.   There were no more
skulking gendarmes, with murderous-looking cutlasses stuck in
their rusty belts, like those of the *bravi* in the " Promessi Sposi."
    In their place I saw, for the first time in Venice, the real
Italian people, enjoying themselves to their heart's content.
Soldiers walking arm-in-arm with gondoliers ;   Garibaldini in
their red shirts, followed by cheering and applauding groups ;
National Guards, belonging mostly to the club and shop-keeping
class, and who, a fortnight since, would have no more presumed
to handle a musket and bayonet than to climb the three tall
masts under the nose of an Austrian patrol, and hoist the Italian
tricolor there.   In their place I saw dozens of organ-grinders
playing Garibaldi's Hymn ; booksellers' shops full of the portraits
of the King, the Princes, and Garibaldi ; legions of ballad singers
yelling patriotic lyrics ; and from every window a kaleidoscopic
display of the national colours.   Among the people nine out of
every ten men you met had the tricolor arranged as a cockade for
their caps or a rosette for their button holes ; the women had
scarves and neckbows of the three hues ; the children wore frocks
and petticoats of red, white, and green ; and almost every adult,
gentle or simple, wore in his hat, or pinned to his breast, a little
piece of white cardboard, bearing the monosyllable " Si," and

signifying that his electoral mind was firmly made up, and that on the ensuing Sunday, when the solemn vote or *plebiscitum* was to be taken, he intended to return to the elaborate question, " Are you desirous that Venetia should be united to the kingdom of Italy under the rule of Victor Emmanuel the Second ? " one conclusive and sonorous " YES."

So much for the enthusiastic side of the picture. Remembering as I did, that I had known Venice as an old curiosity-shop, as a museum of antiquities, as a barrack-yard governed only by the bayonet and the stick, as a city in a state of siege, as a dungeon, as a tomb, I felt very much inclined to fling up *my* cap and burst forth in a series of ecstatic " evvivas " for Victor Emmanuel, for United Italy, for Giuseppe Garibaldi, for " la bella famiglia," which is an Italian equivalent for " our noble selves," for the Lion of St. Mark, St. Theodore, St. Zuliano, San Moïsè, and all our Venetian Saints.

It was as well that I did not fling up my cap, and that I did not break forth into " evvivas." I recollected that it was no affair at all of mine ; and five minutes afterwards I met an English friend, moving in the very first circles, and of a decidedly " codino " way of thinking—that is to say, in his political sympathies, Tory to the backbone. He pointed out to me that Venice was entirely spoilt ; that it had become quite a vulgar and uproarious place ; that the most beautiful architectural monuments were defaced by placards and handbills ; that now the volunteer force was disbanded it had become as ridiculous as it was offensive for the Garibaldini to walk about Venice in their red shirts : that the Italian regular officers gave themselves too many airs, and were not half so gentlemanly in appearance as the Austrians ; that Florian's and Quadri's were now thronged all day by the merest rabble ; that the *plebiscitum* was a sorry farce, seeing that everybody who dared to give a negative vote would infallibly be mobbed, and probably murdered ; that very few English visitors had arrived ; that fewer wealthy Italian families were expected ; that all the enthusiasm of which the Venetians were capable had been expended on the entry of the troops ; and that the visit of the King—if it ever took place, the whîch he considered to be exceedingly improbable—would be a miserable fiasco. My "codino" friend was good enough to add, as with a melancholy grasp of the hand he bade me farewell, that none of the hotels of Venice were more than half full ; that the misery and destitution among the poor of the Canareggio was hourly on the increase ; and that the cholera was more virulent than ever in the narrow and crowded *calli* of the Guidecca.

This was the picture painted from the morose point of view. But, from what I had seen with my own eyes, and heard with my own ears, I preferred to elect the tableau painted from the standpoint of enthusiasm as the genuine one.

XXVIII.

HOMELESS IN PADUA.

O you remember that inimitable description of poor old Major Pendennis, as he appeared at early dawn after dancing attendance all night on Lady Clavering and her daughter at a great London ball? He presented a sight lamentable to view. His beard had grown during the small hours, and pierced bright and stubbly from his aged chin. His cheeks were sunken, his jaw had dropped. The parting of his wig was painfully unnatural, and there were dark rings of *bistre* round his bloodshot eyes. His nose was as sharp as a pen, and the crow's-feet in his countenance could be counted by scores. Flaccid was his white cravat, and dingily yellow looked the shirt-front yesterday so spotless. In a word, rouge, starch, patent varnish, tight-cingled girths, padding, pomatum, Rowland's kalydor and Bully's toilet vinegar, false teeth, and eau-de-Cologne, had all fallen through, and only seventy years and sciatica, and the palsy in perspective, remained. This was Major Pendennis; and this was Padua as I saw her under the pressure of Aurora's rosy fingers, otherwise the bright August morning sun.

The antiquity of Padua is, as you know, immense; and the city really looks its age. She is scarred; she is furrowed; her cornices and architraves have lost all their sharp lines; her walls crumble; the foliage of the old capitals of her old pillars has faded away, and the plinths of the columns themselves have settled down into the earth. Her old inscriptions are three parts illegible; her old gates are rusty; her old windows are boarded up. She is, in fine, a decrepit old place, highly interesting and respectable no doubt, but still belonging to the centuries that shall return no more. Padua yet boasts a famous university, but

Y

from its gates you expect to see issue only grave doctors in
hexagonal caps and gowns of striped black-and-buff velvet, sages
learned in the Taliacotian operation, and demonstrators of anatomy
who had once given lessons to Dr. William Harvey. Padua is a
city where mediæval shrews might be tamed ; where Petruchio
might ride to his wedding on a horse wind-galled, shoulder-shotten,
far gone in the botts, and irrevocably attacked with farcy; and
Grumio confer with the woman's tailor on the subject of slashed
farthingales and bombasted kirtles ; but Padua is not at all the
kind of place in which to look for that frivolous and hysterical
order of recreation known as " going on anyhow."

It was this mode of progression, however, in which Padua had
chosen to move during the past three weeks. *Festa* had succeeded
festa, and one illumination had followed close on the heels of
another. Padua, in short, was still in the heyday of that ecstasy
of delight which followed the departure of the Austrians ; a people
who at home—say, at Vienna, or Gratz, or Brünn—are the jolliest,
best-natured, and most placable to be found anywhere between
Cape Cod and the Carpathian Mountains, but who, abroad, rarely
fail in making themselves as nauseous as nicotine and as insuffer-
able as asafœtida.

I should very much liked to have stayed in Padua, say a couple
of days ; for I love the picturesque city, with its shady arcades,
and its steep flights of stairs, and its façades rich in storied sculpture and heraldic achievements of a proud nobility long since fallen
into the portion of weeds and outworn faces. There was one
capital impediment, however, to making any lengthened sojourn in
Padua—and that was the absence of any place whereat one could
stay. The King of Italy was at Padua. The presence of Royalty
is usually effectual in raising house-rent ; but there were no more
houses, and no more rooms, and no more beds in Padua to be
rented. There was nothing to let. All the hotels were full. I
should not have been mighty particular as to the kind of accommodation to be found ; but I did not hear of a stable, or a billiard-
table, or a cupboard, or even a cottage-floor that was vacant at
Padua and open to take in lodgers.

Beds being unobtainable, there was nothing to do but to walk about Padua, and make believe that you lived there, and were something else besides a homeless vagabond. I confided my valise to an entire stranger—a "facchino" at the diligence-office—simply for the reason that he had *not* mounted an Italian cockade in his cap. All the other "facchini" were flaming in the tricolor, and, in the intervals of fardel-carrying, lurched in and out of the wine-shops grunting "Viva Italia!" or "Viva Garibaldi!" The uncockaded porter did not cry "viva" anybody, but stood with his arms folded, passing sad, waiting until a kind Providence should send him a traveller and the chance of earning a few soldi. He was an old "facchino" and a gray, and had been sweating under burdens, I daresay, for half a century. It did not much matter to him, perhaps, whether it was beneath the trunk of an English tourist or a German hauptmann that he perspired. When you have been carrying heavy loads on your spinal column since the year eighteen hundred and sixteen you are apt to become indifferent to the nationality of your masters. Perhaps the "facchino" sympathised with the departed Tedeschi. Robespierre's landlord wept for him. Haynau was beloved by his valet-de-chambre. The Germans may have been more liberal in "trinkgeld" than the Italians in the "buona mano" to this uncockaded man. At all events, there was something about him that impelled me to confide to him, without exacting any security or guarantee, the precious depository of my other shirt, my socks, and that dictionary. "There is a man," I said, "who is verging on threescore and ten, who is poor and shabby, and yet has courage enough to avow his opinions, and to disdain to screech with the rabble rout. He will not prove a fraudulent bailee. He will not steal my other shirt, nor sell my dictionary to the Egyptians." Nor did he.

Early as it was the flower-girls were afoot—bare-foot be it understood—and made fierce lunges at the button-holes of every passer-by. Shame upon me! the lovers of the romantic will cry, because I look on these bold wenches as nuisances, little inferior to the ragged boys who turn *soubresauts* and the raggeder girls who sell cigar-lights in London streets. But an Italian flower-girl ! she must be, from the romantic point of view, full of poetry, witching sentiment, and all that kind of thing. Only consider Lord Lytton's Blind Girl in the " Last Days of Pompeii." What exquisite songs she sings ; how we sympathise with her when her brutal mistress whips her with leathern thongs ! Alas, were the truth known, I daresay that Pompeian blind girl was a slipshod slut who didn't comb her hair, and bored the life out of Glaucus and Diomed and the young Pompeian nobility to buy her stale bouquets.

I was not in a charitable mood when I made these reflections upon flower-girls in general and the "fioraje" of Padua in particular occurred to me. When you have been travelling all night, and fail to secure a place whereon to lay your head in the morning, the milk of your human kindness is very much given to turn to curds-and-whey. I was irritated, too, to find that the good shops were as yet closed, and that there were at least five hundred establishments open for the sale of bad wine, worse cigars, and postage-stamps ; which last are very useful things in their way, but do not go far towards supplying a tired and hungry man with bed and breakfast.

I should have left Padua with but a sorrowful impression as to its hospitality—even to that hospitality, most cosmopolitan, which is to be obtained by paying for it—had not the Caffè Pedrocchi been open. The Caffè Pedrocchi is the stateliest coffee-house in Italy. It is one of the institutions of Padua, and as famous almost as its time-honoured university. It is a great many stories high, and is I know not how many hundred feet broad and long, and contains I have forgotten how many score apartments, large and small—some of them, especially the one called " La Sala Chinesa," magnificently decorated. In fact, if you wish to see something "right-down handsome" in the way of Corinthian columns, chandeliers, plate-glass, marble tables, crimson-velvet settees, niches with statuettes, and mosaic pavements, you should visit the Caffè Pedrocchi. It is the Alhambra, the Alcazar of Padua ; and the Padovesi are never tired of sauntering in its marble halls, and lounging on its marble stair-cases, and admiring its frescoed ceilings, and expatiating on the glories of its Sala Chinesa.

Who Pedrocchi was, although there is a vague story about him in " Murray," I know not. There is a casino upstairs, which is opened only at the time of the Carnival, when a "ridotto" is held there. Now, what is a "ridotto"? or, if you come to that, what is a "casino," taken in its signification as a place of popular recreation ? A "ridotto" is, I believe, a land relative of a "regata ;" and both are what the Spaniards term a "funcion," and the Americans a "shake up and break down of the High She Quality."

The most marked peculiarity of the Caffè Pedrocchi is this—that, like its brethren at Venice, it never closes. From the 1st of January, until the 31st of December—morning, noon, and night—all the year round, you can obtain refreshment at this large-hearted and indefatigable establishment. You may break-fast, lunch, and sup at the Caffè Pedrocchi ; but at no time, I believe, during its existence—which dates from the invasion of Italy by Attila, King of the Huns—was ever anybody known to dine there. It was at Florian's, in the Piazza San Marco, that the discrowned royalties immortalised in " Candide " met ; every one of whom had come to see the Carnival of Venice, and not one of whom had money enough to pay for his supper. The dethroned princes, I have heard, subsequently came on to Padua, and regaled on *demi-tasses* and *petits verres* at the Caffè Pedrocchi. Their score remains unpaid until this day. It was the then head-waiter's great-grandson who told me so. The unfortunate Charles Edward Stuart consumed a monstrous quantity of cognac on credit ; and Theodore, King of Corsica, was shabby enough to fill the pockets of his threadbare surtout with cigars ere he took diligence *en route* for Gerard-street, Soho, and the London Insolvent Court,

XXIX.

FLORENCE, CAPITAL OF ITALY.

CONSERVATIVE critic once undertook to prove—and did prove to his own entire satisfaction, if not to that of his readers—that the great work of Lord Macaulay was anything but that which it professed to be. He was willing to grant it a romance, a fable, an epic poem, a collection of memoirs, a budget of anecdotes, a repertory of statistics, a dictionary of dates, a bundle of sonnets, or a grand Christmas pantomime; but it could not be considered, so the sage Aristarchus held, a History of England. The world did not agree with Aristarchus; still his snarl remains, to be taken for what it is worth.

Did I ever venture upon criticising works and things immensely above my comprehension, I should be sorely tempted to take up, with regard to the interesting city to which I am paying a flying visit, the line of argument adopted by the Conservative caviller. I might say that Florence is one of the most charming towns I have ever seen, that the beauty of its site can scarcely be rivalled, and that its treasures of art are inexhaustible. I might call it a glorious museum, an unequalled picture-gallery, a refined and cultivated place, a fashionable resort, a picturesque lounge; in short, I might call it everything but that which it calls itself, and that which the solemn decree of the National Legislature has declared it to be—the Capital of Italy.* No; it does *not* look like a capital; and not all the foreigners who are resident or are visitors here; not all the presence of King, Court, Parliament, and diplomatic body; not all the efforts of the pushing and energetic Milanese, Piedmontese, and Swiss shop-

* Written, together with the other articles on Italy, in the year 1866.

keepers who have removed their wares hither from Turin, will
ever give to Florence a real metropolitan aspect.

You cannot create capitals, any more than you can establish
religions, by Act of Parliament. Attempts in that direction
have been made over and over again, but the result has generally
been a more or less humiliating failure; witness Washington and
Ottawa. When Napoleon I. chose to create the kingdom of
Westphalia for his brother Jerome, he, unconsciously imitating
Mr. Haller in "The Stranger," "fixed on Cassel for his abode;"
but all the cooks, aides-de-camp, play-actors, milliners, cham-
berlains, and ballet-girls, imported wholesale from Paris, failed to
make Cassel a capital, and it remained, until the kingdom of
Westphalia itself tumbled to pieces, a dismal, "one-horse" town,
pretentious but contemptible.

Time was, in our own country, when an adventurous spirit,
now by fame forgotten, but once probably well known in the
building trade, declared defiantly that Southend should be the
Queen of Watering-places. He built it; he advertised it; he
puffed it; he ran steamers; he cajoled railways; he beckoned to
lodging-house keepers to come and extort; he offered gratuitous
board and lodging to those interesting members of the insect
world without whose presence no watering-place is complete; he
positively induced shrimps to frequent Southend, and was sus-
pected of emptying a ton of salt into the water every morning to
take off its brackishness; but the thing wouldn't do. Southend
was not arbitrarily to be invested with a robe of brine and a
diadem of seaweed, and she continues to sit solitary and seedy on
the sandhills, while Margate and Ramsgate laugh "Ha, ha!" in
derision, and even Broadstairs genteelly simpers, and Herne Bay
sardonically sneers at the claims of her sandy sister.

Agamemnon was strong, so was Samson, likewise Belzoni. The
power of human volition is tremendous. Faith will remove
mountains, and continuous drippings from wet umbrellas wear out
the steps of the Duke of York's column; but there are some tasks
which baffle proud man, and induce a painful conviction of his
impotence. He may make a poet of Tupper, and a painter of

Raphael Mengs ; he may tunnel the Alps, and bridge the Straits
of Dover ; he may induce the British working-man to drink
Bordeaux instead of beer, and banish the pernicious custom of
smoking from railway-carriages ; he may abolish crinoline and
inland custom-houses ; pull down Holywell Street, finish the
Record Office, and make cabmen and grand-hotel managers civil ;
he may revive the use of embroidered copes in Westminster
Abbey, and turn the beadle of St. Clement's Danes into a thurifer,
an acolyte, or a protospathairos ; but he will never, so far as human
likelihood is concerned, make the real capital of Italy at Florence.

It is a country town ; it always has been a country town, and a
country town it will continue, until the whole of this orb reverts to
the original Proprietor, and all is country, without any towns at all.
Of the myriads of travelling Britons who have been to Florence, and
kept diaries, and printed them, and gone into ecstasies about the
Venus and the Faun, the Flora and the Madonna della Seggiola, I
do not know if there have yet been any who have been stricken
with the amazing likeness existing between Florence and a very
memorable, but purely provincial, English city—I mean Oxford.
At first sight the resemblance may not be striking, and the
analogy may be imperfect. Florence may vie with Rome as the
studio, and surpass her as the workshop of Italy ; but Galileo's
manuscripts and the bibliomania of Magliabecchi notwithstanding,
"Firenze la bella" must yield the palm of deep erudition and
varied lore to Pisa, Bologna, and Padua. You see no capped-and-
gowned undergraduates in the Via de Tornabuoni or the
Cerretani. No dons awe you in the Signoria or the Piazza
Granduca. No proctors in velvet sleeves prowl about accompanied
by watchful bulldogs. The Arno is certainly not the Isis ; for
the hue of the last-named stream is blue, and of the first a muddy
yellow. A violent effort of the imagination would be needed to
transform the verdant labyrinths of the Cascine into Christ-
Church Meadows ; and the Tuscan boatmen are a weak and puny
race, who, although they might, like all other Italians, bear away
the bell for blasphemy, would soon be vanquished, if strength of
lung could carry the day, by the bargees of Iffley Lock,

Nor is the architecture of Florence very Oxonian.   You seek in vain for venerable piles of florid Gothic, or for vast façades in the Palladian style.   Apart from the Duomo, with its towering Campanile, exteriorly a gigantic and most astounding josshouse of variegated marble, and inside as bare and cold-looking as the old Dutch church in Austinfriars ; apart from this, and the Baptistery, the Florentine churches are singularly mean and shabby in outward appearance.   In domestic structures, Florence has its own peculiar style of architecture, and that certainly does not remind the tourist of Oxford.   It rather suggests to him thoughts of the Old Bailey.

The Medici, the Strozzi, the Gherardeschi, the Buonarotti, are names familiar as Guelph or Ghibelline in the annals of Florence ; but I fancy there must be some erasures in the Florentine "libro d'oro," and that the hiatus might properly be filled up with the name of a Jonas.   Assuredly the palaces of the old nobility here look very much as though they had been orginally intended as residences of the governor of Newgate, with private apartments for the governor's guests on each side.   The illustrious Strozzi dwell, for example in a veritable gaol—a colossal pile of granite boulders and barred casements, with a narrow portal uncomfortably suggestive of the debtors' door.   I do not know whether the lady of the actual possessor of the palace and title gives "Wednesday evenings " in London West-end fashion ; but the mediæval Strozzi, to judge from the style of his habitation, must have been very punctual with his Monday mornings—"hang at eight and breakfast at nine," with Il Signore Calcraft as chief butler.

Ferrara is the most murderous town I have yet seen in Italy, and Bologna the most funereal.   It strikes me that in those middle ages, of which we talk so much and know so little, that it was at Ferrara you were preferably poisoned.   At Bologna they buried you, and your assassin was brought to Florence to be fully committed, tried, and executed.   To carry out the Newgate-cum-Horsemonger-lane illusion in the Florentine palaces, the walls are adorned, at a height of about five feet from the ground, with a series of enormous iron rings, pendent to links, and secured by strong staples to the stone. You are informed that these rings were used in the middle ages for securing horses by the bridle, while their cavaliers transacted business with the nobles within. This may or may not be true; but I imagine that animals of a superior race to the equine have been of old time tethered to these grim rings. The Florentines seem very proud of them; and I notice in a new palace, closely resembling Whitecross-street Prison whitewashed, which is in course of erection close to the Strozzi, that copies of the time-honoured Newgate bracelets have been let into the walls.

There is another marked peculiarity of Florentine architecture which I may briefly notice—the extraordinary projecting eaves of the houses in the older streets. With their preposterous eaves and tiny windows the houses look like exaggerated pigeon-cotes. Florence has always been renowned as a great place for gossip and *cancans*. May not that term of "eavesdropper," which has for so long a period bitterly perplexed the learned and chatty correspondents of *Notes and Queries*, spring from the overhanging eaves of Florence, and the necessarily incessant droppings therefrom?

But if there are no undergraduates, no dons, no bulldogs, no town-and-gown rows, how comes it, then, that Florence scarcely ever fails to remind an Englishman of Oxford? For this reason, I take it, that its pure provincialism—which is provincial to the pettiest of Little Peddlingtonism, and countryfied to almost rusticity—is oddly intermingled with the flashy splendour and meretricious bustle of the most expensive town life. By the side of palaces, museums, and churches, are little hucksters'-stalls and poor chandlery-shops; and then come the establishments of tradesmen selling the most sumptuous jewellery, the grandest haberdashery and millinery, the rarest books and engravings, the most brilliant and elaborate nicknacks, at prices which even in Oxford would be thought extortionate. I am not aware whether "tick," either as a word or an institution, has yet become naturalised in Florence; but the tariff adopted by the Florentine jewellers, tailors, and milliners is certainly suggestive of the largest ledgers and the longest credit. Thoroughly Oxonian, also, is the admixture in the streets of individuals whom you know must belong to the cream of the country, with the stolid, listless, narrow-minded *bourgeoisie* of a country town.

Here, in fact, as in Oxford, extremes meet. You have the social steam at its highest pressure, and a considerable quantity of the tepidest water. You have a bottle of champagne just uncorked and flying all abroad in the face of the smallest of small beer. The carriages and pair of the aristocracy, with splendidly-harnessed horses, and coachmen in spun-glass wigs, the fours-in-hand, the tandems and the breaks of Florentine " fast men," the broughams of senators, the basket-phaetons and wicked little black ponies of the Anonymous Estate on their way to the Cascine are jostled, in beggarly by-lanes, by bullock-drays and mules laden with forage, and humble donkey-carts containing the stock-in-trade of travelling tinkers.

Florence is Oxford during Commemoration, and all the big-wigs and *gros bonnets* of the land are holding festival here ; but you know that the long vacation is coming—you know that there are very many weeks in every year when not a big-wig is to be seen in the deserted streets ; when the flashy tradesmen are unable from month's end to month's end to swindle a customer ; when the petty hucksters'-stalls and the little chandlery-shops will reassert their legitimate influence ; when the principal event in each week will be market-day ; when the hotels will become inns, the "ristoratores" farmers' ordinaries, and the caffès tap-rooms ; when his worship the Mayor—they call him a "Gonfa-loniere " here—will be the greatest personage in the place ; and when, in fine, Florence will revert to that which it is really entitled to be called—a town replete with the most exquisite monuments of painting and sculpture, but always a provincial of the provincials. Blaise Pascal might have written his letters from the Boboli gardens ; but you can't make it a capital, try your hardest. As well might Dulwich claim equal rank with Piccadilly because it possesses Alleyn's college and Sir Francis Bourgeois's gallery.

XXX.

Roma Urbs.

" N the heights above Baccano," writes an old traveller, "the postilion stopped, and, pointing to a pinnacle which appeared between two hills, exclaimed, 'Roma!' That pinnacle was the cross of St. Peter's. The Eternal City was before us."

I suppose no man—not being a born idiot or a German bagman, next to an imbecile the most unimpressionable creature in the world, perhaps—ever beheld that cross on the dome of St. Peter's or entered Rome for the first time, without feeling his heart in some manner or another, stirred up within him. "Moab may howl for Moab : everyone shall howl ;" but you have longed, and sighed, and prayed to look upon Rome ; and now your desire is come, and you are full of a happy thankfulness. The image of Rome has been set, long since, "as a seal upon thine heart, as a seal upon thine arm ;" and as "many waters cannot quench love, neither can the floods drown it," so is the love for Rome intuitive, indomitable, and inextinguishable.

English grooms and flunkeys are not given, generally, to become very enthusiastic at the sight of strange cities, and I have known the British flunkey take St. Mark's Place, by moonlight, very coolly, and My Lord's *valet de chambre* bear the Kremlin with perfect equanimity. Nay, I have known a lady's-maid speak superciliously of Seville even during the "feria" week, and pronounce Constantinople to be a "nasty dirty hole." Why should not such criticisms be uttered by our domestics ! They have, very probably, quite enough to do with attending to the wants, wishes, and caprices of their masters and mistresses ; their education, with regard to history, antiquities, poetry, mythology, and the fine arts, has ordinarily been neglected, and they are seldom expected, on their return home, to write octavo volumes descriptive of the sights they have seen abroad. Not but that the *impressions de voyage* of a lacquey might be worth reading. Constant's "Memoirs of Napoleon" are mendacious, but eminently amusing; and who would not like to read a life of Shakespeare by his body-servant—if he ever had one, or a body to be served or anything tangible, or palpable, or unmythical at all ?

I say that the usual train of menials who go abroad with our tourists are perfectly indifferent to the sights they see. There is in most continental cities, some establishment of the nature of an English public-house. Thither the "valetaille" repair in their leisure moments to smoke and drink, and *not* to compare notes as to the monuments of the city in which they are sojourning, but to grumble at and abuse their employers, precisely as they would do at the bars of the dim little taverns which nestle in the purlieus of Grosvenor and Belgrave-squares. With all this I have known gentlemen's gentlemen fall into raptures about Rome, and talk quite learnedly of the Muta Sudans and the Forum of Trajan. By far the most fervent British enthusiast on things Roman occupying a humble sphere of life was a hostler. "There's hevery thing you can wish for in Rome," quoth he. "Hemperors and Popes, and temples and churches, and the Colosseum and the Wattican ; and, bless yer, there aint a 'ossier place out. After 'Igh Park give me the Pincian 'Ill." Rome *is* "'ossy" or "horsey" in good sooth ; but 'tis the English who have made it so.

Everybody is delighted to find himself in Rome. The fervent Catholic rejoices at Rome. It is his Mecca, his Medina, in one. Rome is to him more than Jerusalem ; for in Rome he is still master, and there are no hated Greeks, no loathed schismatics to jostle him while he worships at the Holy Places. Has he not at Rome the Scala Santa, the very steps of Pilate's house ? Is not the Holy Cratch, the manger-board, at Rome ? Are not the Apostle's chains here ? and the very prisons and the tombs of

Peter and St. Paul ; not in the insolent keeping of a Turkish pasha, but under the sacred guardianship of the successor of St. Peter himself ?

The Romanist at Rome *est dans son pays.* He is monarch of all he surveys. To M. Louis Veuillot the foul stenches and miasma of modern Rome are so many sweet perfumes—" Parfum de Rome ;" whereas in the boudoirs of the Chaussée d'Antin and the parterres of Madame Prévost the austere moralist can scent only the most shocking odours. He plumes himself on Rome, for it is the only city in Europe where the shovelled hat takes precedence of the lady's bonnet ; where men in petticoats have the *pas* over women in the like articles ; where a snuffy old Monsignore is a greater leader of fashion than a Russian princess, and a parchment-faced vicar-general from Peru is more run after than a Japanese ambassador. It is nearly the only city where swarms of cowled-and-shaven monks are permitted to pervade the streets ; and where once a year a wooden idol—the Bambino—with twenty thousand pounds' worth of jewels on its wretched little block of a body, is held up by bishops to the adoration of twenty thousand people, in defiance of the pagan memory of Jupiter Capitolinus hard by.

In a word, the Romanist at Rome is in his element. If in his heart and soul he unfeignedly believes—and how shall I dare to say that he does not ?—that the good old Pope* is the Vicar of &c., &c., and the Successor of &c., &c., the believer must feel, while he is in Rome, that he is sojourning in an actual earthly paradise ; for he may see the supernatural Being (elected periodically, by the way, through a conspiracy on the part of several old gentlemen in scarlet petticoats, and one or more foreign ambassadors) driving out daily in a coach-and-four, or trotting about the slopes of the Pincian in a white-flannel dressing-gown and a scarlet-velvet shovel. Fancy the delight of a Moslem at being able to meet Mahomet every day, taking his drives and walks abroad ; and what is the dogma of an uninterrupted succession of Infallible Popes, but a dogma of a perpetual succession of Mahomets ?

* Pius the Ninth.

THE BAMBINO.

Page 350.

The fervent Protestant glories in Rome, but darkly, furtively, and, I fear, somewhat vengefully. His worst fears are now realised ; his darkest anticipations are verified ; and a pretty tale he will have to tell Exeter Hall and the Clapham tea-tables when he reaches home. Idolatory, Paganism, the Scarlet Lady, the Mystery of Iniquity; but it is needless to pursue the theme. The fervent Protestant is shocked, but he takes copious notes. He is horror-struck at the very idea of the Pope, but he is not averse to throwing himself in his way ; and with the pride of conscious. rectitude he relates (when he reaches Clapham) how resolutely he refused to uncover and to kneel as the idolatrous crowds around him did, when the Pope alighted from his carriage on the Pincian for his afternoon trot. Good old 'gentleman ! I have gone down on my marrowbones when he has passed scores of times, and I hope I have had my share in the benedictions he has so liberally dispensed with his two fingers.

There is something, I take it, abominably revolting in crouching down before a hewn idol—the African savage can do no more ; and the Bambino is as hideous as Mumbo Jumbo : but surely there is no harm in an act of reverential courtesy to a patriarchal old priest, whose purity of life and goodness of heart are acknowledged by all the world. You kneel to a good woman, don't you ? You kneel to the Queen. The Pope is king here,* and so long as he can keep his Three Crowns, has a right to the customary obeisances. And finally, as the Pope himself once tersely put it to a recalcitrant heretic, the blessing of an old man cannot do anybody any harm. As for kissing his toe, that is quite another matter : although I have known many fervent Protestants (of a toady way of thinking) ready, and even eager, to perform that ceremony. To sum up, the red-hot and bilious Protestant is rather in a hurry to get away from Rome, in order that Clapham and the columns of his favourite red-hot periodicals, shall be speedily enlightened as to the Idolatry, and the Mystery of Iniquity.

* This was of course written before Rome had become the capital of the new kingdom of Italy.

Abating the Bambino—which idol is to me utterly horrible and sickening—there does not seem to be much that is iniquitous about the silly mummeries and superstitions of ecclesiastical Rome. Everybody who has travelled in Spain, and especially in Mexico, must have witnessed tomfooleries ten times more preposterous and ten times more blasphemous in those countries. I spent the Holy Week of the year 1864 in Mexico City ; and to this day I have never *dared*—even could I find a bookseller bold enough to publish what I wrote—to write a literal account of what goes on in " Juives," and " Viernes Santo " in Tenostitlan.

The English Ritualist makes a joyful pilgrimage to Rome. His heart leaps up when he beholds it. He is mad to see the " functions " of Passion-Week, and Easter, and Christmas, and St. Peter's day. And after that ? Well, I do thoroughly believe that it would be an excellent thing for the old-fashioned Church of England (as you, my good old friend Squaretoes, understand the doctrine and ritual of that Church) could all the ardent young Ritualists in Britain be taken to Rome in a rapid succession of Cook's tours, and be " put through " all the " functions," provided always that they took with them a Dr. William Smith, or an Anthony Rich's " Dictionary of Roman Antiquities " (Muratori or Montfaucon would be too cumbrous), and carefully collated all the Popish " functions " they witnessed with the descriptions of the ceremonies of Paganism.

There are many grave and earnest Ritualists, no doubt—ay, and shrewd and learned men—who have visited Rome repeatedly, and whose extreme views have been rather confirmed than shaken by the investigations of each successive visit ; but I incline very strongly to the belief that among the young fry of Ritualists sheer ignorance and innocent vanity are to an astonishing degree prevalent, and that they know scarcely anything about the model which they profess to copy. And not every ardent young Ritualist can go to Rome. Let them all go, I say, if it be practicable. Let them see the real thing—" all the Fun of the Fair " —for I do maintain that at certain periods of the year ecclesiastical Rome resembles nothing so much as a fair : waxwork shows,

THE BENEDICTION FROM THE LOGGIA.

giants and dwarfs, gingerbread-nuts, and all. I apprehend that if all the frank, cheery, intelligent Englishmen and Englishwomen who are not running crazy about Ritualism, were conscientiously to study *on the spot* the aspect of Ritualism's prototype, the scales would, in a vast number of instances, fall from their eyes, and they would recognise what a sorry tawdry simulacrum of rags and bones and staring paint they had been gazing at and taking for a portent.

But a truce to the *odium theologicum*. Who else delights in Rome ? Who more than the American ? And why ? For the reason, I conceive, that Rome is so very, very old, and that he is so very, very new. I have studied American tourists in every country in Europe, and in every province of Italy; but I never saw them so thoroughly entertained and interested as in Rome. The ancient and the modern city have alike absorbing attractions for them. In very rare instances does the average American care anything about antiquity *per se* —any more, indeed than does our own Mrs. Ramsbottom ; yet the gray old stones of the Forum and the Colosseum seem to exercise over the Transatlantic mind an irresistible fascination.

The Americans are always poking about the tomb of Cecilia Metella, or mooning about the Catacombs, querulously anxious to know what has become of the bodies, and gladdening the hearts of the friar-guides with munificent donations ; or gathering wildflowers, and risking their necks on the summits of the arches of the Baths of Caracalla ; or craning their necks to see the frescoes in the Palace of Titus ; or poking at the pavement with their walking-sticks in the Thermæ of Diocletian ; or vainly "guessing" at the sepulchral inscriptions in the Columbaria. They never seem tired of the statues in the Vatican and the Campidoglio. English visitors I have often seen unmistakably bored at these spectacles ; and many English ladies resolutely refuse to do the antique lions of Rome after the first fortnight. But the Americans are indefatigable and insatiable. They are up early and late. They spend more money in Rome than any other foreign nation. They are the good geniuses of photographers, cameo and bronze-dealers,

z

statuaries, picture-copyists and livery-stable-keepers. Their behaviour at the ecclesiastical "functions" is as the behaviour of most Protestant tourists of the Anglo-Saxon race—simply and brutally indecent. They check off the ceremonies in the Sistine by means of a "Murray" or an "Appleton's Guide-book," and scrutinise the genuflexions of the celebrants through a double-barrelled eyeglass. During the Carnival, they have the best windows on the Corso ; their equipages are the most splendid to be seen on the Pincian.

Until lately the United-States Government maintained a Minister at Rome—not that there was any business to be transacted between the Papal See and the United States of America ; but for the express purpose of "putting through" all Americans who wanted to see the Pope and take tea with the Cardinals. I have known Americans come straight from San Francisco to Rome, and go home again without seeing Paris or London. In addition to a numerous floating population from the States, there is in Rome a resident colony of refined, erudite, and cultivated Americans. An American, Mr. Storey, a distinguished sculptor, antiquary, and scholar, has written the best book, "Roba di Roma," on social and picturesque life in the Eternal City that is extant. But even the floating Americans seem at home in Rome, and come back to the dear old Via Condotti and the jovial Hôtel d'Angleterre over and over again.

The artist in Rome. Why, he is in Eden : for is not here the Tree of Knowledge ? and may he not shake it to the last twig without sin ? Everything appertaining to art is best learnt in Rome. Whatever your graphic vocation may be—are you a painter of history, of genre, of portrait, or of landscape, a sculptor, a modeller, a decorator, an architect, an engraver of gems or an engraver of metals, or a mere draughtsman of maps and plans—you will find exemplars ready to your hand in Rome. If you seek tuition, you will find a master ; if you are a master, you will find disciples. Rome is the inexhaustible milch-cow : no babe need be without a teat. She has *mammæ* for all. And moreover, in Rome, the poorest artist is somebody. The scald word " Bohemian " does not stick to ragged Dick Tinto. On the Seven Hills it is an honourable thing to be a citizen of Prague. The artists of Rome keep no state, live no grand lives, outvie one another in no vain rivalries of dress or equipage. The artist is here, in fact, the secular priest, and his blouse and working-cap carry, in their sphere, as much weight as in another do the shovel-hat, the shaven crown, the cowl, and the hempen girdle.

My Lord loves Rome. Our Lord, you know—his lordship who owns. our land, our skies—at least the fowls that fly in them—and will not allow us, Higgs and sons of Snell as we are, to shoot our rabbits which, he says, are his. My Lord winters in Rome, and has wintered here any time these twenty years ; you may see his sumptuous open carriage, with the bright bays, any day on the Pincian. My Lady and her ladyship's daughters love Rome quite as well ; for here they find the shopping, the society, and the " scan. mag." of London, Brighton, Bath, Cheltenham, Hastings, and Tunbridge Wells.

In a word, who is not charmed with "Roma urbs" ? The classical scholar and the lover of English black-draughts and blue-pills, the antiquary and the connoisseur in painting, the admirer of field-sports and the amateur of monastic institutions, can all find their peculiar tastes ministered to in Rome. Whether you study the bas-relief on a column from a Montfaucon's point of view, or sit yourself on the top thereof and chant doxologies for thirty years as Simon Stylites did ; whether your sympathies lie in the direction of ancient sculpture, of moonlight picnics, of pound-cakes, of palimpsests, or of mulligatawny soup—they have the right sort, an Oriental Club recipe, communicated by a per-verted under-butler at Spielmann's restaurant—whether you like English Bath chaps, or Dunville's V.R. whisky, or alabaster statuettes, or gilt bronzes, or Egyptian obelisks, or the Acta Sanctorum, or stewed porcupine, or photographs, or cameos—you have only to ask for the particular dainty you require in Rome and, so long as you have plenty of money, your wish will be gratified in a moment.

XXXI.

THE STREETS OF ROME.

MUCH sympathy, which would have been better bestowed elsewhere, has been thrown away in bewailing the almost entire disappearance of the streets of ancient Rome. In the first place, persons are apt to forget that, although temples and basilicas, solidly constructed, may endure for a couple of thousand years, and, abating earthquakes, sieges, and the barbarians—to say nothing of princes who strip from old monuments the building-materials for new palaces—may show, at the end of twenty centuries, as few symptoms of decay as the Maison Carrée at Nismes, or the Amphitheatre at Verona, or the Temple of Vesta; here ordinary dwelling-houses are more fragile in their construction, are preserved with greater difficulty, and burned down with greater facility. There may have been Chancery suits, too, under the old Roman civil law which proved as efficacious in ruining house property as any great case of Jarndyce *versus* Jarndyce among us.

Cheops built, and Praxiteles sculptured, for Eternity; but the mass of houses in the mass of streets in this world are but little cockboats launched on the broad river of Time, and doomed, in time, to be swamped or run down by bigger barks. Round about old cathedrals, it is true, the old, old dwelling-houses of our ancestors are curiously tenacious of vitality; and, in spite of all the efforts of the Houses-of-Parliament Commission and Baron Haussmann, some generations may yet elapse before the antique hovels which cling to the purlieus of Westminster Abbey and Notre Dame de Paris disappear. But these are but barnacles sticking to the keels of very old ships; elsewhere, new brooms are being continually made, and the sweeping away of old houses is incessant. The change they suffer, although thorough, is imperceptible, just as a certain school of physiologists tell us that once in every seven years or so, although we think that we have the same heart, lungs, liver, skin, and hair, we get a brand-new set of those organs and tissues. The Poultry, by Cheapside, is abstractedly the same narrow Poultry which Sir Christopher Wren, to his own sore discomfort, was forced to lay down, after the great Fire of London, on the lines of a still older street; yet I question if, the chapel excepted, there are half-a-dozen houses in the Poultry that are a hundred years old.

I have met a great many travellers professing an expectation to find the streets of Rome with precisely the same configuration, containing the same houses, and presenting the same characteristics, as they may have done under the Twelve Cæsars. They require their inn or their greengrocer's-shop to be in exact accordance with the canons of Vitruvius. They look for the "atrium," the "impluvium," and the "alæ." They want statues of the Lares and Penates in the peristyle, fresco arabesques in the "cubicula," "Cave canem" on the door-jamb, and "Salve" on a slab of mosaic to serve as a door-mat; and if they don't find these things, they cry out that Rome is very much fallen indeed; and I have heard fast young gentlemen from the universities declare over their cheroots and punch—they make punch with white rum at the Caffè di Roma, and just tomahawked or dashed with maraschino, after the recipe of the Right Honourable Benjamin Disraeli: it is very good, and might convert Mr. Spurgeon to Romanism—I have heard these fortunate youths, moderns of the moderns, declare Rome to be a " sell," and, as a relic of antiquity, not half so interesting as Chester.

I suppose one might just as well expect to find the old Roman "domus" in modern Rome as to meet ladies and gentlemen arrayed in the "toga," or the "peplum," or the "tunicopallium," followed by their slaves, and surrounded by their freedmen and clients, passing to and fro in the Forum, praying in the Temple of Saturn, or making their way to the games in the Circus Maximus.

We know that such sights, out of the Carnival, are impossible.
We know that the Papal Zouaves are no Prætorians, and that the
Pontifical Gendarmes carry no fasces ; and if we thirst for anachronism, the Swiss Guards in their masquerading canary-bird
dress, the dirty shavelings, and the infinite people in shovel-hats,
should be quite old enough to satisfy the most ardent member of
the Royal Society of Antiquaries.

Still, even those who expect little, and are in consequence
rarely disappointed, those who have taken the portraits of many
cities and dissected many schemes of civilisation, are unable to
suppress something akin to a sigh of regret when they find the
"tabula rasa" which has been made of old Rome—when they
discover that the ruins of the City of the Cæsars are all but
isolated from the City of the Pontiffs—when they behold the
streets of modern Rome and find them so very like modern Clare
Market and modern Whitechapel, only much dirtier, and not quite
so felonious.

Lord Lytton is responsible for much of the sadness thus engendered by the destruction of fondly-cherished illusions. "The
Last Days of Pompeii," sent everybody, in person or imagination,
to that wonderful place. The novel so exquisitely and so truth-
fully portrays the city, that the houses of Glaucus and Pansa, the
theatre, and the gladiators' wine-shop, have become as indelibly
impressed on the readers' minds as the forms of the dead
Pompeians on the hot ashes with which they were stifled. Bulwer
has made Pompeii his own : the "Last Days" are the best possible
guide-book to the disinterred city ; and after a visit to Naples, or
that which is next best, and in some respects preferable—after
careful study of the Pompeian Court at the Crystal Palace—we
come to Rome, and are surprised at not finding " PANSA ÆD." in
red letters over the first private house in the Corso, and feel ourselves aggrieved when, being asked out to dinner, the repast is not
"after the manner of the ancients," with a wild-boar stuffed with
chestnuts and honey, and a sow's bosom served with "garum" to
follow—all to be taken on the "triclinium," with youths from the
Isles of Greece to warble soft melodies in praise of Venus

Aphrodite, and slaves to crown us with flowers while we quaff the Falernian.

I have purposely exaggerated the feeling which I assume many visitors to Rome have experienced; but I am convinced that some such state of mind is very common, and that very few cultivated persons conclude their first day's wandering in the streets of Rome without a sensation of bitter disappointment. Was it for this that they came so far—to see imitation French soldiers in red breeches, and dragoons in helmets with horse-tails after the pattern of the Cuirassiers of the Imperial Guard; to meet everywhere Jouvin's gloves, *chocolat de santé,* and the eau-de-Cologne of Jean Marie Farina; to be told that Mr. Lowe sells Bengal chutnee and family Souchong, and that Mr. William Brown gives the highest exchange for English bank-notes and sovereigns? They may not exactly exclaim that Rome is a " sell," but still they are gravely disappointed. If you wish to see a real Roman house, and—substituting the cloak, the mantilla, and the burnouse for the " toga," the " redimiculum," and the " bardocucullus "—to see people attired after the manner of those of antiquity, you must go to Andalusia or to Algeria; there the " patio " admirably figures the "impluvium," and the hot, vehement, bloodthirsty throng in the bull-ring—I have seen eight thousand people shrieking with exultation over one lamentable horse with his bowels hanging out —completely satisfies the imaginative craving to know what a gala-day at the Colosseum could have been like.

But in modern Rome, Papistry has taken up Paganism, swallowed it, welded it into its own components, and made it bone of its bone and flesh of its flesh. Apart from the huge ruins of the Forum, the Baths, and the Tombs, the Pope's paw is upon everything Roman. If you stumble on an ancient column, it has a saint flaming at the top. If you light on an ancient inscription, it winds-up with some more freshly-cut reminder that the munificence of Somebody " Pont. Opt. Max." has permitted it to escape destruction. The mitre and the shovel-hat have quite extinguished the " pileum." The cupids and genii have gone down before the Madonnas at the street-corners, with their environment of dumpling clouds and more dumpling cherubs. Very often do you see the grim, grimy columns and entablature of a pagan temple chained up, as it were, in the tasteless structure of a Romanist church, which clings to the old marbles and sculpture, strangling them with its flexible claws, like Victor Hugo's devil-fish in "The Toilers of the Sea." Over this absorption Romanists exult, and many devout persons, no doubt, thought it a wicked thing for Cardinal Mai to have scraped away St. Augustine's "Commentary on the Psalms" from the parchment, and exposed Cicero's "Republic," the oldest Latin manuscript extant, which lay beneath.

For my part, while I deplore the havoc that has been made of so many antique temples, basilicas, palaces, fountains, baths, aqueducts, columns, and statues, I do not see the slightest cause for regret in the evanishment of the streets and dwelling-houses of classical Rome. The excavations of Pompeii show us with microscopic distinctness what those streets were like; and it is plain that—all their frescoed arabesques, mosaics, encaustics, bronzes, alabaster, and rosso antico notwithstanding—the Pom-peians must have lived miserably. It is plain that their streets were narrower than the meanest alleys in the meanest Moorish town; that their houses were badly lit and badly ventilated; and that they had every need to frequent such huge baths, such en-ormous theatres, and such a wide forum or gossiping-place, in view of the wretched little hutches in which they were cooped-up at home. Many an English squire's hounds are more amply kennelled than would have been the guests who accepted the hospitality of the patrician whose villa is to be visited every day at Sydenham.

Things at Rome were doubtless all on a grander scale than in the neighbourhood of Vesuvius, yet this is a case in which we are surely entitled to reason from analogy. Pompeii was probably to Rome as Tunbridge Wells was to London, and we certainly look for comfort and even elegance on the Pantiles.* The civilisation

---

*According to Horace, the inns, even at a short distance from Rome, were most miserable.

of old Rome was, it cannot be doubted, grand and sumptuous ; but the old Romans were, for all that, I suspect, a nasty, dirty set of people, who had need to go to the bath so often, seeing what pigsties they wallowed in elsewhere, and who wore their togas until—like the Russian peasants, who send their hats to the village oven to be baked, and thus freed from insect life—they were compelled to send them to the fuller's to be made decent again. Depend upon it, bad as modern Rome is, badly built, badly paved, and but half-lit with gas, ancient Rome was even more intolerable.

Let us not, therefore, beat our breasts and utter the wail of woe because Alaric, Genseric, and others, from the fourth to the sixth century successively performed with Rome the admired feat which in later days was so notably repeated by Field-Marshal Turenne, by Field-Marshal Tilly, and by Generals Sherman and Sheridan, and other famous conquerors, including Genghis Khan and Timour the Tartar, and which is known as knocking a city into a "cocked-hat ;" or because Belisarius gutted the inside of Rome to strengthen the walls outside it ; or because Robert Guiscard and his Normans burnt Rome from the Antonine column to the Flaminian gate, and laid waste the Esquiline hill ; or because the Savellis and the Frangipanis, the Contis and the Caetanis, barbarians within, completed the havoc of the barbarians without ; or because there was an inundation in 1345 which only left the summits of the Seven Hills above water, and an earthquake in 1349, and the Constable de Bourbon in 1527, who was worse than all the Goths and their compounds put together, and another inundation in 1530, with a long succession of Popes before and after, who despoiled and stripped every monument of antiquity to build or to ornament their own churches. " Fust cum smut in the corn," said the New Englander, recounting his experiences as a farmer, "and then cum the Hessian fly, and the next year cum the caterpillars, and they capped the climax of my catastrophe." Popery capped the climax of the catastrophe of Rome. It has left only one of the shabbiest modern cities to be found on the earth's surface ; but the shabbiness and dirtiness of

Rome are things that can be mended, when greater enlighten-
ment and a better government shall prevail.

The best way to inspect the streets of Rome, if you wish to
study as well as see them, is to break your pocket-compass and
burn your maps and guide-books, as Prospero did his conjuring-
apparatus, and, forgetting that such things as ciceroni at a scudo
and a half a day ever existed, take Chance for a Mentor, and lose
yourself. This I contrived to do very effectually, and propose to
commit an account of my wanderings to paper. I must have
halted, now and again, on the way, and brought-up at caffès and
reading-rooms to rest, and I must have slept, and I think I dined-
out yesterday; but walking the streets has been my principal
occupation during the last six-and-thirty-hours, and I have the
satisfaction now of knowing that I have worn a new pair of boots
into a most comfortable state of slipshodedness, inflated my lungs
with a variety of gases—some of them, I am willing to believe,
unfamiliar to British chemists—and acquired an amount of Roman
experience which may prove in the future, I trust, not wholly
unserviceable.

I did not victual for the campaign, for the Roman larder
is admirably supplied, and there is more to eat and drink
procurable in the streets of Rome than in any other city in
Italy. The Romans eat very odd things, it is true, and
some that scrupulous people in England might term nasty
—such as frogs, lizards, and hedgehogs; but at least their
markets are full, and even the smallest wineshop, or "spaccio
di vino," has its "cucina," or kitchen, attached to it. I did
not provide myself with defensive weapons for the excursion,
as nervous tourists still do when they take a trip to Tivoli:
first, because I had no Pontifical licence to carry arms, and
next because I thoroughly disbelieve in the alarming stories current at the table-d'hôtes and in the smoking rooms about brigands,
Sanfedisti, infuriated Dutch Zouaves who stab inoffensive persons
unable to provide them with schiedam, blood-thirsty Antibes
legionaries promenading the back-streets, and bayoneting civilians
of heretical appearance as they emerge from the "botteghe oscure"

where they have been beating down old-curiosity vendors, and felonoius Trasteverini, who sharpen their knives upon stone statues of the Madonna, sprinkle their life-preservers with holy-water, and go out robbing and murdering so soon as the vesper-bell has finished ringing.

I daresay there are back-streets in Rome which are not safe, during the small hours, for people who persist in wearing eighteen-carat gold watch-guards outside their great coats, who won't wear gloves, and will wear diamond-rings on all the fingers of both hands, and who toss for napoleons under every lamp ; but then I daresay the back-streets of Belgravia—or the front ones either, for that matter—would not be much safer to such wayfarers, say between midnight and two in the morning. There are rogues in Rome, as in every other great city ; but pedestrians who are neither foolhardy nor tipsy may penetrate into all quarters of the city without the slightest danger, at all reasonable hours.

I write this, both with a view to correct the false impressions which may be current in England, and to reassure some kind friends of mine who have been writing to me letters of condolence on my alarmingly perilous position in a city infested with bandits, and so soon to be given over to rapine and massacre. We have not yet come to that charming state of things which is chronic in Mexico, where you go to church armed to the teeth, and return from a whist-party with a revolver in one hand and a bowie-knife in the other, walking in the middle of the road, lest an assassin should be lurking under an archway. We have not even come to realise the state of affairs prevalent in London—which I have heard called the metropolis of the world—many of whose most frequented thoroughfares are impassable to decent people, not only after dark, not only at dusk, but often at broad daylight, from the gangs of costermonger " roughs," of blackguard boys and girls, of pickpockets, sharpers, and cadgers, and of common courtesans, who are suffered by a badly-organised police, and an incredibly lax and incompetent municipal government, to infest them. I will say nothing about the state of the suburban London roads at night, save to hint that I would much rather stroll along the Via Appia than Haverstock Hill after ten p.m. I might possibly meet a fox among the tombs ; but I should prefer *that* to a garotter among the trim villa residences.

Unarmed then, unfurnished with provender, and with very little money even in my purse—for foreigners who walk about in Rome are very apt to come home with no gold and silver, but with a large stock of Roman scarves, cameos, and photographs, all picked up, of course, as bargains—I journeyed forth towards my unknown destination. The world was all before me where to choose as I emerged from the Hôtel d'Angleterre. Five minutes' careless strolling either to the north, the south, the east, or the west would bring about, I knew well, the consummation I had in view— that of not knowing where I was ; but I was ambitious, and wished to lose myself thoroughly, and at as great a distance from my habitation as was possible. So I took a cab, and bade the man drive me to the Post-office.

The public conveyances of Rome, I may remark once for all, are generally uncovered, little, light, one-horse calèches, not unlike the St. Petersburg droschkies—not the droschkies on which you sit astride and pull the isvostchik's ears as you wish him to turn to the right or left, but those in which your legs are spread out be- fore you in the normal manner. The Roman " calescini " are passably clean, not at all uncomfortable, and very cheap ; that is to say, a drive to any part of the city within the walls need not cost more than eightpence. For two-horse carriages you pay a lira and a half for a "course," and forty bajocchi, or one-and-sevenpence, for an hour. For excursions " extra muros " there is no settled tariff ; a bargain must be made ; and as foreigners are the prin- cipal patrons for drives beyond the gates, they must expect to be cheated.

If you object to this, I should advise you to hire a carriage, not from the public stand, but from the hotel in which you are stay- ing. In that case you will not be cheated, but simply overcharged. The price of a carriage for an entire day—and which is a really handsome turn-out, with two fiery horses, and a most aristocratic- looking driver in semi-livery—is five-and-twenty francs. You may engage it for half a day; but in the computations of Roman hotel-keepers the day has no first half, the long and the short of which is that if you require a remise for a drive on the Pincian Hill in the afternoon, or to take you to the theatre in the evening, you pay half-a-guinea for it; but if you merely want a drive among the ruins after breakfast, you pay a guinea.

Save when the claims of gentility assert themselves, and I elect to live for an hour-and-a-half at the rate of two thousand five hundred a-year, I prefer the hack "calescino" at eighteenpence the "course." It is very cool and pleasant, and you can see everybody, and everybody can see you, as it was with Brothers the Prophet and the Devil in Tottenham Court Road. As you are usually alone, too, in this vehicle—for it is not genteel to offer a lady one-horse exercise—the "calescino" has something triumphal about it; and, by "making believe" a great deal, as Dick Swiveller's Marchioness did when she put the orange-peel into water and made believe it was wine, you may bring yourself to believe that you are a Conqueror by the name of Cæsar, and proceeding along the Via Sacra in your chariot; Zenobia, Queen of Palmyra, trudging before you a captive, with muddy sandals and shackles on her finely-proportioned limbs, and a host of elephants following you, laden with the spoils of your campaigns. You propose in the evening to paint yourself a bright scarlet, and to sacrifice several of your prisoners to the gods. What scenes in the circus you will have to-morrow with the elephants, and the lions and tigers, and Christians, and other wild animals! Ah, what does that servile person standing on the splashboard of your triumphal chariot venture to whisper in your ear? That you are mortal. What impertinence! Are there no lictors to take him up, or at least cry, "Whip behind"?

That I was mortal I was reminded, and in a very curious manner, not ten minutes after I had entered my "currus triumphalis" at fifteen bajocchi the course. In the maze of narrow streets which hem in the Post-office we got mixed up with a funeral. It was a delightfully fine and warm afternoon, and anything more grotesquely ghastly than this funeral I never saw under a bright sun and a blue sky anywhere. It was a walking funeral. The coffin was a great painted ark, bedizened with rosettes of tinsel and foil-paper, and hung with festoons of paper-flowers and shreds of coloured calico. It looked as though Jack-in-the-Green had gone the way of all flesh which is grass, and was to be buried in professional costume, with my Lord and my Lady as chief mourners; and I am sure that the 19th of December in Rome was very like the 1st of May in less-favoured climates. This ark was borne on painted poles, apparently distrained from barbers' shops, on the shoulders of half-a-dozen lads in long red gowns, beneath which their dirty boots "stole in and out" in anything but the mouse-like manner of the little feet of the bride in Sir John Suckling's ballad; and they swayed to and fro with their burden, and staggered along, now and then halting to trim their bark and adjust their balance, in a fashion which was, to say the least, unseemly.

In a surplice which had evidently not been washed since last Easter, and which was most disgracefully ragged, came a thurifer, with a great crucifix on the top of a pole. There was an old priest in spectacles, and a young priest with many pimples on his face, walking leisurely along, and crooning forth, in that dull, listless, heartless chant which, to heretics, is the most distasteful and irritating of all things in the Romish rite, the Office for the Dead. The old priest had something the matter with his knee-shorts, which compelled him every two minutes or so to stop and hitch them up; and the young priest, at the imminent risk of getting a crick in his neck, was staring at the occupants of the very tall houses on either side the street, droning out his chant meanwhile, and yawning occasionally, as though he found the Office for the Dead rather a bore than otherwise, which I daresay he did. There was a sprinkling of choristers carrying candles, and choristers swinging censers; but the most extraordinary part of the cortège was that which brought up its rear.

A mob—for I can give them no other name—of hulking fellows came clumping along, their features and all but the dim outline of their limbs concealed under most hideous robes and hoods of bright green-baize, with white calico crosses sewn on to the breast. Their cowls, drawn over their faces, with two holes for their eyes to peer through, looked inexpressibly horrible. I have met more than one Trappist monk, and in Spain I have seen the Confraternity of the Passion, who carry images about and wear disguises of fine white flannel; but this rabble-rout of green-baize maskers in Rome staggered me. If anything could add to the incongruity of their aspect, it was this: that the robes of many were too short for them, and that beneath the green-baize vestments I noticed one pair of shepherd's plaid pantaloons, and one of corduroy. They were howling, in a most drearily-demented manner, some litany or penitential psalm of their own, which completely failed to harmonise with the Office for the Dead going on in front.

I asked the driver who these people were, and he informed me that they belonged to one of the innumerable Confraternities of the Dead, who in Rome appear to be a kind of amateur undertakers. According to the driver, they were great rogues; and he even hinted that as soon as they got possession of a corpse their principal endeavour was to extract as many "paoli" as they could out of the bereaved relations: but this, I hope, is not the case. It is certain that they attend condemned criminals to the scaffold quite gratuitously; and the intense horror of death and puerile terror even of the sick-room, which prompt so many Italians to abandon the sick and dying to the priest and the hired attendants, render the intervention of these confraternities necessary. Somebody finds a shroud; a coffin is easily hired for the occasion; and the priests and hooded people do all the rest.

Funerals must be very cheaply conducted in this country; and, abstractedly, there is nothing purer and nobler than the voluntary penance to which these green-baize persons devote themselves in the performance of offices generally found so revolting. Practically, perhaps, it would be better to employ regular undertakers than these howling amateurs. Foreigners are always told that many of the proudest Roman nobles are members of these confraternities, and that the eyes you see blearing through the slits in a hood may belong to a Colonna, an Orsini, or a Pamfili-Doria ; but I scarcely imagine that the green-baize guild numbers many patricians in its ranks. I had a taste of their quality ere long.

I have said that we were mixed up with this funeral. The painted coffin and its carriers, the priests, the cross-bearer, and the choristers, all became inextricably entangled with my "calescino" and its horse, with a string of peasants bearing sacks of charcoal, with a dray piled with pumpkins and drawn by two of the savage buffalo-looking oxen of the Campagna, with a knot of Dutch Zouaves rather the worse—or the better—for their visit to the adjacent "spaccio di vino," and with a contadino on horseback, who, cloaked up to the eyes, and with his shaggy overalls of goatskin, his high-peaked saddle, and huge rowelled spurs, wanted only a coachwheel-hat and a lasso wound round the cantle of his saddle to make him the twin-brother of a Mexican guerillero. You may add to these several priests off duty, and with shovel-hats quite broad enough of themselves to block-up a street of ordinary width·; a select party of young gentlemen returning from some theological day-school, and clad for the occasion in salmon-coloured bed-gowns, also with shovel-hats—nothing religious can be done in Rome without a shovel-hat, and even the Pope wears one, of a bright crimson, like a cardinal's turned up, during the performance of certain rites ; a sprinkling of monks, some barefooted and some clumsily shod, who, in infinite stages of dirt and imperfect shaving, are always hopping about Rome, like pigeons, taking what they can pick up ; and innumerable monks without hoods and shaven crowns, but with brass badges on their breasts licensing them " a domandare in Roma," and who were professional beggars.

These, with the children wriggling about, under and between the legs of the adults, like eels, and a mule, seemingly belonging to Nobody, and who had gotten one eye knocked out, and was wandering about in a dumbly blight manner, the blood trickling from his orbless socket, unable to view—these, with a tribe of furious dogs, and a number of old women, clawing each other's heads on the doorsteps and,

more furious than the dogs, the Confraternity of Death howling
their banshee serenade, made up a picture of modern Roman
life for which I was quite unprepared. For all its frequentation
by the "forestieri," the grass grows between the stones on the
Via Condotti and the Piazza di Spagna; but here there was life
and animation and bustle of quite a turbulent order. It was life
and animation, however, quite two centuries and a half old, and
struck me, as I sat in the hack-cab on the 22nd of December, 1866,
as being life and animation not precisely real and vital, but of a
spasmodic and galvanised description.

A heretic of heretics, I was nevertheless taught in my youth
to uncover my head whenever a corpse passed by. We owe at
least that reverence to the Unknown King. And if Death had
not been there, the Cross at least was. So I took off my hat, an
action not imitated by my driver, so soon as the procession
straggled into view, and I have to record that in Catholic Rome
I got well laughed at for my pains. There is, perhaps, not much
harm either in uncovering when in a public picture gallery you
stand before a picture of the Crucifixion, or the Mother and
Child: but I have always been stared at and grinned at if I
have paid that slight mark of respect to that which I do not
Understand, but which I Revere.

The Confraternity of Death are much to be commended for
their pious zeal; but I am afraid that the familiarity with the
Office for the Dead and other sacred things has engendered
something like contempt for that and other sacred things. At all
events they and the coffin-carriers *and the cross-bearer* indulged *
in a regular slanging-match with the driver of my "calescino"
and the conductor of the dray laden with pumpkins. My driver
gave them as good as they brought, and the result was the
usual torrent of blasphemous Billingsgate, in the comprehension
of which six months' commerce with "gondolieri" and "vetturini"
has rendered me a tolerable proficient. There is a richness and
fulness, a copiousness of scurrility, in the Roman allusions to the
principal personages mentioned in the Scriptures, which I have not
yet heard. The attendant priests did not in any way

A A

reprehend this scandalous scene, but "bullyragged" the driver themselves in good set terms—quite free, however, I hasten to admit, from blasphemy. At last, the dray being enabled to move on, my "calescino" got round the corner of the next street, and then the boys in red gowns began to carry the corpse, and the choristers began to swing their censers, and the old priest began to hitch-up his knee-shorts, and the young priest began to stare up at the windows, and the men in green-baize began to set up a renewed howl, so dismal, that you might have fancied them the very Dogs, and not the Confraternity, of Death.

There is something about funerals irresistibly encouraging to pugnacity. What a row there is whenever an Irishman is buried ! What bloodshed followed the funeral of General Lamarque ! What a frightful riot was that which attended the funeral of Queen Caroline ! How the yeomen of the guard, if Horace Walpole is to be believed, fought for the wax-candles at the funeral of George II ! In modern English society, which is so very genteel, our funeral combativeness is of a subdued and decorous kind ; but bad blood and set teeth have been manifest ere now on the way to Kensal Green. We disparage the cake and wine in undertones, grumble at the gloves, and mutter things sometimes not wholly complimentary to our dear brother departed. I have had myself before now words with a man in a mourning-coach. I once saw two gentlemen—Irishmen by name, and sailors by profession—get out of a " brougham hearse " in the middle of Russell Square and fight, the undertaker waiting for the purpose, and an admiring circle of partisans in hatbands and scarves cheering the combatants on from their cab-windows ; but this slanging-match in Rome, the blasphemy, the Billingsgate, the tawdry coffin, the dirty surplices, the howling mummers in green-baize, and the Cross above all, like the mast of a wrecked ship visible above a stormy sea, made up a spectacle which will never be effaced from my mind.

If New York has been called a city of one street, modern Rome may with equal justice, or injustice, as your architectural taste or prejudices lead you to assume, be described as a city of no streets at all. Of course such sweeping criticisms applied to a metropolis once numbering a million of inhabitants, and now about two hundred thousand,* must to some extent necessarily partake of the nature of paradoxes. In New York, Fifth Avenue and all the avenues, Eighth Street and all the other streets up to Ninety-first Street—if there be such a thoroughfare—the Bowery and Chatham, Wall and William, and the remainder of the streets in the old Dutch quarter of the island of Manhattan, have a clear right, municipally, statistically, and politico-economically, to be termed streets. They are built and numbered, and paved and populated, in due accordance with street-law. Yet, in the opinion of many, who, like Mercier and De Balzac in Paris, or Mr. Peter Cunningham and Mr. John Timbs in London, hold that a street is nothing without social characteristics and historical associations, New York has only one street, and that one is Broadway.

In modern Rome, the paradox is even more sustainable. Broadway is at least a main thoroughfare, a grand artery leading from the heart to the head of the city, a High Street, indeed a trunk-road from which innumerable smaller thoroughfares branch off ;

* The population of Rome, according to the census of 1863, taken a few years before this was written, was computed at 201,161, exclusive of strangers and the French garrison. In 1800 the total number of inhabitants was only 153,000 ; and in 1813, at the conclusion of Napoleon's rule, it had sunk to 117,000. Since that period it has been constantly on the increase, and in 1854 it was 178,042. The calculations as to the population of ancient Rome are, as a rule, the wildest guesses. Some antiquaries put it down at two, and some go as high as three-and-a-half millions. Topographical engineers, taking the extent of the lines of circumvallation as standpoints, declare that there could never have been more than a million of people in Rome. To have done with statistics, I may mention that the ecclesiastical population is composed of fifteen hundred priests, nearly four hundred seminary pupils destined for the priesthood, two thousand five hundred monks and friars, two thousand nuns, and two thousand beadles, sacristans, custodes, bell-ringers, choristers, and other persons of the church-rat order. In this summary of the civilian army of the Pontiff I have not been quite so minute as the German statist who began his table with "Popes, two ; cardinals, thirty-six ;" adding, in a foot-note, "By the other Pope I mean the General of the Jesuits." His "other" Holiness was usually known in Rome as "the Black Pope,'* in contradistinction to Pio Nono, whose habitual attire was white flannel.

but there is nothing arterial about the Corso of Rome. It is
simply a very long, narrow, and dirty lane, with many turnings,
by patiently threading which you may possibly get from the Piazza
del Popolo into a network of filthy alleys which debouch on the
Forum. It is not the highway of Roman commerce. The best
Roman shops are not in the Corso ; and were it not that it is the
most convenient passage for carriages going to the Pincian Hill, it
would be no more the main street of Rome than Holborn is the main
street of London, or the Rue St. Lazare the main street of Paris.

I have, in a preceding page, mentioned the Via Condotti, which
is the principal resort of foreigners, and the chief emporium of the
exquisite nicknacks manufactured by the Romans for the delectation of foreigners and the impoverishment of their purses. The
Via Babuino might also, by a great stretch of courtesy and the
imagination, be termed a street ; so might that of the Fontanella
Borghese ; so—a very large margin being allowed to the admission—might the Vie di Ripetta and della Scrofa. But none of
these are streets, in the rigid acceptance of the word as used by
civilised beings in the nineteenth century.

The would-be dandy of the Regency had a garment made of
Saxony broadcloth with silk linings, which probably cost him
half-a-dozen guineas ; but when he showed it to Brummell, expecting laudatory remarks, the Beau took the collar between his finger
and thumb, and asked the abased neophyte of fashion whether he
called " that thing a coat." So is it with streets. We don't call
Pentonville Hill a street, nor, the Board of Works notwithstanding, do we confer streetal dignity on Hanway Yard, or on that
infirm and incult gap in which the Garrick Club have built their
new house. Vigo Lane is not a street, and never will be. It will take
another half-century to make New Oxford and Victoria genuine
streets ; and even King William Street, Strand, though more than
thirty years old, is still in an incipient and embryotic state, wanting the real *cachet* and *imprimatur* of street vitality.

I have premised so much lest there might be persons yet un-
travelled, but studious of topography, who, on reading this, should
produce a monstrous map of Rome from the pocket of a guide-

THE PIAZZA DEL POPOLO, ROME.

Page 372.

book, flourish it before me, and ask me what I meant when such a viatorial labyrinth had been laid down by the copperplate engraver ; or lest members of the more felicitous classes, who have spent a winter in Rome, should, half-astonished and half-indignant, want to know what I was driving at. " No streets in Rome ? " they might say : " Why, we have been nearly run over half-a-dozen times in the Via dell' Angelo Custode. We have bought West India pickles and Durham mustard in the Via Babuino. We have lost our way in the Via Capo-le-case, and have seen the horse races in the Via del Corso."

With all this I respectfully submit that there are no streets in Rome ; and I would say to the felicitous beings who *have* wintered there, " Ladies and gentlemen, you lived on the Piazza di Spagna, or the Piazza del Popolo, or the Bocca di Leone ; and every morning and evening a carriage came to take you to the Capitol, or the Forum, the Quirinal, the Vatican, the Lateran, the Appian Way, or the Pincian. Do you remember those long dreary drives through by-lanes full of hovels and pigsties, full of dirt and beggars and foul smells ? Surely you could not call those slums streets ! In the afternoon, perhaps, you took a little gentle exercise, or did a little shopping within five hundred yards of your abode ; and in a short time you would find out the principal places for the sale of cameos and mosaics, black draughts, blue pills, photographs, alabaster tazze, French bonnets, and sham Etruscan vases. But within how small a compass were those shops ! You dealt at perhaps twenty, and there should be at least twenty thousand in this huge city."

One of the chief advantages of a paradox is, that it may be qualified, modified, and taken with as many verbal and mental reservations as an oath by a Jesuit. There are few, if any, streets in Rome which are paved, well lit, handsome, commodious, or even commonly decent. There are few, if any, in which three friends can walk arm-in-arm, or in which Materfamilias can sail along surrounded by her olive-branches. In the Corso, for instance, the foot pavement is so narrow, that if a lady halt for a moment to look into a shop she is in imminent danger of being jostled into the

kennel by a Zouave, or a Monsignore, or a barefooted friar, or an
Antibes legionary, or a " trasteverino " with a basket of charcoal
on his back.   As for the Condotto, there is not one inch of foot-
pavement in it.   Streets, indeed, where people can lounge, or even
walk with convenience, are nearly altogether lacking, but on the
other hand, there are some scores of Roman streets not less than
three-hundred-and-fifty years old.   Not that they are picturesque
in their architecture, like the streets of Frankfort, Heidelberg, or
Vienna ; their three centuries and a half only represent an accumulation of dirt, discomfort, rags, and foul smells.

If you will only consent to give the nineteenth century the go-by
—and I own that it is so continually forced down our throats,
both from printed column and from spouting platform, as to have
become a very close imitation of a bore,—and will consent to become thoroughly mediæval, you may take your fill of streets in
Rome, and form a sufficiently accurate notion of the misery and
wretchedness which the non-felicitous classes suffered during those
same middle ages.   Those ages have been unjustly decried, the
sentimental devotees of the past inform us.   There are people who
wish, or profess to wish, for their reëdification.   The amiable Tory
poet, Lord John Manners, has put on record a couplet which,
although not so well known as the famous "old nobility" one,
is even more expressive of his lordship's views in regard to social
progress.   In the sweet volume of lyrics which he published in
conjunction with the gentleman who afterwards turned Papist,
and died Superior of the Oratory at Brompton, his lordship indulges in soft aspirations for the return of the halcyon time when
" the humbler classes once again " shall "*feel the kind pressure of
the social chain.*"

Walk about the streets of Rome, and you will see how
the "humbler classes" felt "the kind pressure of the social
chain," with a vengeance, during the middle ages.   To that
kind pressure, in France, in England, and in Germany, were
due the plague, the sweating fever, the falling sickness, and
the black death which used to swoop down on the kindly-
chained ones periodically, and, where Alaric, Attila, and

Totila had slain only their thousands, would lay their millions low. To the few remaining links of that "kind chain" which still rust and fester at home, we owe Bethnal Green and Spitalfields, and chronic cholera and typhus. Rome has felt the "kind pressure" so long as to have grown accustomed to it, and there are many Ultramontanes, I daresay, who assert that the Romans prefer their backward state of life to the feverish progress of the non-Catholic nations. Would you tell me, if you please, why it is that the most orthodox Catholic cities always stink so intolerably? It is the odour of sanctity, I suppose. Many of the saints smelt more powerfully than pleasantly, and were additionally venerated for that reason. I will mention Seville, Cordova, Toledo, Toulouse, and Vienna. All those cities are orthodox, and in all of them the stench is unendurable. The streets of Rome, the houses of Rome—to the very palaces and museums—reek with such horrible odours that you are very soon led to conjecture that the ever-quoted malaria from the Pontine marshes has been made responsible for a great deal of which it is quite innocent, and that one of the chief predisposing causes of the Roman fever is the inconceivable filthiness of the people and their dwellings.*

These fetid pigsties, these abominable dens, were the kind of places people lived and died in during the middle ages, all the while such splendid churches and palaces were being built, such glorious pictures painted, such beautiful missals illuminated,

---

* There are medical authorities, I know, who maintain a contrary opinion, and who ascribe the unhealthiness of Rome to the desolation of the circumjacent Campagna, the diminution of the population there, and the number of deserted villas, in whose wildernesses of abandoned garden a kind of choke-damp is bred. According to these sages, whenever a large number of persons have been crowded into a confined space in Rome, as in the Ghetto and the densely-thronged quarter about the Capitoline Hill, the salubrity of the situation has been apparent, in spite of the dirty habits of the people. Now, were this statement accepted unreservedly, it would be one of the most powerful arguments ever adduced against soap, small-tooth combs, fresh water, and abundant ventilation. Similar arguments were often heard in England when it was proposed to clear out St. Giles's and abolish Smithfield Market; but I am happy to remember that they did not prevail.

such exquisite bas-reliefs carved in marble and oak and ivory,
such delicate tapestries worked, such rich armoried glass stained,
such brave goblets and tankards chiselled, such gallant suits
of armour and trenchant swords and keen poniards hammered.
All the while the "humbler classes" lived like dogs, were
beaten like dogs, hanged like dogs, bought and sold like dogs,
and died at last, dog-like, in such kennels. There are the very
stalls where they bought their poor scraps of meat, their bunches
of vegetables, their loaves of coarse sour bread. There are the
very taverns where their wine was sold at a mean price to them,
and where, getting hysterical at last with acid drink upon half-
empty stomachs, they dug one another in the ribs with knives,
as they do to this day. There are the same casements stuffed
with foul rags, the same black and crazy staircases, from which
peeped old and weazened faces, or faces young and wan, or
faces bleared by passion and poverty or the greed of other
men's goods ; or at which sprawl and squall, cascading at
last to the kennel below, ragged, frowsy, elf-like children, many
of them maimed by neglect, many of them scarred and seamed
frightfully, more by the hot cinders of the braziers with which
they have been allowed to play than by that other children's
scourge, smallpox, and most of them, up to eight years of age,
more than three parts naked.

I have not yet seen the "humbler classes" in Naples and
Sicily, but up to this writing I have seen nothing so forlorn
and so revolting, so miserable and so degraded, as the "humbler
classes" of Rome. You man in the shovel-hat, who talk so
unctuously about the Virgin Mary—you who have set up
at every street-corner a painted idol, with a lamp before it—
you who fill the minds of your penitents with all kinds of
lying legends about the saints and their miracles—are you,
too, so blind, so ignorant, so stupid, as not to see that in
the lives of these deplorable creatures, fluttering in rags,
wallowing in dirt—in these mothers, who from sheer lethargic
carelessness suffer their babes to become hump-backed and
bow-legged—in these slouching, unkempt men and lads—

in these swarms of beggars, now cringing and now clamorous—in these homes, unfit for human beings, and scarcely fit for hogs, there is one constant, dull denial both of the Mother and the Son of God—there is one standing negative to the tremendous assertions of Romanism in the Basilica hard by? The filthiest streets of Rome are in the Borgo, and the Borgo is composed of the streets immediately surrounding St. Peter's. "*Tu es Petrus*," runs the great inscription in mosaic round the drum of the dome, in letters every one of them as tall as a Life Guardsman—"*Tu es Petrus, et super hanc petram ædificabo ecclesiam meam;*" but underneath the rock of the Church priestcraft has built up a dunghill.

One loses patience altogether with the splendour of the Roman church, when we contrast that splendour with the squalor by which it is environed. At least, among us heretics, consigned by the Romanists to eternal torment, the church goes hand in hand with the trim school-house, full of clean and rosy children, with the hospital, the asylum, and the reformatory. But here there is but one step from Rafaelle's pictures and Bernini's statues to Beggar's Bush and the Cadger's Arms. Bramante's and Fontana's great façades only screen the nest of hovels behind; and all the loathsome losels of the Roman Alsatia wash their rags in fountains adorned with saints and angels. The very steps of St. Peter's, the very corridors of the Vatican, to within the shadow of the halberts of the Swiss guard, are beset by beggars. But is not mendicancy itself orthodox? Did not many of the saints themselves beg? And has not a life of sloth, uncleanliness, and mendicity, otherwise known as "holy meditation," been expressly pointed out by many Fathers of the Church as the direct road to salvation?

There are streets in Rome whose names are more poignant in their suggestiveness than the fiercest satire of Juvenal. The Vicolo Gesù-Maria is close to the Via degl' Incurabili. The Street of the Guardian Angel is the most abandoned place you ever saw out of St. Giles's; the Street of Paradise is a poor imitation of Saffron Hill; and the Street of Death skirts the wall of a grand palace. All the saints have streets named after them; all the articles of religion, all its mysteries, and most of the non-apostolic personages in the New Testament, have their streets, with an occasional Triton, or Dolphin, or Nereid, to make up; and now and then plain truth peeps out to the discomfiture of fiction, as in the "Street of the Old Shoes" and the "Street of the Dark Shops."

But, amidst all these rankling hovels, among all the garbage, amidst all these tatters and tatterdemalions, the three-hundred-and-sixty-four churches and basilicas of Rome rear their sumptuous heads; without, all sculpture and ornate architectural ornament—within, all glowing fresco and radiant mosaic, gilding and embroidery, gold and silver plate. For my part I think it would be much less sacrilegious to sell every Rafaelle and Domenichino to the dealers in the Ghetto—to scrape every particle of gold-leaf off the statues of the Virgin, as the French did at Puebla—to melt down all the silver candlesticks, and despoil the very shrine on the altar of its gems, and apply the ready-money thus obtained to building a few model lodging-houses and a few baths and wash-houses, than to allow Rome to seethe and rot in the corruption of neglect and abandonment, while the monuments of a preposterous idolatry blaze all around in gold and jewels.

XXXII.

A Day with the Roman Hounds.

 " SOUTHERLY wind and a cloudy sky proclaim a hunting-morning," to which I may venture to add that " You all knew Tom Moody, the whipper-in · well." It will be perceived by these quotations from the once-popular anthology of the cover-side—now degraded, I am sorry to say, to a very dog's-eared condition in the " four-penny box " at the book-stalls—that my intent, on the present occasion, is a sporting one; that I purpose rhetorically to array myself in scarlet, and to substitute top-boots for the classical " cothurnus," and that the burden of my song throughout this letter will be " Yoicks ! " " My name is Nimrod, and on the Esquiline hills my father kept his hounds, a noble pack, until—not being a frugal swain—my sire outran the constable, sold his dogs, and went to them himself." To have done with circumlocution, I aspire to give you an account of the great meet of the Roman Hunt as it occurred one day in the month of December, 1866.

If a "southerly wind" be essential to the proclamation of a hunting-morning, the sons of Nimrod in Rome on that day must have had every reason to be satisfied. The sirocco, which is a southerner, with a dash of the easterly, like a Carolinian who has married a lady from Massachusetts, put in a very lively appearance throughout the forenoon. The Roman sirocco is no arid and suffocating blast, such as that awful wind in Algeria which comes scouring in from the Sahara like a *goum* of wild Bedouins, its burnouse laden with impalpable sand, which pierces the lungs of the consumptive even as a sharp scimitar. When the sirocco

blows in Algeria the people hasten to close their doors and
windows, stopping up the very chimneys and keyholes, and remain
in their back-parlours, trembling, till the flying pillar of hot dust
has passed away. But when the Roman sirocco blows we open
our casements, and invite the gentle gale to fan our cheeks and
ventilate our apartments. It is a soft, mild, caressing wind, more
resembling warm milk in a volatilised state than anything else.

In summer the sirocco is said to be both debilitating and
oppressive; but a fortnight before Christmas, and with the
knowledge that your friends in England are being choked with
fog, or rendered despondent in the morning by the appearance of
ice in the water-jug, the balmy south-easter is inexpressibly grateful and refreshing. At least ten thousand times a year we are
informed by didactic journalists that there were people who wept
for Nero—not such a very bad fellow, perhaps, after all—and I
am determined that there shall be at least one bard to sing the
praises of that much-calumniated wind, the sirocco. For the world
is growing very stale and jejune, and paradox has ever a salt
flavour.

With the "southerly wind" came, however, no "cloudy sky."
The cerulean vault might have been taken down bodily—since
this is the city of miracles—and used to crown those enormous
slabs of Russian lapis lazuli in the baldacchino covering the sepulchre, where, outside the walls at Rome, *they say* the Apostle of
the Gentiles is buried. St. Peter and St. Paul! It is not more
shocking and irreverent, perhaps, to breathe those tremendous
names in an article like this than to have them huckstered about
to you by custodes and valets-de-place at so many bajocchi a
piece. "Down dere part of St. Paul be buried; rest of him in de
oder church;" or "A gauche, Excellence, sont les ossements de
St. Pierre, apôtre et martyr." Mr. Kingsley, in his time, was
shocked at the gross familiarity with which the sacred names of
the colleges at Cambridge were bandied about by unreflecting
undergraduates; but Romish and Cambridge ears grow, I suppose,
in time alike hardened. The Ten Commandments here are so
much fresco or encaustic; and the Passion is done in mosaic at so

many scudi per foot. The Trinity has become a trade. Miriam cures wounds, and Pharaoh is sold for balsam.

Yes ; the sky was bluer than any ultramarine that Winsor and Newton could sell at a guinea an ounce ; and, save one little fleecy speck of vapour, wandering like a lost lamb in the fields of Elysium, it was without a cloud. The weatherwise declared the fleecy speck to be a sign that ere noon had passed the southerly wind would shift to the north and the sirocco become a "tramontana," which is a very rude and blustering gale, harsh and penetrating, cracking the lips and reddening the nose, and playing old gooseberry with the ladies' crinolines and the ampler skirts of the Roman clergy. The sun shone bright and strong, to the infinite glee of the "forestieri," but far too brightly and strongly for the Romans, who, in common with other Italians, have a deep-seated reluctance to exposing themselves to the rays of Phœbus. They never walk on the sunny side of the street if they can help it, and the only possible objection that can be taken to the hotels of Rome, which are exceptionally clean, comfortable, and well-managed, is that most of their rooms are as dark as Sir Walter Raleigh's bedroom in the Tower of London. "Murray" tells us of a Roman saying, that "none but Englishmen and dogs walk in the sunshine."* It is very odd how cosmopolitan are these proverbial sayings. Not nine months since I was told at Madrid, that nobody save "un perro o un Frances"—a dog or a Frenchman—walked on the sunny side of the Puerta del Sol. There were numerous Romans, however, yesterday in the Campagna, who were fain to be as dog-like as Englishmen, and not only to walk, but to ride, for a good many hours in the full blaze of the lord of the unerring bow, as Lord Byron calls the Apollo, whose

---

* The Roman doctors would not seem to be quite so strongly prejudiced against solar influences as their patients are, for the faculty in Rome have their own proverbial saying, to the effect that, in rooms where the sun does not enter, the physician invariably must. It is after all a question of season. There are months in the year, in Italy as in Spain, when the sun from a benefactor turns to an intolerable despot. In the hotels in Seville you pay for rooms without sun double the price charged for apartments *al sol ;* and at a bull-fight "un palco à la sombra," or box in the shade, costs twice as much as one in the sun.

bow must have erred sometimes, seeing that it is now hopelessly broken.   You cannot ride to hounds with an umbrella, or
take a stone wall in a brougham ; at least, I fancy that Nimrod and
the *Sporting Magazine* would not approve of such proceedings.

The Roman Hunt is an institution of respectable antiquity, and
probably owes its origin to the great influx of aristocratic English
to the Papal capital which took place after the fall of Napoleon,
and after Sir Thomas Lawrence's pencil and the munificence of
George the Fourth to the Cardinal of York had made the Pope
fashionable, and a winter in Rome the very genteelest of things
to do. It is curious to mark the infinite ramifications stricken
into the English mind, all springing from the common trunk of
our hatred to the First Bonaparte. If Napoleon had used the
Pope well, his Holiness would have probably remained the reviled
and despised " Bishop of Rome ; " but the French Emperor maltreated the Sovereign Pontiff, kidnapped and imprisoned him ; so
genial society in England forthwith "took him up," and he
became the "dear good Pope" whom Belgravian ladies talk so
ecstatically about.

The Roman Hunt fell into abeyance for a period of seven
years. The suspension was due partly to the troubles of 1849,
from which Roman society had never entirely recovered, and
partly to the painful impression made on the mind of the
benevolent Pio Nono by the numerous and sometimes fatal acci-
dents which had taken place in the hunting-field. The truth
was, that the English gentlemen who joined the Hunt imagined
that they could do in the Campagna all that they had been in the
habit of doing with the Quorn and the Pytchley, and that the
Roman patricians who so blithely assumed the scarlet and buckskins—as the costumes " de'veri cacciatori Inglesi "—tried, incited
by noble emulation, to do all that the veterans of Melton Mow-
bray attempted, and more.   The consequence was that, with
melancholy frequency, the noble sportsman's horse would shy at
the stump of a Corinthian column, or fling him neck and crop into
the profundities of a sepulchral monument ; and it was obviously
more classical than convenient to crack your skull by contact with

the broken bust of a defunct Prætor, and be carried to the hospital on a bronze door.

Since 1864 the Hunt has been reëstablished, and with the full concurrence of the Pontifical authorities—a special proviso, however, being added to the permission given by the kind-hearted old Pope, to the effect that the noble sportsmen should be accompanied by a mounted corps of Pioneers, consisting of one contadino on horseback, equipped with an axe and a pick, to cut down hedges that were too tall, and knock down stone walls that were too stiff to leap. The Hunt is placed under the management of a committee of Roman noblemen, and consists of at least one hundred members, each paying a hundred-and-fifty francs a-year, and engaging to keep up their subscriptions for at least three years. Strangers may become annual members, and those staying but a short time in Rome are always welcome at the meet.

I need not say that nine-tenths of the foreigners who thus avail themselves of the privilege are our own countrymen. Now and then a " fast " Yankee, an " illustration " of the Paris Jockey Club, or a Russian prince, makes his appearance in the field ; but the Anglo-Saxon element is by far the predominant one ; and the scene, apart from its wondrous associations of the buried past, is thoroughly English—that is to say, genial, good-natured, and jolly, with just a spice of the national eccentricity—which foreigners mistake for madness—and just a leaven of the national stuckupishness—which foreigners have no name for, but which they laugh at. I do believe there are English people who would give themselves airs in Charon's boats, as young Bibo did, till the stern ferryman hit him over the pate with his oar to teach him humility, and who would use smelling-bottles and eyeglasses in the very dock before Rhadamanthus' judgment-seat. I have seen " stuckupishness " at the top of the Alps and at the bottom of the Catacombs, and I saw it in full bloom at the Roman Hunt.

The meet, which was to be the most brilliant of the season, was announced to take place at the Tomb of Cecilia Metella ; but the actual rendezvous was on a rising knoll in the Campagna—very likely the crest of a partially-sunk tumulus, about a mile farther

oh, to the left of the Appian Way. The Tomb of Cecilia Metella,
and the left-hand side of the Appian Way! What a trysting-
place for foxhounds! Well, they must meet somewhere; and,
given the favourable nature of the locality, we need not inquire
too minutely into its history. The Duke of Wellington kept a
pack of hounds in the Peninsula, and the Great Captain's short,
sharp " Ha! ha!" was often heard as he galloped over the green
slopes of Andalusia. Boabdil and Muley Abbas did not interfere
with Jowler and Boxer, and Tom Moody, a colour-sergeant on
ordinary days, was the whipper-in.

The oldest and the dearest friend I ever had was a great huntsman, and emigrated to South America to re-make the fortune which
he had lost at home. He went to Valparaiso, and did well—principally, I believe, in coal-mines—and I met a Scotchman at Cadiz
who told me that he had known him well in Chili, that his old
passion for the chase had revived, and that he kept a pack of
hounds, all to himself, at the remote " hacienda " where he dwelt,
often without seeing a European face from year's end to year's
end, and went out hunting by himself, monarch of all he surveyed,
like a top-booted Robinson Crusoe. Not a stranger rendezvous
this, among the sierras and pampas and copper-coloured Indians,
than here, among the tombs, with Numa Pompilius looking over
the wall, and Professor Niebuhr denying him round the corner,
while the voice of the late Sir George Cornewall Lewis is heard in
high dispute with Mutius Scævola from the adjacent sepulchres.
Associations à la longue are but adventitious. They may crop up
everywhere. The bluff Leicestershire squire, the sturdy Yorkshire
farmer, have their gatherings among associations as old and as
interesting—now by a Roman encampment, now by a Danish
colony—now by where Druids worshipped the mistletoe, and
roasted people in wickerwork cages—now by where Canute rebuked
his courtiers, or Hardicanute got drunk, or Boadicea was scourged,
or crookbacked Richard fell in fight with Richmond.

I had made up a party, and filled a barouche and pair, and, at
half-past ten, started from our hostelry in the Via Bocca di Leone
for the Tomb of Cecilia Metella. It is, perhaps, unnecessary for

fne to hint to you that your rambling interlocutor is not a hunting-
man, and that he prefers to witness such things as battles, fox-
hunts, and, if possible, shipwrecks, on four wheels, to joining in
them on four legs—that is to say, on horseback. *A chacun son
métier :* and it is not mine to follow the flying fox.

No, I do not hunt. I remember once staying in a country-
house whose hospitable owner pressed me very much to "ride to
hounds," and offered me something which he called a "mount ;"
and I am afraid that, under the influence of *capillaire* and seltzer-
water, late at night in the smoking-room, I promised to "show"
at the meet the next morning. I remember that I received
important letters soon after sunrise, and went to London by the
8.40 train. Is there any harm in admitting that you never
hunted anything bigger than a flea or a guinea. I hope not.
Yet there are some people who grow quite savage, and sneer at
you viciously, because you do not appreciate the delight of
galloping after a wretched vermin at the risk of breaking
your neck, or because you do not understand the slang of the
hunting-field.

How stupid are these sneers ! Can we all of us do everything ?
Suppose I ask Nimrod what a mezzotinto scraper is ; or how he
would use the roulette in half-tones ; and what is the best way of
laying a soft ground, or knocking up a plate which has been over-
bitten ? Suppose I ask Tom Moody how, on a given horizontal,
he would construct an equilateral triangle, or how he would
inscribe, in a given parallelogram, the ellipse known as the
"gardener's oval" ? Ten to one he would know nothing at all
about these things.

Please, then, my noble sportsmen, don't sneer at me because,
until dinner-time on Wednesday night, I did not know what the
"fox's pad" was. Why should I ? I never saw a fox unstuffed
in my life ; but, sportsmen, did you ever see a dolphin, or a shark,
or a brigand, or a wild Indian ? Life is short and Art is long ;
the study of English technology rivals that of the Oriental
languages in abstruseness. I had heard of the fox's brush ; but
this is how I came to hear of his "pad"—the which, I appre-

head, is his foot. "He brought home the fox's pad, did the
captain," quoth a young Englishman at the table-d'hôte, "and he
gave it to the cook to dry on the top of the oven, and, by Jove,
sir, the fellow fried it and sent it up the next morning for breakfast, with chopped parsley. You may smell it in the kitchen now."
I ask, deferentially, what the fox's pad might be, not knowing
exactly whether it was something to eat or something to sit down
upon, and being enlightened, experienced considerable gratification. The English tongue is certainly a most copious one, and
its wealth of synonyms is inexhaustible. The foot of a fox is his
" pad," and that of a dog his " paw." The head of a wild boar is
his " hood," and the tail of a hare his " scut," and the stomach of
a horse is his " barrel."

We drove over the slippery flagstones of modern Rome amidst
a wilderness of old churches, old pictures, old beggars, old women,
and old clothes, and through the old Porta San Sebastiano and
the older arch of Drusus, on to the Appian Way. It is certainly
not wider than that back-lane which leads from Walham Green
to Hammersmith, but it is the most interesting road in the world.
To reach it, by the route we took, you must pass the gigantic
Baths of Caracalla, and the still more gigantic, but more dilapi-
dated, Palace of the Cæsars. You must pass the tombs of the
Scipios, and those of the Pompeys—the Columbaria, so called
from their pigeon-house conformation, where baked Romans are
potted down in such very circumscribed places, that the practic-
ability of being burnt on a fourpenny-piece, and having your
ashes collected on a postage-stamp, and being buried in a porte-
monnaie, at once occurs to you. The first time I visited the
Columbaria the custode took out of a jar—originally, so it seemed,
intended for Bengal chutnee—a handful of little bits of black
stuff, and told me *that* was a Roman senator. Yes; and it might
have been Cleopatra, or Marc Antony, or Alexander, or the Lady
of Shalott, or the costermonger's baby burnt to death in the back-
garret in Bethnal Green last Monday was a fortnight. We pack
very closely, and give very little trouble when we are in a jar,
calcined and powdered fine, that is certain. They might make a

THE ARCH OF DRUSUS.

Page 386.

good pigment for house-painters out of a senator, and consular ashes might be useful in bleaching linen.

Lord save us! what infinite pains these Roman magnificoes were at, not only in these pigeon-cotes, but for miles and miles along the Appian Way, to have elbow-room in their tombs for their stuckupishness, and to let the remotest posterity know what grand folks they were! What myriads of alphabets were there not graven to record their styles and their titles, and the years of their births and their deaths. Not one in a thousand of the inscriptions is perfect; by not one in ten thousand is aught conveyed beyond a hollow noise that has no meaning. Now and then the sound is vocable, and has stress, as in the solemn warning, "Touch me not, O mortals; revere the manes of the dead;" or as in the exquisitely pathetic apostrophe, in which the bereaved mother endearingly implores the "kind fever, the good fever, the holy fever," which has taken two of her children, to spare the two that remain. But time and the barbarians have been as good as the fever, and neither children nor grown-up people, nor the manes of the dead, nor slave nor senator, have been respected; and this Appian Way is but a chaos of charnel-houses, with the Pope's highway running through it, along which post-chaises and hackney-carriages drive.

Do you know the bone-grubbing purlieus of Kensal Green, or the great *Croquemort* promenade on the way to Montmartre or Père la Chaise, or Stonecutter's Row in the Euston Road, or Greenwood Cemetery in New York? Take all the tombs and statues, tear up the vaults, lay bare the catacombs, break them up into fragments large and fragments small, play at nine-pins with them, half hide them in the earth, let grass cover and weeds choke them; grow the acanthus on the Corinthian capital, and let the thistle riot over the cornice— "down with the nose, down with it flat, take the bridge quite away"—from legions of bodiless heads, and shear the arms and legs from legions of headless marble bodies. Let this be a valley of dry bones, of petrified Chelsea and

Greenwich pensioners. Turn the whole chaos loose in the
building-yard of a Lucas or a Cubitt, after a long strike, or
a longer lock-out. Shoot the rubbish of ages there ; sprinkle
with dust and innumerable brickbats, and serve hot, with
trailing vines, and a bright sun, and a blue sky for sauce.
This is the Appian Way.

Never was there such an eloquent rebuke to the pride and
vanity, and ambition of man. You may put the Pontifex
Maximus in your snuff-box, and carry away a vestal virgin
in your waistcoat-pocket. Those tremendous Romans here
attempted to set up a lasting text of the sublime and the
stupendous ; and lo ! Time sits on a broken tombstone, and
reads a lecture on the Infinitely Little. The poorest Paris
gamin shovelled last week into the *fosse commune,* the wretchedest
pauper whom the board can worry and the nurse bully no
longer, and whom the parish undertaker has nailed-up between
four deal-boards and carried off to the paupers' burying-ground,
is of as much account as the Roman Prince who had five
hundred slaves, and a thousand clients, and a fortune of four
millions sterling.

The Via Appia is thronged with beggars. I will not say
infested ; for here they do not seem out of place. They are
in perfect consonance with the decaying scene, with the
decaying Church, with the general "mitycheesiness," so to
speak, and twenty-centuries-old aspect of everything around.
A Carden here might be prodigal of bajocchi ; a Marquis
Townshend, even, induced to bestow a paul upon a poor
widow with a callow brood of brats. There is a very hideous
creature on the Appian Way, a mendicant, who has a sliding-
scale of ailments at his command, and who, in proportion to
your liberality, will get more and more frightfully afflicted.
A gratuitous view may be obtained of him ; but he is then
simply a spiteful idiot, with bandy-legs and St. Anthony's
fire in his face. For two bajocchi he will have St. Vitus's
dance ; for three, his right side will be paralysed ; for five, he
will have an epileptic fit and foam at the mouth.

The "Papalini" tell us that Rome is full of charitable institutions, where every conceivable human ill is ministered to by "nostri poveri monachi"—by those charming monks and nuns whose convents the wicked and atheistical Government are so ruthlessly suppressing. Could not the Pontifical almoners find a corner in one of their admirable hospitals for this deplorable object on the Via Appia ?

Signs of the Hunt began to appear as soon as we were clear of the Arch of Drusus. Outside the city walls there was a great muster of ladies' and gentlemen's steeds ; for the slippery flags of the Roman streets are terribly trying to horses shod for hunting, and prudent Nimrods prefer to mount "extra muros." Many even drive to cover in dogcarts, chars-à-banc, or barouches. There were half-a-dozen English ladies, at least, who did not vault—vaulting is, I believe, the term—on to their crutch saddles until they were well clear of the walls ; but the spectacle then became charmingly equestrian, and the Appian Way was brightened by a most vivacious cavalcade. Gracefully-cut jackets, more graceful English faces,· plumed hats, flying skirts, cambric handkerchiefs in the pocket of the saddle, daintily-varnished boots, tiny gauntleted hands, whips with amber, and coral, and bucksfoot handles—nay, even the famous " ladies' riding-trousers, chamois leather with black feet," were visible among the tombs. The gentlemen made an equally gallant show. With some, the modest pepper-and-salt shooting jacket, with doeskin pantaloons and high boots, were deemed sufficiently "down the road ; " but a goodly proportion of the noble sportsmen had evidently left England with malice prepense as regards the Roman Hunt. They may have aired their "pink " at Pau, in the Pyrenees ; but the full bloom of their Nimrodism had been reserved for the Campagna.

The ladies tell me that there is not a prettier sight to be seen the whole world over than a gentleman in full fox-hunting dress. I think that the prettiest specimen of humanity possible to view is a lady riding in Rotten-row on a fine

May morning ; but, I daresay, were I a lady, that the cynosure of my eyes would be a slim figure in a well-fitting swallow-tail of brightest vermilion, with a shiny chimney-pot hat, a blue birdseye scarf with a horseshoe pin, buckskins fitting like a glove, and top-boots shining like a mirror. The present generation of hunting-men run slim, and have a tendency to moustaches, not innocent of *pommade Hongroise.* Indeed, about many of the dandies of the Roman Hunt there hung a mysterious odour of Truefitt's and Pratt's, the Raleigh Club, and M. Francatelli's *cabinets particuliers.* Yea, even of the Treasury and the Foreign Office, Whitehall.

The Roman Hunt is a highly-select one, principally because the Campagna is rather a long way off for a tenant farmer or a sporting publican, and Mr. Soapy Sponge thinks twice before taking a second-class return-ticket to Marseilles and Civita Vecchia. I did not see Mr. Sponge at the cover-side by Cecilia Metella's Tomb. I did not see Mr. Jorrocks. Squire Western was absent ; but Sophy Western was there, and young Tom Jones—third paid secretary of her Majesty's Legation, Ecbatana—making desperate love to her behind a sarcophagus. I did not see any of the burly, bloated fox-hunters, their scarlet coats smirched by innumerable spills, and stained purple, besides, by after-hunting orgies, with whom we grow so familiar in Luke Clennel's pictures ; mighty hunters before the Lord, riding over five-barred gates all day, and keeping it up to all sorts of hours at night, always cracking t'other bottle, always drinking the "King, God bless him!" with nine times nine, over flowing bowls of punch, waving foxes' brushes over their heads the while in a distracted manner. A tipsy, swearing, Test-and-Corporation-Act-supporting, collar-bone-breaking generation they were, scouting the bare idea of railways, and holding the Elgin marbles in but slight estimation. They drank deep, but they did not smoke, and were far from the frivolous vices of the age of sham science and soda-water. And they won Salamanca and Waterloo, clearly.

There was no meet at Cecilia Metella's Tomb, and the

fox, who must have read the announcement of the rendezvous in the *Osservatore Romano,* was doubtless bitterly disappointed. For, if there be any truth in the good old British theory that the fox likes being hunted, we may expect Reynard to be as punctual as any one else in keeping his hunting appointments. Moreover, the meet was to come off at eleven, and it was now a quarter to twelve. Appealed to, to reconcile this discrepancy, the driver of the barouche pointed to the extreme distance of the Campagna with his whip, and declared that "i cani e tutta la caccia" were "un po' avanti"—a little farther on. So he drove us for another mile and a half along the Appian Way—always among the tombs; but still no meet in sight appeared.

I was sorry, for the sake of Cecilia Metella, with whom I had already formed an acquaintance, and whom I much admire. What a noble old ruin is the mausoleum of Crassus' wife! Battered by the barbarians, converted into a castle, besieged and retaken half-a-dozen times by the more barbarous Roman barons, stripped of its sumptuous shell of marble by the lime-burners ; rifled by Clement XII., to furnish artificial rocks for his monstrous fountain of Trevi ; and at last so utterly given up to abandonment and neglect that its original intent was lost, and it was known only to the country-people as "La Torre del capo di Bove," or Bull's-head Tower, from the white marble bas-reliefs on the frieze, in which festoons alternate with bulls' heads—the Tomb of Cecilia Metella is still one of the most perfect vestiges that remain of ancient Rome, and with the Pantheon and the Temple of Vesta induces the most definite idea of the beauty, the strength, and the magnificence of the structures of this wonderful city. Clements, and Bonifaces, and Robert Guiscard, and the Constable de Bourbon have done their best to devastate it ; but still "the stern round tower of other days," with its garland of eternity, its two thousand years of ivy, stands "firm as a fortress with its fence of stone," and frowns haughtily upon the Campagna, like an indomitable woman.

There is nothing inside the tomb but bats, and, at night, I suppose, an owl or two ; but I could fancy the fox sitting at the bottom on his haunches, and murmuring that it was really very rude of the gentlemen of the Hunt to keep him waiting so long, and that if they meant hunting, they had better look sharp about it. Foxes have feelings as well as other people, which should not lightly be trifled with.

We came on the meet at last, to the left-hand side, as I have already mentioned, of the Appian Way. The sight we saw fully atoned for the delay we had experienced in reaching it. There were the hounds—thirteen couple and a half, I think, they told me—the half being a young dog of piecrust-and-creamy hue, who would wag his tail at the wrong time, and was continually incurring personal chastisement on that account. There were the English gentlemen-riders, and the English lady-riders, and a very fair muster of noble Romans, some of whom appeared in true British scarlet and top-boots, while others favoured us with jackets and jockey-caps of black velvet, and varnished boots reaching mid-thigh. The show of horseflesh was capital ; and as regards the noble sportsmen who had not brought their own hunters with them, but were content to hire them at the rate of forty francs for the day, the exhibition reflected the highest credit on Mr. Jarrett, who appears to be the Quartermaine of Roman livery-stable keepers, and whose little son, in the quietest and prettiest of hunting gear, and mounted on a very strong horse, distinguished himself greatly during the day, and took some of the stiffest leaps attainable.

There was a tent at the trysting-place, and external symptoms, in the shape of hampers of champagne, that something good was going on inside. Not being a subscriber to the Roman Hunt, I could not of course push my inquiries in this direction further. There was a great muster of private carriages—many of the most recherché equipages you meet on the Pincian, with their most recherché occupants, were indeed present—while the "ruck" was made up of yard-barouches, such as our own. The familiar sounds of one's mother-tongue were continually audible; and an occasional "melodious twang" with "I guess," or "O, my!" or "Yes, sir," to give it zest, led to the conclusion that the American as well as the British element was "on hand." After some twenty minutes' giggling and gossipping, and mutual inspection through eye-glasses, the huntsmen, the hounds, and the noble sportsmen decamped from the trysting-place, and the people who had come in carriages hastily alighted in order to follow the Hunt on foot. Then did the historian see sights!

There is a wonderfully droll Irish story of a matchmaking mamma, who is continually striving to delude subalterns in Her Majesty's foot regiments into matrimony, by inciting her daughters to proceed in advance in a country walk, and "show Ensign Somebody how the turkeys walk through the long grass." That matchmaking mamma should have brought her daughters to the Campagna. Ensign Somebody would have proposed at once, had he seen Miss Jemima O'Flynn walking through the thistles. I have not the honour of Miss O'Flynn's acquaintance ; but on inquiring of an English lady with whom I am on speaking terms, . I elicited the fact that walking through thistles, with an occasional variation in the way of climbing a stone wall, was extremely painful to the feet, ruinous to the stockings, fatal to kid boots, and trying to the temper. In addition to the thistles, many parts of the Campagna were knee-deep in wild-flowers, most beautiful to look upon ; and the deep purple of the distant Alban hills was exquisite. With all this, you don't care about having your boots cut to pieces, and your gracilis muscle lacerated by sublatent enemies of Scottish extraction.

The ladies who were best off were some very high-born Italian dames, who had adopted the last new Paris fashion for a walking-dress. It is a marvellous make-up. You wear a hat, to begin with—anybody's hat—a cocked-hat, if you like, but preferably Tom Tug, the jolly young waterman's, glazed, flat-brimmed, and with a blue ribbon round it. The next thing is to go without your gown, and appear in public with your petticoat-skirt, which should be of scarlet quilted silk, like your great grandmother's counterpane, and which reaches no lower than the tops of your boots. Your boots, by the way, are top ones, or rather Hessians without tassels. You wear a jacket, too, if I remember aright, of velvet ; and to be perfectly proper and modest, you wear round your waist, not a fig-leaf, but a curious slashed-and-tagged structure, something like a bustle in duplicate, rigged fore and aft, as the sailors would say, and cut into pendent vankykes. Then, having left your crinoline at home, you borrow a very tall bamboocane from the fifth footman, and go out walking through the thistles. I don't think Ensign Anybody could have resisted *that* sight on Thursday. Unfortunately, most of the ladies so attired were princesses, or, at the least, duchesses, and the ensign would have had but a poor chance. Oh, I forgot one thing ! Although it is so early in the morning, you paint your face an inch thick.

The noble sportsmen were subjected to a test of almost a crucial nature before the real business of the day began. The expanse on which the tent had been erected was separated from the wide waste of the Campagna by a long stone wall of considerable steepness—a very Irish-looking wall, and a very ugly one, to boot. There were no gates in it, and no gaps ; and unless you went a quarter of a mile to the right, and struck the Appian Way, there was no dodging it. The wall, I am proud to state, was taken, in the majority of instances, " in style." The toy-hurdles they set up for the circus-riders at Franconi's could not have been cleared more deftly than was that Roman wall by at least three-fourths of the Actæons and Dianas present ; and, so far as the four-footed participants were concerned, any amount of scudi must be put down to the account of Mr. Jarrett's stable. Now and then a horse would smell the wall, and prudently wheel away from it. One obstinate gray declined to do more than stand with his two fore-feet on the coping, and insinuatingly endeavour to wriggle his rider off his back ; and one evil-tempered animal, a bright bay, fairly showed the wall a clean pair of heels, and bolted back towards the Arch of Drusus.

The whole field, however, got over at last ; at least, that portion who couldn't manage the leaps got *through* the wall. A mob of " contadini," ragged, active and vociferous, started up from the adjacent tombs as though they had been ghouls, and very soon made practicable breaches in the barriers by the simple process of pulling down the loose stones ; for no mortar had been used in their structure. Thus, we pedestrians, too, were enabled to "take" our stone walls and follow the Hunt, to our great internal joy, but to the increasing laceration of our tendon-Achilles. Surely on that hunting-morning the thistles must have savoured all the sweets of vengeance for the injuries inflicted on them by I know not how many generations of donkeys.

This kind of thing went on for a full hour and a half, the noble sportsmen meandering about the Campagna under the guidance of the huntsman, and the pack wagging their tails in unison, or keeping them in a state of quiescence in apparent obedience to the nod or the wink of the whipper-in. It was very pretty to see the ladies "schooling" over the walls, or when there came a hedge with too much brushwood about it, to see the corps of mounted pioneers lop away the impertinent twigs lest the Amazons should scratch their pretty faces as they swept through. There was a dash of the steeple-chase about it, and a suspicion of Mr. Sleary's circus, the audience being unrestricted in their locality. I say that it was very pretty ; but by about a quarter to two I began to grow impatient to hear the hounds "give tongue"—is that the correct phraseology ?—or to hear somebody cry "Yoicks!" or "Hark away!" I began to get weary, too, of the "schooling," and irritated at the corps of mounted pioneers, who was a grisly man, with a black beard, mounted on a black horse, with a black axe, and all manner of sinister-looking implements of a prevailing sable hue, slung at his saddle-bow. He looked like Herne the Hunter, who had emigrated from Windsor Forest to be nearer graves.

At about two o'clock it occurred to me that the excitement of the chase would be very much enhanced if such an article as a fox were added to it. It was very clear, as the condemned criminal remarked to the ordinary when the sheriff looked at his watch, and observed that it was growing late, that the fun couldn't begin without *him*.

An English friend volunteered the information that he had met the fox, the day before yesterday, on quite another road, and going in the direction of the Porta del Popolo, to keep an appointment, it is to be presumed, at a private henroost. For my part, I could not divest myself of the impression that the fox was still squatting snugly at the bottom of the Tomb of Cecilia Metella, lunching off a cold chicken, and repeating that it was very ungenteel behaviour on the part of the gentlemen of the Roman Hunt to keep him waiting so.

There was plenty of cover, both in the underbrush of the slopes and in the inexhaustible graves, and for another half-hour the huntsman went poking about, followed by his dogs. At every moment I expected to see a gentleman with a brush scurry out, and, indeed, I should not have been surprised had he sallied forth, with a shovel-hat and bands, and buckles in his shoes, and, looking up from his breviary, like Don Abbondio in the " Promessi Sposi," calmly inquired what all this clatter was about on the Feast of St. Odille, the eve of St. Nicaise, and the morrow of St. Lucia. But no fox appeared, and in default of Reynard, I was fain to admire the dashing horsemanship of Mr. Jarrett's little boy, and the equally intrepid amazonship of a lady who stuck at nothing, and went at everything, who was capitally mounted, and did not look more than six-and-twenty, and who, I was told, was Miss Charlotte Cushman, the tragic actress. Lady Macbeth foxhunting ! I was quite prepared after this to see the ghost of Cecilia Metella taking the lead, or Galla Placida flying over a five-barred gate.

They found a fox soon after this, appropriately enough, in a tomb ; and here the duties of the scribe come to an end. I may well be excused from accumulating any more solecisms on matters which I do not understand. I trust, however, that the excellent newspaper, *Bell's Life*, had a correspondent in the field, and that this splendid run with the Roman Hounds has been duly chronicled. I was very glad to get back to the barouche, and return to Rome, to lunch, and send my boots, which were rather too elaborately decorated with the Order of the Thistle, to be mended. I have come to the conclusion that hunting is a very abstruse science, and that, in addition to the intense study it requires, you must be born to it.

The Duchess of Berry, it is said, once witnessed a cricket-match gotten up by some Englishmen at Dieppe for her special delectation. After some hours' batting and bowling, in a broiling sun, she asked "when the game was going to begin." She had mistaken all the batting and bowling for mere preparation. Thus may I have made too light of all the meandering and the poking about, and have seen a fox-hunt without being aware of it. I heard in the evening that the fox, though hunted, was not killed. After a sharp run the poor little béast took refuge (always consistent) in another tomb, and they benevolently left him there to be hunted another day. At the last meet an enthusiastic English sportsman insisted that the fox should die the death, and, having some lucifer matches in his pocket, he smoked him out of his earth, and so delivered him to the dogs and secured his "pad." I don't know what lady had the brush. In any case, I still hold the opinion that the animal I saw chevied was not the genuine one, and that the real original fox remains to this moment in the Tomb of Cecilia Metella, picking a merrythought, and observing that punctuality is the soul of business.

Some people are born to do things by contraries. I never saw a cock-fight till I went to Africa, and the only cricket-match I ever witnessed was in the Valley of Mexico. It was quite consistent with the rule of contraries that I should have to wait for a trip to Rome ere I beheld a pack of English foxhounds.

THE END.

H. BLACKLOCK & Co., Printers, 75, Farringdon Road, London, E.C. (7157.)

42, CATHERINE STREET, STRAND,
SEPTEMBER, 1886.

VIZETELLY & CO.'S
NEW BOOKS,
AND NEW EDITIONS.

NEW REALISTIC NOVELS.

FLAUBERT'S MASTERPIECE.

In crown 8vo, beautifully printed on vellum-texture paper, and Illustrated with Six Etchings, by French Artists, price 6s., elegantly bound.

MADAME BOVARY: Provincial Manners.
By GUSTAVE FLAUBERT.

TRANSLATED BY ELEANOR MARX-AVELING. With an Introduction and Notes of the proceedings against the author before the "Tribunal Correctionnel" of Paris.

M. EMILE ZOLA ON "MADAME BOVARY."

"The first characteristic of the naturalistic novel, of which 'Madame Bovary' is the type, is the exact reproduction of life, the absence of every romantic element. The scenes themselves are every day ones; but the author has carefully sorted and balanced them in such a way as to make his work a monument of art and science. It is a true picture of life presented to us in an admirably selected frame. All extraordinary invention is therefore banished from it. One no longer encounters in its pages children marked at their birth, then lost, to be found again in the last chapter; nor secret drawers containing documents which come to light at the right moment for the purpose of saving persecuted innocence. In fact all intrigue, even the simplest, is absent. The story marches straight on, relating events day by day, harbouring no surprise; and, when it is finished, it is as though, after being as it were out in the world, you had regained your home.

"The whole of 'Madame Bovary,' even in its slightest incidents, possesses a heartrending interest—a new interest, unknown prior to the appearance of this book—the interest of reality, of the drama of daily life. It grips your very vitals with an invincible power, like some scene you have witnessed, some event which is actually happening before your eyes. The personages of the story are among your acquaintances, you have assisted at their proceedings twenty times over. You are in your own sphere in this work, and all that transpires is even dependent upon your surroundings. It is this which causes such profound emotion. But there is also to be added the prodigious art of the writer. Throughout, the tone is of an absolute exactitude. The arrangement of the action is continuous as it would be in reality, without a digression due to imagination, without the slightest kind of invention. The life, the colouring, succeed in creating the illusion. The writer accomplishes the prodigy of disappearing completely, and yet making his great art everywhere felt."

BLACKWOOD'S MAGAZINE ON "MADAME BOVARY."

"Flaubert is among the first of social realists. He addresses himself almost avowedly to the senses and not to the feelings. He treats of love in its physiological aspects, and indulges in the minutest analysis of the grosser corporeal sensations. In intelligence and accomplishments, as well as literary skill, he was no ordinary man. He had read much and studied profoundly; he had travelled far, keeping his eyes open, and had made some reputation in certain branches of science.

"Flaubert wrote his great masterpiece 'Madame Bovary' deliberately in his maturity; and the notoriety which carried him with it into the law-courts, made him a martyr in a society that was by no means fastidious. Seldom before has an author concentrated such care and thought on a single work. Each separate chapter is wrought out with an exactness of elaboration to which the painting of the Dutch school is sketchy and superficial. Those who fill the humblest parts, or who are merely introduced to be dismissed, are made as much living realities to us as Madame Bovary herself, or her husband Charles. Flaubert goes beyond Balzac in the accumulation of details. Yet it is clear in the retrospect that the effects have been foreseen, and we acknowledge in the end the vivid impressions the author has made on us.

"Flaubert proposes to set the truth before everything, and we presume he does so to the best of his conviction. He goes to his work as cruelly and imperturbably as the Scotch surgeon in the pirate ship, who is said to have claimed a negro as his share of the spoil, that he might practise on the wretch in a series of operations."

B

NEW REALISTIC NOVELS—*continued.*

*In Crown 8vo, with Ornamental Initials and Vignettes, and a Portrait of the Author,
Etched by* BOCOURT *from a drawing by* FLAUBERT'S *niece. Price 6s.*

SALAMBO.

By GUSTAVE FLAUBERT.

TRANSLATED FROM THE FRENCH "ÉDITION DÉFINITIVE" BY J. S. CHARTRES,
AND PREFACED BY AN ESSAY ON FLAUBERT'S WORKS.

Press Opinions on Mr. J. S. Chartres's Translation of "Salambo."

" Some little while ago there was published an extraordinary bad translation of Flaubert's
'Salambo' [by M. French Sheldon]. By some means (there are so many of these means) it was
puffed as even in our time few if any books so bad have been puffed. Names of all sorts and
conditions of men ('the highest authorities in the land,' said the advertisement) were pressed
into its service. And hand in hand with the puffing went some dark warnings against other
possible translations, which would inevitably be spurious, infamous, and I know not what else.
The reason of this warning is now clear. Another tranlsation has appeared, done by Mr. J. S.
Chartres, and published by Vizetelly, which is much superior to its predecessor."—*The World.*

" We are able to declare that this second translation, the work of Mr. Chartres, and
published by Messrs. Vizetelly, is very much the better of the two. . . . To show the relation of
this translation to its rival and to the original, we shall quote the first few lines of all three.
The beginning of 'Salambo' is a very good test passage. . . . It is hardly necessary to ask which
of the two is nearest to the French. Turn over the page and an abundance of equally instructive
parallel passages are to be found."—*Saturday Review.*

" After being made the subject of an indifferent translation, Salambo has now been dealt with
by a master of the literary art, who has produced such a version of the great Carthaginian
romance as Flaubert himself might have been delighted with. Why, one cannot help asking, ha
the good wine been thus kept to the last ? "—*St. James's Gazette.*

" We said something about the singularly inefficient translation of 'Salambo' by Mrs.
Sheldon, which excited a still more singular revival of the almost defunct art of puffery. Of the
rival version by Mr. Chartres, if it is not positively good, that is because the original is so hard
to translate that little short of actual genius, provided beforehand with an exceptional knowledge
both of French and English, could give a good translation of it."—*Athenæum.*

" As regards the translator's work, which is allowed on all hands to have been a very arduous
task, there is little or no reason to doubt that a good, faithful, and readable rendering has been
accomplished. A very useful appendix has been most thoughtfully and considerately added to
the story ; it contains criticisms of the romance at its first appearance, and replies made to them
by the author. This course was honest, wise, and satisfactory."—*Illustrated London News.*

" The present volume brought out by Messrs. Vizetelly quite deserves the adjective scholarly
Whenever this enterprising firm undertakes a translation it is generally executed in a way above
reproach, and 'Salambo' is no exception to the rule."—*Whitehall Review.*

TWELFTH THOUSAND.

With 32 highly finished page Engravings, cloth gilt, price 3s. 6d.

SAPPHO: Parisian Manners.

By ALPHONSE DAUDET.

UNABRIDGED TRANSLATION FROM THE 100TH FRENCH EDITION.

" The book may, without exaggeration, be described as a glowing picture of Parisian life,
with all its diversity of characters, with its Bohemian and half-world circles that are to be found
nowhere else ; with all its special immorality, in short, but also with the touch of poetry that
saves it from utter corruption, and with the keen artistic sense that preserves its votaries from
absolute degradation."—*Daily Telegraph.*

. *VIZETELLY & CO.'S Edition of "SAPPHO" is the only complete one.
It contains every line of the original work and fifty pages more matter than any other.*

Specimen of the Engravings in DAUDET'S "SAPPHO."

"Alone in the little garden of the restaurant they were kissing each other and eating their fish. All at once, from a rustic arbour built among the branches of the plane-tree at whose foot their table was set out, a loud and bantering voice was heard: 'I say, there, when you've done billing and cooing——,' and the leonine face and ruddy beard of Caoudal the sculptor appeared through an opening in the woodwork of the hut."

NEW ONE-VOLUME NOVELS.

BY THE AUTHOR OF "MR. BUTLER'S WARD."

Second Edition, in crown 8vo, price 6s.

DISENCHANTMENT.

By F. MABEL ROBINSON.

OPINIONS OF THE PRESS.

"'DISENCHANTMENT' is a novel of considerable power. There is not one of the characters which does not become more and more an actual man or woman as one turns the pages. . . . The book is full of humour and the liveliest and healthiest appreciation of the tender and emotional side of life, and the accuracy—the almost relentless accuracy—with which the depths of life are sounded, is startling in the work of an almost unknown writer."—*Pall Mall Gazette.*

"'DISENCHANTMENT' proves Miss Robinson to be capable of high achievement as a writer of romance It contains scene after scene of conspicuous power, and displays that happy combination of the analytic faculty with intensity of human feeling which is essential to the true novelist. It is not often that a young writer creates and vividly portrays three characters so strong and so fine as Philip Preston, his brother John, and Delia Mayne."—*The Athenæum.*

"'DISENCHANTMENT' is a powerful, painful, youthful book. Miss Mabel Robinson has, in very unusual measure, the faculty of keen observation. The pitiful story of Philip Preston's weakness, of his wife's cruelty, and of his half-desperate, half self-sacrificing end, is told by Miss Robinson with a great deal of pathos."—*The Academy.*

"Some of the scenes are given with remarkably impressive power, rendered the more effective by the side-play of widely contrasted characters which, while interesting in themselves, serve to bring out the central portraits all the more fully. The book is altogether of exceptional interest as an original study of many sides of actual human nature. The style, it should be added, is entirely unaffected, and altogether admirable."—*The Graphic.*

"This powerful novel."—*St. James's Gazette.*

"Augusta Desborough and Delia Mayne are finished studies of women who must at some time or other have come under the author's personal knowledge. The book is not crowded with characters, but those which are introduced are of flesh and blood, and drawn from life. The reader makes friends with them, and parts from them regretfully."—*Whitehall Review.*

"There is a great deal of analytical and delineative skill, there is minute realism of the better sort, and there are many charming scenes and touches to be met with in 'DISENCHANTMENT.'"—*Illustrated London News.*

"The work is exceedingly praiseworthy. It is fresh in subject and individual in treatment. Miss Robinson shows remarkable insight into character, male as well as female; and her Philip is as human as her Augusta."—*The Globe.*

"Of all the young novelists of the day, Miss Mabel Robinson is the most promising. 'DISENCHANTMENT' is no idle tale for silly school-girls and foolish women. It is a novel for strong and healthy minds to delight in, and, moreover, it is good wholesome literature. . . . Fine novel as it is, 'DISENCHANTMENT' may be accepted as an earnest of still better things to come."—*Life.*

In crown 8vo, price 5s.

ICARUS.

BY THE AUTHOR OF "A JAUNT IN A JUNK."

In crown 8vo, price 5s.

IN THE CHANGE OF YEARS.

By FÉLISE LOVELACE.

THE NOVELS OF FEDOR DOSTOIEFFSKY.

TRANSLATED FROM THE ORIGINAL RUSSIAN.

Second Edition. In crown 8vo, 450 pages, price 6s.

CRIME AND PUNISHMENT.

A RUSSIAN REALISTIC NOVEL.

By FEDOR DOSTOIEFFSKY.

OPINIONS OF THE PRESS.

The Athenæum.

" Outside Russia the name of Fedor Dostoieffsky was till lately almost unknown. Yet Dostoieffsky is one of the most remarkable of modern writers, and his book, 'CRIME AND PUNISHMENT,' is one of the most moving of modern novels. It is the story of a murder and of the punishment which dogs the murderer; and its effect is unique in fiction. It is realism, but such realism as M. Zola and his followers do not dream of. The reader knows the personages—strange, grotesque, terrible personages they are—more intimately than if he had been years with them in the flesh. He is constrained to live their lives, to suffer their tortures, to scheme and resist with them, exult with them, weep and laugh and despair with them; he breathes the very breath of their nostrils, and with the madness that comes upon them he is afflicted even as they. This sounds extravagant praise, no doubt; but only to those who have not read the volume. To those who have, we are sure that it will appear rather under the mark than otherwise."

Pall Mall Gazette.

" The figures in the grand, gloomy picture are a handful of men and women taken haphazard from the crowd of the Russian capital. They are nearly all poor. The central figure in the novel is one of those impecunious " students," the outcomes of whose turbulent brains have often been a curse where they were intended to be a blessing to their country. He appears everywhere; is never out of sight in the scenes, vibrating between the highest heights and deepest depths of life. The character of Sonia is drawn with consummate skill. She is a figure of tragic pathos. . . . . A strange fascination attracts Raskolnikoff to seek her out in her own lodgings, a bare little room in an obscure street of St. Petersburg; and there, in the haunt of impurity and sin, the harlot and the assassin meet together to read the story of Lazarus and Dives. In that same den Rodia confesses his crime, and, in anguish almost too deep for words, the outcast girl implores the criminal, for God's sake, to make atonement. The subtle skill with which the various characters are delineated make 'CRIME AND PUNISHMENT,' one of the most interesting and curious psychological studies of modern fiction. Sometimes a beautiful poem in prose, in the shape of a dream that is told, lightens up the scene with a golden brightness of sunlight that now and then recalls the best passages in the novels of Turgenieff."

The Spectator.

" There are three Russian novelists who, though, with one exception, little known out of their own country, stand head and shoulders above most of their contemporaries. In the opinion of some not indifferent critics, they are superior to all other novelists of this generation. Two of them, Dostoieffsky and Turgenieff, died not long ago, the third, Lyof Tolstoi, still lives. The one with the most marked individuality of character, probably the most highly gifted, was unquestionably Dostoieffsky. In our opinion his finest work is 'CRIME AND PUNISHMENT.' Though never Zolaesque, Dostoieffsky is intensely realistic, calls a spade a spade with the most uncompromising frankness. He describes sin in its most hideous shapes; yet he is full of tenderness and loving-kindness for its victims, and shows us that even the most abandoned are not entirely bad, and that for all there is hope—hope of redemption and regeneration. Dostoieffsky sounded the lowest depths of human nature, and wrote with the power of a master. None but a Russian and a genius could draw such a character as Rodia Raskolnikoff, who has been aptly named the 'Hamlet of the Madhouse.'"

The Academy.

" Raskolnikoff, the St. Petersburg student-hero of this story, who finds his guardian angel in Sonia, a poor girl, whom the poverty of her family and the drunkenness of her father have driven into the streets, is not bad in the ordinary sense of the word. He is only mad and poor, and given to what he calls psychology, and, in a frenzy of madness, privation, and philosophy, he murders a female usurer and her sister. . . . . Besides Raskolnikoff and Sonia, the chief characters in 'CRIME AND PUNISHMENT' are his mother, his sister, and her three lovers—Razoumikhin, a fellow student, Looshin, a low-minded official, and Svidrigaïloff, a wild sensualist. These three last, especially Razoumikhin, who is a sort of Russian George Warrington, are ably drawn. There are many passionate scenes in the book, one of them, between Svidrigaïloff and Raskolnikoff's sister, in which the latter fires at her lover with a revolver, is sketched with great, and, indeed, revolting, power. Nor is 'CRIME AND PUNISHMENT' devoid of humour, or of almost Juvenalian satire, upon the present condition of society in Russia."

Now Ready. In crown 8vo, with Portrait and Memoir, price 5s.

INJURY AND INSULT. By FEDOR DOSTOIEFFSKY.

TRANSLATED FROM THE ORIGINAL RUSSIAN BY F. WHISHAW.

To be followed by

THE FRIEND OF THE FAMILY, & THE GAMBLER.
THE IDIOT.   THE BROTHERS KARAMASOFF.
UNCLE'S DREAM, & THE PERMANENT HUSBAND.

THE NOVELS OF COUNT LYOF TOLSTOI.

"Count Lyof Tolstoi presents us with spirited and felicitous studies of the intrigues prevalent in the highest spheres of Russian society, and of their centre of gravitation, the Court. Herein he is in his native element; he has seen both the court and the army—has held a position at the one the same as in the other. . . . . Count Tolstoi amuses himself in taking every part of the human puppet to pieces. Never yielding to emotion, this doctor at every minute of the day is feeling the pulses of all whom he meets, and coldly noting the state of their moral health."—*Viscount de Vogüé.*

Now Ready. In crown 8vo, 5s. each volume

"War and Peace" Series:

1. BEFORE TILSIT.   2. THE INVASION.
3. THE FRENCH AT MOSCOW.

Now Ready. In one volume, crown 8vo, 780 pages, 7s. 6d.

ANNA KARENINA.
A REALISTIC NOVEL.

"As you read on you do not say, 'This is *like* life,' but, 'This *is* life.' It has not only the complexion, the very hue, of life, but its movement, its advances, its strange pauses, its seeming reversions to former conditions, and its perpetual change, its apparent isolations, its essential solidarity. It is a world, and you live in it while you read, and long afterward ; but at no step have you been betrayed, not because your guide has warned or exhorted you, but because he has been true, and has shown you all things as they are."—*W. D. Howells, in Harper's Monthly.*

In crown 8vo, with a Portrait and Memoir of Count Tolstoi, price 5s.

CHILDHOOD, BOYHOOD, AND YOUTH.

THE MERMAID SERIES.

"I lie and dream of your sweet MERMAID wine."
Master Francis Beaumont to Ben Jonson.

Preparing for Publication,

AN UNEXPURGATED EDITION OF

THE BEST PLAYS

OF

THE OLD DRAMATISTS,

UNDER THE GENERAL EDITORSHIP OF HAVELOCK ELLIS,

In half-crown monthly vols., post 8vo, each vol. containing about 400 pages, bound in cloth with cut or uncut edges.

ALTHOUGH a strong and increasing interest is felt to-day in the great Elizabethan dramatists who are grouped around Shakspere, no satisfactory attempt has hitherto been made to bring their works before the public in a really popular manner. With the exception of such monumental and for most readers inaccessible editions as those of Dyce and Bullen, they have either been neglected or brought out in a mutilated and inadequate form. Some of the most delightful of them, such as Middleton and Thomas Heywood, and even Beaumont and Fletcher are closed to all, save the few, and none of them are obtainable in satisfactory editions at moderate prices. In the MERMAID SERIES it is proposed to issue the finest examples of the Elizabethan Drama, those which, with Shakspere's works, constitute the chief contribution of the English spirit to the literature of the world.

The MERMAID SERIES will appear in half-crown monthly volumes, two of which will be published during November. The Editors who have promised their assistance to the undertaking include men of literary eminence, who have already distinguished themselves in this field, as well as younger writers of ability. The first volume will contain a general introduction by Mr. J. A. Symonds, dealing with the Elizabethan Drama generally, as the chief expression of English national life at one of its points of greatest power and expansion.

Each volume will contain on an average five complete Plays, prefaced by an Introductory Notice of the Author. Great care will be taken to ensure, by consultation among the Editors, that the Plays selected are in every case the *best* and most representative—and not the most conventional, or those which have lived on a merely accidental and traditional reputation. A feature will be made of plays by little known writers, which although often so admirable are now almost inaccessible. The names of the Editors will be sufficient guarantee for the quality of the selection. In every instance the utmost pains will be taken to secure the best text, the spelling will be modernised, and brief but adequate notes supplied.

In no case will the Plays undergo any process of expurgation. It is believed that, although they may sometimes run counter to what is called modern taste, the free and splendid energy of Elizabethan art, with its extreme realism and its extreme idealism—embodying, as it does, the best traditions of the English Drama—will not suffer from the frankest representation.

Carefully etched Portraits of those Dramatists of whom authentic portraits exist will be given as frontispieces to the various volumes, and every pains will be taken to ensure typographical accuracy and excellence, and to produce the series in a satisfactory manner in every respect.

The following is the proposed Order of Publication—

MARLOWE. Edited by HAVELOCK ELLIS. With a General Introduction by J. A. SYMONDS.

MASSINGER. Edited by ARTHUR SYMONS.

MIDDLETON. With an Introduction by A. C. SWINBURNE.

BEAUMONT AND FLETCHER (2 vols.). Edited by J. St. LOE STRACHEY.

WEBSTER AND CYRIL TOURNEUR. Edited by J. A. SYMONDS.

SHIRLEY. Edited by EDMUND GOSSE.

DEKKER. Edited by ERNEST RHYS.

ARDEN OF FEVERSHAM and other Plays attributed to Shakspere. Edited by ARTHUR SYMONS.

THOMAS HEYWOOD. Edited by J. A. SYMONDS.

FORD. Edited by HAVELOCK ELLIS.

To be followed by BEN JONSON (2 vols.), CHAPMAN, MARSTON, WILLIAM ROWLEY AND FIELD, DRYDEN, OTWAY, LEE, CONGREVE, &c.

MR. E. C. GRENVILLE-MURRAY'S WORKS.

Second Edition, in post 8vo, 434 pp., with numerous Page and other Engravings, handsomely bound, price 10s. 6d.

IMPRISONED IN A SPANISH CONVENT:
AN ENGLISH GIRL'S EXPERIENCES.

"Intensely fascinating. The *exposé* is a remarkable one, and as readable as remarkable."—*Society.*

"Excellent specimens of their author in his best and brightest mood."—*Athenæum.*

"Highly dramatic."—*Scotsman.* "Strikingly interesting."—*Literary World.*

"Instead of the meek cooing dove with naked feet and a dusty face who had talked of dying for me, I had now a bright-eyed rosy-cheeked companion who had cambric pocket-handkerchiefs with violet scent on them and smoked cigarettes on the sly."—*Page 75.*

New and Cheaper Edition, Two Vols. large post 8vo, attractively bound, price 15s.

UNDER THE LENS: SOCIAL PHOTOGRAPHS.
ILLUSTRATED WITH ABOUT 300 ENGRAVINGS BY WELL-KNOWN ARTISTS.

CONTENTS: — JILTS — ADVENTURERS AND ADVENTURESSES — HONOURABLE GENTLEMEN (M.P.s)—PUBLIC SCHOOLBOYS AND UNDERGRADUATES—SPENDTHRIFTS —SOME WOMEN I HAVE KNOWN—ROUGHS OF HIGH AND LOW DEGREE.

"Brilliant, highly-coloured sketches. . . . containing beyond doubt some of the best writing that has come from Mr. Grenville-Murray's pen."—*St. James's Gazette.*

"Limned audaciously, unsparingly, and with much ability."—*World.*

"Distinguished by their pitiless fidelity to nature."—*Society.*

AT THE ETON AND HARROW CRICKET MATCH: *from* "*UNDER THE LENS.*"

MR. E. C. GRENVILLE-MURRAY'S WORKS—*continued.*

Seventh Edition, in post 8vo, handsomely bound, price 7s. 6d.

SIDE-LIGHTS ON ENGLISH SOCIETY:

𝔖𝔨𝔢𝔱𝔠𝔥𝔢𝔰 from 𝔏𝔦𝔣𝔢, 𝔖𝔬𝔠𝔦𝔞𝔩 𝔞𝔫𝔡 𝔖𝔞𝔱𝔦𝔯𝔦𝔠𝔞𝔩.

ILLUSTRATED WITH NEARLY 300 CHARACTERISTIC ENGRAVINGS.

CONTENTS:—FLIRTS. — ON HER BRITANNIC MAJESTY'S SERVICE. — SEMI-DETACHED WIVES.—NOBLE LORDS.—YOUNG WIDOWS.—OUR SILVERED YOUTH, OR NOBLE OLD BOYS.

"This is a startling book. The volume is expensively and elaborately got up; the writing is bitter, unsparing, and extremely clever."—*Vanity Fair.*

"Mr. Grenville-Murray sparkles very steadily throughout the present volume, and puts to excellent use his incomparable knowledge of life and manners, of men and cities, of appearances and facts. Of his several descants upon English types, I shall only remark that they are brilliantly and dashingly written, curious as to their matter, and admirably readable."—*Truth.*

"No one can question the brilliancy of the sketches, nor affirm that 'Side-Lights' is aught but a fascinating book ..... The book is destined to make a great noise in the world."—*Whitehall Review.*

Third Edition, with Frontispiece and Vignette, price 3s. 6d.

HIGH LIFE IN FRANCE UNDER THE REPUBLIC:

SOCIAL AND SATIRICAL SKETCHES IN PARIS AND THE PROVINCES.

" Take this book as it stands, with the limitations imposed upon its author by circumstances, and it will be found very enjoyable. . . . . The volume is studded with shrewd observations on French life at the present day."—*Spectator.*

" A very clever and entertaining series of social and satirical sketches, almost French in their point and vivacity."—*Contemporary Review.*

" A most amusing book, and no less instructive if read with allowances and understanding."—*World.*

" Full of the caustic humour and graphic character-painting so characteristic of Mr. Grenville-Murray's work, and dealing trenchantly yet lightly with almost every conceivable phase of ocial, political, official, journalistic and theatrical life."—*Society.*

MR. E. C. GRENVILLE-MURRAY'S WORKS—*continued.*

Second Edition, in large 8vo, tastefully bound, with gilt edges, price 10s. 6d.

FORMING A HANDSOME VOLUME FOR A PRESENT.

PEOPLE I HAVE MET.

Illustrated with 54 tinted Page Engravings, from Designs by FRED. BARNARD.

CONTENTS :—

The Old Earl.	The Rector.	The Doctor.	The Bachelor.
The Dowager.	The Curate.	The Retired Colonel.	The Younger Son.
The Family Solicitor.	The Governess.	The Chaperon.	The Grandmother.
The College Don.	The Tutor.	The Usurer.	The Newspaper Editor.
The Rich Widow.	The Promising Son.	The Spendthrift.	The Butler.
The Ornamental Director.	The Favourite Daughter.	Le Nouveau Riche.	The Devotee.
The Old Maid.	The Squire.	The Maiden Aunt.	

THE RICH WIDOW (reduced from the original engraving.)

"Mr. Grenville-Murray's pages sparkle with cleverness and with a shrewd wit, caustic or cynical at times, but by no means excluding a due appreciation of the softer virtues of women and the sterner excellences of men. The talent of the artist (Mr. Barnard) is akin to that of the author, and the result of the combination is a book that, once taken up, can hardly be laid down until the last page is perused."—*Spectator.*

"All of Mr. Grenville-Murray's portraits are clever and life-like, and some of them are not unworthy of a model who was more before the author's eyes than Addison—namely, Thackeray."—*Truth.*

"Mr. Grenville-Murray's sketches are genuine studies, and are the best things of the kind that have been published since 'Sketches by Boz,' to which they are superior in the sense in which artistically executed character portraits are superior to caricatures."—*St. James's Gazette.*

"No book of its class can be pointed out so admirably calculated to show another generation the foibles and peculiarities of the men and women of our times."—*Morning Post.*

An Edition of "PEOPLE I HAVE MET" is published in small 8vo, with Frontispiece, price 3s. 6d.

A BUCK OF THE REGENCY : *from "DUTCH PICTURES."*

" Mr. Sala's best work has in it something of Montaigne, a great deal of Charles Lamb—made deeper and broader—and not a little of Lamb's model, the accomplished and quaint Sir Thomas Brown. These ' Dutch Pictures ' and ' Pictures Done With a Quill' should be placed alongside Oliver Wendell Holmes's inimitable budgets of friendly gossip and Thackeray's ' Roundabout Papers.' They display to perfection the quick eye, good taste, and ready hand of the born essayist—they are never tiresome." —*Daily Telegraph.*

VIZETELLY'S ONE-VOLUME NOVELS.

CHEAPER ISSUE.

"The idea of publishing cheap one-volume novels is a good one, and we wish the series every success."—*Saturday Review.*

2s. 6d. each.

FIFTH EDITION.

THE IRONMASTER; OR, LOVE AND PRIDE.

By GEORGES OHNET.

TRANSLATED WITHOUT ABRIDGMENT FROM THE 146TH FRENCH EDITION.

"This work, the greatest literary success in any language of recent times, has already yielded its author upwards of £12,000."

THIRD EDITION.

NUMA ROUMESTAN; OR, JOY ABROAD AND GRIEF AT HOME.

By ALPHONSE DAUDET.

TRANSLATED BY MRS. J. G. LAYARD.

"'Numa Roumestan' is a masterpiece; it is really a perfect work; it has no fault, no weakness. It is a compact and harmonious whole."—Mr. HENRY JAMES.

SECOND EDITION.

THE CORSARS; OR, LOVE AND LUCRE.

By JOHN HILL, AUTHOR OF "THE WATERS OF MARAH," "SALLY," &c.

"It is indubitable that Mr. Hill has produced a strong and lively novel, full of story, character, situations, murder, gold-mines, excursions, and alarms. The book is so rich in promise that we hope to receive some day from Mr. Hill a romance which will win every vote."—*Saturday Review.*

The Book that made M. Ohnet's reputation, and was crowned by the French Academy.

SECOND EDITION.

PRINCE SERGE PANINE.

By GEORGES OHNET. AUTHOR OF "THE IRONMASTER."

TRANSLATED, WITHOUT ABRIDGMENT, FROM THE 110TH FRENCH EDITION.

"This excellent version is sure to meet with large success on our side of the Channel."—*London Figaro.*

BETWEEN MIDNIGHT AND DAWN.

By INA L. CASSILIS, AUTHOR OF "SOCIETY'S QUEEN," &c.

"An ingenious plot, cleverly handled."—*Athenæum.*

"The interest begins with the first page, and is ably sustained to the conclusion."—*Edinburgh Courant.*

ROLAND; OR THE EXPIATION OF A SIN.

By ARY ECILAW.

"A novel entitled 'Roland' is creating an immense sensation in Paris. The first, second, and third editions were swept away in as many days. The work is charmingly written."—*The World.*

EIGHTH EDITION, CAREFULLY REVISED, AND WITH A SPECIAL PREFACE.

A MUMMER'S WIFE. A Realistic Novel.

By GEORGE MOORE, AUTHOR OF "A MODERN LOVER."

"A striking book, different in tone from current English fiction. The woman's character is a very powerful study."—*Athenæum.*

"A Mummer's Wife, in virtue of its vividness of presentation and real literary skill, may be regarded as a representative example of the work of a literary school that has of late years attracted to itself a good deal of notoriety."—*Spectator.*

"'A Mummer's Wife' holds at present a unique position among English novels. It is a conspicuous success of its kind."—*Graphic.*

THIRD EDITION.

COUNTESS SARAH.

By GEORGES OHNET, AUTHOR OF "THE IRONMASTER."

TRANSLATED, WITHOUT ABRIDGMENT, FROM THE 118TH FRENCH EDITION.

"The book contains some very powerful situations and first-rate character studies."—*Whitehall Review.*

"To an interesting plot is added a number of strongly-marked and cleverly drawn characters."—*Society.*

THIRD EDITION.

MR. BUTLER'S WARD.

By MABEL ROBINSON.

"A charming book, poetically conceived, and worked out with tenderness and insight."—*Athenæum*

"The heroine is a very happy conception, a beautiful creation whose affecting history is treated with much delicacy, sympathy, and command of all that is touching."—*Illustrated News.*

"All the characters are new to fiction, and the author is to be congratulated on having made so full and original a haul out of the supposed to be exhausted waters of modern society. . . . ."—*Graphic.*

THE THREATENING EYE.

By E. F. KNIGHT, AUTHOR OF "A CRUISE IN THE FALCON."

"There is a good deal of power about this romance."—*Graphic.*

"Full of extraordinary power and originality. The story is one of quite exceptional force and impressiveness."—*Manchester Examiner.*

THE FORKED TONGUE.

By R. LANGSTAFF DE HAVILLAND, M.A., AUTHOR OF "ENSLAVED," &c.

"In many respects the story is a remarkable one. Its men and women are drawn with power and without pity; their follies and their vices are painted in unmistakable colours, and with a skill that fascinates."—*Society.*

THIRD EDITION.

A MODERN LOVER.

By GEORGE MOORE, AUTHOR OF "A MUMMER'S WIFE."

"Mr. Moore has a real power of drawing character, and some of his descriptive scenes are capital."—*St. James's Gazette.*

"It would be difficult to praise too highly the strength, truth, delicacy, and pathos of the incident of Gwynnie Lloyd, and the admirable treatment of the great sacrifice she makes. The incident is depicted with skill and beauty."—*Spectator.*

"Kiss me, dear," said Athenaïs.

*In large crown 8vo, beautifully printed on toned paper, price 5s., or handsomely
bound with gilt edges, suitable in every way for a present, 6s.*

An Illustrated Edition of M. Ohnet's Celebrated Novel.

THE IRONMASTER; OR, LOVE AND PRIDE.

CONTAINING 42 FULL-PAGE ENGRAVINGS BY FRENCH ARTISTS, PRINTED
SEPARATE FROM THE TEXT.

PRINCE ZILAH.

By JULES CLARETIE.

Translated from the 57th French edition.

"M. Jules Claretie has of late taken a conspicuous place as a novelist in France."—*Times.*

THE TRIALS OF JETTA MALAUBRET.

(NOIRS ET ROUGES.)

By VICTOR CHERBULIEZ, OF THE FRENCH ACADEMY.

TRANSLATED BY THE COUNTESS G. DE LA ROCHEFOUCAULD.

"'Jetta Malaubret' deals with the experiences of a young girl who is taken from a convent and deliberately plunged into a sort of society calculated to teach her the utmost possible amount of worldly wisdom—to say nothing of worse things—in the shortest possible time. The characterization and dialogue are full of piquancy and cleverness."—*Society.*

In post 8vo, with numerous Page and other Engravings, cloth gilt, price 3s. 6d.,

NO ROSE WITHOUT A THORN,

AND OTHER TALES.

By F. C. BURNAND, H. SAVILE CLARKE, R. E. FRANCILLON, &c.

" By the aid of the chimney with the register up Mrs. Lupscombe's curiosity was, to a certain extent, gratified."—*Page* 19.

In post 8vo, with numerous Page and other Engravings, cloth gilt, price 3s. 6d.

THE DOVE'S NEST,

AND OTHER TALES.

By JOSEPH HATTON, RICHARD JEFFERIES, H. SAVILE CLARKE, &c.

ZOLA'S REALISTIC NOVELS—*continued.*

The following Volumes will be published during the Autumn :—

HOW JOLLY LIFE IS!
From the 44th French Edition.

THE FORTUNE OF THE ROUGONS.
From the 24th French Edition.

A LOVE EPISODE.
From the 52nd French Edition.

HIS EXCELLENCY EUGÈNE ROUGON.
From the 22nd French Edition.

THE CONQUEST OF PLASSANS.
From the 23rd French Edition.

The following are published, in large octavo, price 7s. 6d. per Vol.

Each Volume contains about 100 Engravings, half of which are page-size.

1. NANA.   2. THE ASSOMMOIR.   3. PIPING HOT.
DESIGNS BY BELLENGER, BERTALL, CLAIRIN, GILL, VIERGE, &c.

THE BOULEVARD NOVELS.
Pictures of French Morals and Manners.
In small 8vo, attractively bound, price 2s. 6d. each.

NANA'S DAUGHTER.
By ALFRED SIRVEN and HENRI LEVERDIER.
From the 35th French Edition.

THE YOUNG GUARD.
By VAST-RICOUARD.
From the 15th French Edition.

THE WOMAN OF FIRE.
By ADOLPHE BELOT.
From the 30th French Edition.

ODETTE'S MARRIAGE.
By ALBERT DELPIT.
From the 22nd French Edition.

BEAUTIFUL JULIE & THE VIRGIN WIDOW.
By A. MATTHEY.

Vizetelly's Sixpenny Series of Amusing and Entertaining Books.

In picture cover, with many Engravings.

MATRIMONY BY ADVERTISEMENT;

AND OTHER ADVENTURES OF A JOURNALIST.

By CHARLES G. PAYNE.

Uniform with the above, and by the same Author, profusely illustrated.

VOTE FOR POTTLEBECK!

THE STORY OF A POLITICIAN IN LOVE.

CECILE'S FORTUNE. By F. DU BOISGOBEY.

THE THREE-CORNERED HAT. By P. A. DE ALARCON.

THE BLACK CROSS MYSTERY, By H. CORKRAN.

THE STEEL NECKLACE. By F. DU BOISGOBEY.

THE GREAT HOGGARTY DIAMOND. By W. M. THACKERAY.

CAPTAIN SPITFIRE, AND THE UNLUCKY TREASURE.
By P. A. DE ALARCON.

YOUNG WIDOWS. By E. C. GRENVILLE-MURRAY. 50 *Engravings.*

THE DETECTIVE'S EYE. By F. DU BOISGOBEY.

THE STRANGE PHANTASY OF DR. TRINTZIUS. By AUGUSTE VITU.

A SHABBY GENTEEL STORY. By W. M. THACKERAY.

THE FIDDLER AMONG THE BANDITS. By ALEXANDRE DUMAS.

Other Volumes are in Preparation.

In One Volume, large imperial 8vo, price 3s., or single numbers price 6d. each,

THE SOCIAL ZOO;

SATIRICAL, SOCIAL, AND HUMOROUS SKETCHES BY THE BEST WRITERS.

Copiously Illustrated in many Styles by well-known Artists.

OUR GILDED YOUTH. By E. C. GRENVILLE-MURRAY.
NICE GIRLS. By R. MOUNTENEY JEPHSON.
NOBLE LORDS. By E. C. GRENVILLE-MURRAY.
FLIRTS. By E. C. GRENVILLE-MURRAY.
OUR SILVERED YOUTH. By E. C. GRENVILLE-MURRAY.
MILITARY MEN AS THEY WERE. By E. DYNE FENTON.

In demy 4to, handsomely printed and bound, with gilt edges, price 12s.

A HISTORY OF CHAMPAGNE;

WITH NOTES ON THE OTHER SPARKLING WINES OF FRANCE.

By HENRY VIZETELLY.

CHEVALIER OF THE ORDER OF FRANZ-JOSEF.
WINE JUROR FOR GREAT BRITAIN AT THE VIENNA AND PARIS EXHIBITIONS OF 1873 AND 1878.

Illustrated with 350 Engravings,

FROM ORIGINAL SKETCHES AND PHOTOGRAPHS, ANCIENT MSS., EARLY PRINTED·
BOOKS, RARE PRINTS, CARICATURES, ETC.

"A very agreeable medley of history, anecdote, geographical description, and such like matter, distinguished by an accuracy not often found in such medleys, and illustrated in the most abundant and pleasingly miscellaneous fashion."—*Daily News.*

"Mr. Henry Vizetelly's handsome book about Champagne and other sparkling wines of France is full of curious information and amusement. It should be widely read and appreciated." —*Saturday Review.*

"Mr. Henry Vizetelly has written a quarto volume on the 'History of Champagne,' in which he has collected a large number of facts, many of them very curious and interesting. Many of the woodcuts are excellent."—*Athenæum.*

"It is probable that this large volume contains such an amount of information touching the subject which it treats as cannot be found elsewhere. How competent the author was for the task he undertook is to be inferred from the functions he has discharged, and from the exceptional opportunities he enjoyed."—*Illustrated London News.*

"A veritable *edition de luxe*, dealing with the history of Champagne from the time of the Romans to the present date. . . . An interesting book, the incidents and details of which are very graphically told with a good deal of wit and humour. The engravings are exceedingly well executed."—*The Wine and Spirit News.*

MR. HENRY VIZETELLY'S POPULAR BOOKS ON WINE.

"Mr. Vizetelly discourses brightly and discriminatingly on crus and bouquets and the different European vineyards, most of which he has evidently visited."—*The Times.*

"Mr. Henry Vizetelly's books about different wines have an importance and a value far greater than will be assigned them by those who look merely at the price at which they are published."—*Sunday Times.*

Price 1s. 6d. ornamental cover ; or 2s. 6d. in elegant cloth binding.

FACTS ABOUT PORT AND MADEIRA,

GLEANED DURING A TOUR IN THE AUTUMN OF 1877.

By HENRY VIZETELLY,

WINE JUROR FOR GREAT BRITAIN AT THE VIENNA AND PARIS EXHIBITIONS OF 1873 AND 1878.

With 100 Illustrations from Original Sketches and Photographs.

BY THE SAME AUTHOR.

Price 1s. 6d. ornamental cover ; or 2s. 6d. in elegant cloth binding.

FACTS ABOUT CHAMPAGNE,
AND OTHER SPARKLING WINES.

COLLECTED DURING NUMEROUS VISITS TO THE CHAMPAGNE AND OTHER VITICULTURAL DISTRICTS OF FRANCE AND THE PRINCIPAL REMAINING WINE-PRODUCING COUNTRIES OF EUROPE.

Illustrated with 112 Engravings from Sketches and Photographs.

Price 1s. ornamental cover ; or 1s. 6d. cloth gilt.

FACTS ABOUT SHERRY,

GLEANED IN THE VINEYARDS AND BODEGAS OF THE JEREZ, & OTHER DISTRICTS.

Illustrated with numerous Engravings from Original Sketches.

Price 1s. in ornamental cover ; or 1s. 6d. cloth gilt.

THE WINES OF THE WORLD,
CHARACTERIZED AND CLASSED.

In small post 8vo, ornamental scarlet covers, 1s. each.

THE GABORIAU AND DU BOISGOBEY SENSATIONAL NOVELS.

" Ah, friend, how many and many a while
They've made the slow time fleetly flow,
And solaced pain and charmed exile,
BOISGOBEY and GABORIAU ! "

Ballade of Railway Novels in " Longman's Magazine."

IN PERIL OF HIS LIFE.

" A story of thrilling interest, and admirably translated."—*Sunday Times.*

" Hardly ever has a more ingenious circumstantial case been imagined than that which puts the hero in peril of his life, and the manner in which the proof of his innocence is finally brought about is scarcely less skilful."—*Illustrated Sporting and Dramatic News.*

THE LEROUGE CASE.

" M. Gaboriau is a skilful and brilliant writer, capable of so diverting the attention and interest of his readers that not one word or line in his book will be skipped or read carelessly."—*Hampshire Advertiser.*

OTHER PEOPLE'S MONEY.

" The interest is kept up throughout, and the story is told graphically and with a good deal of art."—*London Figaro.*

LECOQ THE DETECTIVE. Two Vols.

" In the art of forging a tangled chain of complicated incidents involved and inexplicable until the last link is reached and the whole made clear, Mr. Wilkie Collins is equalled, if not excelled, by M. Gaboriau."—*Brighton Herald.*

THE GILDED CLIQUE.

" Full of incident, and instinct with life and action. Altogether this is a most fascinating book."—*Hampshire Advertiser.*

THE MYSTERY OF ORCIVAL.

" The Author keeps the interest of the reader at fever heat, and by a succession of unexpected turns and incidents, the drama is ultimately worked out to a very pleasant result. The ability displayed is unquestionable."—*Sheffield Independent.*

DOSSIER NO. 113.

" The plot is worked out with great skill, and from first to last the reader's interest is never allowed to flag."—*Dumbarton Herald.*

THE LITTLE OLD MAN OF BATIGNOLLES.

THE SLAVES OF PARIS. Two Vols.

" Sensational, full of interest, cleverly conceived, and wrought out with consummate skill."—*Oxford and Cambridge Journal.*

THE CATASTROPHE. Two Vols.

" A plot vigorously and skilfully constructed, leading through a series of surprising dramatic scenes and thrilling mysteries, and culminating in a sudden and complete exposure of crime and triumph of innocence. ' The Catastrophe ' does ample credit to M. Gaboriau's reputation as a novelist of vast resource in incident and of wonderful ingenuity in constructing and unravelling thrilling mysteries."—*Aberdeen Journal.*

INTRIGUES OF A POISONER.

" The wonderful Sensational Novels of Emile Gaboriau."—*Globe.*

THE COUNT'S MILLIONS. Two Vols.

" To those who love the mysterious and the sensational, Gaboriau's stories are irresistibly fascinating. His marvellously clever pages hold the mirror up to nature with absolute fidelity; and the interest with which he contrives to invest his characters proves that exaggeration is unnecessary to a master."—*Society.*

THE OLD AGE OF LECOQ, THE DETECTIVE. Two Vols.

" The romances of Gaboriau and Du Boisgobey picture the marvellous Lecoq and other wonders of shrewdness, who piece together the elaborate details of the most complicated crimes, as Professor Owen with the smallest bone as a foundation could reconstruct the most extraordinary animals."—*Standard.*

IN THE SERPENTS' COILS.

" This is a most picturesque, dramatic, and powerful sensational novel. Its interest never flags. Its terrific excitement continues to the end. The reader is kept spellbound."—*Oldham Chronicle.*

THE DAY OF RECKONING. Two Vols.

" M. du Boisgobey gives us no tiresome descriptions or laboured analyses of character; under his facile pen plots full of incident are quickly opened and unwound. He does not stop to moralise; all his art consists in creating intricacies which shall keep the reader's curiosity on the stretch, and offer a full scope to his own really wonderful ingenuity for unravelling."—*Times.*

THE SEVERED HAND.

" The plot is a marvel of intricacy and cleverly managed surprises."—*Literary World.*
" Readers who like a thoroughly entangled and thrilling plot will welcome this nove with avidity."—*Bristol Mercury.*

BERTHA'S SECRET.

" ' Bertha's Secret ' is a most effective romance. We need not say how the story ends, for this would spoil the reader's pleasure in a novel which depends for all its interest on the skilful weaving and unweaving of mysteries, but we will repeat that ' Bertha's Secret' is very well worth perusal."—*Times.*

WHO DIED LAST? OR THE RIGHTFUL HEIR.

" Travellers at this season of the year will find the time occupied by a long journey pass away as rapidly as they can desire with one of Du Boisgobey's absorbing volumes in their hand."—*London Figaro.*

THE CRIME OF THE OPERA HOUSE. Two Vols.

" We are led breathless from the first page to the last, and close the book with a thorough admiration for the vigorous romancist who has the courage to fulfil the true function of the story-teller, by making reflection subordinate to action."—*Aberdeen Journal.*

Lately published Volumes.

THE MATAPAN AFFAIR. — A FIGHT FOR A FORTUNE.

THE GOLDEN PIG; OR, THE IDOL OF MODERN PARIS. 2 Vols.

PRETTY BABIOLE.— THE CORAL PIN. Two Vols.

THE THUMB STROKE.—THE JAILER'S PRETTY WIFE.

THE ANGEL OF THE CHIMES.—HIS GREAT REVENGE.

[Two Vols.

In double volumes, bound in scarlet cloth, price 2s. 6d. each.

NEW EDITIONS OF THE
GABORIAU AND DU BOISGOBEY
SENSATIONAL NOVELS.

1.—THE MYSTERY OF ORCIVAL, AND THE GILDED CLIQUE.
2.—THE LEROUGE CASE, AND OTHER PEOPLE'S MONEY.
3.—LECOQ, THE DETECTIVE.   4.—THE SLAVES OF PARIS.
5.—IN PERIL OF HIS LIFE, AND INTRIGUES OF A POISONER.
6.—DOSSIER NO. 113, AND THE LITTLE OLD MAN OF BA-
TIGNOLLES.   7.—THE COUNT'S MILLIONS.
8.—THE OLD AGE OF LECOQ, THE DETECTIVE.
9.—THE CATASTROPHE.   10.—THE DAY OF RECKONING.
11.—THE SEVERED HAND, AND IN THE SERPENTS' COILS.
12.—BERTHA'S SECRET, AND WHO DIED LAST?
13.—THE CRIME OF THE OPERA HOUSE.   17.—THE CORAL PIN.
14.—THE MATAPAN AFFAIR, AND A FIGHT FOR A FORTUNE.
15.—THE GOLDEN PIG.   18.—HIS GREAT REVENGE.
16.—THE THUMB STROKE, AND PRETTY BABIOLE.
19.—JAILER'S PRETTY WIFE, AND ANGEL OF THE CHIMES.

In small post 8vo, ornamental covers, 1s. each ; in cloth, 1s. 6d.

VIZETELLY'S POPULAR FRENCH NOVELS.

TRANSLATIONS OF THE BEST EXAMPLES OF RECENT FRENCH
FICTION OF AN UNOBJECTIONABLE CHARACTER.

*" They are books that may be safely left lying about where the ladies of the family can pick them up
and read them. The interest they create is happily not of the vicious sort at all."*
SHEFFIELD INDEPENDENT.

FROMONT THE YOUNGER & RISLER THE ELDER. By
A. DAUDET.
" The series starts well with M. Alphonse Daudet's masterpiece."—*Athenæum.*
" A terrible story, powerful after a sledge-hammer fashion in some parts, and wonderfully tender, touching, and pathetic in others, the extraordinary popularity whereof
may be inferred from the fact that this English version is said to be ' translated from the
fiftieth French edition.' "—*Illustrated London News.*

SAMUEL BROHL AND PARTNER. By V. CHERBULIEZ.
" Those who have read this singular story in the original need not be reminded of that
supremely dramatic study of the man who lived two lives at once, even within himself.
The reader's discovery of his double nature is one of the most cleverly managed of surprises, and Samuel Brohl's final dissolution of partnership with himself is a remarkable
stroke of almost pathetic comedy."—*The Graphic.*

THE DRAMA OF THE RUE DE LA PAIX. By A. BELOT.
" A highly ingenious plot is developed in 'The Drama of the Rue de la Paix,' in
which a decidedly interesting and thrilling narrative is told with great force and
passion, relieved by sprightliness and tenderness."—*Illustrated London News.*

MAUGARS JUNIOR. By A. THEURIET.
" One of the most charming novelettes we have read for a long time."— *Literary World.*

WAYWARD DOSIA, & THE GENEROUS DIPLOMATIST.
By HENRY GRÉVILLE.

"As epigrammatic as anything Lord Beaconsfield has ever written."—*Hampshire Telegraph.*

A NEW LEASE OF LIFE, & SAVING A DAUGHTER'S
DOWRY. By E. ABOUT.

"'A New Lease of Life' is an absorbing story, the interest of which is kept up to the very end."—*Dublin Evening Mail.*
"The story, as a flight of brilliant and eccentric imagination, is unequalled in its peculiar way."—*The Graphic.*

COLOMBA, & CARMEN. By P. MÉRIMÉE.

"The freshness and raciness of 'Colomba is quite cheering after the stereotyped three-volume novels with which our circulating libraries are crammed."—*Halifax Times.*
"'Carmen' will be welcomed by the lovers of the sprightly and tuneful opera the heroine of which Minnie Hauk made so popular. It is a bright and vivacious story."—*Life.*

A WOMAN'S DIARY, & THE LITTLE COUNTESS. By
O. FEUILLET.

"Is wrought out with masterly skill and affords reading, which although of a slightly sensational kind, cannot be said to be hurtful either mentally or morally."—*Dumbarton Herald.*

BLUE-EYED META HOLDENIS, & A STROKE OF DIPLO-
MACY. By V. CHERBULIEZ.

"'Blue-eyed Meta Holdenis' is a delightful tale."—*Civil Service Gazette.*
"'A Stroke of Diplomacy' is a bright vivacious story pleasantly told."—*Hampshire Advertiser.*

THE GODSON OF A MARQUIS. By A. THEURIET.

"The rustic personages, the rural scenery and life in the forest country of Argonne, are painted with the hand of a master. From the beginning to the close the interest of the story never flags."—*Life.*

THE TOWER OF PERCEMONT & MARIANNE. By GEORGE
SAND.

"George Sand has a great name, and the 'Tower of Percemont' is not unworthy of it."—*Illustrated London News.*

THE LOW-BORN LOVER'S REVENGE. By V. CHERBULIEZ.

"'The Low-born Lover's Revenge' is one of M. Cherbuliez's many exquisitely written productions. The studies of human nature under various influences, especially in the cases of the unhappy heroine and her low-born lover, are wonderfully effective."—*Illustrated London News.*

THE NOTARY'S NOSE, AND OTHER AMUSING STORIES.
By E. ABOUT.

"Crisp and bright, full of movement and interest."—*Brighton Herald.*

DOCTOR CLAUDE; OR, LOVE RENDERED DESPERATE.
By H. MALOT. Two vols.

"We have to appeal to our very first flight of novelists to find anything so artistic in English romance as these books."—*Dublin Evening Mail.*

THE THREE RED KNIGHTS; OR, THE BROTHERS'
VENGEANCE. By P. FÉVAL.

"The one thing that strikes us in these stories is the marvellous dramatic skill of the writers."—*Sheffield Independent.*

Bradbury, Agnew, & Co., [Printers, Whitefriars.

www.ingramcontent.com/pod-product-compliance
Lightning Source LLC
Chambersburg PA
CBHW030042130726
47901CB00007BA/1700